"Masterful storytelling, I believed every breathtaking word. The glamour and contained hysteria of backstage Broadway and Hamptons royalty, a tragic and unavoidable link to the craven underbelly of syndicated crime. The vulnerability of celebrity life told in delicious detail, with amazing twists of imagination, gripping suspense and deep caring …
Like intimate friends, I yearn to spend more time with all the characters, the good, bad, ugly and the beautiful--and relive each incredible moment. Pure pleasure, pure entertainment, I relished every moment …"

--Cynthia Scott, Media Executive Producer/Creative Director

A WALKING SHADOW

A WALKING SHADOW

Deborah Fezelle & Sherry Yanow

Published 2014 by Shorehouse Books
Printed in the United States of America

Cover designer Wendy Prince

ISBN 0-692-33828-4
EAN-13 978-069233828-5

"Life's but a walking shadow, a poor player
That struts and frets his hour upon the stage,
And then is heard no more: it is a tale
Told by an idiot, full of sound and fury,
Signifying nothing."

William Shakespeare
MACBETH, Act V Scene v

For Chris, my "Andrew" *Deborah Fezelle*
For great teachers who inspire *Sherry Yanow*

Acknowledgments

Katherine Fasbender Bos
Wendy Prince
Rufus Malone Jr.

PROLOGUE

Gianni Fosselli shot out of the house and sprinted after his son. Gasping for breath, he ran like the wind itself, his feet sinking into ground soggy with melting snow. He could make out the dog just ahead of Anthony, his silver collar reflecting the moonlight. The boy's white scarf whipped behind him as he dashed for the fence.

And then Gianni saw McDeare on the other side of the barrier, yelling for Anthony! Lyle Barton was next to him, McDeare's accomplice. Dashing towards her son, the boy's mother materialized out of the darkness, the locked gate swinging open!

The faccia di merda would not lay one perverted hand on Gianni's precious son. But first, he would silence the whore. Gianni thanked God his gun was loaded, swiftly turning the weapon on Jessica.

In the moonglow, Gianni could see McDeare suck in a breath as he realized the game was over. Gianni directed Anthony to call his dog. When the boy refused, Gianni raised his voice, ordering him to do as he said. The dog lowered his head, barking furiously at Gianni.

As Anthony finally complied, Gianni smiled warmly at his son. He thanked him in front of McDeare and Jessica, wanting them to understand at last how blood told. McDeare was an outsider here, no relation to Anthony Fosselli.

Cocking the gun, Gianni willed his trembling hand still, his moment approaching. He instructed his son to take the frenzied creature into the house. Now. He waited for Anthony to retreat so his father could do what was necessary. The boy played dumb. Gianni shrieked at him to run to the house!

Snarling, the dog leapt for Gianni's throat. The gun fired, a bright flash--

Bolting upright in bed, Gianni Fosselli wiped beads of perspiration from his forehead.

Mio Dio, another nightmare yanking him out of his sleep.

*

It was a new day, the nightmare behind him. The man who now called himself Max Callaban, the man everyone thought dead, stepped back and surveyed his handiwork. The most important room in the house was finished, all in blue. His son's room. Satisfied, Max turned out the lights and headed downstairs. The Victorian house was coming together bit by bit. Passing a gilded mirror in the lower hallway, Max paused, his new image looking back at him. A shaven head, his swirl of dark hair gone. Green contact lenses, his brown eyes erased. He threw back his shoulders. He looked fit. He didn't look like Gianni Fosselli. Not anymore.

There was nothing like restoring an old house to get you back in shape. Especially a house with a personality of its own. The old Victorian rang out with random echoes of laughter. Windows sagged open in the middle of the night. Cold spots leaked. And that haunting recurring dream—racing after Anthony into the yard. McDeare and his cohorts on the other side of the fence. A dog. Dogs were a filthy nuisance … Max chuckled. His imagination was too vivid. The place had character, that's all.

Max poured himself a grappa from the living-room bar. Strolling onto the front verandah, he surveyed his property, five rolling and leafy acres in northeastern Ohio. The land stretched out like the mid-Atlantic, the autumn foliage a confetti of rust and sienna and pumpkin and mustard. The sun was beginning to sink, turning the pond molten silver.

It was peaceful here, the perfect place to raise a seven-year-old boy. A place with stable family values, as America called it. People went to work at eight every morning and returned home at five. They attended church on Sunday and said grace before dinner. They celebrated the changing of the seasons and the holidays, just like their parents and grandparents before them.

Ambling back indoors, Max headed for a glassed-in side porch he'd turned into his office. He still had a few minutes before leaving. Sitting in front of his iPad, Max read THE NEW YORK POST'S gossip section one more time:

Jessica Kendle and Nick McDeare to Wed New Year's Eve

Beautiful stage and screen star Jessica Kendle will marry best-selling suspense author Nick McDeare in a New-Year's Eve candlelight ceremony at the Long Island mansion of famed Broadway producer William Rudolph. The guest list of over four hundred includes renowned political figures and Broadway luminaries. This will be the hottest ticket in town as New York City ushers in the New Year.

This is the second marriage for both parties. Mr. McDeare, a renowned former investigative reporter for THE WASHINGTON POST, has been divorced for many years. His son from that marriage died of leukemia. The author of five novels, Mr. McDeare has won the prestigious Arthur Conan Doyle Award and been nominated for a Pulitzer for his work at the POST. Ms. Kendle, a Tony Award winner, was married to Broadway star Andrew Brady until his murder two and a half years ago. She has a seven-year-old son. After nearly a three-year hiatus, Ms. Kendle is due to return to Broadway in a musical revival of TO HAVE AND TO HOLD.

In a twist worthy of any drama, Mr. McDeare is Mr. Brady's long-lost older brother, given up for adoption at birth. The brothers were reunited via a phone call shortly before Mr. Brady's death. Mr. McDeare was instrumental in the apprehension of Gianni Fosselli, his brother's killer and the biological father of Ms. Kendle's son. Mr. Fosselli later died at sea in an escape attempt from a cruise ship. During the course of his investigation, Mr. McDeare and his sister-in-law fell in love. Quite a coup for Ms. Kendle. Mr. McDeare, long considered a confirmed bachelor, has left behind a trail of broken hearts. Apparently, he just hadn't met the right woman until now.

Max stared at Jessica's cut-crystal features, the sapphire eyes smiling into the camera, spun-gold hair framing her face. An angel's face. Nicholas looked the devil next to her, amber eyes fierce under knit brows, strands of ebony hair spiking his forehead. Max's gaze shifted to the little boy in a framed picture on his desk, his dark curls and cleft chin a mirror image to Max's at that age. Only the boy's eyes were his mother's, blue jewels that changed colors with his mood.

Jessica Kendle Brady, Anthony's whore mother.

"Mr. Callaban?" Carlo Nori stood a few feet away. "I brought the car around. Whenever you're ready."

"I'll be there in a moment." Max motioned. "My bag's by the back door." Carlo was a connected man, part of Roberto Martinelli's extended family. He'd been sent by the crime boss to protect Max.

Dropping the iPad into his briefcase, Max slung the satchel over his shoulder. He reached into a drawer and grabbed a small box. His calling cards, the primary reason for this brief trip. It was time to set the dominoes in motion.

*

It was a brisk autumn morning, a light wind churning the inlet. Roberto Martinelli strolled along the pier of his Long Island estate, a Cuban cigar clamped between his teeth. He loved the change of seasons, the never-ending cycles of life and death.

A reedy man with slicked-back hair hurried across the garden's expanse. Aldo Zappella clapped Roberto on the back. "So, how was Jersey City?"

"Excellent. The camera I ordered arrived. A Canon, cost a fortune. They were practicing with it when I got there. And the girls insisted on modeling the special wardrobe I ordered from Italy. Another fortune."

"But it gives you pleasure."

"True." Aldo knew Roberto well. And he never judged. He was too loyal to judge.

"So how did they look in these designer clothes?"

Cupping his fingers to his lips, Roberto blew a kiss into the air. "Perfection."

Aldo laughed. "Good."

"Now," Roberto spit a piece of tobacco to the ground, "what's this important news you have for me?"

"Fosselli arrived last night to work out the details. He wants to take the kid at the wedding."

"Not a problem."

"In the meantime, he wants a glimpse of his son. And what he didn't tell me was he plans to fuck with McDeare. He asked too many questions. His hatred's eating him up."

"Poking a sleeping rattlesnake." Roberto shook his head. "I'd hoped Fosselli was smarter than that. Now we need someone to watch McDeare." Puffing on his cigar, Martinelli paced towards the water. "Get Clint Vaughn."

"That old shit? Roberto--"

"Vaughn's a chameleon. No one sees him. And keep Fosselli in line."

"You want Carlo should report to us?"

"Fosselli and I go back too far. He's an honorable man. We deal with Fosselli directly."

"Roberto, there has to be someone better than Vaughn. Anyway, he's semi-retired."

"He's been semi-retired ever since he got his PI license. Vaughn's natural habitat is a bar and his main diet is a bottle of scotch. But the lazy SOB always comes through for me, and he loves money. I don't want any screw-ups this time. Not with McDeare."

*

Hands stuffed in his pockets, Nick McDeare clipped home, the late afternoon sun warm on his face. Rounding East Seventy-Fifth Street, Nick headed towards Fifth Avenue. The Brady brownstone rolled into view, slate gray and neatly framed by a ribbon of black wrought-iron fence. Nick flicked the gate open, catching a speck of trash on the front steps. He bent down to pick it up.

What the hell?

It was a matchbook. And not any matchbook. This was a refugee from Oceano, Gianni Fosselli's former restaurant, playground for the rich and famous. Now extinct, like Gianni.

Nick turned the familiar matchbook over in his hand, a drawing of a cruise ship set against a tropical sunset. How did this particular book of matches home in on this particular brownstone?

Trying to ignore the kick to his gut, Nick brushed a hand through his hair. Okay, someone who used to frequent the restaurant and lived in the area accidentally dropped the matchbook on his way past the brownstone. It blew onto the stoop. New York City streets were littered with trash and packed with pedestrian traffic. No big deal.

Pocketing the matches, Nick fished for his keys and turned the locks.

*

From behind a Victorian lamppost down the block, Max Callaban smirked at the shock on McDeare's face.

Excellent.

This was just the beginning of his hell.

Custom made for Nicholas McDeare, Max Callaban was adding a tenth circle to Dante's nine.

CHAPTER 1

Clint Vaughn spent last night at Hanratty's, celebrating the wrap of a cheating husband case. After a rewarding evening of booze and pool following two all-nighter stakeouts, he'd fallen into bed at dawn like a dead man. His cell squawked at five p.m. Groping for the phone, Vaughn crawled out from under a mound of blankets. "Yeah?"

"It's Aldo. Our friend has a job for you. He'll make it worth your while."

Groaning, Clint sat up. You didn't say no to Roberto Martinelli. Aldo barked instructions and hung up. Clint staggered to the bathroom, just big enough to turn around. If you kept your arms down. "What an asshole you are, Aldo." He swallowed three aspirin with a large glass of water. His throat was parched, his tongue coated with cotton balls from the bottle of scotch he'd inhaled.

The grizzled image in the mirror didn't interest Clint. His sandy hair had turned to dirty ice. His face had more layers than a canyon. His pale blue eyes were slits. But he could still reel in the ladies and he didn't need any of that Viagra shit, so what the hell?

He made an obligatory phone call before heading back to Hanratty's for a pastrami on rye and a bottle of scotch. Revived, Clint drove across town to check out his new quarry. This time it was some arty-farty celebrity. Who the hell was Nick McDeare?

*

Nick McDeare was playing chef tonight. He eyed the collection of food on the kitchen counter. Let's call it Asian fusion. Mary, Jessie's live-in housekeeper and surrogate mother to them all, was gone for the weekend so Nick had taken charge. To begin, a delivery of crispy spring rolls, edamame, and vegetable udon noodle soup from Amoy's. Nick had made the entrée from scratch, setting out a platter of salmon and eel sushi next to sweet potato and shrimp tempura.

Jessie filled two flutes with Pinot Blanc. She looked exhausted, another long day at rehearsal. She was driving herself hard for opening night.

"Sit." Nick pulled out a stool at the granite counter. "Did you eat anything all day?"

"Two chocolate bars and a turtle?" Jessie made short work of the starters, dropping an elbow onto the counter and smiling. "Mmm. I feel much better."

Reaching back, she rewrapped her ponytail into its tie, wispy blond strands framing her face.

"What would you do without me, Kendle?" Nick cleared away the takeout, setting out their dinner plates and chopsticks.

"You are so good to me. I think I'll marry you."

"Since you're being so agreeable, there's something I need to ask you ..." Nick motioned to the slew of new wedding RSVPs fanned out on the counter with the mail. "Do I know any of these people? Do you?" He took a sip of wine.

"Funny, I've been asking myself the same question." Jessie flashed him a weak smile.

"It's not too late to elope," Nick said, staring at her over the rim of his glass.

Her eyebrows shot up. "You're kidding. Over two hundred RSVPs already. They're all coming. And we've got another two hundred to go. Thanks to our respective agents."

Draining his glass with one swallow, Nick filled another flute, a headache beginning to ping. How had falling in love with Jessie turned into a ten-ring circus?

"It's just a few hours out of our lives," Jessie said in a little voice. "We can't back out now."

"Are you sure about that?"

"You want to call it quits because the wedding's too--"

Leaning over the island, Nick kissed Jesse on the mouth, smoothing the hot words into a throaty purr. He finally drew back, his lip twitching. "That's better."

"Yeah," she murmured. "Much. Better that is."

"You know I love you. You know I want to marry you."

"You're lucky you're a good kisser."

"It's not luck."

"And they say actors have the ego. Listen, I would've been happier getting married at the courthouse. You know that."

He did. It wasn't Jessie's fault everything had snowballed out of control in the past eight weeks. His agent Liz and her agent Jeremy had talked Bill Rudolph into offering his mansion. It had been impossible for Jessie to say no, not after everything the producer had done for her. Like a pair of gremlins, the agents had leaked wedding tidbits to the rags and social media for Jessie and Nick's "own good." As if they needed more paparazzi on their doorstep.

Reading his mind, Jessie said, "The ceremony's an hour out of our lives. We say our vows and then we party before we head off to London. What's so bad about that? By the way, Mary bent my ear before she left for her sister's." Jessie snared a piece of sushi with her chopsticks. It dropped onto the island before it reached her lips.

"I can't take you anywhere, can I?"

Making a face at him, she got it right on the third try. "Anyway, Mary made me promise you'd settle on a best man by the end of this weekend."

"I'm asking Lyle."

"Lyle for you, Abbie for me. Anthony as ring bearer. No one else. That part we keep simple."

"Simple's good."

*

Being Chief of Detectives at Midtown North meant long hours. Sometimes it meant being married to the job instead of the wife. Lyle Barton stared at the reports on his desk. Paperwork, the part of the job he hated. It was nine forty-five. Barb had called twice, reminding him Dina was waiting for his help on her science project. Lyle scrubbed a hand over his long face, skin as slack as a hound dog's.

Draining his tenth cup of mud, he got up and stretched his taut frame, his eyes drawn to faded splotches on the floor. Steve Bushman had swallowed his gun in this room, in front of him and McDeare. Barton still had a hard time dealing with his partner's collusion with Martinelli. Especially at night, in his dreams. Who was he kidding? His nightmares.

At his cell's buzz, Barton clicked on. McDeare. "What's up?"

"I was wondering … how much would you hate being my best man New Year's Eve?"

"It depends."

"On what?"

"On what I have to wear." Silence. "McDeare? You there?"

"You're going to hate it a lot."

"A tux?"

"Worse. Tails."

"Why don't you just invite Queen Elizabeth while you're at it?"

"Very funny. The whole thing's gotten out of hand. But I need a best man."

Tails. "Yeah. Okay. Only for you, McDeare."

Barton could hear Nick laughing as he hung up. Funny. Lyle Barton, Nick McDeare's best man. He'd hated the arrogant SOB when he first met him. Life was one surprise after another.

*

His heart thumping as if he'd been scaling Mt Everest at a dead run, Nick woke with a start. Frantic, he scanned the bedroom for Anthony before he realized it was just a dream, a horrible dream. He'd been imprisoned in a cage, watching helplessly as Gianni grabbed Anthony, struggling and kicking. The boy was terrified, shrieking for Nick.

Those damned Oceano matches.

Nick glanced down at Jessie, nestled against his shoulder. She needed her sleep before rehearsal that day. They had the house to themselves for the weekend. Besides Mary being gone, this was Anthony's sleeepover weekend at Eric's. Jessie didn't have to sneak from her bedroom up to his fourth-floor suite at night. No disapproving looks from Mary in the morning. Carefully disentangling himself from her arms, Nick reached for his robe. He shuffled downstairs, pausing on the second floor. Early dawn shafted through the open doorways of the old two-room nursery under reconstruction.

Work would be finished within days. Nick wandered into the space. The wall separating the two rooms had been knocked down, creating an enormous open area for Nick's office, the place he'd pen his novels. Floor-to-ceiling bookshelves lined a wall. A desk faced arched windows, overlooking the back garden's curving cobblestone walkways and stone benches and fountain.

Next on the list were the master bedroom and sitting room, due for a total makeover. Nick and Jessie wanted no shadows from the past looming over their future.

Ambling to the windows, Nick stared down at a blood-red cardinal at the bird feeder. This house had such history. Jessie had been born in the brownstone, in her mother's family for generations. When Jessie was thirteen and her mother died, Mary Bodine had moved in, becoming a member of the family. Jessie's father had raised Andrew here as his foster son when Chelsea Brady passed away. Jessie had married Andrew and raised Anthony here, Andrew the only father Anthony had ever known. Now Nick was adopting Anthony, the papers already filed and signed. He'd steer him into adulthood, freeing him from Gianni's reign of terror.

It was fitting.

Gianni had killed Nick's brother. Nick was raising Gianni's son.

The monster had to be turning over in his grave.

*

Max Callaban's car had been trailing Anthony ever since the boy left his home yesterday afternoon. Max had watched as Anthony climbed into a dark limo, driven by an athletic black man wearing a three-piece suit. Anthony had seemed overly friendly with the chauffeur. Since when did his son fraternize with the help? And when did Jessica hire a car and driver?

The limo had pulled in front of a luxury building on East Sixty-Second Street, the driver escorting Anthony into the lobby. Max and Carlo had returned to the high-rise this morning, just in time to see Anthony emerge with another young boy and a woman who looked like the boy's mother.

Had Jessica farmed their son off on someone for the weekend so she could fornicate with the degenerate McDeare in private? *Che cosa la scopata?*

*

Anthony used to be thrilled to go to the movies with Eric Pemberton and his mom on Saturdays. He'd loved sitting in the dark theater eating buttered popcorn and drinking grape soda. He'd picture how he'd photograph things in the movie with the fancy old camera Uncle Nick had given him. It even used film.

But today he'd rather be playing soccer with Zane Harwell, his new friend at his new school. Besides, Anthony was too old to go to the movies with someone's mom. Zane lived around the corner from the movies downtown, and his mom let him go with his friends.

What he really wanted to see was the cool movie about aliens. But instead they were seeing a stupid cartoon about a lion. Anthony shoved popcorn into his mouth and stared sullenly at the floor. He was too old for-- Anthony froze. Someone was watching him. He could feel it.

Sliding up in his seat he peeked over his shoulder. No one was looking at him except an old lady, sitting next to a little girl. Anthony twisted around, trying to see everyone's face. Mrs. Pemberton leaned forward and glared at Anthony.

Hunkering down in his seat, Anthony fingered a ring on his right hand that Uncle Nick had given him. It had belonged to his son Jeffrey. Anthony's daddy Andrew had died and Uncle Nick's son Jeffrey had died, but now he and Anthony had each other. They'd chosen each other for a father and a son. Gianni didn't

- 8 -

count, and he was dead anyway. Whenever Anthony was afraid, he touched the ring and felt safe. He knew Uncle Nick would always protect him.

On the walk home with Eric and his mom, Anthony still had the creepy feeling someone was watching him. Uncle Nick had told Anthony he'd enrolled him in his new private school with his new adopted last name—he liked printing it out in capital letters, ANTHONY MCDEARE—because Andrew Brady was a celebrity and in the news. That's why the kids at the old school had teased Anthony—because he was Andrew Brady's son, Anthony Brady. Uncle Nick and Anthony's mom were celebrities, too, but it was Andrew Brady who was in the news the most because he was dead. Now Anthony was afraid he was a celebrity, too, even with a new name. Was someone following Anthony who knew about him?

Why couldn't he be a normal kid with normal parents? Why did he have to have three dads when other kids had one or two? It made Anthony so mad sometimes. Gianni popped into his mind again. But Gianni was dead. He was being a baby.

Pushing his fear away, Anthony raced for the marble lobby of Eric's apartment building, ignoring Mrs. Pemberton's cries to slow down.

*

"Okay, hold it," Quill Llewelyn shouted. Jessie watched the director sprint up the theater aisle and onto the stage. He clapped his arm around her. "Jessie, you have to fight those tears."

"I'm sorry, Quill," Jessie swiped at her wet cheeks. She was standing in front of a flag-draped coffin. Her character Christine had lost her precious son in the Vietnam War. But all Jessie kept seeing was Andrew's coffin in real life. "I know what you want. I'm trying. I just--I keep seeing Andrew."

"Look, honey," Quill soothed in that lilting Welsh accent, "I know how hard this is for you. Let's try it again, okay? If you see Andrew, use your grief. You want to be strong for Andrew, right?" Quill dashed back down the stairs, his long blond hair flying. He yelled over his shoulder to the rehearsal pianist. "Mimi, follow Jessie. If she stops and starts, just follow her."

Her hands on her hips, Jessie paced in a tight circle. Andrew. Of course. Andrew had always fallen apart whenever Jessie cried. He never knew how to stop the tears. She'd hang onto that. Jessie looked at the coffin. Instead of seeing her husband inside, she pictured him on the other side, pleading with her to stop crying.

Taking a deep breath, Jessie inched towards the casket, eyes on the flag. Her voice quavering, she began the opening stanza of "Not This Boy, Not My Son" a cappella. Her voice cracked. She closed her eyes and filled her lungs with air. Focusing on the coffin, she launched into the second stanza, the piano accompanying her this time.

Kneeling in front of the casket, Jessie pictured Andrew's eyes urging her to stay strong. Her voice steady, she smoothed out the flag as if she were straightening her son's collar. Jessie spread her arms, trying to hug the coffin, trying to hug her son.

Her voice caught in her throat. Burying her face in the flag, Jessie balled it in her fists as she fought for control. When she lifted her head, her eyes drifted skyward. As she rose from her knees, she railed at God for taking her son, begging him to take her instead. Her voice was strong and full-bodied. As Jessie built the song, her voice intensified and rose to a crescendo, her world telescoping into the moment, into Christine Mackey's skin.

When she finished, everyone in the theater broke into applause. Jessie blinked, back in the real world. Quill leapt onto the stage and hugged her. "You nailed it, Jessie. There won't be a dry eye in the house. Now go home and sleep on your day off. In two weeks, we open."

*

On a whim, Nick had ridden with Willie to pick up Jessie after rehearsal. The cast had recently moved from a rehearsal studio downtown to Dickason's, producer Bill Rudolph's theater complex in the heart of Times Square. Jessie's musical was being staged in the Rodgers and Hammerstein Theater, one of several in the modern arena.

Sitting in the last row of the darkened theater, Nick was amazed at how Jessie transformed onstage. The beautiful woman who was an endearing klutz in real life turned into a picture of fluid grace on the stage. Sliding down the seat, Nick had fought the image of his own lost son as Jessie sang an emotional song about her dead child. Jeffrey had died four years ago, but the ache was forever there.

The director brought the rehearsal to an end. Before Nick could reach the stage, Jessie's leading man bounded up the stairs to her side. Josh Elliot looped his arms around Jessie, kissing her forehead. Nick halted, watching as Jessie dropped her head on his shoulder.

Spotting Nick, Josh whispered something to Jessie before moving away. She lifted her head and smiled at Nick. "What a nice surprise. How long have you been here?"

"Not long." Nick stepped onto the stage.

"What's wrong?"

"Nothing." Nick draped his arms around her from behind. "That song, Jess," he whispered in her ear.

"You saw it? Oh God, it'll be so much better." Jessie whirled out of his embrace and said goodbye to Josh. "Come on," she told Nick. "My bag's in my dressing room. Let me show you around and then we can go home."

While Nick followed Jessie into the stage wings, she gave him a guided tour, pointing out the scenery flats and turntables on stage right and left. With a single rotation a whole new room would revolve into view. Jessie showed him the stage manager's booth, where the show would be called. Quick-change rooms were directly off both wings.

Jessie led Nick into the green room, the cast's communal gathering place, before they headed down a smaller hallway to Jessie's dressing room. Nick rambled around the cozy space, a mirror outlined in white bulbs on the dressing table. Blond wigs nested inside mounted open cupboards. A clothing rack ran along a wall, already holding some finished costumes. A framed picture of Anthony and another of himself sat on a side table next to a comfy couch. "No Andrew?"

"In the green room. I have to learn to go it alone now."

"You're not alone. You've got me. Always."

"And I love you for it." Jessie reached up and pressed her lips to his mouth. Drawing back, she said, "Let's stop at Amoy for take-out and spend the night in bed. It's our last chance before Anthony comes home tomorrow. What do you say?"

"I say you're brilliant." Nick reached into his pocket for his cell. "Peking Duck, sesame noodles, and spicy shrimp dumplings?"

"And scallion pancakes." Jessie grabbed her jacket and dance bag. "And that yummy eggplant with the ground pork."

Josh Elliot popped his Viking blond head into the room. "Jessie, just remembered. Don't forget we have that interview with the Entertainment Channel Monday after lunch." He winked at Nick.

Phoning in their order, Nick kept an eye on Josh. Was he that dumb, blond, and good natured, or was he good at acting that dumb, blond, and good natured?

He just knew he didn't like the son of a bitch. And he bet he dyed his hair.

*

Clint Vaughn had tailed Nick McDeare from the brownstone to the theater. He was parked down the street in his beat-up Chevy, his eyes fixed on the stage door. The bright marquee lights over the theater kept attracting his attention.

JESSICA KENDLE & JOSH ELLIOT
IN
TO HAVE AND TO HOLD

A WILLIAM RUDOLPH PRODUCTION

An hour later McDeare emerged with Jessica Kendle and climbed into the limo, stopping at a Chinese restaurant on East Fifty-Eighth Street before returning home. Clint double-parked half a block from the brownstone and speed-dialed Aldo. "I'm on McDeare. Looked him up on the Internet. He's some hot-shot author." Also vaguely familiar looking, and not from his book covers. The only thing Clint read was a racing form.

"He used to be an investigative reporter. A good one."

"What's this about?"

"The less you know, the better."

"Bullshit. What's this about?"

Aldo cleared his throat. "You know who Jessica Kendle is?"

"Hey, dumb fuck. I'm tailing them, remember?"

"Keep talking to me like that and you'll end up as landfill."

"Ooh, I'm scared."

There was a pause before Aldo said, "The real father of Jessica Kendle's son is going to abduct him New Year's Eve, with your help. In the meantime, I want your eyes on McDeare."

"I need more details."

"Look them up on the Internet. Dumb fuck." Aldo hung up on him.

Late that night Clint sat at his computer, slowly draining a bottle of scotch. It hadn't taken more than one Google search to discover Gianni Fosselli was Anthony Brady's biological father. The man had gone ape-shit and murdered Andrew Brady

- 11 -

when he'd discovered Brady had kept him away from his kid. Two years later, Fosselli had been arrested and killed in an escape attempt.

Supposedly.

Fosselli had played everyone for a fool, courtesy of Roberto Martinelli. Chuckling, Clint turned out the light and crawled into bed. Martinelli had orchestrated a brilliant sting. No surprise. Roberto was one of the smartest men Clint had ever known. They went back a long way. Clint had saved his fat ass on more than one occasion.

Growing up in the same Brooklyn neighborhood, Clint and Martinelli had been neither enemies nor friends. Both had had scrapes with the law, and both had kept their mouths shut. Later, Clint had joined the Marines, developing into a crack sharpshooter and sniper. Martinelli had become another kind of soldier, one who answered to organized crime, joining the Cappadore family. His skill had lain in his ability to get a job done without leaving a trace to the pile of corpses behind him.

Clint and Roberto had put their respective skills to common use more than once, to their mutual satisfaction. The two youths from Brooklyn had merged on the same path, their silent friendship a bond most people never understood. Clint didn't like Roberto and he didn't hate Roberto. He had too much money for his own good, but he'd trust him with his life.

As long as he played by the rules.

As for Aldo Zappella, Clint regarded him as an infinite source of amusement. Aldo took life much too seriously.

You let the good times roll, or you might as well be dead.

CHAPTER 2

A seductive touch. Jessie's eyelids fluttered open. Nick was staring down at her in the morning light, his eyes hazy. "Mmm," she whispered, curling her leg up around Nick's waist.

"The day is ours." He pressed his naked body to hers. "To do with as we will."

At her cell's jangle, she ordered, "Don't move."

"You've got sixty seconds."

It was Deidre Pemberton, Eric's mom, apologizing for calling on a Sunday morning. While Jessie said hello, she drew her leg further up Nick's back, tickling him with her toes, both silently laughing.

"Jessie," Deidre said. "You know I adore Anthony. He's always been a perfect little gentleman. But this weekend there've been some problems. I'm sorry. My chauffeur will be bringing your son home in a few minutes."

"... What happened, Deidre?" Jessie shot up. Nick stilled, watching her.

Deidre said that Anthony had resented her authority all weekend. She ticked off bad behavior at the movie and walking home, and he broke a Lalique vase tossing a football in the living room. "And then," Deidre said, her voice quickening, "in the middle of the night I found the boys in my husband's den watching a slasher movie on television. Those kinds of movies are blocked on Eric's bedroom TV."

"Deidre, I'm sorry. This kind of behavior doesn't sound like Anthony. Of course, I'll pay for the vase--"

"I don't care about the vase. It's Anthony I'm concerned about. I hope you understand if I feel it best we halt these weekend sleepovers for now."

Ending the call with apologies, Jessie reminded herself to send Deidre a new vase tomorrow. She and Nick threw on their robes and were waiting for Anthony in the kitchen when he returned home. "Start talking," Jessie said. "I just got a call from Mrs. Pemberton."

"What's the big deal?" Anthony didn't seem surprised. He opened the refrigerator and stuck his head inside. "Hey, Mom, will you ask Mary to buy us some new drinks? I want sports drinks."

"Anthony, we're not talking about Mary's shopping list." Jessie closed the fridge door. "We're talking about your behavior."

"I broke a vase. I said I was sorry. Mrs. Pemberton's stuck-up."

"Anthony! That's disrespectful." But Jessie smothered a snicker. Deidre Pemberton was a social climber and a snob.

"What about the movie late last night?" Nick asked.

"Eric and I watched television, no biggie." Anthony trotted to the pantry and studied its contents. Nick and Jessie exchanged arched eyebrows behind his back. "We need energy bars. The kind with football players on the wrapper."

"Anthony," Jessie said, "the kind of energy you need right now is a change in attitude. You know you're not allowed to watch those movies."

Anthony's calm demeanor disintegrated. "Everyone at school watches them. Why can't I be a normal kid? Is that a crime around here?!" He charged up the stairs, followed by the sound of his bedroom door whapping shut.

"What's going on with him?" Jessie stared at Nick. "My God."

"Your sweet little boy's growing up."

"Do kids just change their personalities overnight? Since he started his new school and met this friend Zane, he's--"

"Anthony's life hasn't been exactly normal." Nick folded his arm around her shoulder. "He's been to hell and back—Andrew, Gianni, the media circus, celebrity parents. I'd be more worried if Anthony bottled it up instead."

"You think he should talk to a therapist?" Jessie trusted Nick's insight. And Anthony adored Nick. There was a special bond there, something she didn't share.

"Let's keep a close eye on him. And we should ground him for a week. You want to be the bad guy, or should I?"

"You do it. I'm getting a headache."

*

By Monday morning Nick needed a workout, the kind you got pounding the pavement. After Jessie left early for the theater, Nick threw on sweats, stretched his legs, and headed outside.

It was a brisk fall morning, perfect for a long run. Concentrating on his breathing, Nick started out at an easy clip, waiting to feel his muscles settle into a greased rhythm. He trotted down Fifth Avenue, heading for the park entrance at Seventy-Second. Traffic was heavy during rush hour, including the sidewalk. Nick nimbly wove his way around pedestrians.

Something clipped the back of his neck. Nick stopped in his tracks, spinning around. There, on the sidewalk—a pack of ... Oceano matches. Nick picked it up, quickly scanning the mass of people streaming down the broad avenue, a stew of strangers. It was impossible to know where the matches had come from.

Someone was toying with him. No way was this random. Gianni was dead. Who else would want to torment Nick? With Oceano matches?

When Nick got back home he made a decision. Jessie would be out tonight— plans with Abbie after rehearsal. Nick called Lyle and asked to meet. The cop chuckled. "I've been looking for an excuse to get out of tonight's school conference. McGowan's Pub at Forty-Fifth and Eighth at seven. The best corned beef in town."

*

"Are you okay with this, Jessie?"

"Not exactly. How about you?"

Shrugging, Josh plopped onto the prop bed with her. "It's raw for a family musical, but I've done worse Off Broadway."

Quill had just sprung a revamped scene on Jessie and Josh--less than two weeks before opening. Jessie snorted, flipping through the new pages. "I don't think we're in a family musical anymore. I can't let my son see this scene." But Anthony wasn't the reason her blood pressure was spiking off the charts.

"So. What do you think?" Quill strode onto the stage.

"I'll just speak my mind." Jessie glanced at Josh. "I don't think this scene belongs in this musical."

"Jessie," Quill said, leaning against the prop dresser, "the old scene wasn't working. It was hokey. The play opened in the early seventies. It had to be updated."

"I know that, but—"

"Listen, we changed so many other scenes that this one stood out, and not in a good way. Now it'll be erotic. Hip. Do what you have to do to make it your own. I can guide you, but I want this to come from the two of you. It'll be more intimate and real that way. And just so you know, while you're up there on the turntable," Quill looked skyward, "the chorus will be on the stage floor doing their own gyrations. Why don't you rehearse with Mimi while I work with the chorus?"

As Quill gathered the chorus, Jessie stared at the stage floor. Once upon a time she and Andrew were America's sweethearts, Mr. and Mrs. Apple Pie. Now Quill expected her to simulate making love—graphic sex--wearing a bit of fabric no thicker than a flower petal. Anthony would never be able to see this play.

And Nick ... Nick.

*

It had turned into a beautiful autumn evening when Nick set out on foot to meet Lyle. The temperature had dropped into the upper forties, bringing out the first glimpse of suede, leather, and fur trim on the chic streets.

Ignoring the stares of recognition, Nick strode down Fifth Avenue, taking in the city. Yellow cabs' horns blended with the diesel whoosh of buses in an endless traffic jam. Doormen stood sentry over posh apartment buildings lacing the avenue. Central Park nestled between glass and steel towers, its trees dripping crimson leaves into the chill air. The famed Plaza Hotel held court across from the park's greenery. Saint Patrick Cathedral's ornate spires held their own against gleaming office buildings.

Nick cut across Rockefeller Plaza, passing the NBC Building. Soon the lower courtyard would morph into an ice rink, crowned by a glittering pine tree. Emerging onto Sixth Avenue, he heard someone call his name. He'd been on too many talk shows. Nick kept moving.

"Nick, it's Kristin." Nick glanced over his shoulder. Kristin Wallingford was running to catch up to him, wobbling in stiletto heels. Nick halted. The flight attendant hustled to his side, out of breath. "I thought that was you," Kristin gasped, dropping her shopping bags and patting her ample chest. "What are you doing in New York?"

Eyeing his ex-girlfriend, one of a multitude of ex-girlfriends, Nick crossed his arms. Not exactly an endangered species. "And what are you doing in New York?"

"Just got transferred back to the States from London. What a surprise! You look great. I was going to call you tomorrow when I got back to Washington."

"Why would you call me, Kristin? What part of 'We're finished' didn't you understand the first time?"

"I, well, I figured you'd cooled down by now over my, um, fit of jealousy."

"Fit of …? You destroyed Jessie's private property and knocked me unconscious."

"I know you, Nick. You can't stay mad at me for long. And I knew Jessie Kendle wouldn't turn into anything serious." Kristin broke into a grin, brushing her juggernauts against Nick's arm. "In fact, I'd like to invite you to a party at the British embassy Saturday night."

"I guess you haven't heard," Nick drawled, stepping back. "Don't you read the papers?"

"You know me." Kristin shrugged. "I get the news walking down the aisle of a Boeing 777. I miss something earth-shattering?"

"Just that I'm marrying Jessie nothing-serious Kendle on New Year's Eve."

Nick's words knocked Kristin a step backwards. "This has to be a joke. Why would you get married? I mean, you can't keep your pants zipped for more than five minutes."

"You always did have a penchant for hyperbole."

"Whatever that means. That poor woman. I feel sorry for her."

"You didn't feel too sorry for yourself when it came to your own hands unzipping my pants, did you?"

"You bastard." Kristin's eyes narrowed. "You knocked her up, didn't you? This is one woman who refuses to let you wiggle out of your responsibility. Jessica Kendle's too big for even the great Nick McDeare to use, abuse, and toss away."

"You're pathetic."

"That's funny. You, Nick, you're pathetic. One day you're going to break Jessie's heart like you broke mine. You can't help it. You are who you are. She'll find that out."

"Have a nice day." Turning on his heel, Nick jogged across the busy avenue.

When Kristen yelled after him that he hadn't heard the last of her, he didn't turn around.

*

"I'll be a couple of hours, Willie." Jessie's driver opened the limo's back door for her. "In fact, why don't you go home? Abbie and I will catch a cab."

"Nice try." Willie grinned. "It's my job to take you everywhere. I'll grab a bite and you page me when you're finished. I can take Miss Forrester home, too."

Jessie smiled at the soft-spoken man as she emerged from the back of the car. She gave up and agreed to page Willie. She had to admit having Mary's nephew around was a godsend. He was a formidable six feet five and as charming as a prince.

The trendy Park Avenue restaurant was a giant chessboard of shiny black and white marble squares. It made Jessie slightly dizzy. Abigail Forrester was already nursing a glass of white wine when Jessie dropped into a seat across from her. "Sorry I'm late. Major problem at rehearsal."

Laughing, Abbie fanned a hand through a mahogany mane thick enough to knit a scarf. "Jessie, we've been best friends for twenty years. I love you like a sister, but you've never once been on time. So what's the problem?"

Jessie ordered a glass of Pinot Grigio from the waiter. She pushed her menu aside, sweeping her silverware to the floor with a clatter. The waiter sprang away from a bouncing knife. "Oh God, sorry." After her utensils were replaced, she continued, "The problem's a revamped love scene sprung on Josh and me today. An extremely graphic love scene."

"Oh come on, you still have lots of time. You're a pro. You can do it."

"That's not what's bothering me. I'm ... not comfortable with it."

"Is it tacky?"

"It's actually very sensual. It takes place on our wedding night."

"Ooh," Abbie purred, "you get to strip down with Josh. I've been dying to do that for years. Details. I want details. That man is hot. Like a Norse god."

"Abbie, I'm not joking. I have to strip down, as you say, to a flimsy teddy before he flings me on the bed. And then I slither around on the sheets like Bathsheba and entice him to join me. After which, we simulate making love high over the stage while the chorus cops their own feel down below. I hate it."

"You're serious, aren't you?" Abbie leaned across the table. "After everything they put us through at Juilliard, wearing a teddy and faking a good screw is child's play. Do you remember when we all had to switch clothes with each other in Jerry's scene class? We--"

"Oh, don't remind me," Jessie groaned. But she started to laugh. "I never got the point of that."

"The point's exactly what you need in this situation. Lose all inhibition. Have fun with it." Abbie sat back. "What's really bothering you? You're the shyest actress I've ever known, but this is more than modesty."

"It's Nick." Jessie's wine was delivered and she took a sip, contemplating her words. "He's jealous of Josh."

Abbie cackled. "A little jealousy's healthy."

"I don't think so. Nick is ... Nick."

"Look, you know I adore Nick. Since I've been back I've come to love him as much as I loved Andrew. I even worked with him to, uh ... anyway, there's a reason he's a legend in the PI biz."

"I can't believe a famous lipstick model got a PI license. You're crazy, you know that? Even if it was to— Well." Jessie didn't want to revive her Gianni memories any more than Abbie. Nailing Gianni Fosselli as Andrew's killer was the reason Abbie had secretly worked for Nick.

"Hey, I wrapped a cheating-husband case," Abbie snapped her fingers, "like that. And I uncovered an embezzler. And then I, uh, back to the point--before he met you, everyone knows Nick McDeare juggled women like a waiter doing noon tables in a Times Square deli."

"Yeah, but this isn't about Nick the lady killer. It's about his body language whenever he sees me around Josh." And it was only going to get worse when he saw this new scene. Nick was not a marshmallow like Andrew, easy to handle when they hit a rough patch. Nick was more like a wall of steel.

"Jessie," Abbie said patiently, "what I'm trying to say is Nick didn't care who he hurt before he met you. Maybe now he knows how they felt. And that's a good thing. It'll make him more sensitive."

"More sensitive." Uh huh.

*

Lyle and Nick were on their second round of drinks in McGowan's back booth. It was a cop's bar, cheap and friendly, run by a former NYPD inspector. Probably the only establishment in New York Lyle knew of that hadn't been robbed.

"I agree." Lyle took a swig of his draft. "Two sets of Oceano matches turning up in your proximity's no accident. So you think it's our friend Roberto Martinelli?"

"On the face of it, who else? But why?"

"Because he's an SOB. Because you caught Fosselli and ended the don's cushy money-laundering business at Oceano."

"Except it's not his style." Nick took a gulp of bourbon. "Martinelli would come after me directly or forget about it. This person's playing games. But if not Martinelli, who?"

"Aldo Zappella? Zappella's a nasty crud, a street fighter who worked his way up the hard way in that family. You caused him a lot of trouble. Maybe he took it personally, thinks you made him look like a fool. He handpicks Ian Wexley to be fingered for Andrew's murder. Jessie's former lover, a creep with a grudge against her and Andrew. The same man who married Aldo's sister and made her life hell. And you blow the whole scheme to pieces. He must hate you for that mess. And Jessie."

Nick met Lyle's eyes. "If Aldo's behind this and he has Martinelli's backing, Jessie could be in real danger. We all could."

Would they ever be rid of Gianni Fosselli and his mob connections? Barton grimaced. "Take some extra precautions. Make sure Jessie's driven everywhere. The same with Anthony."

"Done. I spoke to Willie after I got back this morning."

"And I'll talk to Kersey in the Nineteenth, the brownstone's district. He can put an unmarked car on your street for a while."

Their mile-high corned beef sandwiches on soft rye were delivered. Barton smiled at the mound of French fries and sour pickles. "My arteries are hardening just looking at this. I'll die young but happy." He bit into his sandwich and glanced up at Nick, staring moodily across the room. Lyle swallowed, in heaven. "I'll take care of it, okay? I'll pay an office visit to Martinelli and Zappella tomorrow morning."

"This won't stop with a personal visit. You know what we need?"

"Yeah. A second sandwich." Lyle took another bite of his corned beef, on sensory overload."

"We need to get something on Martinelli, something we can use for leverage. He has to be involved in this. I know it. We need to block him."

"No offense, but you're fucking nuts. What do you get on a Mafia don? Murder? Martinelli's too insulated. RICO likes him where he is. Keep the big fish around so you can reel in all the little fish." Barton reached for the spicy mustard, slathering another layer on what was left of his sandwich.

"I need something so explosive," Nick mused, as if Lyle hadn't spoken, "that he'll never come near my family again. Something so damaging he'll rein in anyone else who even thinks about bothering us. Something personal."

"Good luck." Lyle took another bite and chewed slowly, groaning with pleasure.

"And we can forget about RICO. You're right. If they haven't gotten him by now, they never will." Nick leaned across the table, a pale light flickering in his eyes. "Look, you and I got Fosselli in months, when the NYPD got nowhere in two years. Maybe we can do the same thing with Martinelli. There has to be something. Everyone has baggage. Especially a Mafia kingpin."

Lyle stopped chewing. "Stop worrying about Martinelli. Let me handle this. I don't want you to end up dead."

"Thanks."

"I want to wear tails at your wedding."

*

When Nick returned home, he found Mary asleep on the sofa in the downstairs study, an open magazine on her stomach, the TV on. A lone hurricane lamp on the bar lit the homey room. The fire in the grate had burned down to embers, fireflies against the dark brick.

Eyeing the large oil painting over the mantel, Nick's own image stared back at him, Nick with Andrew at his side, both men in tuxedos. It had been a present from Jessie, the artist working with two separate photos. "It's not over, Andrew," Nick said. "Not until the shadows are gone for good."

Nick climbed the stairs, rapping a knuckle on Jessie's door before entering. She was sleeping, tinsel hair wisped across her face. He crossed the hall to check on Anthony. The boy was whimpering in his sleep, his head moving spastically. "Hey, Bongo," Nick urged, "wake up."

Anthony jerked upright, looking around in a panic. Nick dropped to the bed. "Bad dream?"

"Gianni. I heard you call me Bongo, and I woke up."

Bongo, Andrew's pet name for the boy. Nick would never let Anthony forget Andrew, the man who had raised him and loved him. "Want to talk about it?"

"I was on the playground at school. Gianni was watching me. He was there, staring at me. His eyes were spooky."

"Gianni's dead. He'll never hurt you again."

"But … the dream I had about him chasing after me came true, remember? Sometimes dreams happen!"

Nick knew all about those dreams. There were the good dreams, when Andrew had visited him and Anthony after his murder, coming alive for them. And there were the bad dreams, Anthony plagued by nightmares about a menacing man who chased him, a man who turned out to be Gianni in real life. When Gianni told Anthony he was his real father, the boy had run from him as fast as he could, straight into traffic.

"The other day," Anthony gulped, "when I was at the movies with Eric and his mom, I felt like someone was watching me, too."

Anthony was a bright and intuitive child. Nick went cold. His sixth sense wasn't something to be dismissed. But this time there was no dream Andrew to watch their backs. Andrew had said his farewells and disappeared from their lives with Gianni. Keeping his voice calm, Nick said, "Lie back down. How about if I tell you more stories about growing up in Japan?"

"Okay. Tell me about the funny stuff. Like the food."

"Did I tell you about the time I brought a stray mutt home and he ate my mom's whole platter of home-made gyoza?"

"What's geeoh…?"

"Dumplings. They take hours to make …"

A half hour later Nick crawled into bed, exhausted. But his mind was racing laps. Thank God they had Willie. Tomorrow he'd ask the driver to accompany Jessie everywhere and keep a low profile. He didn't want to alarm Jessie. She was a wreck, obsessed with opening night and now Anthony's problems, too. The last thing she needed to hear was they might have a stalker. And Anthony … He needed to have a serious talk with him without scaring the poor kid to death.

*

In a frenzy, Jessie awoke before dawn. She raked her hair off her face and looked around wildly. It was only a dream. Thank God. Jessie flew up the stairs to Nick's suite, sliding into bed and melting her body against his warm back. He stirred and rolled over. "You're shaking. What's wrong?"

"A bad dream." Jessie wrapped her arms around him, breathing in his soapy scent.

"Want to tell me about it?"

The image was still in her head. She was leaving the theater when a gunshot rang out. A man crumpled to the ground, a scarlet pool seeping beneath him. Nick, was it Nick? Jessie screamed, crouching beside him …

"Jess?"

"I just want to forget about it," she whispered. "It's silly now. I know what brought it on. A fan last night when I left the restaurant. More like an anti-fan."

"What happened?"

Jessie could still picture the giant of a man with a mop of black hair yelling at her. "Any more of Andrew's brothers out there for you to marry, Lady Kendle? Going to get Nick McDeare killed, too?" Jessie squeezed her eyes shut. "It was nothing. Willie stepped in and took care of it."

"You're sure it was nothing?"

"Yeah." Jessie hesitated. "Just someone trying to get too close. Fans seem more aggressive these days. Or maybe I never noticed because I always had Andrew at my side."

"The public's definitely more aggressive. Social media, celebrity TV, they feel like they know you. I see it myself." Nick stared thoughtfully at her. "Look, you're about to open on Broadway. You're famous. I want you to be extra careful. Since we've got Willie, let's use him. He's an ex-cop. I want him to accompany you in and out of the theater and anywhere else you go. Don't worry. He'll make himself scarce. You'll have your privacy. But I want him around just in case, okay?"

"Sure. Sounds like a plan." Lifting up, Jessie kissed Nick, her touch tentative. Their lips parted, and she twined her fingers through his hair, combing it from his eyes before kissing him again, this time with heat. As the early morning sun spangled into the room, nothing existed for Jessie but Nick loving her. That's the way it would be from now on. Nick was her future.

*

Max was glad to be home in Ohio. It was a new day, evening to be exact, and time for dinner. He and Carlo had left Manhattan last night, after Carlo's award-winning confrontation with Jessica in front of that restaurant. Too bad Jessica's thug of a driver had interrupted them. What kind of chauffeur behaved in that fashion, stepping in and pushing a fan away?

After topping off his Mediterranean salad with shavings of Parmesan cheese, Max grabbed a loaf of crusty garlic bread and carried his dinner to the dining-room table. Dimming the chandelier and lighting two tapers, Max slipped a New York Philharmonic CD into his sound system.

He seated himself, filling his crystal flute with Italian Bolla and arranging his linen napkin. Whether alone or with company, dinner was an event. But first ... Max unfolded himself from his chair and slipped on the cardigan sweater he kept in the hall closet, protection against the room's chill. Ah, better. He sat down and took a sip of wine, finally beginning his meal.

His cell buzzed, interrupting his tranquility. Max dug the phone out of his pocket and glanced at the screen. Maybe the New Year's Eve plans were set. "Good evening, Aldo."

"What the hell are you up to? Barton paid Roberto and me a visit earlier today. He wanted to know about some Oceano matches that turned up around McDeare."

"He's asking the wrong people." Max laughed.

"Where are you?"

"Back in Ohio. The adventure's over. For now."

"Roberto says to cut the crap. No more games. You hear me?"

Max put down his wine glass hard, swearing at the bloody stain that splashed over the white lace tablecloth.

"A faint chuckle echoed through the room. "And just what do you find so amusing, Aldo?"

"Does it sound like I'm laughing?"

CHAPTER 3

"Stop the games?" Aldo was a fool, a *scemo*. Max managed to hold onto his temper, his voice silky smooth. "Where's the fun in that?"

"If you want our help getting your boy back, stay in Ohio until the time comes."

Max steadied his breathing, calming himself. That ghostly chuckle—merely electrical noise on the other end of the line. He covered the scarlet stain with a cloth napkin, letting Aldo chatter on. "We respect our mutual ties ... Max, but not to the point of attracting attention and compromising business."

Ah, yes, business. Ties stemming far back to his own father's treachery in Italy. Roberto had dealt with Paolo Fosselli's greedy business betrayal his own way. And Gianni Fosselli had kept a complicit silence, for which Roberto had let him live and rewarded him handsomely. It was tragic his father had been foolish enough to make Mama his accomplice ...

Breaking off a piece of garlic bread, Max ignored another distant chuckle. "How are the plans for New Year's Eve progressing?"

"We got our hands on the guest list. Two British brothers by the name of Hawthorne mailed their regrets. We just sent a note saying they had an unexpected change of plans and will be happy to attend after all. We want a man to assist you that night."

"Someone won't notice we're not the Hawthorne brothers?"

"They're suits from McDeare's publishing house, names on a letterhead. We got a man in London watching the Hawthorne mail. He'll snatch the entry passes for the Rudolph mansion that night."

"Excellent. Thank you."

"By the way, Roberto wants to know if the work's begun on your face?"

Sessions with a discreet plastic surgeon in Cleveland had already been scheduled. The dimple in his chin would disappear, his eyes would alter shape, and his cheeks would become more prominent. Max had also been working with speech and voice tapes to eliminate his Italian accent.

"By New Year's Eve," Max assured Aldo, "even my own son won't recognize me."

The crackle of a laugh died as he clicked off.

Static. Shoddy American workmanship.

*

It had been a long day for Nick. After putting in four hours on the new book that morning, he'd met his agent Liz Scott for lunch to discuss the manuscript's progress. THE SILVER LINING was a fictionalized account of Andrew's life and death, the main characters altered to protect their privacy. Nick was going to surprise Jessie with a tribute to Andrew. He'd never written a book this fast, in just two months, but the research was all in his head. He'd lived the events and breathed the danger. All he had to do was let it flow through his fingertips onto the keyboard.

Nick had wasted the rest of the afternoon at a salon called Marcel's. He and Barton had been forced to stand still for hours as a silly man measured and fussed, fitting them for tails. When Nick and Lyle had finally been sprung from hell they'd headed for the nearest bar to toss back a few. Lyle's mood had been darker than his own. By the time Nick returned home, he was feeling no pain.

Now Mary stood in the middle of the kitchen, her back stiff, copper skin flushed. Anthony was slumped in the breakfast nook, looking cranky.

"I don't know who I'm more angry with," Mary declared. "You or Jessie. I go to the trouble of making a nice meal, and you disappear for hours and Jessie's locked in a bedroom upstairs." She turned her dark eyes on Anthony. "Go get Josh and your mother. We're eating right now, with or without them."

Muttering under his breath, Anthony stomped up the stairs.

"Josh?"

"They've been rehearsing upstairs. If you want dinner, you better sit down. I'm in no mood."

Neither was Nick. He wove his way to the dining room. Sure enough, five places had been set at one end of the long oak table. Nick dropped heavily into the seat at the head of the table. He'd always loved the dining room's medieval aura, the beamed ceiling, carved oak trim, and ornate chandeliers. The room evoked ancient kings and their absolute powers

Studying his distorted reflection in a spoon, Nick envied their ability to banish fools from court and chop off heads.

*

Josh Elliot managed to get through the awkward meal by politely ignoring McDeare, smiling in the gaps of silence, and praising Mary's cooking. A brooding Nick filled his and Anthony's plates with lamb chops, baked potatoes, and broccoli, letting Jessie take care of herself and Josh. Mary focused on cleaning her plate and talking about the weather.

The atmosphere lightened when Nick disappeared upstairs before dessert. After coffee and Mary's cherry cobbler, Jessie threw on a poncho and walked Josh outside. "I want to apologize for Nick," she said quietly. "He had a fitting for the wedding this afternoon. He hates all the fuss. Nick's not--"

"Look, Jessie, don't apologize for him," Josh said lightly. "It's just that he's so different from Andrew. It's hard to believe they were brothers. Of course, he's a writer. They live in their own worlds."

"Nick's slow to open up to strangers. You'll get to know him as time passes." Jessie gazed at him, her hair glinting sliver under the full moon, eyes gauzy with mystery. "I wouldn't be surprised if you two became friends. Nick had the same reaction to Lyle Barton, and now Lyle's his best man."

Josh smiled back at her. Jessie had stolen Josh's breath away with her frosty beauty when he'd met her backstage years ago. Only being married to a star the magnitude of Andrew Brady had prevented him from making a play for her. But Nick McDeare, prince of darkness? Jessie could do better. Anyway, Josh always fell in lust with his leading ladies. It came with the territory.

"Aw, I'm sure you're right, Jessie." Broadening his smile, Josh's eyes twinkled. "We'll probably become friends."

*

Jessie stepped into Nick's suite, hearing the shower's rush. Maybe Nick's rotten attitude would be washed down the drain. The room was a mess. Clothes were flung over the furniture. Papers tumbled from the cluttered desk onto the floor. The wastebasket overflowed. Five half-empty water bottles crowded the dresser next to the contents of Nick's pockets. Nick's gold pocket watch gleamed in the mix of loose change, a family heirloom preserved by his birth mother Chelsea for her elder son. Nick did have a sentimental streak, even though it killed him to admit it.

Hearing the shower snick off, Jessie headed for the bathroom. Nick stood in front of the sink, a towel wrapped around his torso, wet hair hanging in his face. He met her eyes briefly in the mirror before running a comb through his hair.

"You were rude tonight."

"Was I?" Nick squeezed toothpaste onto his toothbrush. "He stared at his reflection as he brushed.

"Don't be flip." Jessie leaned against the doorframe, crossing her arms. "Did something happen today to put you in such a lousy mood, or was it Josh?"

Nick stopped brushing. "You don't think it was just my surly self making a guest appearance?"

"Stop evading the question."

"Why would Josh put me in a lousy mood?" Nick spit out his toothpaste and rinsed out his mouth.

"You tell me."

"Where did you find that tailor for Barton and me?"

"Is that what's bothering you, the tailor? Your agent Liz found him. He's the 'in' man for celebrity weddings these days."

Turning around, Nick stared at the floor. When he looked up, his eyes were guarded. "Why were you rehearsing here tonight?"

"Why the inquisition?" He continued to stare at her. "Okay. Quill threw a new scene at Josh and me yesterday. Our characters' wedding night. Neither one of us is comfortable with it so we wanted some private time to work out the kinks."

"So you and Josh took a quickie between the sheets?" Nick brushed past her into the sitting room.

"Don't be ridiculous! This is a play. We're acting."

"I'm going to bed."

"Wait a minute." Jessie blocked his path. "We need to talk about this. This is my job. Do you think I'd fool around with Josh while Anthony and Mary were waiting for you downstairs?"

"Would you fool around with Josh if they weren't?"

"Do you really think so little of me?" Jessie could feel her face growing hot. "Think of what you're saying!"

Nick looked at her for what seemed like an eternity. And then his expression softened. "Jess," he rasped. "Come here."

Thank God her Nick was back. Jessie pressed her head against his chest, his arms wrapped around her. He smelled like shampoo and toothpaste.

"I can be such an ass. I'm sorry. Forgive me?"

"Maybe."

"I'll make it worth your while." He knuckled a finger over her jaw. "I promise."

*

If there was one thing in life Lyle Barton prized besides his family, it was his ability to read people, an invaluable asset for a detective. And what his people instincts had picked up today had him on edge. Pacing his den, Lyle couldn't sleep, his mind as frenzied as a hornet's nest.

He'd kept his promise to Nick and paid a visit to Martinelli and Zappella that morning at the leather-import office, one of Martinelli's legitimate business fronts. They'd been surprised when Lyle brought up the Oceano matches. That surprise had been followed by a hint of anger.

So where was the anger directed? It wasn't with each other. Aldo had shot Martinelli a knowing look.

Which meant ... someone else had showered Nick with matches. And Martinelli and Zappella suspected they knew who that someone was. An underling trying to grab the big boss's attention? Barton doubted it. That kind of unsolicited attention could get you disappeared.

Only one other person would get his kicks from taunting Nick with Oceano matches. Just one.

That crazy thought had been eating away at Lyle all day, all through the wacky fitting with the talky tailor, all through his gloomy session with Nick at the bar. It was too abhorrent to discuss with Nick. Lyle wasn't even comfortable discussing it with himself.

First he needed to pore through the records on Gianni Fosselli's escape and death until he could recite every line by memory. He needed to check and double check every fact about that day until he knew them as well as he knew his middle name was Zachariah. He needed to learn everything he could about Roberto Martinelli and how his mind worked. Without telling him why, he needed to share that information with Nick and pick his brain for his own insights into the mob boss. And only then would he allow himself to think the unthinkable.

Was it possible Martinelli was the mastermind behind the hoax of all hoaxes?

Had Gianni Fosselli survived that explosion at sea?

It didn't matter how late it was or how long it took. Lyle needed a favor. He made a call to an old friend from the Academy.

It ended up taking over a week.

*

The sun had set before Nick knew it. Three days before opening night, and Nick was holed up in his new office, a man obsessed with anything but Jessie's Broadway debut. Not to mention he should be scrambling to get his manuscript in by Christmas, but that wasn't what was taking up every waking moment either.

Nick swore. All that paled next to his family's safety. From the day he'd spoken to Lyle about Martinelli and those Oceana matches until today, he'd been focused on one thing: finding the key to Martinelli's closet.

The closet that hid the skeletons.

Fluent in several languages, Nick had spent the entire day devouring Italian newspapers, digging into public records, even scouring the Italian Internet and social media for anything new he could scrounge up on Martinelli.

Scanning his files, Nick reviewed what he'd learned to date. Roberto had been born in Sicily, coming to the United States as a child. The oldest of four children, he'd joined the Cappadore family as a teenager, quickly moving up through the ranks. Unlike his criminal peers, Roberto seemed to have no vices: no drinking, no womanizing, no gambling. By the time he was forty, he was next in line to take over when Godfather Cappadore died. And now Martinelli was the last don left from the decimated crime families of New York City.

Roberto had been the focus of dozens of investigations, but never indicted. He kept himself so well insulated the law could never touch him. His men were fiercely loyal. Any traitor or threat to his power vanished, usually quietly. He had a slew of anonymous journalists, judges, and politicians in his pocket. Not one was ever identified. He kept an eye on their welfare, and they kept on eye on his. His picture was never in the paper, on the Internet, or broadcast on TV. The man had more pull in New York City than the mayor. He never needed to worry about being elected. Easier to murder the opposition.

Martinelli had married late, at thirty-five. His wife Marcella was the daughter of a mob scion in Genoa. There were no children, and the couple was rarely seen in public together. Marcella was shy, dowdy, and docile. Close to her large family across the Atlantic, she spent many months every year in Genoa caring for her aging mother.

That was Roberto Martinelli's official story. As sterile as pasteurized milk. Nick had yet to ferret out the unauthorized biography.

At his cell's buzz, Nick picked up. Barton. He had something for him.

*

Slouched behind the wheel of his weather-beaten Chevy day after day, Clint Vaughn had memorized the occupants' routines. The little boy went to school, wearing a navy blazer over khaki pants. Jessica Kendle went to rehearsal. McDeare jogged every morning, rarely venturing out for the rest of the day unless it was to meet a man Aldo had identified as Lyle Barton. A cop, the only interesting cog in this wheel. The black woman left the brownstone to run errands and go shopping. A group of workmen arrived in the early morning and didn't leave until the evening.

A boring family. No one came home drunk or consorted with anyone who belonged in a police lineup. No bookies paid a discreet visit. No flamboyant theater types pranced in at all hours for drugs or orgies. If McDeare was fooling around on Kendle, Clint couldn't see any sign of it. Not unless he had a bimbo stashed under his bed with the dust bunnies. These people belonged in a loaf of white bread. Clint hated white bread. If your life wasn't exciting, you might as well be a plant.

The best part about this stakeout was that Clint had finally figured out why McDeare looked familiar. All it took was a little blast from the past. Now THAT was delicious.

His cell buzzed. "Yeah? ... Stop calling me. When I have something you'll know it."

It was after nine. Clint had intended to leave a half hour ago but Barton had suddenly shown up, still inside. Barton and McDeare making like Butch and Sundance made Clint's fillings ache. Aldo insisted the men were just friends. But Aldo was an idiot. A cop was a cop and this one was Chief of Detectives. And tonight Cochise had carried a thick manila envelope into the brownstone. Sketches for the latest wedding attire? Clint snickered. He didn't think so. He squirmed behind the wheel. Something was up.

Barton emerged fifteen minutes later. Surprisingly, he bypassed his double-parked car and approached a dark sedan parked further down the street. The passenger window lowered. Barton leaned down and conversed with someone. An unmarked police car. How had Clint missed that?

What the fuck was going on?

*

For approved eyes only, Martinelli's RICO files. Nick skimmed the folder Lyle had brought him. The man was a magician. Nick's stomach growled. He'd worked his way through dinner again. He needed a short break.

Setting the Martinelli dossier aside, Nick headed for the kitchen. He devoured left-over ham and sweet potatoes in ten minutes flat, blessing Mary's culinary skills. On the way back up to the office, he stopped by the master bedroom suite. The workmen had left only an hour ago.

Nick strolled throughout the cavernous room. A carved wooden king-sized platform bed had been constructed, the special-order mattress and box springs on order. On the opposite wall, floor-to-ceiling bookshelves were taking shape. Best of all, a beauty of a marble fireplace was nearly restored. The bathroom now had a hot tub. And the dressing room had doubled in size, holding a dressing table, closets, cedar storage, and overhead racks. A suite fit for royalty.

At the sound of raised voices across the hallway, Nick headed for Anthony's room. He found Mary and Anthony arguing about the TV. "Anthony," Nick said calmly, "it's almost ten o'clock. Turn off the TV and go to bed."

"No. And you can't make me." Anthony punched up the sound on the remote, a car chase blaring. "You're not my real dad and Mary's not my mom!"

The kid was having a rough time. Hamlet, the Siamese cat, reclined like the Sphinx next to him. "Mary," Nick said, "please go downstairs. I'll handle this."

"Gladly," Mary hurried from the room.

Crossing his arms, Anthony told Nick, "I liked things how they used to be. I want Daddy to be alive. Not a ghost."

"We all want that, Anthony. But we can't change what happened."

"I wish we could. I wish magic was for real and Daddy was back, not you!"

Flicking off the television with the remote, Nick told himself this outburst had been coming for a long time. "You don't want me to be your father?" he asked gently. "If that's how you really feel, I'll stop the adoption papers for now. We can talk about it later, when you feel better."

Breathing hard, Anthony wouldn't look at him.

"I love you, Anthony, and I always will, no matter what." Nick touched his shoulder. "So does Mary. Mary's a member of this family and so am I. I'm your uncle, and I'm marrying your mother. Now you need to get under those covers and turn out the bedside light. It's time for bed."

In a huff, Anthony did what he was told, turning away.

"Good night, Anthony."

Silence. Nick hoped Jessie was having a better night than he was.

*

Lyle Barton didn't mind the drive to Queens at this hour of the night. Rush hour was long gone, and he could breeze home in under twenty minutes. He'd love to live in Manhattan, but who could afford it? Not a civil servant with a daughter who needed braces and a math tutor.

What a day. Barton had sat at his desk for hours, going over the police report on Gianni Fosselli's death at sea. It was a grueling read, no matter how many times he reviewed it. His partner Bushman, AKA Cobra to the mob, had helped Fosselli escape from jail, leaving three dead bodies in his wake. Including Fosselli's own nephew Eduardo Santangelo, the hit man Martinelli had hired to get the job done. Lyle had ordered Detectives Manganaro and Loman to search the Milano, a cruise ship the fugitive owned before selling the line to Martinelli. After heading out to sea, Mario Manganaro had spied Fosselli at a speedboat's wheel, just after it was lowered over the liner's side by two of the crew. Mario aimed his gun at the boat as it raced away, inadvertently hitting the gas tank and causing an explosion. Barton had delegated Manganaro and Loman to investigate the incident. The finished report was detailed and thorough.

But that afternoon Barton had taken Mario to lunch, drilling him with questions. Was Mario one-hundred-percent certain that Fosselli was the man in the boat? Yes, he was certain. Was Mario one-hundred-percent certain that Fosselli hadn't survived the explosion? Yes. He and Loman had been immediately taken out in a lifeboat to survey the wreckage. No one could've survived the blast. There'd been nothing left of the craft but charred splinters. They'd found one shoe floating ...

The shoe. Barton had picked up the phone and asked desk officer Steinmetz to quietly check the size and make of that shoe. An hour later, Steinmetz had come through. A size twelve. An inexpensive American brand. And Lyle's gut had begun to hurt. Gianni was allergic to cheap. And he bet all his clothes were Italian made. Especially the shoes.

Later that afternoon, Lyle's old Academy buddy had finally shown up in his office. Preston Kramer was a part of the RICO team, the resident expert on Martinelli. Press hand delivered a thick manila envelope, eyes-only copies of the Martinelli file Lyle had begged for over a week ago. Against rules and regulations, but it happened. One day Press would ask Lyle for a favor, and he'd get it.

Barton had made another copy for Nick and dropped it off on his way home. And a fine piece of luck he'd made the trip to the brownstone. His conversation with Kersey's surveillance team—finally in place after cutting through departmental red tape--had been enlightening. The cops and pigeons weren't the only squatters on the street. A man in a dark Chevy had also taken an interest in the block. The plainclothes team had spotted him earlier in the day and snapped his mug with a telephoto lens. Copies would be sent to Lyle's e-mail. Another wrinkle in a shitty day.

Lyle sped across the Queensboro Bridge. Tomorrow morning the Milano would be in port for its weekly turnaround. Barton intended to board the ship and ask a few questions. All a prelude to the question he couldn't stop asking himself as he darted through traffic.

Was Gianni Fosselli dead?

Or was Gianni Fosselli ... not dead?

Jesus Christ.

*

As the stage went to black, Jessie dashed into the wings. Spotting her dresser's silver topknot, she made a beeline for it, shimmying her sheath off her hips as she ran. Nora had the ball gown accordioned in her hands, ready to slip over Jessie's head. This was the fastest costume and wig change in the show, requiring completion in twenty seconds. While Nora jiggled the zipper up the back of the flaming red ball gown, the wig master James flicked off Jessie's old wig and fitted the new one.

The orchestra vamped, Jessie reaching for her glass of champagne on the prop table. The outline was there ... but no glass. Panicking, Jessie scanned the long table. No glass! Where was Esther, the prop mistress?

Hearing the orchestra's relentless vamp, Jessie had no choice but to sprint for the stage. She collided with a stagehand, her spike heel coming down hard on the man's foot. Ignoring his yelp, Jessie zeroed in on the white gleam of Josh's tuxedo shirt in the darkness. She reached out for him, her heart pounding like a heavy metal band, grateful when Josh's hand clasped hers.

As the lights came up, Jessie whispered, "No glass." She was supposed to make a toast. This was a major faux pas. It was only an evening dress rehearsal, but Quill treated dress rehearsals as performances, inviting select people to sit in and share their impressions. Bill Rudolph himself was in the house tonight, along with several major investors.

Josh came to her rescue, ad-libbing, "My wife!" He chuckled and looked around at the other party guests on stage. "She begged me all day to let her make the toast, and then she forgets her glass. Here, Christine, have mine. We've shared everything else over the past twenty years."

Taking the glass from Josh, Jessie kissed his shoulder. When she looked back up she blinked, his face out of focus. Swallowing hard, she gazed out over the house and lifted her glass to make her toast.

But the rows of colored gels lining the ornate ceiling turned into a blur of fuzzy colored dots that floated downward like streamers.

The glass slipped from her hand as darkness folded her up.

Jessie felt an arm circle her waist before she had the sensation of falling through the rabbit hole like Alice.

CHAPTER 4

The front door slammed, followed by a patter of footsteps on the stairs. Swinging around in his office chair, Nick glimpsed Jessie buzz down the hallway. What was she doing home at this early hour? "Jess?" Her bedroom door swung shut.

Willie appeared in his doorway. "Jessie fainted at rehearsal, Nick. Mr. Rudolph was there. He set her up for an appointment with his doctor tomorrow morning."

"Is she all right?"

"I'm no doctor, but I think she's just run down. She confessed she hadn't eaten since breakfast. No wonder she fainted."

Nick thanked Willie. He stuffed the Martinelli file into his desk drawer and headed for the master bedroom. Jessie sat on the platform bed's bare wood frame, chin cupped in her hand.

"Are you okay? What's this about fainting?"

"I just forgot to eat today, that's all." She sighed dramatically. "My understudy's finishing the dress rehearsal. Do you believe it?"

"That's why you're in a snit? Your understudy?"

"That woman's been dying to step into my shoes for weeks, classic Eve Harrington. The minute--"

"Eve Who?"

"Harrington. ALL ABOUT EVE? A movie about a starlet who worms her way into Bette Davis' theatrical shoes?"

"Haven't seen it." Nick shrugged.

"How can I marry a man who's never seen ALL ABOUT EVE?" Jessie clapped her hands to her head. "Andrew and I could quote every line."

"I'm not Andrew."

"I know."

"I'll make you the same offer I made Anthony," Nick said evenly. "He's not sure he wants me to be his father. Maybe you'd rather not have me as your husband?"

"What made Anthony say a thing like that?"

"You didn't answer my question."

"I'd better talk to him."

- 33 -

Springing up, Jessie dashed for the doorway and lost her balance. Nick grabbed her before she crumbled to the floor. "My God, what's wrong with you?"

"I'm so tired." Sobbing, Jessie clung to Nick, her stage makeup staining his T-shirt. "I have the mother of all understudies out to get me, watching me constantly. The other day I caught her trying on my costumes. And Anthony's turning into a different child. I barely have time to eat. I can't get a good night's sleep. I hate sleeping upstairs in my old room. The mattress sags. The whole room makes me feel like I'm five. I want my bed back."

"Why don't you sleep in one of the other bedrooms on the third floor?"

"I hate those rooms."

"It's at least another week before you can move back into the master bedroom."

"I know." She sniffled.

"Isn't there a single bed in this house besides your own you can sleep in comfortably?"

"Just one."

*

Anthony couldn't sleep. He wanted Uncle Nick to be his father more than anything in the world. Even Zane thought Uncle Nick was cool. And Zane was smart. He went to their private school on a scholarship, not because he was rich.

Fingering the ring Uncle Nick had given him, Anthony thought how it made him feel like he was never alone. He liked to pretend it was a magic ring. But now he felt lonelier than ever.

Rolling onto his side, Anthony stroked Hamlet. One day he'd take pictures of Hamlet for a book about cats. Zane would write the story. Zane and Anthony had met on the school paper. Anthony wished he had a brother and sister like Zane did.

"You still like me, don't you, Hamlet?" The cat lifted his head, staring at Anthony. He jumped to the floor and strutted from the room, tail straight up like a ruler.

Even Hamlet was mad at him.

*

Ham with pineapple, sweet potatoes, and buttered baby peas. Comfort food, Jessie's best medicine. Nick planted the dish in the microwave.

"Nick." Mary stood on the back staircase. "What's going on? I heard Jessie come in, but she's not in her bedroom."

"She's up in my suite. Which is where she's going to sleep until the master bedroom's finished."

"And where will you sleep?" Mary clomped downstairs.

"With Jessie." The microwave pinged. Nick placed the plate on a tray, beside a bottle of water.

"There's an impressionable young boy in this house."

"Listen, this situation's ridiculous. Jessie and I are getting married in a couple of months. I'll explain it to Anthony in a way he'll understand."

"I don't like—"

"Jessie fainted at rehearsal tonight."

"What?" Mary's hand flew to her chest. "Is she all right?"

"She will be. She's exhausted and run down."

"No wonder, what with her running up to your suite all hours of the night."

Softening his tone, Nick said, "Jessie sleeps best with me. She agreed if I explain it the right way, Anthony will be okay. With the master bedroom torn up, this is the obvious solution."

"Anthony isn't even eight years old. What will he think?"

"Anthony lived through Andrew's murder. He survived being hit by a car. And he managed to handle learning the truth about Gianni. I think he can deal with our sleeping arrangement."

*

Clint kept his cell pressed to his ear as he watched the bartender refill his glass. "Thanks, Howie." He took his drink to a deserted booth. Hanratty's was quiet tonight.

"Well ...?" Aldo snapped on the other end of the line, "It's midnight. What the hell did you call me about?"

"The cops are watching the Brady brownstone. In an unmarked car. What's going on?"

"I ... don't know. It's probably because the Kendle woman's opening on Broadway. Fans and the press. Keep me posted."

Aldo had no intention of being straight with him. It was up to Clint to cover his own ass.

At which he was a master of the universe.

*

Careful to stay on Mary's good side, Nick stacked Jessie's empty dishes in the dishwasher and stowed the tray in the pantry. As he turned out the lights, he spotted Anthony standing at the foot of the stairs.

"I'm sorry, Dad," Anthony said. Nick took a step forward. Anthony rushed into his arms. "Don't stop the adoption," Anthony whispered. "Please. I love you, Dad."

Nick leaned back to look Anthony in the eye. "Dad?"

"Uncle Nick's too long to say all the time. And Zane calls his dad Dad."

"I love you, too. Son." Anthony grinned. "How about a nightcap?" Nick asked. "You get that sports drink, and I get bourbon. I put it on Mary's list. Don't tell your mom I let you stay up this late."

"Let me drink mine from the bottle, okay?"

As they settled onto stools at the island, Nick said, "I want to talk to you about your mom."

"Is she okay? I heard her come home early."

"She'll be fine. She's just ... been under a lot of pressure lately. Working long hours. It's getting to her."

"She wasn't like this before when she was in a play. When Daddy was alive."

Daddy, the man who could recite ALL ABOUT EVE. Andrew was still haunting him. He was probably roaring with laughter. "Listen, I think that's part of the problem," Nick began carefully. "She's missing your daddy just like you are. This is the first time she's done a play without him." Nick took a gulp of his bourbon. "Anthony, your mom hasn't been getting enough sleep. She had to move out of her bedroom for the renovation, and she hates it. So she's going to sleep up in the suite with me ... until we get married."

"She goes upstairs in the middle of the night anyway," Anthony whispered. "She doesn't think I know. Don't tell her, okay?"

"Um, cool. It's just between us." Nick squashed a smile. Kids saw life in straight lines. It was the adults who got lost in the scribbles.

"Night, Dad." Anthony yawned.

His son jumped down and climbed the stairs.

Dad.

*

Barton strode through the West Side Cruise Ship Terminal the next day. He flashed his badge to the security guard and asked directions to the captain's quarters onboard the Milano.

Five minutes later he surprised Captain Vincenzo Verde having lunch in his cabin. Introducing himself, Barton studied the captain. Distinguished looking, dark hair going white, crow's feet from a lifetime of squinting at the horizon. A captain's captain. "Don't bother to get up, Captain." Lyle closed the door. "Andrew Brady's murder happened under my watch. So did Gianni Fosselli's escape. I have a few questions about Fosselli, if that's okay with you."

The captain was fluent in English according to Mario, but Verde stumbled through his answers about the day in question. When Lyle showed him a picture of Gianni, the captain verified it was Fosselli aboard that day. He'd threatened the lives of Verde's family if the captain didn't accede to his demands, including ordering two of his crew to lower the lifeboat for his secret guest.

Lyle thanked Verde and returned to the terminal, descending the escalator to the Milano's crew entrance. He showed his badge to the officer on duty and asked to see the two crew members who'd lowered the lifeboat, reading the names from his notebook. The yeomen appeared quickly. Neither looked old enough to shave. Neither spoke English. The officer offered to act as an interpreter. Lyle had no choice but to trust his rough translation.

The two crew gave brief accounts of lowering a man in a powerboat over the side of the ship in mid-ocean that night. They were following the captain's orders. Both nodded vigorously when Lyle showed them Fosselli's picture. Yes, that was the man. They were as nervous as two pigeons with a hawk, visibly relieved when dismissed.

It looked like Fosselli was dead, everything happening according to the report. No one could've survived that explosion. So why was everyone afraid of his cop self today? It didn't add up.

Barton descended the gangway, heading for the escalator. He halted as the duty officer ran to catch up to him. "Lieutenant, I'm thinking you should know something," he said in a thick Italian accent. "I, ahem, I am one deck above when the boat swings out that night. On the bridge wing. It's raining very much and the man is wearing goggles, but his profile looks a small difference from *Signor* Fosselli. I worked for the line many years now. I know what Fosselli looks like. This man's nose, it is larger. And ... well, he doesn't sound like *Signor* Fosselli. He sounds like an Americano with faking the Italian accent. I can tell the difference. You know?"

The words slowly sinking in, Barton nodded. His mouth went as dry as the Sahara.

"I, ah, I appreciate it much if you say nothing to my superiors. I don't know for sure--"

"I understand," Lyle said hoarsely, jotting down the man's name and willing his hand not to shake. He pocketed his notebook. "Please don't discuss what you just told me with anyone either. If anyone asks, you forgot to tell me how hard it was raining."

Watching the officer walk back to the ship, Lyle wished to God he didn't understand. His life had just turned into a horror movie, the kind where the monster never dies.

Worst-case scenario, Gianni Fosselli was never on the Milano.

Worst-case scenario, Gianni Fosselli was alive.

*

The appointment with Dr. Logan confirmed Jessie was run down. She needed rest and nourishment. He gave her a vitamin injection. No more skipping breakfast. No more candy bars for lunch. Jessie promised to be good. Nick had overseen her dinner last night, then drawn a bubble bath and given Jessie a massage that left her purring. She'd slept well in his bed, the sleeping situation resolved.

This morning, Mary had taken charge of breakfast, standing over Jessie while she devoured a clutch of eggs and toast and sausage. Mary sent Jessie to rehearsal with a huge lunch basket. Willie promised to see that she finished it, including dessert.

After she left the doctor's office, Willie drove her to rehearsal. With the countdown at twenty-four hours before she stepped in front of the critics, Jessie began to feel like her old self. She ran a hand over her stomach. But she'd eaten too many eggs this morning. And she never should've put that sausage in her mouth. What was wrong with her? Sausages were full of grease. And toast wasn't necessary. Eating enough to keep from fainting didn't mean she had to stuff herself. In fact, no more scallion pancakes. Nothing fried. Ever. Mary didn't understand. She'd never heard the words organic or grains or low fat or kale. Jessie decided she'd eat half her sandwich, hide the other half, and toss out the extras. No dessert.

Her costumes were skintight. Nora, her dresser, had to jiggle the zipper up the red ball gown yesterday. Three days ago it had slid up smoothly. Her understudy was built like a Barbie doll and she had age on her side, just twenty-five, not one wrinkle or extra fold of flesh on her. Jessie had caught Valentine York looking her up and down more than once. Running a finger over her jaw line—was it sagging?-- Jessie vowed to do extras sit-ups and crunches and curls in the brownstone's exercise room later. She'd get on the bike, too. Maybe hire a personal trainer.

Jessie could take care of her physical well being by eating just enough to stay healthy and fit. But her nerves were another story. The thought of appearing on a stage without Andrew at her side was consuming her with fear. Jessie knew what stage fright felt like. This was different. This numb feeling every time she pictured stepping out on that stage had nothing to do with eating or sleeping or even acting. It was beginning to scare her.

*

Tired, Abigail Forrester dragged home from her meeting with a new lipstick-marketing firm. She was afraid today finally marked the beginning of the end of a long, profitable career. Abbie's plump lips had graced the covers of magazines and television commercials for over ten years. She'd been the number-one choice of every lipstick executive in the business. Now younger girls with collagen-enhanced lips were pushing her out. It was depressing to be considered over the hill at thirty-five, but it was a brutal industry. Which was one reason she'd gotten her PI license and apprenticed with her uncle in L.A.

Jogging into her luxury building on West Seventy-Second Street, Abbie collected her mail and took the elevator to her apartment. She kicked off her shoes and began sifting through her letters at the kitchen counter, a lot of bills and a residual check from a lipstick commercial. The last item looked like an advertisement sample, judging by the thick feel. Abbie ripped it open, and gasped.

A pack of Oceano matches slid into her hand. What ...?

The envelope was typed. Abbie sank onto a chair. No return address, the postmark Buffalo, New York. Sick memories stirred. Abbie had known Gianni well when they'd all lived in New York years ago. Jessie had introduced them, her father working for the Fosselli family's shipping line as a cruise director. Bewitched by Jessie as she matured into a beauty, Gianni had tried to use Abbie to keep track of her. But Abbie had seen through him, always. He was obsessed with her best friend.

When Andrew had been murdered, Abbie suspected Gianni from the get-go. Which was the other reason she got her PI license, so she'd know what she was doing when she went after Andrew's killer. It had been serendipity she met up with Nick, determined to solve his brother's murder. Abbie had worked undercover for Nick and played Gianni, dating him, even accepting his underhanded marriage proposal designed to win custody of Anthony. And all the while she'd been feeding Nick incriminating information to help trap the maggot.

Gianni had hated her at the end, when he discovered her role in his downfall, his explosive temper revealing the terrifying man who lived inside the slick exterior. Springing up, Abbie sealed the envelope and matches in a plastic bag. She'd talk to Nick at Jessie's opening tomorrow night.

*

Gliding through his greenhouse, Max Callaban chatted on a disposable cell with his sister Luciana in Italy. As a precaution, he always discarded the prepaid phone the same day he used it, picking up a new one from a supply ordered in bulk. When he hung up, he reminded himself to send Luci a new supply of disposables, also to be tossed after use. Max routinely used prepaid cells for any calls except to Roberto Martinelli and Aldo Zappella. Roberto and Aldo were as secure as he was, no worries there.

Clicking off, Max surveyed the vegetable garden, the tomatoes, zucchini, and eggplant, all thriving. Even the scallions and peppers were doing well. The greenhouse's restoration had been worth the hours and backbreaking labor.

Attached to the main house, it ensured that Max and Anthony would be self-sufficient throughout the long Ohio winter.

He and Carlo had returned from Buffalo yesterday, completing several errands and arranging for various gifts to be sent. Using the whore Abigail to convey his respects to McDeare had been a delightful inspiration. At his other cell's buzz, Max dug it from his pocket. Aldo. "We have trouble," the man grated. "Barton was hanging around the Milano this morning, asking questions about your escape."

"Why, after all this time?"

"Those fucking matches. Listen to me carefully ... MAX. Just in case you didn't understand me before, English your second language and all. This is a reminder. No more pranks. No more matchbooks. Or you get your boy on your own." The man clicked off.

Okay, no more matches. Max had moved on to better things anyway.

Wrapping his arms around himself, he shivered. With fall this cold, what would winter bring?

*

Nick entered the RICO files into his computer's desktop, analyzing every tidbit, only pausing when his cell rang. "You are such a hypocrite," a woman said in German.

"Greta?" Nick hadn't heard from the hot little fraulein since he'd hung up on her months ago.

"Ah, you remember me! What a shock. I just heard a silly rumor you're getting married."

"And where did you hear this?" Nick asked in Greta's native tongue.

"It was on television. Why would they tell such stories?"

"It's not a story. I'm getting married New Year's Eve."

Cursing in German, Greta began to sputter.

"Greta ... Greta. Take a pill. Chill. And then take me off your speed dial." Nick clicked off, chuckling. The truth was that no one had been more surprised than Nick when he'd decided to ask Jessie to marry him. Unless it was Jessie. Womankind would get over it. Nothing was going to go wrong with Jessie and him. He wouldn't give Gianni the satisfaction, not even in hell.

Hearing the front door open, Nick glanced at his watch. Almost midnight. He met Jessie in the kitchen. "How was the final dress rehearsal?"

"Awful," Jessie groaned. She put the kettle on for tea.

"Relax. Not another word until you're feeling better." Nick sat Jessie on a stool. He took over, pouring the steaming hot water over a chamomile tea bag and sweetening it with sugar.

Jessie took a tiny sip and sighed with satisfaction. "May I speak now?"

"I like you obedient."

"Don't get too used to it."

"I won't. Tell me what happened?"

"A light crashed to the stage during the song about my dead son. Then one of the turntables had a glitch rotating. It jerked so much Josh lost his balance and fell off."

Picturing the schmuck falling on his ass, Nick smothered a grin.

"The orchestra was out of synch with the chorus on the theme song. The mike failed at the top of the second act. My skintight ball gown ripped down the back when I sat down. But the best? The best was the stage manager putting castors on the couch so they could move it on and off the stage faster. I sat down and slid into the wings like skates on ice."

Nick burst into laughter. "Sorry, I don't mean to laugh but--"

"No, go ahead, laugh. I did. Thank God for that old saying: Bad dress rehearsal. Good opening night. Because it can't get any worse!"

*

After pouring an Amaretto, Aldo Zappella sank into a tub chair across from Roberto. The Martinelli study was swept for bugs on a regular basis, the one room the two old friends could speak in freely.

Roberto opened his humidor, selecting a rare Cuban. "So. You think Barton knows?"

"At the very least he suspects. He's got cops watching the brownstone. We know he questioned Captain Verde about Fosselli. And a security guard at the pier saw that officer, uh, Bocco, talking to Barton privately on the lower level. Bocco was on the bridge that night, had a clear view of the lifeboat and men. And he's an old-timer, known Fosselli for years."

"It looks like we have a problem." Martinelli sniffed his cigar before biting off the tip.

"Do we send Barton a warning? Scare the wife or the kid?"

"With his dead partner in the mix, it's personal now. It'll never end for Barton, not when he suspects the truth." Roberto took his time lighting the cigar, a cloud of sweet smoke encasing them. He looked long and hard at Aldo.

"You can't mean—" Aldo leaned forward. "... A cop?"

"We wait, but not too long. I know this man. He won't tell McDeare until he's sure of himself. We have a small window in which to act and escape with clean hands."

"Roberto. That may be easier said than done."

"My friend, accidents happen all the time."

CHAPTER 5

It was after six. Opening night curtain was seven. And Jessie had asked him to stop backstage. Nick quickly straightened an indigo tie over his black shirt, shrugged on a slate gray suit jacket, and dashed downstairs.

Yelling goodbye to Mary and Anthony, he hurried towards Willie and the waiting limo. Willie let Nick out in front of the theater, clearing a path for him through the gala crowd packed behind velvet ropes. Ticket-holders were mixed with opening-night gawkers. The TV cameras were whirring, reporters doing sound checks and blaring into microphones, the network's parked vans choking off traffic.

The guard at the stage door buzzed Nick through. Stepping into the green room, he paused. The space was crawling with people: actors in full costume and makeup; guests in designer suits and beaded gowns; stagehands in jeans and T-shirts. As Nick squeezed through the sideshow, he felt dozens of eyes watching his progress, heard whispers echoing his name. Nick flattened himself against the wall as a multiple flower delivery barged ahead. He finally reached Jessie's dressing room and opened the door to chaos.

Jessie sat at her dressing table conferring with Josh and the director. Several women were fussing over Jessie's shoes. Stagehands delivered a parade of special PLAYBILLS for Jessie's autograph. Floral arrangements kept arriving like parts on a rolling assembly line. They covered the top of every cabinet in the room. "My God," he muttered, "who died?"

An austere woman with a silver topknot and a pince-nez on her nose shot him a withering look. "It's opening night. No jokes about dying." She put down the wedding veil she'd been steaming and squinted at him. "You must be Nick. My God, you look just like your brother!"

"You knew Andrew?"

"I've been Jessie's dresser for years." Her dour expression melted into a smile. "I adored Andrew. Name's Nora. Make yourself at home. Quill's giving Jessie and Josh some last minute notes. He's almost finished."

Sliding his hands into his pockets, Nick lounged against the wall. Jessie's attention was rooted on the director and Josh. At Nora's gesture towards Nick, she flashed him a quick smile. Josh glanced at Nick over his shoulder before turning back and resting his hand on Jessie's shoulder. Ass.

A woman with bright red hair and magenta glasses padded through the doorway, stacked garments piled over each arm. Her dress was covered with rows of safety pins, and she wore pink bedroom slippers. "Costumes are all pressed, Nora," she said, jamming the clothes on the rack. "Tell Ms. Kendle I let out the seams on that red ball gown. She won't have to worry about flashing an audience again."

"Thanks, Gloria," Nora said, rearranging the costumes.

"Listen, that gown looked like it was taken in recently, but I didn't do it. Maybe a mistake, one of my new girls. You'd have to be a midget for those measurements. I'll talk to them," Gloria added, shuffling out.

The next character in the carnival materialized, a tall man with a rugged build and wavy brown hair, darting walnut eyes, broad nose. He asked Jessie for her valuables. Jessie dropped her wallet and a diamond necklace with matching earrings and bracelet into a large metal box. She kept her eyes on Quill the whole time, absorbing his words.

The backstage bandit turned to Nick.

"You want my valuables, too?"

"We lock these up during the performance." He studied Nick. "You're Nick McDeare, right? I'm George Penfield, stage manager. I knew your brother. See you at the party." Without waiting for a response, he strode from the room.

"Okay, you two," Quill said to Jessie and Josh, "it's up to you now. I have the utmost faith in you." He kissed Jessie's cheek and clapped Josh on the shoulder. "Come on. I want to show you your new position in that dinner scene." The director winked at Jessie before leaving. Josh pressed his lips to Jessie's forehead before following Quill. Nick rolled his eyes.

As Nick pushed himself away from the wall, a young man with porcelain skin glided into the room. His jet-black hair was silky, artful wisps framing a face as angular as a geometry lesson. Lean and well built, a snakeskin belt decorated his narrow waist. Nick estimated he was about five-nine and all whiplash muscle. The man was gorgeous. Aphrodite glanced at Nick with pure aqua eyes that matched his tight polo shirt. A second later, a tiny orange dog with a plumed tail danced into the room.

What next? A gorilla in the bathroom?

"Is that wig secure enough, love?" the beauty asked Jessie in a soft voice.

Jessie bobbed her head from side to side. Not a single hair in her blond French twist moved. "It's fine."

The canine approached Nick, sniffing his shoes. It sat down, eyes glued to Nick's face, open mouth a grin.

"Where's the veil, Nora?" Nora handed the man a short veil and he carefully placed it atop Jessie's wig, delicate fingers pinning it down with hairpins.

"James," Nora said, touching the young man on the shoulder, "this is Nick McDeare, Jessie's fiance."

James looked at Nick's image in Jessie's mirror. "Hello. I'm James Lovelock."

Nodding, Nick asked, "Who's this?" He glanced down at the powder puff licking his shoes.

"That's Cosette. Stop that, baby cakes," James crooned. "She's named after the character in LES MIS. The first show I worked on."

"James designed all the wigs in the revival," Nora said, straightening the veil over Jessie's shoulder. "And Jessie won't let anyone but James handle her wigs during the performances. Quite a coup for a young man. Most wigmasters are old farts."

Jessie laughed. "James will always look twenty-eight."

"I keep telling Jessie it's all about skin care," James said. "I just took a short vacation. Wore a hat and oodles of sun block." He swung around to look at Nick. "You have great skin. And even better hair." He reached out and touched the feathery tendrils on Nick's forehead. Nick jerked away. "If you ever want to sell some of those shiny locks, sweetie, I'll pay top dollar." James turned back to Jessie. "Okay, see you after the opening number." Kissing her cheek, he added, "Have a good one, love." James scooped up Cosette, and skated from the room.

Rising stiffly in her beaded wedding gown, Jessie turned around, finding Nick's eyes. She smiled up at him. Nora smoothed out the dress's billowing folds as Jessie approached Nick. "Could you please give us a minute, Nora?"

"Sure. I want to check the quick change room anyway." Nora left, closing the door.

"I had no idea." Nick shook his head.

"I'm sorry. It's crazy around here. I'd forgotten what opening night was like." Jessie reached for his hands.

"Why didn't you give this to the stage manager?" Nick fingered Jessie's engagement ring, three princess diamonds.

"I convinced Quill to let me wear it. It makes me feel like you're with me."

"I will be. Every minute."

"Ten minutes please," a disembodied voice announced. "Ten minutes."

"I've never been this nervous." Jessie bit her lip. "Not like this. It's more than stage fright."

"You told me nerves are good, remember?" Nick slid his arms around her waist, careful of the gown. "They keep you on your toes."

"It's been so long since I've gone before an audience. Another lifetime ago. Andrew was the one who led. I followed."

"That's not true. You walked out on stage at the Tonys last summer, minus Andrew. In front of a live TV audience. Every eye in the country was on you. You were magnificent."

"But --"

"It's like riding a bike, swimming. Your instincts take over. Your training kicks in. You'll see."

Jessie splayed her hands on his lapels. Lifting up, she kissed him. "Oops." Grinning, she rubbed his lips with her thumb. "You don't want to walk around wearing red lipstick."

"Are you kidding? I'd fit right in here wearing full makeup. It's, ah, interesting, this world you live in."

"Not exactly your world, is it?"

"It's what you do, Jess. Your career. I'll adapt." Nick spied three floral arrangements on the dressing table. The one in the center was from him, lilies and white roses in an ebony Ming vase. The same arrangement Nick had given Jessie the night he proposed.

Jessie followed his eyes. "You can't even tell I knocked over the vase, can you? See, it didn't even crack."

Laughing, Nick said, "And the others?"

"Bill sent the red roses. An old tradition."

"And the yellow roses? Didn't Andrew always give you yellow--"

"They're from Josh." Jessie's face constricted. "I guess-I guess he thought they'd make me feel like Andrew was with me."

Swallowing his disgust, Nick glanced at the wall clock. "I should go. You'll be great tonight. Go be brilliant." Nick kissed Jessie softly and headed for the green room, remembering to wipe the lipstick from his mouth.

"Excuse me, you're Nick McDeare, right?" A stunning platinum blond blocked his path. Her hourglass figure was squeezed into a low-cut gold gown, a considerable portion of her creamy breasts popping out.

Nick halted and stared, moving his eyes up to her face with an effort. "Yes."

"I'm Valentine York, Jessie's understudy," she said in a breathy voice. "I've been dying to meet you." Valentine held out her manicured hand, her round blue eyes fixed on his as if nothing else in the world existed.

Taking her hand, Nick said. "It's nice to meet you, Valentine. You're learning from the best."

Valentine's smile faded as she removed her hand.

"Nick?" Nora interrupted. "That door will take you into the outer vestibule."

Shooting Valentine a lazy smile, Nick pushed through the door. It was a glittering crowd. Sequins. Jewels. Pearls. Crystal. All the sparkles in the world concentrated in one room. Nick gave his ticket to the usher and moved into the lobby, scanning the audience for Abbie.

He found her talking to a coiffed man who smelled like a bottle of bug spray. Abbie smiled graciously at the man and sidled away. "I'll never get that cologne out of my hair or clothes. Ugh. Believe it or not, I used to date him. Now I'm turning into a spinster."

"I don't think so." Nick looked down at Abbie's clingy fuchsia gown, low-cut and backless. "Come on. Let's find our seats."

As they were led down front by an usher, Nick heard his name whispered repeatedly. He took his seat, seventh row center on the aisle, stretching his legs into the walkway. The house lights flickered.

"Remind me at intermission," Abbie whispered. "There's something I want to talk to you about."

*

"Lyle?" Barb Barton poked her head into his home office. "Our dinner reservation's at nine."

Tonight was the night, a Sunday. Barb had been nagging for an evening out together. Dina was sleeping over at a girlfriend's. The city was quiet on Sundays. Lyle saw enough hustle on the weekdays.

"There's plenty of time. I'm in the middle of something," he said, staring at his computer screen. No reply. A sigh and Barb's heavy footsteps on the stairs. It couldn't be helped. This was important.

Lyle scanned his screen, details of his interviews aboard the Milano. He was starting a new file on Fosselli, amassing every hint that indicated the man might be alive. The shoe. Captain Verde's stammering answers. The yeomen's' nerves. That officer, Luigi Bocco--Lyle had memorized his nametag—and his chilling observations about the visitor lowered over the side of the ship that night. Fosselli? Or a look-alike?

If it had been a double, was he supposed to have made it safely to the steamer idling a short distance away? Lyle doubted it. If the man was an impostor, Lyle suspected his fate was death, making the police assume the Fosselli saga was over. So who was the poor schlub? Someone who'd wronged Martinelli and thought the charade would cancel out his sins? Someone who had no idea he'd never come home again? Someone who wore a size-twelve, inexpensive, American-made shoe?

And then there was Manganaro. Mario had blown up the speedboat with that gunshot to the gas tank. Did he work for the mob like Bushman, another dirty cop? He was a paisano under the skin. Lyle trusted no one, not after Bushman's treachery. Tomorrow he'd take Manganaro's history apart, piece by piece.

But what if Manganaro had been a lucky accident? What if someone else onboard had intended to destroy the boat? There'd been a horrific rainstorm that night. Most of the passengers had been inside eating dinner, few witnesses to the gunshots. All had been questioned and cleared. Or maybe there'd been a bomb planted aboard the powerboat, waiting to be detonated.

Bolting forward in his chair, Lyle rapidly typed his thoughts into the computer.

In the end, all that mattered was whether Gianni Fosselli was alive.

If Fosselli drew breath, Nick, Jessie, and Anthony were in grave danger.

*

A habit dating back to Juilliard, Jessie walked the stage. She needed to feel at home on the set, listen to the buzz on the other side of the dress curtain and get a sense of the audience.

Closing her eyes, she took in the discordant notes as the orchestra warmed up, pumping her adrenaline. The chatter of the chorus in the wings. The vibration of air conditioners working to balance the heat from the stage lights.The whiff of fresh paint as flats and scenery were touched up. And Jessie's own stage makeup, the smell of greasepaint, an aroma more intoxicating than the scent of flowers in a dressing room.

"Places please," George Penfield called. "Places for Act One."

When Jessie opened her eyes, she spotted Valentine York standing in the wings. The two women locked eyes. Josh appeared, pausing and looking from one to the other. He leaned over and whispered in Valentine's ear. She turned on her heel and headed in the direction of the green room.

Handsome in his tux, Josh walked towards Jessie. "That bitch knows she's supposed to watch from the back of the house. She's trying to psyche you out, Jessie. Ignore her."

Thank God Josh couldn't see her knees knocking together under her gown. And there he was, as relaxed as a cougar sunning himself on a rock. She shook her head. "You have nerves of steel."

"You'll be fine as soon as you sing your first note." Josh rubbed her shoulders.

"That's what Nick said."

"He's been onstage?"

"He's a writer. Creative personality. Same thing."

"Really?"

George interrupted them. "Save the chitchat for later, guys. I called places."

Feeling her stomach lurch, Jessie pictured all the critics out there ready to play God.

"You and me, Jessie." Josh squeezed her hand. "We're in this together." Jessie hugged him. He was right. She didn't have Andrew, but she had Josh.

Heading upstage, Jessie and Josh each moved into place on separate turntables as the stage lights went to black. The audience broke into applause on the other side of the curtain. That would be for the conductor. There was a moment of silence before the overture began, sending Jessie's pulse racing.

Jessie grabbed a handle on the back flat and looked across at Josh, spotting his white shirt in the darkness. Hanging on, she focused on Josh as the turntables lifted them high over the stage. The set decorator had installed hidden handles in case she panicked. She was panicking, but it wasn't from a fear of heights. Good God, could she do this? Down below, the minister and chorus took their places on the darkened stage.

The dress curtain was pulled. The stage lights came up, and the chorus began the theme song. Jessie took a deep breath and prayed for her character to settle over her. Josh's turntable rotated and the spots targeted him as he began his verse. A moment later Jessie's turntable began its slow rotation. The spotlights hit her, their warmth settling into her bones. As Jessie inhaled to sing, the audience broke into applause, an ovation that swelled. Jessie hadn't expected it. She froze in place as the orchestra vamped. She waited … and waited … listening for the applause to peak and start to fade.

And then she began her song. Christine took over and Jessie flickered into nothingness. She was in perfect voice, strong and clear. Her nerves disappeared and her knees steadied as the adrenaline raced through her body.

It was a high like no other, a soaring above the clouds.

She was home again.

*

The pictures had arrived in his morning e-mail. Barton stared at surveillance photos of the man in the Chevy on East Seventy-Fifth Street. It had taken Lyle less than fifteen minutes to put the images into the system and come up with an ID. Clint Vaughn, PI.

Vaughn had one arrest and wrongful conviction ten years ago. For the murder of one Benny Dykstra, a drug kingpin in Brooklyn. Pleading not guilty, Vaughn had claimed he was near the murder scene doing surveillance in a missing teen case. An unregistered Smith and Wesson semiautomatic pistol was found in a dumpster near

Vaughn's car. Its ammunition matched the bullet in Benny's heart. Vaughn swore he'd never seen it.

Barton vaguely remembered the case. Two months after Vaughn was sent to Rikers, a rival dealer in custody copped a plea and confessed to the murder. Oscar "Foxy" Foxwell, DEA, received a commendation and promotion for his work on the case, and Vaughn walked. The dealer ended up dead, knifed at Rikers during breakfast, his head landing in a bowl of Cheerios. Lyle had crossed paths with Foxy during a drug bust near the river a year ago. He'd give the man a call tomorrow and feel him out about Vaughn.

According to his profile, Vaughn specialized in chasing down philandering husbands. Chances were good the PI had no interest in the brownstone. He was on the street for a different reason, a different family. Just to make sure, Barton would question Mr. Vaughn.

"Lyle!" Barb yelled down the stairs. "It's seven-thirty!"

*

Taking a deep breath, Jessie released the air slowly. The next scene was the rewrite. The bedroom scene. The one her son could never see. Jessie had come up with only one way to make this scene work for her. It was radical because it took her out of character. As the lights came up on the stage, Jessie focused on the love song as she and Josh frantically peeled each other's clothes away.

In Jessie's mind, it wasn't Josh standing in front of her in his briefs. It wasn't her character's husband David Mackey either. It was Nick. Nick was the one who laughed with amusement as she blushed in her skimpy teddy. It was Nick who lifted her into his arms and flung her on the bed. Oh, God, her teddy ripped halfway up one side, exposing more skin. Fat, she was too fat.

No one saw as Jessie rolled over the split. It was Nick she seductively beckoned to join her under the sheets. It was Nick who tossed the duplicate teddy and briefs into the air. And it was Nick who was making passionate love to her as she stretched her hand high over their heads to admire her rings.

Nick's engagement ring sparkled back at her. As her arms folded back around Christine's husband's neck, it was Nick Jessie held.

*

Applauding heartily at the end of the hotel scene, Nick could feel Abbie's eyes on him. "What?" he asked, his face a mask.

"A pretty hot scene, wouldn't you say?"

"So?"

"Josh was really throwing himself into it."

"Shut up, Abbie." The lights came back up on the next scene. Nick slumped down in his seat, the image of Jessie and Josh in bed together branded on his brain in living color. Were they naked under those sheets? Is that why Jessie had wanted to rehearse in a real bed at home? So she could get used to being naked with Josh-- or was she already used to it?

The image ate away at Nick throughout the rest of the first act. He escaped out front at intermission while Abbie headed for the ladies' room. Nick streamed through the crowd, keeping his head down. Emerging into the lobby, he felt a wave of cool air hit him and made his way to the street.

Bill Rudolph was schmoozing with a group of people under the theater's overhang, talking to one man in particular. The tall producer's mane of silver hair and tanned face stood out in any crowd. Nick came to an abrupt halt. The man talking to Bill ... average height, coming up to Bill's chest ... A head of thick curly salt-and-pepper hair, blunt features, dark eyes. Stocky. His diamond ring caught the marquee lights. He wore a beautifully cut suit under an open cashmere coat. Nick looked harder. Roberto Martinelli, in the flesh. He recognized him from the RICO file. What the hell?

Martinelli caught Nick's eye. The two men stared at each other before Roberto turned back to Bill, the echo of a smile on his face.

*

Only ten minutes late, Barton maneuvered his SUV over the Queensboro Bridge and across Fifty-Ninth Street into Manhattan. The restaurant would honor their reservation. He'd flash his gold shield if he had to.

His mind was a jumble of conflicted thoughts. Should he tell Nick his suspicions about Fosselli? Nick was under a lot of pressure. His manuscript was due by Christmas. He was getting married in a royal extravaganza of a wedding. If Nick didn't tell Jessie about Lyle's hunch, the guilt would eat him up. And if Nick did tell Jessie, she'd flip out at the thought of Gianni being alive. Maybe for nothing. Maybe Fosselli was as dead as Andrew Brady. Lyle couldn't rely on one vague eyewitness and a shoe to determine the truth.

Lyle decided to wait. He needed more proof before tearing Nick and Jessie's lives apart all over again.

*

Rudolph and Martinelli drifted back inside the theater. Martinelli. Here. Goddamn. Nick paced like a hopped-up tiger in a cage. Every time Nick paced to the right, he found his eyes drawn to a small brunette, and he looked a little longer, a little more distracted. She had short shaggy hair, her head lowered as she studied her PLAYBILL. Nick stopped pacing. He shook his head. She looked like ... But Bree had to be chasing down a story in Syria or Pakistan or some hot spot across the world. She couldn't be at a Broadway opening.

The woman looked up and met Nick's gaze. Brianna Fontaine moved to his side. "Hey, Nick. I figured you'd be here."

He hadn't seen Bree since she'd abruptly left Hong Kong, and him, years ago. Nick found his voice. "Last I heard, you were in the Middle East. This is the last place I'd expect to run into you." He smiled thinly. "Are you doing theater reviews for THE NEW YORK TIMES now?"

"Bill and Marcy Rudolph are my godparents. I'm here for them." Bree's eyes met Nick's. "Small world, right? I'll even be at your wedding."

"You will?"

"Since Bill and Marcy are hosting." Nick kept a lock on his jaw, keeping it from falling open.

"Honestly, Nick, I never thought I'd be talking to you again."

"You said as much in the letter you left me in Hong Kong."

"You hurt me." Bree shrugged. "The paper wanted to transfer me. I was glad to get out of there."

- 48 -

"You haven't changed at all." Bree was the same brutally honest woman he'd remembered. And she was one of the best reporters in the field, fearless, with an instinct that couldn't be taught.

"Apparently you have. Tell me something. Is this marriage to Jessica Kendle for real? You're serious?"

"It's for real. I'm serious."

"I've kept track of you. Your novels. Andrew Brady. Catching his killer. I've also heard through the grapevine you think Roberto Martinelli was involved."

"Always the reporter, hmm?"

"Just like you. He's here tonight. Martinelli."

"I saw."

"Here's something you probably don't know. Roberto, Bill, and I are all neighbors. I grew up in Southampton, Long Island, remember?"

"The enclave of the super rich and privileged," Nick said smoothly. Of course. That explained the Martinelli-Rudolph connection. Martinelli lived in a palace in Southampton. Nick had seen a picture in the RICO dossier. "I remember. Daddy was a mere FBI profiler but Mommy's side of the family shipped over on the Mayflower. They own half of New England. It's a small world."

"There you are." A man joined them. Yves Leveaux, the French Pulitzer Prize winning photojournalist. Nick had crossed paths with Yves before. Yves had looked the same for twenty years. Five-o'clock-shadow, scruffy chestnut hair, rumpled jacket, sleeves pushed up.

"Good to see you again, Nick," he said, his accented voice nasal. Yves extended his hand. "I hear you're marrying that luscious creature up on the stage tonight. Congratulations. An amazing talent." Yves slipped an arm around Bree. "Brianna and I are discussing the subject ourselves. Of course, first I have to make a little sojourn to the Middle East."

Her gaze almost defiant, Bree looked Nick straight in the eye. The marquee lights flickered, and they all moved indoors. Yves clasped Nick's shoulder. "Maybe we can catch up at the party, yes?"

Nodding, Nick headed down the aisle for his seat, trying to process it all. Rudolph and Martinelli. Bree and Martinelli. Rudolph, Bree, and Martinelli.

Nick slid into his seat, Abbie waiting for him. "Nick, I really need to talk to you about something." Nick stared at Brianna and Yves chatting with a couple in the opposite aisle.

"Someone sent me a pack of Oceano matches in the mail yesterday," Abbie said.

"What?" Nick's head swiveled.

The lights began to dim. "We'll talk at the party."

CHAPTER 6

"I must be putting on weight," Jessie told Nora. "First the ball gown. Now the teddy." The intermission was nearly over, Jessie in costume for the second act.

"Don't be ridiculous," Nora soothed. "You're skin and bones. Gloria thinks one of her girls took in that red dress by mistake. She's got some pretty green apples on this show." Nora examined the ripped teddy closely. "Looks like it was already torn and stitched together at the last minute. No wonder it gave way. I better show this to Gloria."

After Nora left, Jessie finally had a moment to herself. She wanted to refocus on Christine before she went back on. Except for the teddy malfunction, Jessie was glowing. Every moment, every scene, every song, had never been better.

Jessie pulled Nick's flowers closer, blocking Josh's yellow roses. She'd told Josh she loved his thoughtfulness. But in truth, the yellow roses were a painful reminder of who was missing tonight. Jessie buried her face in Nick's white blossoms. "It's not the same without you, Andrew," she whispered. "How am I doing solo?"

You're brilliant, Jess. Jessie felt a hand on her back.

"Andrew?" Jessie's head shot up, and she whirled around. But there was no Andrew. There would be no more ghostly dreams where she could touch him or hear his voice. That little window had closed forever.

The intercom crackled. "Places, please. Places for Act Two."

*

Glancing at Abbie in the darkened theater, Nick was clutched by a feeling of dread. The Oceano matches …

The play began, abruptly shutting out real life. Christine and David Mackey got word their son had been killed in Vietnam. The scene shifted to the graveyard and the service, complete with taps and a twenty-one-gun salute. The other characters faded from the stage into the shadows. Jessie gracefully glided into the bright spotlight to sing the haunting song about her dead son.

Nick found himself choked up. Jessie was riveting, a powerful and brave force standing center stage, light radiating from her as if she were an angel. How could a sound that large come from a woman that small? She looked … translucent. Swallowing hard, Nick noticed a large man across the aisle reach for his handkerchief and wipe his eyes. Abbie was sobbing. Soundlessly, he handed her his handkerchief.

When the song came to its conclusion, Jessie propelled upward to scream at God. The entire audience sprang to its feet with her. Nick had never witnessed such an emotional reaction in a theater. Jessie owned that stage. If any actor had ever held an audience in the palm of her hand, it was Jessica Kendle.

*

Forget Martinelli and Fosselli, Lyle told himself. Not in his favorite steak house. Concentrate on Barb sitting across from him over dinner instead. Her bright blue suit set off her carrot-top hair and green eyes. She looked as beautiful today as the day Lyle had married her. She had him laughing hysterically over her most recent sitcom moment. Her chewing gum had fallen from her mouth as she'd been jogging on the treadmill. The capper? She'd gotten her hair caught in the contraption while trying to retrieve it.

Their sirloins and braised mushrooms arrived just as Lyle's cell buzzed. Harry Steinmetz. He had to answer this. Midtown North's daytime desk officer told Lyle the dossier Barton had requested on Manganaro was finished. Lyle had no choice but to swing by and get it tonight. Harry had done this ASAP, on his own time. It was almost ten. Harry lived in Brooklyn, an hour away.

Barton looked down at his juicy steak, pink in the middle, seared on the outside. He watched Barb deflate as he asked the waiter for a doggie bag.

*

Jessie had never taken a curtain call without Andrew at her side. They'd been a team, taking their bows together. Josh bounded out to thunderous applause. Taking a deep breath, Jessie made her way to center stage and dropped her head. The audience went wild, rising to their feet, whistles ringing out with shouts of "Brava!" Overwhelmed, Jessie dropped her head again. She looked back up, all the way to the second balcony, beaming. Still, they wouldn't stop. Her eyes filled with tears as she sought out Nick in the audience. The look of pride in his smile as he applauded made the tears overflow.

The stage lights blinked out and came back up. Jessie was alone, the star taking a solo call. Looking again at Nick, she found him scanning the house, as if searching for someone.

*

When Nick finally made his way backstage, he ran into a crowd spilling out of Jessie's dressing room. Pushing his way through, he caught sight of Jessie, surrounded by Bill Rudolph, Quill Llewelyn, and a dozen others. She was having an animated chat with Jeremy Irons and Kathleen Turner.

Abbie burst into the room, interrupting as if the two stars didn't exist. "You were fabulous, Jessie. Just incredible! I've never seen you better. Listen, I'll wait for you in the car, okay? This room's an oven." Abbie slithered towards the door, grabbing Nick's hand on her way out. "We'll talk at the party, gorgeous."

"Abbie, wait--" But she was gone.

Spotting Nick, Jessie excused herself, reaching for his hand. "Hi," she whispered.

Dozens of eyes were watching them in that small room. Jessie shot Nora a look. While Jessie said goodbye to Irons and Turner, Nora shooed everyone else out.

"I'm going to jump in the shower," Jessie whispered to Nick. "Then we can talk alone."

While the stragglers meandered into the hallway, Nick read the cards on the flowers, famous names mixed with strangers. One arrangement caught his eye, two black orchids in a blood-red vase. Nick grabbed the card and envelope.

"Break a leg. Break two. From an old friend." The envelope was from a florist in Buffalo. Nick brushed a hand over his forehead. Thank God Jessie hadn't seen the card. He crumbled it into his pocket. First the matches. Nick's, now Abbie's. Anthony's fear of being watched. Martinelli here on opening night, smiling at him. A floral curse.

They had a stalker.

Nick would find the son of a bitch. And then he'd kill him.

*

It had been one shitty day. On his stool at Hanratty's, Clint Vaughn tossed back scotch after scotch. He'd been up and out early, heading across town on foot. No more stakeouts by car, not with the cops watching the brownstone. His instincts were right on. The police presence on East Seventy-Fifth Street had been beefed up, an unmarked car cruising by at random.

The television over the bar was blaring. A fag with gelled hair custom-cut by locusts was gabbing about Jessica Kendle's performance that evening. Kendle was the next messiah of the theater, blah, blah, blah.

Clint was beat. After his trek on foot, he'd spent the rest of the day on the Internet, trolling for info on Fosselli and McDeare. Fosselli had been hot celebrity news when Oceana opened with a splash, the gossip columnists dredging up juicy tidbits. According to his bio, Fosselli's father had been a big shot in an import-export leather goods business, headquartered in Genoa. Gianni's mother and father had been found shot to death by their son after a robbery at their villa. He'd been visiting on break from culinary school, his younger sister Luciana in secondary school.

Motioning to the bartender, Clint signaled for his tab and a bottle to go. Leather goods happened to be one of Roberto's legitimate businesses, headquarters also in Genoa. Was that the Gianni-Roberto link—Martinelli's Magnifico Leathers?

It wasn't hard to put together a plausible scenario. Let's say Gianni's father worked for Martinelli. Let's also say he was skimming the books and the wife was with him during the hit. Forget the robbery story. Robbers didn't commit double murders. That was Roberto's game. So the son stumbles onto the carnage and Martinelli's cappo lets him live if he keeps his mouth shut. Martinelli gambles the grateful shipping heir will be useful one day. Meanwhile, according to Google, the sister leaves school early, marries a charming con man, and is left a single mother at the age of eighteen. The son is named Eduardo.

The theory worked. Clint swallowed down the last of his scotch. The newspaper murder investigation on Andrew Brady claimed Gianni sold the lucrative cruise line he'd inherited from his grandfather to Martinelli for a song right before

Brady croaked. The reporters cited anonymous sources, AKA Nick McDeare, intrepid reporter.

Pagano Industries was the cruise line's technical owner of record, but Roberto was a master at using paperwork to hide his non-legit businesses. Clint drummed his fingers on the bar. The papers also insinuated Fosselli's real payment was one dead Andrew Brady. Very cleverly accomplished, according to said sources. Aldo Zappella's sister Paula was married to Ian Wexley, actor on the skids. Also Jessie's former lover and the man first arrested for Andrew's murder. The perfect stooge, having his own axe to grind against Andrew. When McDeare torpedoed that scheme and Gianni and his nephew Eduardo were finally arrested for Brady's murder, Gianni had kept Martinelli's name out of it.

Martinelli would've generously rewarded such loyalty, orchestrating Fosselli's escape from jail and later making arrangements to kidnap his son. Eduardo, on the other hand, had been eliminated by Martinelli after foolishly threatening to talk. Clint silently toasted himself for piecing the bodies into a bloody puzzle.

His search on McDeare was a lot sexier. Adopted at birth. Raised in Europe and the Far East. Successful investigative reporter and writer, winning fame and fortune. A hot rep with the ladies, not that that was any surprise from what Clint knew. Judging from McDeare's past, Jessica Kendle Brady would not be the only moist morsel in his bed, not as long as there was another delectable piece of ass out there.

In Clint's experience, there always was.

*

As Willie maneuvered the limo through traffic towards Roxy's, a theatrical restaurant on West Forty-Fifth Street, the restaurant's crimson and gold canopy slid into view. Jessie eyed Abbie and Josh, lounging back on the opposite seat, deep in conversation about his performance. When she'd discovered his date was home with strep throat, Abbie had declared the star of the show couldn't be seen alone at the opening-night gala. She'd been his one-woman entourage ever since.

Jessie's brow creased. She and Nick had never had the chance to discuss her performance. A never-ending migration in and out of her dressing room had made it impossible to finish more than one sentence at a time. And Nick seemed distracted. As the limo pulled to a stop, Jessie flipped on the intercom. "Willie, let Abbie and Josh go in first. Nick and I will hang back a minute." She flipped up the opaque screen between the driver and his passengers.

"Jessie," Josh said, "I think—"

"What you think," Nick said softly, "is irrelevant."

"Now, boys ..." Abbie laughed

Nudging Nick's foot with her own, Jessie whispered, "Behave."

"Jessie Kendle's back," Abbie said, "and wants to make an entrance. We will, too, won't we, Josh?" Willie swung the limo door open. Abbie reached for Josh's hand. After hesitating, he followed her onto the sidewalk, squaring his shoulders for the swirling crowd and flashing a surfer smile. The limo door slammed shut, abruptly stifling the street noise.

"I'm sorry about tonight, Nick. The chaos and the craziness."

"It's your night." Nick stared through the tinted window at the TV news vans outside the restaurant.

"I never noticed before … because I had Andrew, but none of this, tonight, I mean, it doesn't mean anything if you're alone."

"I know alone." Nick met her eyes.

"Are you with me? I see that look on your face. You're someplace else."

"I'm sorry if it seems that way. I am with you. You know I am. Always."

Her man of many moods. Jessie stretched up and kissed Nick on the mouth. "Mmm," she whispered, "Better?"

"That's not playing fair."

"Since when have either of us ever played fair?" Jessie kissed him again. Nick sank into the kiss, crushing her against the creaking leather cushions. They finally pulled back, fighting for breath. "Now," Jessie inhaled, suddenly nervous, "about my performance tonight? You never said."

"Was that a bribe? You really are adorable, you know that?"

"I need to know." Nick's approval was more important than she'd realized, her heart thumping. "Please. Tell me."

Looking solemn. Nick took her hand. "Okay, you want the truth so I'll give it to you. Unvarnished. You were fantastic. You held that audience in the palm of this little hand." He pressed it to his lips.

"And …? My songs? How did I sound, really? Do you believe that my teddy ripped? My God, I thought I'd die. I think Quill needs to talk to the conductor about moving in on my solo a few beats too fast. Do you think the lighting was too--"

"Jessie, you were great! What more can I say? You were perfection. Perfection cannot be parsed and dissected."

"But you're a writer. You should--"

"Sometimes words just don't cut it."

"Try," she begged.

"You really sound like an actress, you know that?"

"Don't evade the subject."

"Okay, you want to know more? Here's how I felt about your performance tonight. This is what I have to say about the passion you brought to that stage in the performance of a lifetime."

"I'm listening."

"Make sure you do." Nick gently cupped her face with his hands.

"Tell me already."

Slowly, Nick lowered his head and covered her mouth with his. He kissed her with enough heat to melt a thermometer. After Nick set her free, Jessie rested her head against his chest and smiled.

A kiss was worth a thousand words.

Maybe more.

*

Nick tucked Jessie's hand in his as they entered the two-tiered restaurant. With its heavy dose of red and gold, Roxy's was known as a jewel box. It reminded Nick of a gaudy eatery in Hong Kong. At the sight of the show's star, the crowd broke into applause. Cameras flashed as Nick took a step back to give Jessie her moment alone. Instead, she clasped his hand tighter. 'You know me," she whispered. "I can trip over my own feet when I'm not onstage."

Bill Rudolph hurried over to them, smiling for the photographers. "Come, my darlings," he said. "You're seated at my table." He led them across the thick carpet, past the dance floor and orchestra to a round table in the center of the room. Nick nodded hello to Marcy Rudolph and Quill Llewelyn, bypassing Abbie and Josh. He halted at the sight of Bree Fontaine and Yves Leveaux smiling back at him.

Bill introduced Yves and Bree to Jessie. "Nick, I understand the three of you know each other from your work."

"Our paths have crossed a number of times," Nick said dryly.

"You were magnificent tonight, Miss Kendle," Bree said, her voice dripping syrup as she sized up Jessie.

"Please," Jessie said sweetly. "Call me Jessie." Nick eyed his fiancee. She was wearing her humble actress smile. Nick reached for a glass of champagne and swigged it down.

*

Lounging in bed, Max Callaban flipped the TV channels on his satellite dish. The New York stations were raving about TO HAVE AND TO HOLD and Jessica's starring role. Max wasn't surprised. What was acting, after all, but perfecting the art of lying to an audience?

Flipping off the television, Max tucked his hands behind his head. The oaks outside the bedroom windows were shedding their last leaves, silver limbs waving in the moonlight. Winter was just around the corner. Winter, which meant Max would soon be reunited with his son.

Max's mind drifted back to Jessica. Had she liked her black orchids? Max chuckled. Tonight was her big night, her triumphant comeback. Let Jessica have her moment. It wouldn't last much longer.

*

Josh Elliot felt his fury building like hot gas under a rising rocket. The press was treating Nick like he was Jessie's co-star. They'd been photographed together, interviewed together, and trailed as if they were royalty. Now the reporters were interviewing Nick solo, like the jerk knew anything about anything. This was crap. Josh was Jessie's leading man. It was time to change the music.

While Nick was pontificating to a reporter, Josh seized his moment. "Hey, Jessie," he said, interrupting her conversation with Marcy Rudolph, "how about a dance with your leading man?"

As Jessie smiled and took his hand, Josh caught Nick's dark expression. The gaggle of photographers immediately gravitated towards the two stars on the dance floor like the wave in a football stadium.

*

Brianna Fontaine skillfully receded into the background as she soaked up the activity around her. Her pretty tablemates were an eclectic bunch, a gathering of enormous egos and clashing dynamics.

Earlier, she'd smothered a smile, watching Josh Elliot watch his leading lady. Her gleaming blond hair loose and dipping over one eye, Jessie wore a strapless turquoise swirl of chiffon and silk that drew masculine eyes like a black hole sucking in gravity. Jessie didn't seem to notice Josh's eyes riveted on her while they danced now, the press all over them.

Meanwhile, Josh's date had been doing cartwheels to catch Josh's attention. She seemed to know all the players at this little social drama, including Bill. Another actress? She looked like one.

A statuesque blond in a scarlet dress had visited their table early in the evening before dinner, rubbing up against Bill Rudolph like a cat on a leg. Bill had introduced her as Valentine York, Jessie's understudy.

Another grouping consisted of Jessie's hand-picked lackeys, the table next to theirs. Amused, Bree had observed Jessie playing the gracious star and visiting the table between courses with Bill, introducing him to a beautiful young man she said was her wig master. Then Jessie had chatted with her dresser for a few minutes, before sitting down again.

As for the ice queen herself, Jessie was a mass of contradictions. One minute she smiled easily, chatting with a reporter, the picture of confident grace under pressure. The next she knocked over a wine glass and Nick called over a waiter to clean it up. She played with her fork, her prime rib congealing on her plate. She nibbled at her salad, but looked longingly at her untouched baked potato. A woman obsessed with her body? She probably weighed herself in ounces. Jessica Kendle couldn't wear more than a size two.

Bree looked down at her own figure. Shapely but average. Her hips were narrow, but her breasts were full, something Nick had always admired. Now he slept with a piece of fluff that belonged on top of a wedding cake?

Her glance drifted to Nick, back at their table after a reporter had hijacked him. He closed his mouth around a piece of rare roast beef. No one kissed like that man. No one. Bree could still taste him, the hint of bourbon on his tongue, the .... She had to stop this. He was marrying Jessica Kendle, every male's unavailable fantasy female.

Time for some air. Bree rose.

*

Sipping his bourbon, Nick watched the figures on the dance floor. He absently fingered the crushed note in his pocket that had accompanied the dressing-room's black orchids. Josh was showing off for the cameras, playing Fred Astaire and sweeping Jessie across the floor. Nick eyed Bree's empty seat. He'd watched her leave the room. On impulse, Nick sprang up.

He found Bree pacing the sidewalk. "Mind if I join you?"

*

Mario Manganaro's folder open in front of him, Barton sat at his desk. Barb had gone quiet on the ride into Brooklyn, her anger finally erupting on the way home. She'd headed upstairs without a good night, Lyle's promises to make it up to her echoing in her wake. He'd even vowed to leave his cell at home next time.

And then he'd lost himself in the last hour, going over Manganaro's police career and personal history. There was no dirt, not one tie to Martinelli or any other member of organized crime, not a speck of wrongdoing or sketchy activity in his personal or professional life. Not one complaint in his jacket. Nothing but commendations. Even his cell records were clean.

So when Mario had taken out Fosselli's speedboat, he'd been an NYC detective trying to stop a prisoner from fleeing. At least Barton had a definitive answer to one of his questions.

But the big question was still out there, looming like a bad omen. Who was in the speedboat--Fosselli ... or a look alike?

*

Abbie found herself alone at the table. Josh was working the press with Jessie. Marcy Rudolph had gone to the ladies' room. Bill and Quill were on their cell phones, trying to get word on the reviews.

And Nick had disappeared. Right after Brianna Fontaine had disappeared. Abbie suspected they'd done a lot more than work together in the past. The way Bree looked at Nick ... And the way Nick looked away from Bree .... With every female instinct she possessed, Abbie knew he'd slept with the woman. But had it been more than a casual fling?

As for Jessie ... Abbie tapped her fingers on the table. Right now Jessie seemed to be searching the room for someone.

*

Emerging from his limo, Roberto Martinelli told his driver to take the car home. "I'll page you in the morning."

Martinelli hurried into Bottoms Up, his strip club in the Bronx. He was immune to the heavy beat of the music, the thick cigarette smoke. He moved quickly through the dim lounge with its shadowy silhouettes fixated on the girls on stage.

Passing the private rooms in the back, Martinelli entered his office, hanging out the Do Not Disturb sign. He locked the door, turned on a lamp and headed for a private exit leading into the back alley.

Roberto climbed behind the wheel of a dark green Honda and maneuvered the car through a quiet neighborhood before coming out onto a busy intersection. Crossing into Manhattan, he sped down the West Side Highway and snagged the Holland Tunnel into New Jersey. Ten minutes later he cruised into the parking garage of a luxury apartment building in Jersey City.

*

Jessie found a seat at a table empty for the moment. Everyone still at the party was dancing or milling about the room. Several people had already left--Gloria, James, George, and Patty Hines, who played Christine's mother. Valentine had disappeared before dinner. The women at the table had parked their handbags on their chairs or under the table. Jessie was tired. And nervous. The reviews were due any moment. Nick must have gone outside for some air at exactly the wrong time.

Smoothing a hand over her hair, Jessie jiggled a foot. She kicked a purse. Jessie peeked under the tablecloth. The clasp had opened and everything was spilling out. Quickly looking around, Jessie ducked under the table and shoved everything back inside the beaded bag, tucking it neatly under the chair.

Straightening up, Jessie spotted Nora pushing through the crowd towards her. She was wearing an emerald beaded tunic with matching balloon pants, her topknot lacquered in place. "Jessie, Gloria cornered me before she left. She said she handles all your costumes personally. She swears your teddy was in mint condition when she washed it this morning."

"I'm gaining weight. What other explanation is there?"

"If you lose any more weight you'll be invisible. I have to run. I'll see you Wednesday matinee. And I'm going over every one of your costumes with a magnifying glass." Nora pecked Jessie on the cheek before rushing away.

Jessie scanned the room. No Nick. She and Andrew had always left the party early, opting to read the reviews in private. She tensed at the thought of being caught out in the open when they came in.

Wait--she spotted Nick as he crossed the dance floor, deep in conversation with that woman from the TIMES. Jessie didn't like the way the reporter had looked at her when they met, appraising her like she was a shiny goldfish dripping in fins, no brain. Bill Rudolph suddenly appeared, a thick stack of newspapers in his hands. Jessie sprang up and interrupted Nick and the woman as they approached the table, almost colliding with her.

"Sorry, uh, Beth? Nick, I want to go, right now. Can you page Willie? I'll explain on the way home. Please."

*

Slouching at the table, Josh fumed over the way Jessie had run out. He'd envisioned reading the reviews with his leading lady over a glass of champagne. Without the obnoxious Nick McDeare smirking at him. This was supposed to be Josh and Jessie's night. They were in this together, or had Jessie forgotten?

A beaming Bill passed out newspapers around the room. When he reached the head table, his smile faded. He quickly handed Josh a stack and moved on. Josh felt his stomach tighten.

Ten minutes later, Josh and Abbie were in a cab heading uptown to her apartment.

*

Bree was anxious to get home after the reviews came out. She was thrilled for Bill, another hit on his hands. But with Nick gone, the party's glitter dulled. Yves had been bored out of his mind all evening, more than ready to leave.

As their cab sped downtown, one thought kept playing in Bree's mind. On Wednesday morning Yves would fly across the world on assignment and be gone at least a month. And at noon on Wednesday, Bree had a date to meet Nick for lunch. Today was Sunday, Wednesday around the corner. Bree's heart was beating too fast for her health.

She'd fallen in love with Nick McDeare in Hong Kong.

And tonight she'd realized nothing about that had changed over the years. Nothing.

CHAPTER 7

Willie pulled the limo to a stop in front of a Times Square newsstand. "You stay put," he told Nick and Jessie. "I'll get the papers."

The brisk autumn wind twirled Willie's coat as he hurried from the car. Turning to Jessie, Nick finally asked her what was wrong.

"Nothing. It's just … reading the reviews alone is an old tradition I'd like to continue."

"Alone? You want me to walk home?"

"You know what I mean. I don't like having a crowd watching my reaction."

But she could lie in bed naked with Josh under a spotlight and give a rousing imitation of making love in front of hundreds of strangers. Actors. Which reminded him-- "By the way, your understudy made a point of introducing herself to me, but she didn't stay long at the party. She didn't even sit down to dinner."

"Ha. She usually takes off the minute we finish rehearsals. I'm surprised she showed up at all."

Opening the back door, Willie handed Nick four early-morning editions of the metropolitan papers. A moment later they were heading uptown.

"Are you alone enough?" Nick asked, holding up the TIMES. It didn't take long to find the review. The headline was in bold print.

JESSICA KENDLE, THE BRIGHTEST LIGHT ON BROADWAY

He quickly skipped the introductory background, his eyes dropping down to the meat of the critique.

After a three-year hibernation, Jessica Kendle returned to her roots tonight, opening in the William Rudolph revival of TO HAVE AND TO HOLD at the Rodgers and Hammerstein Theater. And what a splendid return it is! From her opening song as a nervous young bride on her wedding day, Ms. Kendle proves she's an indelible force on the stage.

Near the end of the second act, the Tony-Award-winning actress jerked the audience to its feet as one body, belting out a gut-wrenching lament about her dead son. It was electrifying, a moment of pure stage magic and a pinnacle in Ms.

Kendle's career. This is a performance not to be missed. She is riveting, alternately vulnerable, sexy, strong, funny, and deeply moving.

Josh Elliot, on the other hand, falls short in the role of the husband. While Mr. Elliott has a powerful voice and is an adept dancer, he lacks the depth and nuance with which Ms. Kendle layers her character. One can't help wondering what Andrew Brady might have done with the role. Mr. Elliot is ...

Jessie pushed the paper away. "Oh God. They compared Josh to Andrew."

Which was no surprise. Nick opened THE NEW YORK POST, quickly scanning the review. "Pretty much the same here, except they really hated Josh." Was he smiling? He hoped he wasn't smiling.

"Stop it."

"What?"

"That nasty smile of yours. This will devastate Josh. He's never gotten a bad review before."

"He's never worked opposite you before."

*

Josh downed the brandy Abbie gave him. "Mind if I have another?"

"Here," Abbie said, "have the whole bottle." She dropped down beside him on the couch. "You okay?"

"No." Josh shrugged, feeling shell-shocked. "Was I that bad tonight? Tell me the truth."

"I thought you were great. That's the truth."

"I don't understand. I've felt good about my work since our first rehearsal. How could I've been so wrong?"

"You know what I think?" Abbie leaned against him. "This is all about Jessie. Her return to Broadway after Andrew's death is huge. The critics focused on Jessie and didn't pay attention to you. It's not your fault. It's not Jessie's fault either."

Springing up, Josh headed to the picture window and looked out. Fifty-six floors below, the wind churned the Hudson's waters. The lights of the George Washington Bridge flickered in the distance. "I'll tell you something. I thought Andrew was a great actor, one of the best. But Jessie ... Jessie always seemed secondary to Andrew."

Josh took a gulp of brandy. "When Bill asked me to do this show and told me Jessie would be playing Christine, I thought, great, this is my moment to shine. But from the first rehearsal, I was blown away by Jessie's brilliance. I think without Jessie, well, Andrew might not have looked so good."

"You just discovered the secret of Andrew Brady's talent. The woman behind the man." Abbie sauntered over to Josh. "Tell me something. Are you in love with Jessie?"

Taking her hand, Josh looked into Abbie's warm eyes. "Not at the moment."

*

"My God, Jess." Combing his damp hair back from his eyes, Nick gazed at Jessie. She was still breathing hard after their lovemaking, her lips parted, her eyes fastened on his. Nick pulled her into his arms, covering them with a sheet. They lay in silence as their breathing leveled off to the normal range.

"Two whole days off," Jessie whispered, "and more time for us. Not counting the interviews, and that TODAY thing. It'll be quick. I love working an Off-Broadway schedule."

Mondays and Tuesdays Jessie would be home. Nick liked it, too. But she paid for the luxury, doing double performances on Wednesdays, Saturdays, and Sundays.

"So," Nick murmured, keeping his tone light, "what's it like to bed two men in one night?"

"What do you mean?"

"You and Josh. Naked in bed together."

"You think we were naked?"

"That's what it looked like."

Jessie chuckled. "Ever hear of duplicate costumes?"

"Dupli-- ?" Nick started to laugh. Okay. They weren't naked. Still ...

"Nick?"

"Hmm?"

"Tell me about Beth."

"Bree?"

"Yeah. Her."

"... What do you want to know?"

"Were the two of you lovers?"

"A long time ago." Nick searched her eyes.

"Was it serious?"

"I didn't know the meaning of the word until I met you." Nick traced Jessie's lips with his finger. "More to the point, what difference does it make? It was a lifetime ago."

Jessie gazed at Nick a moment longer before nestling into his arms. "Night, Nick."

Nick pressed his lips to her forehead. He'd see Bree on Wednesday. Maybe they could erase the past and start over.

*

Several nights later, Roberto Martinelli stood at the penthouse deck window, high above the Jersey shoreline. The five-bedroom condo had been a good investment. He felt miles away from his Long Island estate, far from the New York decision making and the worries. Within these walls he entered a different world, employed a different ... talent. One he'd discovered he was surprisingly good at. No one suspected. No one ever would. This was Roberto's secret.

He stared across the Hudson, the lights of lower Manhattan still blazing in the middle of the night. The city that never slept. The skyline rankled Roberto, the missing twin towers of the World Trade Center a gaping wound. Roberto had lost nineteen employees when the south tower collapsed that sunny September morning, their only crime showing up for work. The memory still whipped the acids in his gut. But the gleaming One World Trade Center that had risen in its wake was a masterpiece of stark beauty and--

"Roberto?" a woman's melodious voice called from behind him. "It's bedtime," she teased. "They're waiting for you in all their glory. To do with as you will."

"Be there in a moment."

Still staring at the Manhattan skyline, Martinelli said a silent prayer for the innocents who'd died September eleventh. He'd snuffed out many lives during his career, but his victims always earned their demise, one way or another. It was always a business decision. One more decision would be executed—Roberto's lip twisted--shortly. Lyle Barton.

*

Awakening to a soft kiss, Nick cracked one eye open. Jessie loomed over him, dressed in jeans and a sweater.

"Hey, Rip Van Winkle, just wanted to let you know I'm leaving."

"Stay."

Jessie laughed. "We can lounge in bed tomorrow. Today's Wednesday, remember? A matinee. And I'm stopping at Bill's office for a copy of the show's CD. Jeremy says another talk show called. I want to know how I sound before I have to talk about myself on TV."

The bedside clock read ten-forty-five. He had to get moving, too. Nick sat up, brushing the hair out of his eyes. "I'll see you at the theater between shows. Anthony and I are bringing you dinner?"

"It's easier. I can't venture out in between shows without being mobbed. Mary's out grocery shopping. I told her to keep it non-fattening."

"Like you have to worry." Nick reached over and squeezed Jessie's waist.

"Don't squeeze my fat." Jessie playfully twisted away.

"You didn't mind my squeezing it last night."

Blushing, Jessie headed for the hallway. "Goodbye," she shouted over her shoulder, closing the door behind her.

Women and their weight. Although Bree used to eat twice what Nick consumed, and she never mentioned the word diet.

After a shower and shave, Nick threw on a suede jacket over slacks and a turtleneck. Clipping down the back stairs to the kitchen, he poured a cup of coffee.

"Hey, stranger."

Nick spun around. Abbie sat in the breakfast nook, nibbling an orange muffin. She was wearing a wraparound turquoise top and skinny jeans that molded her body like the skin on an apple. Only Abbie could get away with that outfit and not look like a hooker. "How did you get in?"

"Jessie was going out when I was coming in. I bought Anthony some frames at a flea market," she said, waving them in the air, "for his photos. But I also wanted to talk to you."

"About your little gift? I gave Barton your matches and the envelope when he dropped by on Monday. He doesn't expect to find any prints." Nick had also given Barton the card attached to the black orchids. And during the opening night party, Nick had arranged for a messenger service to deliver the orchids to Midtown North. Might as well dust the vase for prints, too.

"No, smarty, it's not about the matches, even though it still sends a chill up my spine. Let me know if you find out anything more."

"Uh huh." Abbie didn't need to know Jessie's orchids and Abbie's matches had both come from Buffalo. Once Abbie got involved in something, she could be a pain. And the fewer people involved, the better. He glanced at his pocket watch.

"Am I keeping you from something?"

"I'm on a schedule." Nick ignored Abbie's pointed stare. "So? What else is up?"

"I wanted to let you know I've taken Josh off your hands."

"I didn't know Josh was on my hands."

"Right. I reeled him in on opening night. I also wanted you to know Jessie invited Josh and me to join you for dinner today between shows."

"Fine." Nick took another swallow of coffee and set his cup in the sink. "Have to run." He headed for the hallway.

"Where are you off to?"

"Errands."

"Can I tag along?"

"Then I'm meeting a friend for lunch."

"So that's why you're dressed up. And you smell good, too."

"It's called soap. Tell Josh to try it sometime."

*

Adding a sports drink to his tray, Anthony moved out of the lunch line in the school cafeteria. He spotted Zane Harwell motioning him to a table. Anthony slid onto the bench across from his friend and looked at his tray. Beef macaroni, green beans, and chocolate pudding. Yuck. Maybe if his mom tasted it, she'd let Mary make him lunch and stop nagging about a hot meal.

Zane pulled a peanut butter and jelly sandwich and a thick slab of apple pie from a sack and dug in. Eyeing Anthony's tray, he made a face. "Even my dog wouldn't eat that. Toss it and we'll split my lunch."

Grinning, Anthony took his tray to the counter and slid it towards the Hispanic woman cleaning up. "You didn't eat a thing," she scolded. "It's a crime to waste food like that."

A big kid was watching them, a star on the soccer team. Anthony didn't think a cafeteria lady would talk that way to Oliver Boardwell. Anthony squared his shoulders. "Even a dog wouldn't eat this. It-it sucks."

Someone gasped. Anthony whirled around. Gina Fusciello stared at him. Anthony didn't like Gina. She was Italian, just like Gianni. Even her names were like Gianni's. She was always getting in his face because she was a year older and his boss on the school paper. "You used a bad word," she said.

"Shut up, Gina."

"Who's going to make me? You?" She giggled. "You think you're cool 'cause you're hanging out with Zane Harwell. But you're just a nerd whose real father killed your stepdad. My mom told me you're not Anthony McDeare. You're not even Anthony Brady. You're Anthony Fosselli."

"I am not!"

"And my mom said your mom's marrying a playboy. My mom says he wants everything his brother had. Like--"

"Shut up!" Anthony could feel his face go hot and his breathing get faster.

"Like your—"

Anthony pushed Gina. She crashed into a stack of clean trays, toppling them over towards the startled dishwasher.

Gina righted herself and started to cry. "I'm telling Mr. Yablonski!" She ran from the cafeteria, holding her shoulder.

Breathing harder, Anthony quickly looked around. The monitors were talking to each other, standing by the glassed-in garden. They never glanced his way over the cafeteria noise. The Hispanic lady gave him a dirty look, but she kept on working. She had a lot of dishes. Oliver Boardwell winked.

Anthony swaggered back to his table. Let Gina tell the headmaster. Anthony didn't care. He didn't care if everybody knew about Gianni anymore. So what? Anthony thought of a bad word he'd heard Zane's brother Dylan say. Fuck. Fuck Gianni.

What he was angry about was something else. Nobody talked about his dad like that.

*

In Clint's line of work, you never knew when a little extra information would come in handy. So he sat in front of a computer at his battered desk, studying an Internet fan site for Nick Mcfucking-celebrity McDeare.

The man wouldn't know the real world if it bit him in the ass. Writing from his ivory tower. A different bimbo on his arm for every award and PR event. One of PEOPLE'S most eligible bachelors. Jessie Kendle would be lucky if McDeare made it down the aisle. Or maybe she'd be luckier if he didn't.

The downstairs buzzer droned. Clint didn't have visitors. But the building did, junkies pushing every bell and trying to rob the place. Clint unbolted his door, shoving the pole-bar lock aside. He trotted down the steps and approached the windowed vestibule.

"Yeah?" Clint opened the door a crack.

"Clint Vaughn?"

"Who wants to know?"

"Lieutenant Barton. NYPD." The cop produced his shield.

Before opening the door wider, Clint made a show of sizing up the detective, as if he hadn't seen him before. Solid build, like he was poured from a concrete mixer. The cop wore a crumbled trench coat with ink stains on the right pocket and loafers that belonged on a bum.

"Could we talk somewhere a little more private?" Barton asked, stepping into the hallway.

"What's this about?"

"Just want to ask a couple of questions. Nothing major."

Shrugging, Clint started up the stairs, Barton a few steps behind. Clint pushed open his door and headed to the desk, quickly closing out his computer screen window. Bye-bye, McDeare.

Barton paused in the doorway, fingering the pole lock. "I haven't seen one of these babies in years."

"It was here when I moved in."

"And that was …?"

"When Indians roamed Upper Manhattan."

He waited while the detective ambled around the living room, flitting from object to object like a housefly. "You've been spotted on East Seventy-Fifth Street, Mr. Vaughn. Sitting in your car by the hour. You want to tell me why?"

"None of your business."

"It's my business when a celebrity who's been stalked and harassed lives on that block."

"A celebrity?"

"Yeah. So what's up?"

"I'm a PI, on a job."

"Your client is …?"

"Uh-uh. Client confidentiality. But I can tell you this much. He's no celebrity. Just a schmuck banging some sweet meat behind his rich wife's back."

The two men stared at each other. Barton nodded and headed for the door. "Thanks for your time, Mr. Vaughn."

Clint locked the door behind him. Barton had gotten a good look at him. He'd have to disguise himself at the wedding, even though it would be a mob scene. Better to take precautions. He wasn't shadowing McDeare anymore so no more notice from that end of the McDeare business. He'd told Aldo exactly where he could shove his surveillance.

*

Climbing behind the wheel of his double-parked car, Barton pulled out his notebook and scanned his scribbles.

Foxy had confirmed Vaughn's innocence in the Dykstra homicide over breakfast yesterday. Clint Vaughn had been in the wrong place at the wrong time. According to Foxy, Vaughn didn't have the cojones to pull off a drug lord's assassination. You wanted to get the goods on a cheating husband—Vaughn was your man. They'd nailed the right guy.

After meeting Vaughn in person, Barton tended to agree. Vaughn was a sketchy operator, looking for a quick buck.

*

Abbie parted with Nick outside the brownstone. She hurried towards Fifth Avenue as Nick moved in the other direction. Peeking over her shoulder, she waited for him to turn the corner onto Madison Avenue before jogging after him. She was just in time to see Nick climb into a taxi. Abbie hailed a cab and told the driver to tail him, ignoring the man's curse.

Nick got out at Seventh Avenue and Twenty-Fifth Street, heading east. Yelling at her driver to stop, Abbie scrambled out of the taxi mid-block. The cabbie stopped swearing when she flung an extra twenty in his face. She caught sight of Nick entering a pre-war apartment building. Abbie secreted herself in the doorway of a dry-cleaning shop and waited.

Her heart sank when Nick emerged five minutes later with Brianna Fontaine. The reporter had dressed with care, wearing sleek leggings, leather boots, and a funky coat with faux leopard trim. They headed towards Sixth Avenue. Abbie trailed a half block behind, halting when they ducked into a Spanish bistro on Twenty-Third Street.

What the hell was Nick's problem?

*

Nick speared the last clam from his paella and met Bree's eyes. It had all come down to this moment. "Look," he said softly, "I understand if you want to walk away. I mean, I know this was a surprise. But for old times' sake ..."

Bree pushed her plate away and took a sip of sangria. "You haven't changed. You know exactly how to push my buttons. Why am I such a sucker for your sweet talk?"

Smiling, he knew he'd won. "It's my special talent." Nick bit into the clam, chewing slowly and swallowing. "We need to be honest with each other from the get-go. I don't want a rerun of our Hong Kong finale."

"Me neither." Bree stared at Nick thoughtfully. "I can't say no to you. God help me, yes."

The waiter cleared their plates. Nick held out his hand and Bree clasped it. "You won't be sorry." He felt the old rush of excitement, the thrill of the chase.

"That remains to be seen. Truthfully, I'd been dreading coming back to New York. But then you appeared out of nowhere." She released his hand and laughed, staring at the ceiling. "I don't know which is more lethal. Being around you or uncovering a terrorist cell in Afghanistan."

"I'll take that as a compliment." Nick's cell rang. "Excuse me." He clicked on. "McDeare."

"Mr. McDeare, Durwood Yablonski, Grantham Academy's headmaster. Anthony has detention today, until four o'clock. I wanted to call his mother but the boy insisted on you. I'd like to have a conference before Anthony goes home. Under normal circumstances an uncle wouldn't--"

"I'm on my way." Nick rang off and checked his pocket watch. Almost three-thirty. "Sorry. Have to run. Trouble at Anthony's school."

"Anthony? Your nephew?"

"My son."

"I don't understand."

"I'm adopting Anthony." Nick tossed some bills on the table and rose.

"Nick, is that ... never mind."

"What?"

"You'll get angry. Anyway, it's none of my business."

"Come on. If we're going to be seeing each other, you might as well get it out now."

"Me and my big mouth ... Okay. Is this, uh, really more about Jeffrey than Anthony? I mean, do you think you should--"

"You think I'm trying to replace Jeffrey with Anthony? You should know me better than that." Bree was right about one thing. It was none of her business. She'd never had a child. How could she understand that one son, no matter how precious, could never begin to take the place of another? Nick started for the door.

"Nick, wait. I'm sorry." Bree ran after him, catching up outside the restaurant. "Look, you have to remember I was around when Jeffrey was sick. I saw what it did to you every time he was in the hospital. I know the kind of hole it had to leave in your life when ..." She sighed. "I'm glad you have Anthony. You're great with kids. Remember that time in Japan when we got stuck in line with the school tour from hell? All those giggling little girls and Nick McDeare? You become a different creature around children."

"Meaning I'm an SOB creature otherwise?"

"Your words."

"Fair enough." Nick took her hand, cracking a smile. "We're on for Saturday?"

"Saturday."

Kissing her on the cheek, Nick lingered over Bree's scent of elixir and incense. It brought back the old days. He could never breathe in incense after Hong Kong without thinking of Bree's eyes, light brown with emerald chips, and how they looked under an Asian moon.

*

Late October and the trees had already shed their leaves, their branches dark lace against a milky sky. Lyle made the winding drive out to Long Island to talk to Roberto Martinelli, a home visit this time. Thanksgiving was only weeks away. Barb's family would be coming down from Boston for the holiday. Lyle figured he could put up with his mother-in-law for a few days in exchange for her candied yams and turkey.

He parked at the apex of the horseshoe drive. The manicured estate showcased Martinellli's stone mansion in solitary splendor. The construction must've wiped out an entire quarry. A maid showed Barton into the foyer, bigger than Lyle's first floor. Aldo Zappella appeared, informing Lyle that Mr. Martinelli was out for the day.

"In that case," Lyle said, "maybe you can help me."

"Sorry, Lieutenant, but I'm busy." Aldo didn't bother to conceal the contempt in those small dark eyes, his thin face almost effete but for the jutting nose. His sister Paula, the poor fool who'd married Ian Wexley, had gotten the looks in that family.

"Oh, this won't take long," Lyle said pleasantly, ambling around the hallway and peeking into rooms. Looked like Martinelli used Marie Antoinette's decorator. "I was just wondering if I should file a missing person's report?"

"Don't have a clue what you're talking about."

"I'll enlighten you." Still ogling the furnishings, Barton wandered back to Zappella. "That man killed in an escape attempt from the Milano in a powerboat last August? Has anyone been asking his whereabouts? You know. The Fosselli look-alike?"

The eyes gave it away. Aldo didn't move a facial muscle, but it was over. Lyle had seen those eyes on scum busted in the middle of a drug deal. He'd seen that look on an infamous serial killer. Nailed climbing into his car when he thought he was home free after slaughtering his tenth hooker and stuffing her body parts into four garbage cans. Barton was sure he'd worn that same look when he realized his partner Bushman was working for the mob. That disconnect between what you expect and what you got—it was always in the eyes.

"Well?" Lyle drawled.

Zappella found his voice. "Lieutenant, if this is supposed to be some kind of joke, it's not funny. Gianni Fosselli died that night. You know it, and I know it. Now if you'll excuse me, this ridiculous conversation is over."

The drive back into Manhattan was a blur as Lyle allowed reality to sink in.

He'd been right.

Gianni Fosselli—a dead man--was alive.

He beat his fingers on the gearshift as he sat at a light. All right. He had a job to do. Get to the basics. How did he prove Gianni was among the living? How did he ferret out the son of a bitch? No one would believe him. Not the police commissioner. Not the feds. Not even his own detectives.

At least McDeare would believe him. Wouldn't he?

*

Stationed inside a vegetable market across Twenty-Third Street, Abbie stared over a mound of eggplants through a dirty front window. At Nick and Bree. After they split in separate directions, Abbie plodded down the street, heading towards Seventh Avenue and the subway.

Was Nick cheating on Jessie? Or having lunch with a friend? The good part was Nick had met Bree in a restaurant, not a hotel. It had been a long lunch, but old friends would linger to reminisce. And Nick had kissed the reporter on the cheek, not the lips.

Tucking her shoulder bag closer to her side, Abbie neared the subway station. The more she thought about it, the sillier her suspicions seemed. Nick and Jessie were getting married. Why would he fool around now? Was Nick having second thoughts? But he was in love with Jessie. Abbie was as sure of that as she was sure you didn't mix stripes with plaid.

Okay, she'd test Nick. Tonight at the theater she'd ask him outright whom he'd met for lunch. In front of Jessie. If he admitted it was Bree and Jessie acted like it was no big deal, there was nothing to worry about.

Abbie scampered down the station steps and slipped her Metro card into the turnstile, rushing to the platform at a train's rumble and blast of wind. Meanwhile, there was Josh to look forward to. He was great in bed. With her lipstick career tanking and no one standing in line to hire a PI, Josh was something to do. Literally. Jostling against passengers, Abbie joined the other sardines on the crowded train, the door whoosing shut behind her.

*

"You should've seen Barton's face. He knows." Aldo took a slurp of Compari, the ice cubes rattling.

"Then move on it." Bored, Roberto stared out the floor-to-ceiling study window, wishing he were back in Jersey City.

"I have. Barton's wife and daughter are at a party Saturday afternoon. He'll be home alone."

"You know this how?"

"A bug in the kitchen. And get this, we got in with a key."

"You're shitting me."

"The daughter has a college math tutor, Barton's godson. Came by Monday afternoon. The kid likes his booze. So he got a new drinking buddy Monday night."

Joey Three Fingers slipped him something in a dive near Fordham and stole his key chain. The moron even had Barton's key marked. It was copied and back in his pocket before he knew it was missing."

"Barton trusts the kid with a key?"

"He's like family, you know how it is. A computer whiz, does work for Barton on the side. Something about hooking up the home computer to the police system. He comes and goes."

Roberto nodded. The wife and child would be untouched. No need for collateral damage. He was not a heartless man despite his reputation. Roberto Martinelli was no monster. He was a patriot. An astute businessman. And he had feelings like everyone else. He even liked children.

*

Lyle climbed into his SUV and headed home. It had been a long day, half of it in his car. First Vaughn. Then Zappella.

Barb had sausage and peppers waiting for him. Dina was excited about her best friend's birthday party on Saturday, going into double digits at ten years old. She was bubbling over about the gift she'd bought, a jeweled collar for the Lab puppy the girl's parents were giving her. Dina had created a special puppy card for Grace on the computer.

Listening patiently, Lyle savored every morsel of his dinner. After living in the belly of the beast all day, it was a relief to come home to family.

CHAPTER 8

The session with Yablonski was an exercise in frustration. Willie was waiting for Nick and Anthony after they left the Academy. As the limo inched into traffic, Nick closed the partition between driver and passengers. He turned to Anthony, handsome in his uniform blue blazer and tie. But the image of a perfect little boy in a perfect private school was at odds with reality.

"Why wouldn't you tell Mr. Yablonski and me why you pushed that little girl, Anthony?"

Shrugging, Anthony turned away, staring out the window.

"Did she push you first? Or maybe she--what's her name again?"

"Gina Fusciello,"

"Did she call you a name?"

"No."

Gina Fusciello. Italian. "Did she say something about Gianni to you? Something that bothered you?"

"Kind of. But that's not what made me mad."

"Was it something about Andrew?"

Anthony shook his head.

If this wasn't about ... "It was about me, wasn't it?"

Swiping a sideways look at Nick, Anthony turned back to the window.

"It's okay, Anthony. You can tell me the truth."

"I'm not going to let anyone say anything bad about you. I'll stay after school every day if I have to." Anthony hunched into his seat.

So much for celebrity. His rep with the ladies had infiltrated the halls of a grammar school. Anthony had to deal with Andrew and Gianni's notoriety, and now Nick's, too. No wonder he was having problems.

Clearing his throat, Nick said, "That means a lot to me. I feel the same way about you. But neither of us can go around hurting people just because we don't like what they say."

"It's not fair! Gina doesn't even know you."

"Look, you're going to hear things about my past from time to time. Some of the things are true. No one's perfect, especially me. We've talked about this. When you're famous, people know things about you, or they think they do. You and your mom are my life now. That won't change. That's what counts."

"I'm sorry I pushed her. She just makes me so mad sometimes."

"Lots of times people make me mad. Sometimes I wish I could push them, too." Nick paused. "How about we make a pact? Let's promise we'll just laugh at anything people say about us. Whatever anyone else thinks, that's not our problem." Nick held out his hand. "I promise."

Anthony stared at Nick. He slid his hand into Nick's and shook. "I promise, too."

"Good." Nick pulled the boy into a bear hug.

"Dad? Can we not tell Mom about this? Please? She'll just get mad, and she doesn't understand. I promise I'll never push a girl again."

Another secret from Jessie, stacking up like pancakes. "On one condition. I want you to be on your best behavior from now on. Starting tonight, when we take dinner to your mom. Deal?"

"Deal. Um, one more thing? Could you talk to Mom about lunch? I want Mary to make my lunch. I hate cafeteria food."

"Let me guess. Zane brings his lunch from home."

"Yeah."

"Okay, why not? I hated cafeteria food too. It's the same all over the world, Bongo. "

*

Tightening the sash on her silk robe, Jessie settled into the easy chair in her dressing room, waiting for Nick and Anthony. She rubbed her scalp, reveling in no wig. There had been no more wardrobe mishaps since Nora had become inspector general. Thank God for Nora. A good dresser was hard to find, and Nora was the best in the business. Nora and Jessie had been together since that long-ago day when Jessica Kendle had first set foot on a Broadway stage.

Jessie had received another standing ovation at the matinee. Bill had a hit. It was exhilarating. And it ate up all her energy. She'd forgotten what performing onstage took out of you, not to mention what was going on backstage. Jeremy was setting up an interview for her with a TIMES reporter for an Arts and Leisure interview. NEW YORK MAGAZINE was after him for a photo spread and PLAYBILL wanted a follow-up feature. Brat Pitt had just left her dressing room after slipping into the matinee, and Jeremy said Al Pacino was going to be in the audience tonight. He'd love to meet her. And something about a pile of movie scripts coming her way.

Meanwhile, Jessie was starving, but she didn't dare eat. She'd caught Valentine watching her backstage during a quick costume change. She could swear the understudy was hoping the zipper would snag on Jessie's cellulite as Nora had jiggled it up the slinky sheath.

That had done it. Jessie complained to the stage manager about Valentine hanging around backstage. But George had coolly reminded Jessie he had more pressing things on his mind than an understudy. Jessie longed for the days when Quill was in charge. He popped in occasionally, but he'd soon be heading to London to direct a new play in the West End. So Valentine still stared at her every performance. But Jessie didn't want to go over George's head to Bill. Not yet.

As her dressing room filled up for dinner, Jessie stopped brooding. Abbie and Josh arrived on Nick and Anthony's heels. Jessie looked longingly over the contents of the picnic basket Nick and Anthony brought. Mary had packed a hearty salad. Mixed greens. Beveled cucumbers. Matchstick black radishes. Cherry tomatoes. Green pepper and celery. Baby shrimp. Slices of filet mignon and honey-baked ham. Wedges of hard-boiled eggs. Black olives. Shredded English cheddar and baby Swiss. Crumbles of gorgonzola. Mandarin oranges and seedless grapes. Bacon crisps. Home-made croutons. An assortment of dressings. And a basket of homemade buttermilk biscuits with sweet butter and honey.

The days of stuffing her face like a monkey over, Jessie daintily filled a plate with vegetables. Crunchy stuff, a lot of cucumbers and peppers. No olives. She drizzled fat-free vinaigrette over the top, careful not to use more than a teaspoon. Her robe's drooping kimono sleeve knocked over the bottle of Italian dressing and Abbie wiped it up, reminding everyone Jessie couldn't go without spilling. Anthony thought that was very funny. Jessie chewed each piece slowly, relishing the tart taste. She popped one shrimp into her mouth, plus a grape. Two. She used to enjoy eating. Now each bite reminded her of the sleek image she had to present to the world.

Anthony was more interested in his mother's dressing room than the food. Jessie patiently answered his questions, while Nick fixed a plate for the boy. Nick ate only a portion of beef, but Abbie and Josh piled their plates. "Full from your lunch, Nick?" Abbie asked, closing her lips around a biscuit.

"Mary made you a special lunch?" Jessie asked.

"No," Abbie said casually. "Nick met a friend for lunch. Where did you eat?"

"Who did you meet?" Jessie asked.

Nick swallowed before answering, "Michael. It's been a while since we've seen each other."

*

"The TIMES is giving me until Thanksgiving to get settled," Bree said into her cell. "The first in my series is due early December."

"How's the apartment coming along?" Yves asked.

"I emptied a few more boxes today." Now that Bree was based in New York, she and Yves had bought this apartment two weeks ago. It made sense. They were both tired of living out of a suitcase and needed a home base. Bree stared out at the high-rise opposite her window, stacked blocks of smoked glass crisscrossed with strips of steel.

"You need to get out more. Maybe spend a weekend at your mother's."

"I'm going out there Saturday and staying a few days. Mummy and husband number four are in Australia for a few months. I thought I'd get a jump-start on my articles in the countryside. Plus I can jog on the beach. I hate running in the city, the exhaust."

"Wish I could join you." His sigh filled the silence. "Well, I better go. The sun will be up soon and I want some shots of Islamabad at dawn."

"Promise you'll be careful."

"I will. Love you." Yves said goodbye.

Staring at her laptop screen, Bree felt as guilty as a teenager sneaking around under the football stadium with one guy while she was an item with another. Even though it wasn't quite the same. Yves had called right after she'd sent Nick a long e-mail.

Even after all these years, she was hopeless. Bree knew she'd always care more about Nick than he cared about her.

What the hell was she getting herself into this time?

*

It was a relief for Abbie to be in a cab heading home. She hadn't been able to eat after Nick's lie about lunching with his reporter friend Michael. She'd left quickly, saying she didn't feel well, nixing Josh's suggestion he come over after the show that night.

Josh had shot her a sharp look after Nick's lie. He must have picked up on something. Abbie wouldn't underestimate that Ken doll face again. She couldn't risk the chance of seeing Josh tonight. If he coaxed her to tell him what was wrong …

Abbie shook her head. If Josh thought Nick was cheating on Jessie, he'd tell Jessie the dirt and go after her himself. There was no doubt in Abbie's mind Josh was another man hot for her best friend Jessie Kendle. Abbie had seen it happen ever since high school. Males of all ages tripped over their running shoes when it came to Jessie's icy fire or fiery ice or whatever the hell it was.

So she'd keep quiet and investigate on her own. She needed irrefutable proof. And what if she got it? Jessie would be shattered. Losing Andrew had almost destroyed her. How many blows could a woman take and not lose it? Damn Nick McDeare and his womanizing games to hell.

*

Early Saturday morning, Nick threw on sweats and an Orioles baseball cap. Time for a run to clear his head and put his life back in order. He'd been in freefall ever since Abbie tripped him up at the theater last Wednesday. He needed a good five miles.

It was cold but the sun was strong. Nick jogged past Starbucks towards Fifth Avenue, thinking about his life since the day those matches had shown up. Twice. Since the black orchids had arrived. Since Abbie had gotten her own matches. Since Martinelli had smirked at him at the theater. Since he'd renewed things with Bree. Since his talk with Anthony's headmaster. Problems were multiplying as fast as spam.

Nick reached Central Park at Seventy-Second. He pumped across Strawberry Fields, sprinted around the reservoir, and passed Alice in Wonderland and the merry-go-round before heading back home. He hated the lies to Jessie. He jogged in place at a stoplight before it turned, oblivious to the garbage trucks and early-morning street sweepers. And he hated Abbie getting in his business and making things worse. She meant well, but she was going to mess everything up.

Breathing harder, Nick spun around the corner. He breezed past a dog walker with an Afghan, two spaniels, a greyhound, and a terrier jerking his arms out of their sockets. Nick wiped a hand across his forehead and pushed through the brownstone's gate, his cell jangling. "McDeare," he panted.

"It's Lyle. Listen, I have to talk to you about something important. I don't want Jessie to overhear us. She's at the theater all day, right?"

"Yeah." Nick tried to steady his breathing.

"I'll come by around noon, okay?"

"I'll be out all day. Not back until late this evening."

"Tomorrow? Jessie has another matinee, right?"

"Tomorrow's good. Early afternoon. What's up?"

"Not over the phone. We need to talk, Nick. I'll see you tomorrow."

*

"Jesus, Barb, why don't you cut through the back yards instead of walking all the way around the block?" Lyle would never understand women.

"Yeah, Mom," Dina said. "We're already late for the party. Grace called twice. Come on!" Dina clasped a gaily-wrapped package in her hands.

"Civilized people don't cut through the neighbors' yards," Barb said firmly. Lyle followed the women out onto the front porch, telling Dina to have fun.

"I'll bring you a piece of cake, Daddy."

Before returning to his computer, Lyle watched his girls with their heads of shiny red hair trot down the sidewalk. He got back to work, doing a search of new rentals and sales since August in all five boroughs, making a list of single men. It was probably a waste of time. But Gianni could be right here. He wouldn't put it past the prick to enjoy his own private joke on the NYPD.

Barton had pondered not telling Nick about Gianni. He'd thought of nothing else the past few days. He'd finally decided the man should be warned. And Lyle needed help. This was too much to handle alone.

His cell rang. Barb. "What's up?"

"We -- Grace's -- card. My cell needs --- charged. Can you -- -- it?"

"A card?"

"Yeah. It's -- Dina's -- We'll -- -- behind -- Goldblums' house."

The line went dead. The birthday card for Grace? In Dina's room, Lyle surmised. And he was supposed to meet them behind the Goldblums'. He headed upstairs to his daughter's room. What a mess, no card in sight. He called Barb's cell but it went straight to voice mail. Her battery had died. How many times had he nagged his wife about keeping her cell charged?

*

"So?" Aldo muttered into his cell. "It's done?"

"Soon. I let myself in a few nights ago when they were all out. It's set to go as soon as I press a button. Just watched the woman and the kid walk out the front door. Barton went back inside. I'm out of here in a few minutes."

"Good job, Joey. I'll let the boss know." Aldo clicked off.

*

"But we play with my camera on Saturdays," Anthony complained to Nick. "And we were going to toss a few balls and work on my swing."

"Sorry, Bongo." Nick shrugged on a crewneck. "It can't be helped. I have some research to do for my book."

Anthony sighed dramatically as he edged towards the suite's door. "Hey," Nick called after the boy. "I have to meet with Lyle after lunch tomorrow, but then how about I help with your swing and we'll develop some of your photos. And we'll take dinner to the theater for your mom between shows."

"Promise?"

"Promise."

"Can I have Zane over this afternoon? We could practice out back."

"Fine with me as long as you clear it with Mary." Anthony's face broke into a smile as he left the room. Nick felt like a jerk. He'd never lied to the boy until now. Lies were the gift that kept on giving. Cursing, he grabbed for his pocket watch and wallet when Abbie called his cell.

"Hey, gorgeous," she purred. "Are we bringing dinner to the work force today?"

"No can do, Abbie." Nick swallowed his anger. "I'm working all day."

"Maybe tomorrow then."

"Tomorrow Anthony and I have something special planned. Maybe Wednesday, okay? Have to go. Talk to you soon." His pocketed his phone. Abbie was going to be a problem.

Nick flew down the stairs. He was meeting Bree at a Hertz location. Driving to her mother's house would take less time than the Long Island railroad.

*

Exasperated, Lyle jogged out the back door and met Barb and Dina in the Goldblums' back yard. "I couldn't find the card in that mess. And what have I told you about your cell, Barb?"

"Not now." Barb shook her head at her husband. "Look, you go to Grace's and explain why we're late to her mother, okay? Come on, Dina. You can get your birthday card, and I'll get my charger." They started off towards their house. "I'm cutting across the backyards. Satisfied?" Barb yelled over her shoulder.

"I wasn't planning on making an appearance at a kid's birthday party. You do it. Why do you need the phone anyway?"

"My mother's calling to make plans for Thanksgiving. You want your turkey, don't you?"

*

Abbie dialed the brownstone's private line. "Hi, Mary. Nick's not answering his cell. Could you get him for me?"

"He just left. Can I give him a message?"

"He said he was working today."

"Doing research. Got a message?"

"No message. Thanks." Abbie collapsed into a chair, cursing men. "Research, my ass."

*

"They'll be here any minute," Lyle told Mrs. Bishop and Grace. "It's been a crazy day. Dina forgot your--"

A thunderous explosion rattled the window frames, nearly rocking him off his feet. On instinct, Lyle grabbed Grace, sheltering her. "What the--?" He glanced at the distressed children. They began to catch their breath one by one, terror taking root. One little girl started shrieking hysterically, unable to catch her breath.

"Everyone okay?" No injuries he could see, just shock and tears. Lyle raced for the back door, their cries rising behind him.

Across the lawns and down the block, black smoke billowed into the air. Smoke and flames. Coming from ... Lyle began to sprint, his pace picking up speed, his heart galloping faster than his legs. He cut across the back lawns and onto his block, sideswiping neighbors pouring out of their homes and staring in shock at the smoke. "Please God, no, no, please, no ..." His next-door neighbor grabbed him, forcing Lyle to skid to a stop.

His home was engulfed in jagged flames and acrid smoke. Lyle coughed, his eyes stinging and tearing. Burning debris littered the yards and the roofs of nearby houses. The shriek of sirens drew closer.

Lyle clutched his hair, the horror choking him. He turned to his neighbor. "Did you see Barb? Dina?" He looked around the yard frantically. Where were they? They had to be here. Empty. He stared at the inferno, a roaring red mountain range eating away his life. NO! Breaking free, Lyle darted around the blaze, screaming for his wife and daughter. The rear half of his house collapsed in on itself.

"B-A-R-B!"

*

Jessie and Josh took their final bow, the heavy brocade and velvet curtain sweeping down over the stage. "Thank God that's over," Jessie whispered. They headed for their dressing rooms.

"That audience was brutal. The ladies-who-lunch from Jersey and the Island. I think they were still out to lunch."

"Too many martinis at Gallaghers." Jessie giggled. "Or maybe it was Quill's revisions."

"Well, this ain't BRIGADOON. Nick bringing you dinner?"

"He's doing research. I'll grab a salad from the vending machine."

Whipping off his tie, Josh grinned down at her. "I'll join you in a few minutes. Poor Jessie, so popular she can't venture out for dinner. I put on a Mets cap and I'm invisible."

Making a face at him, Jessie found Nora and James waiting for her. She shimmied out of her finale costume and flopped down at the dressing table.

"Jeremy phoned," Nora said. She pulled a piece of paper from her pocket. "Let's see ... He said the TIMES called about the Arts and Leisure interview. That talk show wants you. Michael Douglas's assistant sent a note about next Saturday evening's performance—he'd love to stop by afterwards." Nora took a breath. "Jeremy said he's also had calls from the POST, PEOPLE, and USA. He wants to know what he should tell them."

"That I'm dizzy?"

"Whew," James said. "Things are hopping in Jessieville."

"James, this wig felt really loose today."

Unpinning the wig, James inched it off Jessie's head and examined it closely. "Well, no wonder, love. There's a six-inch rip across the crown. How did that happen? It's a fast wig change at the end--maybe I pulled on it too hard."

"Let me see that." Nora took the wig from James. "This looks like it was cut."

Grabbing the wig back, James studied it. "You're right. It's a clean slice. Normally, the netting would give way, forming holes, but this --"

The dressing-room phone rang. Nora answered and handed it to Jessie. "Mary."

Massaging her scalp, Jessie took the phone. "Everything okay, Mary?"

"It's Lyle, honey." Mary's voice was so thick Jessie could barely understand her. She choked back a sob. "On the news. His house. There was an explosion. Gas … His wife and— They, they're gone. Oh, that poor little girl."

Chills shrouded Jessie's shoulders, working their way down her spine. "Oh my God, my God. Lyle … is he--"

"He's fine. He was next door or something."

In a flash, Jessie was back in the ICU. That moment when Andrew's heart stopped beating, when she realized he was gone forever. "Nick," she cried. "I need Nick."

*

"So you grew up in this room?" Nick wandered around Bree's childhood bedroom. "Pretty nice for a kid." The room was the size of Nick's entire apartment back in DC. Queen-sized bed. Built-in desk and bookshelves. A couch. Rust? Dark orange? Something like that. No pastels for Brianna Fontaine. The room was as bold and brassy as the woman she'd grown into.

Nick perused the bookshelves. All the classics. And games. Backgammon. Risk. Battleship. Chess. "No Barbie dolls?"

"I loathed Barbie." Bree ambled over to Nick.

Her eyes were twinkling. And that cute little smile he remembered. Her lips pressed together, one corner higher than the other. Her lips. Nick remembered when they used to share a cigarette after sex. The good old days before he'd quit. He'd take a deep drag, the filter still radiating the warmth of Bree's lips.

She read his mind. "It's been a long time since we've shared a cigarette together, hasn't it?"

"It has." He met her gaze.

"Today's packed with been-a-long-times. Makes me think of that cigarette. Sharing the afterglow …"

Nick could light up right now. Instead, he paced to a telescope perched in front of the bay window. "You're full of surprises. I never pictured you a star-gazer."

"Don't you remember that time in Hong Kong when we took the tram up to the Peak? It was such a clear night."

"I had other things besides stars on my mind that night."

"You did." Bree cast him a sideways smile.

Turning to the window, Nick saw the bay rippling with enough glossy shimmers to pass for a Monet. The shoreline curved into a half moon, studded with two other mansions off in the distance. This part of Southampton was a gated community, ultra private. Nick squinted through the telescope at one property in particular. The back of Roberto Martinelli's estate hosted a tennis court, a five-car garage, an ornate swimming pool, and a boathouse and private pier.

His cell rang, a muffled hum. Scanning the room, Nick pinpointed the chair, his jacket. He retrieved the phone from its pocket, checking the screen and turning away. "Hey, Jess. Matinee over?"

"Nick, I-I, God." She broke into sobs, her words jumbled. "I have news, horrible. About Lyle."

"Calm down," he said quietly. "Try to tell me, okay? What happened?"

"I'm sorry. … It's Lyle. There was a gas explosion in his home. Barb, oh, God, Barb and Dina are dead. They're dead."

"What?" A wash of fear and horror settled in Nick's gut, an internal scream … Nick shivered, tamping it down. Quickly, he pulled himself together, focusing on the facts. "Lyle? Lyle's okay?"

"Yes. He wasn't home. That's all I know."

Dear God. Nick yanked a hand through his hair.

"I'll see you after the show. We need to talk, be there for Lyle."

"I'll be waiting for you." He clicked off and turned to Bree. "Lyle Barton, the cop I told you about? His wife and daughter were killed in a gas explosion at home."

Bree's mouth opened. They stared at each other.

"I have to go. I'm sorry."

"I'll drive you into Manhattan."

"I'll take the train. As planned."

"Don't be ridiculous." She put her hand on his arm. "The train will take hours. You need to get to your friend. I'll stay in Manhattan tonight. Come on. We can listen to Ten-Ten-WINS on the car radio."

*

"God damned son of a bitch!" Roberto shouted. He paced his study. "Who the fuck did you get for this job?"

"Joey Three Fingers," Aldo croaked. "You can count on him like you count on garbage to stink."

"I want the shithead gone. You hear me? What a royal fuck up." His blood pressure had to be spiking up a mountain peak. Screw it. He'd pop an extra Topril.

"Calm down, Roberto. I'll take care of it. This could be a blessing in disguise."

"Get the hell to church for a blessing! Are you out of your ever-fucking mind? What are we, in the business of murdering children?!"

"Listen to me. Barton knows we mean business now. He'll back off."

"You dumb shit, this cop never gives up. Now he's got nothing. He won't care about anything but revenge, a scorpion looking for a warm body to sting. And he'll come after us! Fucking RICO has their heads up their asses, but not Barton. And if he gets McDeare involved--"

"He won't. Clint Vaughn says McDeare writes all fucking day."

"That was his last surveillance. Who the hell knows now? Barton made him!"

"The explosion looks like an accident, remember? A gas leak. Buildings blow up all the time like that. And even if someone asks questions, why should the cops come after us? Anyone could have done this, any slug Barton's ever sent away. That's what we were counting on."

"We were counting on Barton being dead. Not his wife and an innocent child. If he starts talking about Fosselli being alive, the road leads back to us."

"He'll look like a nut if he starts babbling a dead man's alive. He knows that."

"What about that ship's officer who talked to Barton?"

"Taken care of. He's got kids back in Italy. He doesn't want to go to their funerals."

Maybe Aldo was right. Barton would look crazy if he ranted about Fosselli being alive. Anyway, Roberto couldn't go after Barton again, not yet, for one very good reason.

"Okay." Roberto turned to Aldo. "For this to keep looking like an accident, Barton has to be left alone. For now. We off him tomorrow, we might as well call a press conference and announce we fucked up. So change of plan. I want Clint Vaughn stapled to Barton. If the man farts, I want to know about it."

"But you just said-- Barton made him."

"Which is why he's perfect. Barton will never suspect I sent the same man twice. Whatever BS Vaughn gave him will look legit. And if McDeare gets involved, plant him. Right beside his pain-in-the-ass brother."

"Can we off Jessie Kendle, too? The whole family's giving me a headache."

*

Groaning with pleasure, Max Callaban stirred basil leaves into the marinara sauce, inhaling the succulent mixture. Every ingredient came from his greenhouse: fresh herbs, plump tomatoes, sweet onions, and peppers. This would be his best batch yet. He was lining an entire shelf in the pantry with jars of marinara for lasagna, one of Anthony's favorite dishes.

As Max added a dash of Cabernet to the sauce, Aldo called.

"Barton figured out you're alive. We tried to take care of the problem. Got his wife and kid instead."

"*Maledicalo.*" Max slumped against the counter.

"You, uh, might want to rethink your plan. Barton's going to have cops swarming all over that wedding."

The plan was perfect. Stealing Anthony in the first hours of Jessica's unholy union with McDeare. Turning their celebration into a horror show. "No. The plan remains in place."

"Don't be a fool. Barton will be looking for you."

"They'll look right at me and not see me."

"Take the boy some other time."

"We proceed as planned. And trust me. Even you won't recognize me."

*

"Stop here," Nick directed Bree. She pulled over to the side of Madison Avenue, the brownstone around the next corner. Nick stared out the window, trying to regroup. "Look, I won't be able to come out to the house too often. They'll get suspicious. How much research can I have at this late date? But we can meet in town."

"I understand."

"I'll let you know about Wednesday. I'll try to make it, but until I reach Barton--"

"Text me when you do."

"I will." Nick leaned over and hugged her. "It was a good beginning for us."

"Better than Hong Kong."

Nick squeezed Bree's hand before exiting the car. He headed up Madison and called Barton. It went straight to voice mail again. Bree had taken a detour through Queens on their way into the city, passing Lyle's house. But there was no house. Just a pile of rubble, cordoned off by police tape, a few firemen sifting through the debris.

*

Parked at the bar, Clint worked on a half-finished plate of Hanratty's special nachos and a double scotch. Overhead, a television reporter who looked like he was in junior high excitedly described what had happened at Detective Lyle Barton's home. He babbled that a charred chimney was all that remained standing.

The bartender shook his head. "That cop must've pissed off somebody big time."

The damn cell cawed. Clint longed for the old days when you couldn't be bothered every five minutes by a cell phone. The future wasn't always what it was cracked up to be. "Yeah?"

"I know you're in a bar, Vaughn," Aldo hissed. "Listen close. Change of plan. Our boss wants you to attach yourself to that cop, Lyle Barton."

Sliding off his stool, Clint retreated to an empty corner. "Does this have anything to do with a little barbecue in Queens?"

"Fuck you, ass wipe. Just do it. *Capice*?"

Silence. "Tell our boss I'm on it. Ass wipe. For ten times my normal fee because he already made me once." Clint clicked off on Aldo's obscenity.

Back at the bar, Clint drained his glass. It didn't take a nuclear physicist to figure it out. A hit on Barton winds up in the toilet. Zappella fucked up.

Signaling Jake for another round, Clint crunched a nacho. He didn't give a shit about risk, not for this kind of money.

CHAPTER 9

A soft patter of morning rain hit the window. Roberto stared across the Hudson at the jagged Manhattan skyline, a geometric dance in steel and glass. This was the real heart of America. A country that let a man make something of himself if he had the drive and the smarts, no matter what his beginnings. Roberto had come up in the world with nothing but his own ambition. He used his hard-earned fortune to live well.

This Jersey City penthouse gave him an escape. He could forget about the off-track-betting problems in Brooklyn, the shylocks in Harlem, his dealers getting busted all over, and the headache of Barton and McDeare.

Aldo had been phoning with daily updates from Clint for the past nine days. Barton was entrenched in the Brady brownstone, the funeral over. The next few days would tell the story. Maybe losing his wife and kid had destroyed the cop. Aldo had street smarts, a pragmatic common sense Roberto valued. Maybe he was right. Maybe Barton's light would go out. Some men just needed a push, and they were never the same again.

Or maybe Barton needed to refuel, and McDeare was his lifeline.

If McDeare or Barton made trouble for him, he'd make a business decision and eliminate the threat. Roberto tightened the sash on his robe. It's how he'd gotten where he was today. You had to protect yourself, or you were a dead man.

Nothing personal.

*

Two mugs of coffee in hand, Nick paid Lyle a visit. Barton was living in a wrap-around corner suite on the third floor, facing both the front and back of the house. Nick stepped gingerly through the open doorway, the floor littered with empty bottles of alcohol.

The funeral had been two days ago. Barb's parents and his fellow cops had paid their respects and left. Lyle had no family, not anymore. Nothing left but his credit cards, his wallet, and the clothes on his back that day. So far, the police investigation had turned up nothing.

Barton was staring out the back window. He shifted his gaze when Nick entered, taking the mug Nick planted in his hand. Barton's face was so scored with grooves of pain it hurt to look at him.

"Thanks." He poured in a slug of whiskey. "I love Irish coffee." He slurped it down, turning his attention to the window again.

"Lyle. We need to talk."

"Yeah." Barton remained focused on the window, unmoving.

"Okay. Uh, right before the … You were going to come over to tell me something. Something important you made a point of telling me you didn't want Jessie to hear. I don't want to bother you, but if it's related to the situation … Do I need to know what that was all about?"

The silence lingered. Lyle tipped back the mug, took another swallow of laced coffee. He finally turned to face Nick. "I've been waiting to tell you," he said in a monotone. "You need to know. I figured it out. I discovered the truth. That's why--" His voice cracked.

"Figured what out?"

"Those matches. And Jessie's flowers." Lyle cleared his throat. "They weren't Martinelli's work."

"Who then?"

"Gianni Fosselli. It was a Fosselli look alike on the Milano that night. The man is alive, Nick. He's ALIVE."

What …? Nick dropped into a chair. Weighing his words carefully, he put aside his mug. "Look, you've had a terrible loss. You're not thinking clearly. Maybe we should wait to--"

"No. You have to listen to me. It's time." Lyle slumped into a recliner and dully listed his findings, one by one. His first visit to Martinelli and Zappella and their reaction to the matches. Aldo's reaction later. Barton's conversation with Captain Verde and the two yeomen. The officer who insinuated it hadn't been Fosselli aboard the ship. The shoe.

"A shoe? Gianni was probably wearing the janitor's shoes. That's how he made his escape from lockup, wearing the dead guy's uniform. Or Aldo bought him a cheap pair to make his run."

"Or he changed into his own clothes after Bush chauffeured him to a drop-off point. And the fool masquerading as Fosselli didn't have his taste in footwear."

"It doesn't prove anything."

"Explain how one week after I visit Aldo to let him know I'm onto the Fosselli scam, they put a hit on me. I'm right, Nick. You know I am. And who the hell else would harass you and Abbie with Oceana matches and send those flowers to Jessie opening night? How much more personal can it get? It's Gianni Fosselli. The undead."

Tell him California had just sunk into the ocean. Or the Cubs won the World Series. But a monster rising from the grave … Nick mashed a hand over his face. Maybe it added up. Made sense. Nick's gut told him Lyle was right even as his mind screamed no.

Gianni. Alive.

Only one thing mattered if that was true. And it scared the shit out of him. "Jessie and Anthony," Nick croaked. He shook his head. He couldn't say the rest.

"Your family's lives are in danger." Lyle leaned forward. "You need to focus on keeping them safe. You have to tell Jessie. Right now. She needs to know the threat out there. And Willie. Show him Fosselli's picture. He's a decorated ex-cop. He'll know what to look for, what to do if the situation arises."

Jessie finally had her life back. If she thought Gianni was lying in wait, the fear and dread would settle over her like smog, infiltrating every breath. She'd lock herself in the house again, her career shot. All the progress since Andrew's death, gone. She might regress to drinking too much, sleeping pills, one pill too many ... "I'll tell Willie, but not Jessie."

"Are you listening? You saw what they did to me! To my wife, my little--" Lyle looked away, his voice cracking.

"No," he said softly. "I know what's best for Jessie." Nick rubbed a hand over his eyes. "Who else have you told about this? Who else knows?"

"No one. Just you." Lyle's voice dropped to a harsh whisper. "Martinelli will be on me like a hawk on a mouse, waiting for my next move. You can be sure he knows I'm here, that I'm telling you everything. I go to the commissioner, we're all targets. Martinelli needs to think I'm slinking away. Giving up. It's the only way to keep everyone safe."

"Lyle," Nick said hoarsely, "this is my fault. If it weren't for me, you never would've started asking questions, gone to Aldo. I'm the reason—"

"That's crap." Lyle shot out of his chair, his face turning red. "This is Gianni's Fosselli's doing!"

"Shhh," Nick urged.

Lyle lowered his voice. "Fosselli went after you and you did the only thing you could. You came to me for help. And he's not done yet. Let's not play the blame game. Let's find the son of a bitch."

"I don't know what to say." Nick eyed the ceiling, the guilt riding heavy in his heart.

"Say you'll help me nail Fosselli."

"You know I will. Or die trying."

"Okay." Lyle sat back down. "Here's my plan. The department will insist I take a leave of absence. That works for us. I want to put every ounce of energy into finding Fosselli. It all begins with Fosselli. The tail's wagging the dog. We have to get the tail."

Springing up, Nick paced to the back window. They were back to where they were last spring. Andrew's killer was a free man. Gianni Fosselli. "You really think they know you're here?"

"From now on, we assume we're followed every time we step out that front door. They blew it. They'd be stupid not to watch us. And they're not stupid."

A light rain was pattering the window. The back yard's wrought iron fence glistened with winking droplets, the stone path washed clean. Chickadees and finches shared Mary's feeder. And Gianni Fosselli was alive. Everything happened according to its natural order except that. A dead man was alive.

"Look," Lyle said, "we nailed Eduardo Santangelo and Gianni Fosselli the first time, my partner sabotaging our every step. We can do it again."

"Martinelli knows where Gianni's hiding." Nick's gaze wandered to the brownstone abutting their back property. Shades were lifted on the third floor, an elderly woman framed in the window. "He may be untouchable, but he's the key to Fosselli. We need a bargaining chip, something to shake Martinelli off our case. Make him cut his ties to Gianni and forget about us."

"The first thing we need is a way out of this house without a shadow."

"Have you spotted anyone on the street?"

"A PI on a cheating-husband. I questioned him, before the— Anyway, he's not connected. Martinelli would never send someone I already made. But I know someone is watching. Nick, Anthony's what Gianni wants. You know it, and I know it."

"I have to talk to the boy. Somehow, I have to teach him how to stay safe without scaring the spit out of him. I've put it off too long."

"I've been thinking. I have an idea. Something for Anthony. I have to make a call. Remember when Anthony was in the hospital last summer and you and Jessie discovered ..."

*

Coffee cup in hand, Abbie flipped on her computer and sank into her desk chair. She had to get her mind off the funeral, the sight of that child's coffin ...

She wiped her eyes and typed Brianna Fontaine into the computer's search engine, skimming her bio. Born with a silver ladle in her mouth. Parents divorced early. Raised by a wealthy socialite mother on Long Island. Father a famous FBI profiler. Attended the best schools, graduating from Columbia's School of Journalism cum laude. Hired by the TIMES and sent overseas on assignment. Lebanon. Afghanistan. Israel. Columbia. And Hong Kong.

Abbie focused on Hong Kong. Nick and Bree had solved the murder of a fellow journalist, an AP reporter. Their apprehension of the killer had been the basis of Nick's award-winning novel THE GREEN MONSTER. And Nick's investigative series for THE WASHINGTON POST had nabbed him a Pulitzer Prize nomination.

Okay, onto Nick McDeare. Like most celebrities, Nick had collected a slew of unofficial websites, swirling with juicy tidbits. Abbie went looking for sex and scandal. She found Nick McDeare's "Trail of Broken Hearts" at McDearesdears.com. Abbie scrolled through scores of photos of luscious women, all with knockers out to there. Nick dated a Miss USA? And more than one European princess. Ah, here it was. A picture of Nick and Bree at a party in Hong Kong. His arm slung around Bree's shoulder, Nick gazed at her, amber eyes soft ... Had Brianna Fontaine been more than a casual fling? Was he hooking up with a past love?

Today was Sunday. Jessie's next matinee was Wednesday. That's when Nick would make his move. Abbie would be ready.

*

Parking herself at the kitchen table, Bree was about to answer Nick's e-mail on her laptop. She looked out over the Hampton bay. Rain blurred the images, melting the landscape into a child's finger-painting. She was worried about Nick. He was juggling too much, his focus slipping. And creampuff Jessie couldn't be helping.

What was it about Jessica Kendle that Nick found so addictive? Jessie was the kind of unobtainable woman Nick usually obtained and discarded. Nick didn't belong married. He was meant to roam free.

If anyone knew that, it was Brianna Fontaine. Nick had hardly been faithful during the six months they'd dated. Not that he'd ever promised exclusivity or tried to keep his out-of-town jaunts secret. When Bree had finally forced herself to investigate and face the truth, she'd been devastated, pushed that harsh note under his door, and left.

She'd never know what Nick would've said had she confronted him. But she suspected he wouldn't have apologized for a damn thing. Nick would be bored stupid by Jessie Kendle within two minutes after the wedding.

Back to the e-mail ... Bree's fingers flew over her keyboard. She expressed her concern. She was supportive. The poor man didn't need another female cross to bear

*

Bored, Anthony had nothing to do. There was nothing on TV. It was raining out. Mom was at the theater. Dad was locked in Lyle's room. Zane was in New Jersey visiting his grandmother. Mrs. Pemberton wouldn't allow Eric to come over. Anthony had conquered his new computer game, killing all the green jellies before Olaf zapped him. His iPad was boring. He'd gone down to the basement and tried to set up the new Batter-Man equipment Dad had bought him. But the instructions had too many big words. Dad would have to do it. Zane said he had a good arm. Anthony flexed the muscle on his right arm, feeling it harden. Now he needed to learn how to hit.

Anthony stared at the picture of Daddy on his bookshelves. Daddy Andrew. Until a few months ago, his first dad had visited him in his dreams. He'd sit on the bed and make him laugh and tell him things that came true. Anthony closed his eyes, picturing him laughing.

Climbing onto his bed, Anthony tried reading a book, but his eyes kept closing. He was so sleepy ... Daddy Andrew was sitting in the chair by the window. But he wasn't laughing. He looked scared. He didn't say anything. He just kept pointing over his shoulder. What did that mean? Why couldn't Daddy just talk to him?

*

When Jessie got to the theater, Nora gave her another list of calls Jeremy had sent over by messenger. Three talk shows and all the New York stations wanted to book her. "Listen," Nora added, closing the door, "I've been thinking. I don't like what's going on with your costumes and wigs. And remember that missing champagne glass during dress rehearsal? Esther's the best prop mistress on Broadway. She doesn't make those kinds of mistakes. Too many accidents. I've been thinking. It can't be coincidence."

Forcing out the words, Jessie said it at last. "You think it was sabotage?"

"If it is, one person comes to mind. Valentine York."

Jessie hesitated, speaking slowly. "She spooks me, Nora. She's always around, watching me." Jessie slipped off her sweater, tossing it onto a chair.

"I've heard rumors." Nora handed Jessie her makeup shirt. "I knew she was going to be trouble. Too bad Carmella Watts got pregnant. She was always great as your understudy." Nora patted Jessie's shoulder. "Look, I know you got a lot on your mind these days with your friend Lyle. Let me take care of this. I'm going to do a little snooping between shows."

"There's more, Nora," Jessie confided. "I didn't want to bother you with this, but a few days ago when you were home sick, the handle to my dressing room door came off in my hand before the show. I couldn't get out. I had to yell bloody murder before Josh finally heard me. And our friend George, he shrugged it off."

*

The next Wednesday morning found Abbie parked in a borrowed car a block down from the brownstone, a powerful camera with a telephoto lens at her side. Earlier that morning, Willie had chauffeured Jessie to the theater for her matinee. Abbie was counting on Nick to slip out to meet Bree. The bastard. Abbie wore a curly platinum blond wig and horn-rimmed glasses. No makeup. Very few people had seen Abbie without makeup. Not even those who shared her bed.

*

"I talked to Willie," Nick told Lyle quietly, huddled with Barton by the front door. "He knows everything. He's licensed to carry. He'll be armed from now on." Nick checked his watch. "I have to run."

He breezed out the door and hustled down the street. Working out the logistics with Lyle was the easy part. The hard part was the lies to Jessie, replicating like DNA. It was killing him. And they wouldn't be ending anytime soon. Not until he knew his family was safe.

*

Clint Vaughn spotted the blond sitting in her car, her eyes glued to the Brady residence. Who the hell was she? An undercover cop? One of McDeare's ex-bimbos? She wasn't working for Martinelli. Clint had checked with Aldo.

Even though he was shadowing the cop now, he'd still ended up back on the same dull street. Didn't matter. His cheating-husband cover was gold. For the fortune Martinelli was paying him to sit on his ass day and night, he could handle boredom.

Blondie pulled away from the curb and trailed McDeare, striding down the street. An ex-bimbo for sure.

*

From the vantage of his bedroom window, Lyle watched Nick head down Seventy-Fifth Street. A blue Lexus followed him, lady driver. So Martinelli had sent a woman. His first sight of their shadow.

Lyle spotted Clint Vaughn again, sitting in his car down the block. The PI was still trying to catch the cheating husband. What a dreary life.

*

Abbie wasn't surprised when Nick grabbed a taxi to Brianna Fontaine's apartment. He was inside for hours, the schmuck.

As Nick hailed a cab home, he glanced up at a window in the building and waved. Abbie shifted her lens upward. There she was. Brianna looked down at Nick like Rapunzel at her prince. The bitch had the nerve to look forlorn. Poor her. That's what you get for having an affair with an about-to-be-married man. Abbie snapped some frames before the skank disappeared from sight.

*

Jessie threw on her robe and headed for the vending machines. Most of the cast and crew were at the Italian street fair on Ninth Avenue between shows today. The theater was blissfully quiet.

On her way back to her dressing room, Jessie glanced into the chorus girls' room. She halted. A woman stood at one of the mirrors, playing with her hair and admiring her reflection. Jessie looked closer. Correction. She was fussing with a wig. "Is that yours, Valentine?"

Valentine York jumped and whirled around. "Um, no." She quickly yanked off the wig, placing it back on an empty Styrofoam head. "I just wanted to see how I'd look as a brunette." She turned away, fluffing her sheet of glistening golden hair back into place, each shiny strand capturing the light as if she were in a shampoo commercial.

"You shouldn't be in here." Jessie said, shooting Valentine a pointed glance. Jessie spun on her heel and marched back to her dressing room. She'd let the chorus girls know what had happened as soon as they returned. And she'd tell George once again that Valentine York had stepped over the line. How much time did she give it before she went over his head and had a talk with Bill?

But there was no time to pursue it today. She and Nick had come up with a plan for Lyle's future. A new home for their friend.

*

Sitting Lyle down in the family room for a talk after Jessie got home, Nick went over their idea with him, Jessie laying the groundwork. Jessie thought they were doing a grieving friend a favor, giving him a new home and avoiding the press in the process. Nick knew better. They were playing a deadly game of hide and seek with Roberto Martinelli.

"So," Jessie was saying to Lyle, "the brownstone behind us on Seventy-Sixth Street is owned by Gertie and Herb Skolnik, an elderly couple. Gertie just put the ground-floor apartment on the market, and I'm buying it. I talked her into donating the money to the Andrew Brady Foundation. Like I said, it's yours. Gertie loves the idea of a cop living on the ground floor."

"I won't take charity," Lyle said. Nick idled at the window, avoiding his glance. He and Jessie had known that would be a sticking point. Jessie had enthusiastically figured it all out.

"Of course not," Jessie said lightly. "You'll pay a monthly maintenance fee to Gertie. She has a gardener and a plumber and a handyman. Once I buy it and the paperwork's done, the rest is up to you. And we'll all have a back way out of here to beat the reporters. We sneak through the connecting fence between our yards and walk out through your condo onto Seventy-Sixth. I want you to live there, Lyle. I mean it."

"So do I," Nick said, turning from the window and giving Lyle a hard stare. It was the only way to be free to do what they had to do. And Lyle knew it.

*

Slipping a Cuban cigar from his humidor, Roberto Martinelli skimmed it under his nose. Sighing with satisfaction, he parked himself in his easy chair, lighting up.

Outside, dusk was descending over the Southampton bay, the smoky sky turning to charcoal. Thanksgiving was only a week away, November sliding by unnoticed. Where had the time gone? His days were full of problems, business decisions involving millions of dollars, delicate political issues within the organization, questions of life and death, the kind of turmoil the ordinary man couldn't begin to understand. It would take a Churchill, a Roosevelt, or a Kissinger to appreciate the enormous weight he carried on his shoulders.

The condo in Jersey City was what saved Roberto, fulfilling a secret fantasy. The outside world would never understand. Even his wife Marcella, the daughter of an Italian Mafioso who well knew the man she'd married—she didn't suspect this. She would be appalled. Only Aldo knew the truth, a man he trusted with his life.

At a knock on the door, he grunted, and Aldo entered. "Vaughn reported in this afternoon."

That buzz-saw voice fractured Roberto's pleasant thoughts. He fingered the antacid tablets in his pocket. "So?"

"It's been a few weeks now, and Barton sticks close to the brownstone. When he does leave it's at night. Sometimes he goes down to that cops' bar on Eighth Avenue. Sometimes he heads to the first watering hole he can find. But here's the problem. While Vaughn's tailing Barton, McDeare could be slipping out."

Roberto fingered the aspirin vial in his other pocket, a headache beginning to knock at his skull. Gianni Fosselli was turning into one fucking pain-in-the-ass crisis after another. But the cruise line was paying off, the fleet delivering wave after wave of highly profitable shipments of cocaine, contraband ivory, and tortoise. Fosselli had included secret deck plans when he sold the line to Roberto, complete with ingenious hiding places. Theirs was a two-way street, and Roberto valued his allies and their loyalty.

"They're onto us," he told Aldo. "They know we're watching them, and Barton's a decoy."

Aldo dropped into a chair. "I think this whole surveillance's a fucking waste of time."

"Never underestimate the enemy. That was Stalin's mistake with Hitler."

"Huh?"

"Never mind. Tell Vaughn to tail McDeare."

"Roberto, he's—"

"Pay him twice what he's getting now. He'd kill his own mother for the right price. Put a woman on Barton. Someone he'd never suspect. Get Hinkie Bozzoli. She's like dogshit on a shoe, impossible to rub off. Tell her to report to Vaughn."

"Why not wire the brownstone again?"

"Brilliant. We got caught last time. They'll be watching for it."

"How can I convince you to just drop this? Barton's washed up. Every man has his breaking point. Losing his wife and kid flattened him."

"Barton figured out Fosselli was alive. A week later we put a hit on him and kill the wife and kid instead? He's playing us. I got a sixth sense about this. Trust me."

CHAPTER 10

"They said they'd have it done by Thanksgiving," Jessie marveled to Nick, "and they did. With two days to spare." Jessie eyed the refinished master bedroom's pine green walls, the woodwork trim restored. The platform bed's duvet was a swirl of rich earth tones. Oriental throw rugs sprawled across the high-gloss wooden floors. It was perfect.

Clasping her hand, Nick led Jessie into the sitting room. "Let's get our stuff and move in." Nick shot her a grin.

"I don't know." Jessie inhaled the scent of fresh paint and polish and wood. "Maybe we should wait until we're married. Make it an official new beginning, you know? The sitting room's great, isn't it?" Jessie gazed happily at the mushroom walls, soft leather couches, and overstuffed chairs in cool mint green. There was a wet bar, sound system, and a TV as big as a movie screen. Recessed window seats overlooked the back garden.

Lyle appeared in the sitting room doorway and asked for a minute. He cleared his throat. "Uh, this condo thing with you, Jessie, my moving in tomorrow--I want to keep it quiet." Lyle brushed a hand over his wiry hair. "I have my reasons. To the outside world it looks like I'm still living here for a while, in the brownstone. No one can know. Okay?"

Did he think it would look like he was living beyond his means? Or maybe he was afraid the press would catch on to their escape hatch. Jessie covered her surprise and smiled. "Sure, Lyle. Whatever you want."

Before he left the room, Lyle asked Nick to meet in his office when he got a chance. Something about which TV cable service to sign up for.

*

"I have to say it again." Lyle locked the office door behind him and Nick, speaking in a low voice. "I don't like deceiving Jessie. She should know the real reason we need to keep the new place a secret. That it's imperative Martinelli thinks I'm still in the brownstone with you. You need to fill her in about Gianni. This isn't right. It's going to come back to haunt you."

Nick got that stubborn look. "Jessie's a wreck with the play and the holidays and the wedding. She can't handle this now. I know what I'm doing."

"If you're wrong--"

"I'm not."

Lyle let it go. He could barely muster the strength to go after Fosselli and save Anthony. God help him, but he didn't have the reserves to save Nick from Jessie, too.

"Your call. I asked Kersey to pull his plainclothes team from the block. We'll do our own surveillance from now on. We don't need anyone to uncover the hole to our burrow."

*

Holiday chaos reigned in the brownstone. Nick hid in his office. Mary and her sister Violet were preparing for Thanksgiving dinner tomorrow. Barton disappeared after breakfast into his new apartment. Jessie had three days off for the holiday. She insisted on helping in the kitchen, to Mary and Violet's horror. Nick was glad she had something to focus on. Jessie had been moaning for days about Valentine York stepping into the role of Christine, even though holidays off had been written into her contract.

Saying he needed to check out a location for his book, Nick escaped for a few hours to see Bree. Jessie smiled and kissed him as she hand-washed the fine crystal. Nick felt like a shit. As he hurried down the hallway he heard glass shatter, followed by a litany of Mary's curses. Nick pushed through to the street, relieved to be out of hell's kitchen.

Later, as dusk settled over New York, Nick slumped at his desk. His hours with Bree had been well spent, taking his mind off Jessie and Thanksgiving and a houseful of guests tomorrow. Nick couldn't remember last Thanksgiving, but he had a feeling he'd never forget this one. For one thing, Jessie had invited Josh Elliot. She said he was dating Abbie.

*

Jessie surreptitiously locked herself in the master bathroom and dialed the theater, asking to be put through to Nora. The matinee would've come down by now. "Nora, it's me. Are you alone?"

"Her Highness went down the street for something to eat, but she'll be back any minute."

"How's it going? I take it no glitches with costumes or props."

"You take it right. Valentine wouldn't sabotage herself."

Jessie felt a chill shiver up her spine.

"Josh said Valentine forgot some lyrics and screwed up those tricky dance steps in the first act finale, you know, that rumba. He covered for her, an embarrassment. Typical understudy. You don't rehearse, you trip all over yourself. Tomorrow's going to be a nightmare with two understudies in the leads."

"Anyone who spends Thanksgiving going to a musical instead of stuffing themselves with turkey deserves understudies. Don't let Valentine work you too hard."

"I'm not putting myself out, believe me. She's sickeningly sweet. Everything's thank you and please, like she's some silly thing off the farm. Have to go," Nora whispered, "she's back."

*

Restless, Nick stared out the window. Lights were on in Barton's new digs across the way. According to plan, Lyle would keep on trudging out the brownstone's front door every now and then for Martinelli's benefit, always to a bar. Nick gave him a call. "Want some company?"

"Come on over." Barton came into view, silhouetted in a window. "I have a few things that might interest you. I'll leave the door open."

A few minutes later, Nick let himself in through the screened-in porch. He wandered into a miniature version of the brownstone kitchen. "In here," Lyle yelled. Following his voice, Nick spotted a bedroom and living room towards the front of the house. He found Lyle in the study, sitting in front of a computer at a battered desk.

"Where'd you get this stuff?"

"Steinmetz. Out of storage at Midtown North. He spent the afternoon wiring me into the NYPD system. I ordered a mattress from a catalog. Delivered today. Listen, I've been going over the missing persons reports from August and September. I think I found our Milano look-alike. Frank Panfiglio, a small-time felon. His wife reported him missing two weeks after Fosselli bought it. She told the police he was working for Aldo Zappella and never came home. Zappella was questioned, denied knowing Panfiglio."

Nick eyed the man's picture. Same shape face as Gianni. Same thick black hair. Almost the same nose. "He's a ringer, especially from a distance. What about the officer you spoke to on the Milano? You reached him for a formal statement?"

"I decided against it. Don't want to tip off Martinelli." Lyle pulled a small box from a desk drawer and removed the lid. Inside were two medallions on sterling silver chains and a tiny metal gizmo on a key chain. "This is to protect Anthony."

"You're kidding."

"Just listen. The smaller medallion's for him. It lists his allergy, the one you and Jessie found out about when he was in the hospital. There's a lock on the clasp, can't be removed. Your medallion says penicillin, your allergy."

"I can take it off?"

"Yeah. Now, if you're both wearing the medallions, that little transistor compass on the key chain acts like a homing device when you turn it on. Your medallion vibrates and the compass points in Anthony's direction. If Anthony disappears we can find him within a hundred miles. That's the catch. A hundred miles."

Picking up his medallion, Nick flipped the switch on the key chain's transistor. The arrow swung towards Anthony's medallion. He nearly jumped out of his shoes when his disc vibrated. "Who did this? James Bond?"

Barton snorted. "It helps to have friends in low places. A snitch owes me. A computer whiz owes him. I told the guy what we wanted and he inserted computer chips into the medallions keyed into this homing thing. Only Bill Gates could understand it. Anyway, the vibration's strong because the two medallions are close together. The further apart they are, the weaker it gets."

"Amazing."

*

Max Callaban rose on Thanksgiving morning and stared at his image in the mirror, passing a hand over his face. The plastic surgery was complete. Tomorrow the doctor in Cleveland would remove the bandages from his forehead and around his eyes. Max would also pick up his custom-made tuxedo for the wedding. He'd made a reservation at the Southampton Holiday Inn for a certain guest two nights before the ceremony. That's where he'd rendezvous with a man named Clint Vaughn.

Making his way downstairs. Max began to prepare the holiday meal. He wanted to integrate American holidays into his lifestyle so Anthony would grow up celebrating all the right customs. Capon with a wild cherry foam. A medley of winter squash. Homemade pumpkin tortellini stuffed with porcini mushrooms. And a peanut butter crème brulee for dessert. Thanksgiving dinner with a new-wave touch.

Better to save his old-fashioned recipes for a belated Christmas meal with Anthony. Anthony's palate would have to be trained for finer culinary fare. Mary was a simpleton cook. Anthony would acquire better taste with time. How could he not? His father was one of the premiere chefs in the world. Blood always told.

*

"Okay, heads up, guys. Food coming through." Jessie carried appetizers into the study, the males in the house watching a football game on TV. Jessie placed the food on the coffee table. Chilled prawns with cocktail sauce. Fried calamari. Curried deviled eggs. Buffalo wings. And Mary's special Jamaican meatballs. Two bags of chips and a bowl of onion dip had already disappeared. Also a case of chilled Lowenbrau.

"Honey, do you mind?" Nick asked, tipping to the side to see around her. "You're blocking the TV."

Shrieking, Josh and Willie leapt up, staring at the television.

Jessie watched her son, sitting like a little man beside Nick. Anthony kept glancing up at him. Did Nick realize how much the boy idolized him?

Lyle would join them for dinner. Or so he'd said. He'd slept in his apartment for the first time last night. Mary had invited him over for breakfast that morning, but he'd spent more time staring out the window than eating. Jessie remembered too well her first Thanksgiving without Andrew.

Back in the kitchen, Jessie plopped down on a stool next to Abbie, working her way through the women's appetizer plate like there was no tomorrow. The woman never gained weight. Jessie hated her.

*

Abbie joined the men for some touch football in the back yard. Nick, Anthony, and Abbie versus Josh and Willie. Abbie was ready to concentrate on the fun things in life. Like Josh. Whatever had been going on with Brianna Fontaine and Nick, if anything, was over. She'd been watching the brownstone faithfully whenever Jessie had a matinee and Nick rarely went anywhere anymore.

Licking her lips, she watched Josh score a touchdown, his muscles rippling in a cut-off sweatshirt. The man was a sex machine in bed.

Willie checked his watch. "I was due at LaJeanne's, like thirty minutes ago. She's going to kill me. Sorry, guys." Willie messed up Anthony's curls and said his goodbyes.

"Dad, when's Lyle coming over?" Anthony tossed the football to Nick. "Josh needs someone on his team. Should I get him?"

Looking up, Abbie said, "I thought he was upstairs resting."

"He's over there." Anthony pointed to the brownstone abutting the Brady property. "Lyle has the whole first floor."

Abbie caught the look Nick cast Anthony. Inching closer to Nick, Abbie whispered, "When did Lyle move in there?"

"Hmm?"

"Lyle. When did he move in?"

"Who keeps records?" Nick turned his head. "Come on. Let's play everyone! Anthony and me against Abbie and Josh." Nick punted the ball. Josh leaped into the air, caught it, and began to run. He ran right through Nick.

Barely noticing, Abbie swore to herself. No wonder she hadn't caught Nick meeting Bree. He'd been sneaking out the back way through Lyle's new apartment onto Seventy-Sixth Street!

Minutes later Nick had the ball and sprinted for the end zone. Josh tackled him. The two men slid on their stomachs, cutting a swath through the grass. A cell phone shrilled over their grunts.

Breathing hard, Nick quickly snatched his phone from the back steps. He glanced at Abbie and turned his back to her, lowering his voice. Was the intrepid reporter calling him all hours of the day now? On Thanksgiving? Was Nick McDeare a sex addict? OMG.

*

After the game Nick limped into the house, fingering his bloody elbow through a rip in his sweatshirt. His jeans were shredded at both knees and his ribs felt like someone was using them for xylophone practice. Josh grinned. "Hey, Jessie, maybe Nick needs a gym membership for Christmas so he can get into shape."

"Listen you, sh--"

Quickly blocking Nick, Jessie nudged him towards the stairs, reminding him to call Lyle about dinner before the Rudolps arrived.

After a hot shower, every drop of water a bullet to his ribcage, Nick dialed Barton's cell. "Bree just called. I set it up for us. And dinner's about to be served."

Ten minutes later, Nick returned to the kitchen. "Lyle isn't joining us," he told Jessie quietly. "I didn't push."

"Nick," Bill Rudolph said, appearing in the doorway. "Josh tells me he pummeled you in a football game out back."

*

By the time everyone had washed, changed, and sat down to dinner, Jessie was relieved to see Nick's dark mood had lightened. He was wearing black slacks, a black blazer, and an amber silk shirt that matched his eyes. From the other end of the table, Nick winked at her and lifted his wine glass in a toast.

Running a hand over her new teal dress, Jessie smiled back. Nick had delighted her a few days ago with the wispy silk garment, his taste impeccable. It was from a Fifth Avenue boutique where the price of a designer dress could buy a small car.

Jessie had carefully placed Josh on one side of herself, Marcy Rudolph on the other. Bill and Anthony sandwiched Nick. Mary, Violet and Abbie sat in the center seats. They'd outdone themselves with a spectacular dinner. Roast turkey with cornbread and sausage stuffing. Candied yams with bourbon, marshmallows and walnuts. Cranberries with kirsch. Waldorf salad. Mashed potatoes with cream cheese and chives. Spinach soufflé. And homemade French rolls.

With amusement, Jessie watched as Anthony insisted on serving himself, opting for the same things Nick chose. She stuck with the turkey and salad and one tablespoon of yam. And half a roll.

The chatter was all about the wedding, in between exclamations about the food and reaching for second helpings. The wedding party would lodge at the Rudolph mansion the night of the rehearsal and dinner. Selected guests were invited to stay in the thirty bedrooms the night of the ceremony. Jessie fretted about falling on her way down the aisle with Bill, who was giving her away. Bill laughed, promising he wouldn't let that happen.

Everyone was in such a good mood, Jessie decided the time was right to broach a touchy subject. "Nick," she said casually, "I'd like Josh to sing at the beginning of the ceremony. Mmm, please pass more of the cranberries, Bill. Yummy."

Nick stared at Jessie, a forkful of food in hand. "Why not? It's already a three-ring circus. What's another clown?"

"Takes one to know one, Bozo," Josh said. "I'd be happy to, Jessie. I'm flattered."

"And to think this dead turkey was alive," Nick said, looking at his fork, "and gobbling turkey songs on the barnyard stage just a week ago."

Jessie angled Nick a look. He scooped some stuffing and looked innocently back at her.

"Must be nice to have a few days off from the show, Jessie," Marcy said, biting into a crisp roll. "When do you return?"

"Saturday."

"That reminds me, Jess," Nick said, swallowing quickly. "Lyle's driving up to Boston, something about a case that crossed state lines. I volunteered to keep him company for a few days. A DNA expert wants his statement. I thought the drive would be good for him."

"Sure. I'm buried at the theater both days anyway."

"Wow," Abbie said sarcastically, "Nick's giving up a few days on his manuscript? He's been such a busy boy lately."

Jessie raised an eyebrow.

Excusing herself, Mary got the house phone. A call for Jessie. The woman said it was important, wouldn't leave her name. Few people had Jessie's private number. But she wouldn't put it past Nick's agent to call with advice about not upsetting his routine so he could get his manuscript in on time. Liz knew no boundaries.

Moving away from the noise, Jessie carried the phone into the study. "This is a friend, Miss Kendle," whispered a female voice. "Nick's cheating on you. He's screwing another woman. I bet he's buying you special gifts each time he fucks her. Get rid of him. For your sake and your little boy's."

For a minute, Jessie couldn't think. The globe had tilted on its axis and she was falling off, floating into space. She took a deep breath. "Who are you, and how did you get this number?"

"I know you don't believe it," the voice said sadly, "but I'm a friend. Don't bother with star sixty-nine. I'm calling from a pay phone."

"A friend doesn't slander the man I love."

"He doesn't love you back. He can't love any woman. I know!"

"Kristin Wallingford." Jessie's lips thinned. "What the hell's wrong with you? Get some help. Who did you trick this time to get this number?"

"Just watch out he doesn't break your heart." There was a click.

Putting a hand to the heart Kristin was so worried about, Jessie's mind raced. Jeremy was the only link to her private number. Agents were on a lot of celebrity websites. Kristin could've found his office number and tricked it out of him. Jessie sank into a chair, numb. If Kristin called again she'd have the number changed.

What Kristin had said … Jessie stroked a hand over her dress's delicate fabric, its butterfly design a work of art. Nick had given her this exquisite silk dress for no reason at all. But Nick had changed. She trusted him.

Dessert should be served. The mince pie … Jessie trotted back to the kitchen, picked it up, and headed for the dining room. She stopped in her tracks. She'd trusted Andrew, too, but he had harbored a terrible secret during their marriage. He'd surreptitiously broken up her relationship with Gianni and let her blame Ian Wexley. Years later, that secret had opened the way to multiple deaths, including his own, nearly destroyed Jessie, and put Anthony in danger. Could she really rely on her instincts when it came to men?

Tipping up her chin, Jessie marched into the dining room. Nick had seen what Andrew's secret had done to her.

He'd never betray her trust.

*

When the guests were gone and the kitchen back in order, Nick volunteered to take over a basket of food Mary packed for Lyle. He found Barton in the bedroom, fully clothed and sprawled snoring on the floor mattress. A half-empty bottle of scotch next to his pillow kept him company.

Nick placed the basket in the bare refrigerator and left for home. On his way upstairs he checked on Anthony. The boy was standing at the window, staring out into the darkness. "Anthony?"

Anthony spun around. "It's Daddy again," he whispered. "Daddy Andrew."

"A dream?" Nick's breath caught.

"Not like before. It's different."

"How?" Nick patted the bed and Anthony slid beneath the covers.

"He can't talk." Hamlet jumped onto the bed, snuggling next to Anthony. "He's always sitting in that chair by the window. He keeps pointing over his shoulder and he looks scared. I thought maybe he was telling me somebody was watching me."

Composing his face, Nick said calmly, "Do the dreams feel real, like before?"

"Except he can't talk. I think he's trying to tell me something."

Was Andrew trying to warn Anthony? "Maybe Andrew just wants to make sure you're always safe," he said gently, "and he's telling you to watch your back. That's why he's pointing over his shoulder."

"Watch my back. Like from a soccer ball hitting me?"

If only it were that benign.

Hamlet lifted his head, focusing on something invisible across the room. He catapulted off the bed and darted into the hallway, crouching low. Anthony didn't notice, turning onto his side and staring at Andrew's picture on the bookcase.

At a blast of cold air, Nick tucked the blankets around Anthony's shoulders. "You feel it?" Anthony asked. "Daddy's still here. He's protecting me."

There was no use denying it, not to Anthony. They'd been through this before with Andrew's ghostly visits. "I think so, too," Nick said evenly. "And since he wants you safe, tomorrow you and I are going to have a long talk about taking precautions. I have something special for you. You know how that ring's magic, how it keeps you safe when I'm not around?"

"I think I'm too grown up for magic." Anthony eyes looked too old for his face.

Nick heart sank. He'd be damned if he let Gianni steal Anthony's childhood. "Anthony, no one's ever too old for magic. You have to trust in it. And what I'm going to give you tomorrow will keep you even safer than that ring." Nick brushed Anthony's hair off his forehead. "Now get some sleep." Nick headed for the door.

"Dad?" Nick swung around. "After we talk tomorrow will you toss me some balls so I can practice my swing?"

"You bet. Night."

It was impossible to fall asleep that night. Nick stared at the ceiling, Jessie nestled peacefully beside him.

Andrew was trying to get through to them.

That's as far as Nick's magic went these days.

*

"Lyle had them specially made," Nick said. He showed Jessie the medallions the next morning before breakfast, reminding her they'd discussed getting Anthony one last summer. "Lyle," Nick added casually, "thought we should take it a step further. He had a homing device inserted into Anthony's." Nick demonstrated how the medallions worked.

"You're scaring me." Jessie eyes widened. "Is this really necessary?"

"Lyle says parents are taking extra precautions these days. Look how many people insert a chip into their pet. I bet Anthony thinks it's cool."

"You don't think this will frighten him, after everything he's been through with Gianni?"

"I think knowing the truth will make Anthony feel safer."

"I don't know."

"Honey," Nick said smoothly, "we're both celebrities. We have money. What if someone kidnapped Anthony for ransom? Or he got lost in a crowd like any kid? We'd be able to find him this way."

"I know what this is about now." Jessie's eyes were shining. "You and Lyle both lost a child. So you want to make sure we don't lose Anthony. I love you for this. I think it's a great idea."

*

Later that night, Anthony turned out the bedside lamp and settled under the covers. Clasping his medallion around his neck, he smiled. He and Dad had spent the whole day together. Dad tossed him balls in the backyard and showed him how to adjust his swing.

But Mary got mad when they almost broke the kitchen window, so they went to the park. They had fun until some dumb girls wanted Dad's autograph. They wouldn't go away so he and Dad took a cab to the West Side for pizza. Then they went to Riverside Park and sat on a bench and fed the pigeons the crust. That's when Dad gave him the medallion and told him how it would keep him safe. And he locked it on Anthony's neck with a special key.

They sat there a long time. Dad taught him what to do if a stranger ever took him. A boy at Anthony's old school got into a stranger's car last year, and they still hadn't found him. Dad said celebrities' kids had to be extra careful. That's why Anthony needed the medallion. The talk scared him a little. But Dad said he'd never be lost if he kept it around his neck. Dad made him repeat all his instructions to make sure he knew what to do if anyone ever kidnapped him. Anthony promised to memorize them. It was a lot to remember.

Closing his eyes, Anthony went over the rules again, repeating them over and over. And then he heard a voice join in, saying the words with him. Anthony's eyes popped open. It was Daddy Andrew, sitting in the chair. He was talking but his mouth wasn't moving.

His face was serious and ... he was wearing a medallion just like Anthony's.

CHAPTER 11

As the sun rose over the East River Saturday morning, Abbie got comfortable in her borrowed Lexus. This time she was parked on East Seventy-Sixth Street, Lyle's block. Her friend Eden was in Europe for six months, and the car was Abbie's to use. She'd come prepared. One camera, a camcorder, binoculars, one bottle of water, and a twenty-four-hour food supply. The only thing missing was a high-powered rifle to kill Nick McDeare, the schmuck. This was the day she'd catch Nick and Bree in the act.

Abbie had begun planning this encounter as soon as she realized what Nick was up to. With Lyle's help. Unbelievable. Lyle may've suffered a tragedy, but that was no excuse. While Abbie had helped Jessie clear the table after Thanksgiving dinner, she'd casually asked what Lyle was driving these days. A rented Bronco, Jessie said. And wasn't it nice their garage was adding the Bronco to the Brady's list of vehicles for him?

Last night Abbie parked the Lexus overnight in the same garage. Sure enough, the Bronco was next to the Brady limo. It had been easy to attach a tracking device under Lyle's rear bumper on her way out this morning. No self-respecting PI was without one these days. Abbie looked down at the GPS tracking screen on her console. It displayed a color map of the streets around the garage, a red blinking light indicating the location of the Bronco.

It was a good bet Lyle would drop Nick at Bree's apartment before heading off wherever on his own. Meanwhile, she'd done her homework. Yves had a sister named Monique who lived in New Haven. Abbie would tell Bree's doorman she was Monique, gain access to the apartment, and catch Nick and Bree in the act. And then she'd make Nick McDeare wish he'd never been born, the cheating sack of shit.

In the meantime, Abbie waited, watching the Skolnik brownstone. Nick and Lyle emerged at eleven, carrying small overnight bags. Lyle looked terrible, eyes ringed with circles, jaw scruffy.

A moment after Abbie trailed the men to the garage, the Bronco appeared, heading east. Lyle hooked south on Park, taking Nick to Bree's— Wait. At Sixtieth Street, Lyle headed east again and crossed the Fifty-Ninth Street Bridge into Queens. Maybe Nick had been telling the truth and they were really going to Boston?

Doggedly, she followed the Bronco. Two hours later Abbie had traversed almost the entire length of Long Island, all the way to Southampton. Were Nick and Lyle checking out the wedding site? Abbie pounded the steering wheel in frustration, careful not to beep the horn.

When the Bronco approached a gated community's guard booth, she hung back. Nick spoke to a guard who waved them through the lush entryway. Abbie followed the tracker's blinking light as it moved far into the private development.

Now what? She could try feeding the guard Bill Rudolph's name, but he looked formidable, no senior citizen filling the empty hours after retirement. Abbie scanned the area. That nine-foot iron fence was spiked on top. She was in good shape, but she wasn't that good. She'd have to be patient and see what happened next. Not her strong suit.

*

Slouched in his car down the street from the Brady home, Clint studied the off-track betting form. He'd played a hunch yesterday and won a bundle on a little filly named Jessie's Joker. A knock on the passenger window made him jump. Hinkie Bozzoli glared at him. Clint unlocked the door, and the sour woman slid in. "Stay put, Hinkie. Those are orders."

"What a fucking waste of time. Barton doesn't leave that brownstone except to slink out to a bar twice a week and toss back multiple shots of Glenlivet."

"Get back in your car. Until Aldo tells us otherwise, we're stuck."

Hinkie cursed and climbed out of the Chevy. In truth, Clint agreed with the hag. It had been almost a month since Barton's wife and kid had been killed. The cop was on leave from the force, and he hadn't made a move in Martinelli's direction. He wasn't seeking revenge on anything but his liver.

*

The stage lights snapped to black. Jessie crawled off the prop bed and dashed for the wings, Josh heading to the opposite side. Nora held out the wraparound robe for Jessie to slide into. While Nora twisted the strings around her waist, Jessie stepped into her backless heels. Josh was already in place on stage. Jessie sprinted towards him. Just as she hit her mark, the heel of her shoe broke off. Off balance, she stepped on her robe, her momentum carrying her forward, the robe pulling her backwards. Jessie toppled, hitting the stage floor with a splat as the lights came up.

Josh started to laugh. Jessie looked up at him and couldn't help giggling. The audience began to catch on and responded, their titters sweeping across the house in a wave.

"My mother bought those shoes for me," Jessie ad-libbed.

"And your mother advised against marrying me. You think this is a sign?" Josh ad-libbed back.

The audience was laughing uproariously.

With ease, Josh helped Jessie to her feet. Jessie grabbed the discarded shoe and flicked off the other one. Walking over to a fancy wastebasket by the bed, she held the shoes high and dropped them into the container with a clatter. "That's what I think of my mother's advice."

As the audience broke into applause, Jessie moved smoothly into Josh's arms. The scene continued as rehearsed.

At intermission Nora showed Jessie the broken shoe. "This was no accident," Nora said slowly. "Look. The heel was broken off and reattached with cheap glue. Forget going to George. He's not listening to us. Break a leg has taken on a whole new meaning in this show."

Nora was right. Jessie shivered. She could have broken her leg or an arm if she'd landed the wrong way.

*

"You're sure about this, Nick?" Bree greeted him in the mansion's foyer, opening the door at his knock. "It seems risky."

"I told you, it's fine. This is our big night." Nick jogged inside, leaving the door ajar. "Anyway, you're the one who likes to take all the risks." He grinned. "It's one of the things I find so sexy about you."

"Stop it. I'm serious."

"Am I interrupting?" Lyle appeared in the doorway. He managed to make a pair of new jeans and a T-shirt look like they'd come out of a trashcan. The trench coat already had an ink stain on the pocket.

"About time you got off your cell." Nick was anxious to get the preliminaries over with. It hadn't been easy to convince Bree to include Lyle. "Come on in. Lyle Barton," Nick motioned, as Lyle closed the door behind him, "meet Brianna Fontaine."

Extending her hand, Bree told Lyle she was sorry for his loss. "I've heard a lot about you."

Lyle took Bree's measure. She was wearing snug jeans and a blue sweater, hair tousled, just a hint of lipstick. Lyle gave a short nod and got down to business. "Okay," he said, "show me the set-up Nick talked about."

"Follow me." Bree headed down the hallway.

Hesitating, Lyle eyed the alabaster living room to their right, original Impressionist artwork on the walls, abstract metal sculptures, one wall a window of sheer glass overlooking the bay. "How can you stand this place?" he whispered to Nick. "It's a museum."

"You'll get used to it." Nick led Lyle into Bree's bedroom. Bree was waiting, flicking a hand through her hair.

"Jesus," Lyle said. "This looks like an FBI stakeout."

"I'll take that as a compliment." Nick circled the room, explaining the equipment. The telescope, he pointed, was aimed directly at the rear of Roberto Martinelli's estate, which bordered the mirrored inlet opening into the Atlantic. Next to it was a high-speed camera with a telephoto lens on a tripod. The sound system was set up next to the window. Lyle took in the huge speakers and elaborate console, leading to a snake pit of cables on the floor.

"You spared no expense." Lyle looked impressed. He glanced at the desk. "And you've been busy." The desk sported an elaborate computer system with stacks of printouts. Nick kicked some trash out of the way, knocking over the wastebasket. Empty cartons of Chinese take-out, dirty napkins, plastic utensils, and fortune cookies scattered across the floor.

"This is more your style, McDeare. A garbage heap."

"It's my style, too." Bree gave a laugh. "Actually, this is orderly." She righted the trashcan, stuffing the garbage back inside. "Nick and I get tunnel vision when we're working."

"And Martinelli," Nick pointed out the window, "is in that tunnel." Nick stared at Roberto's jeweled estate. All the answers were there, the house that held the key to his family's welfare.

Lyle turned to Bree. "So what's in this survelliance for you, if I'm not being rude."

Bree eyed Nick.

"Go ahead," he said. "I told you. You can trust him."

"Okay. The TIMES brought me back to New York to do a series of in-depth exposes on corruption in the city. Bumping into Nick gave me a starting point. I'd heard whispers of Martinelli's involvement in Andrew's death." She glanced quickly at Nick and away again. "I have history with Nick, so I was naturally interested when the news broke. Plus, Martinelli was my neighbor growing up. When Nick filled me in on the missing pieces, I knew I had my first series of articles. It's been a long time since the head of a New York family's been brought down."

"Explain to Lyle how you've gone about this from your end."

"I started watching Martinelli's grounds through the telescope. Roberto and Aldo Zappella like to walk along that boat dock and talk. So," Bree smiled, "I rowed over in the middle of the night and planted a voice-activated bug on the waterfront side of Martinelli's boathouse."

"Christ." Nick thought Lyle's eyes were going to bug out of his head.

"I told you she was good," Nick said. "Sorry, Bree, go on."

"See, that's what the sound system's for," Bree said, "to pick up their dialogue. So far they haven't discussed Fosselli, just their business down at South Street, off-track betting, drug shipments, boring shit like that." She looked up at Nick. "This morning they mentioned Jersey City again."

"That's what, the third time?"

Nodding, Bree looked at Lyle. "It could just be about a business associate. Or it could be something else."

"Jersey City's a perfect hideout for Fosselli," Barton mused. "A high population of Italians, only a short PATH train ride away. I'll make some calls. See if I can get my hands on new apartment sales or rentals since August."

"Smart," Bree said. "Anyway, whenever a car leaves the Martinelli garage or estate, the still camera's programmed to take photos. The clicking alerts me. I get in my car and wait for Martinelli's limo outside the gate."

"Dangerous," Lyle said.

"I'm careful. I rent a new car every week, wear a wig, a cap, a hood, glasses, whatever. In the last few weeks I've seen parts of the Tri-State area I didn't know existed. I got lost in Riverdale the other day. Most nights he goes out, he heads to Bottoms Up."

"Martinelli's been doing a lot of overnights there," Nick told Lyle, "that strip club he owns in the Bronx. He pays a visit a couple times a week and always early

Saturday night, like clockwork. Which is why we've put this plan together for tonight."

"I hope it's worth lying to Jessie."

"You know I think it is." Nick avoided Bree's eyes. She didn't have to say anything. Nick knew she didn't approve of him marrying Jessie. They'd grown closer working together, but Jessie was not a topic for discussion. His love life was none of Bree's business.

"Okay, fill me in on the rest of the details. Besides wearing a wire, what else?"

"We get to the club ahead of him tonight," Nick said. "I have a disguise, plus a camera built into a button. While you and Bree wait in the car, I enter, wearing the wire I asked you to bring. This could be a big break. I thought it was worth a lie."

"Go on."

"With your help, I'll check out exactly what Martinelli's up to inside that place, trace his movements." Nick's fingers beat a tattoo on the desk. "So, you're in?"

"With a catch. You stay in the car. I wear the disguise. I brought my own, with my own camera. That's why I grew this Brillo on my face. I wear the wire."

Nick stared at Lyle. "Bullshit. This—"

"Save it," Lyle said, using his cop voice. "I worked the decoy squad when I made detective. No street punk ever made me. Who knows what's going on in there? Bottom line, I have the wire. I have the authority to make whatever we hear or see stick. It's a good plan. The only difference is I carry it out."

"Nick, he has a point," Bree said slowly.

"Et tu, Brute? Fuck it. Fuck you both."

*

"Here you go, Jessie." James Lovelock placed a Cobb salad on Jessie's dressing table. "The Rabbit Patch makes the best Cobb in Manhattan. I got one, too."

Cosette leapt up on the dressing table, sniffing Jessie's salad.

"Cosette, no, baby cakes. That's rude. Get down. Besides, we're not staying." The dog jumped down, fixing liquid eyes on Jessie.

Jessie scratched behind the dog's ears. Anthony had been begging for a dog. "Why don't you join me? I'm eating alone today. Unless you have other plans?"

"Just filling my stomach between shows." James sat on the divan and took the lid off his salad, feeding the dog a flake of tuna. "Where's Josh and the yummy Nick today?"

"Josh had errands. And Nick drove up to Boston with Lyle Barton."

Cosette swallowed the tuna and grabbed an olive.

Jessie burst out laughing.

"Silly dog," James said. "She loves olives, pickles, taco chips, and cantaloupe."

"Our cat loves Chinese or Japanese."

Valentine York ambled by Jessie's open door, halting their conversation. James sprung to the door and closed it. Sitting back down, he lowered his voice, "Nora says Valentine's your prankster."

"The woman's out to get me. I told George about my shoe this afternoon. He won't lift a finger."

"George is flexing his muscles with Quill out of the picture. You could have broken your leg. Or worse."

"It's scary," Jessie admitted.

"You need to catch her red-handed."

" … I have an idea. But I'll need your help. And Nora's."

*

The sun was dipping below the horizon, but no sign of Nick or Lyle. What the hell were they doing in there? A three-way? Abbie had inspected every car that left the gate in case Nick had switched to another vehicle. Nothing.

Maybe it was time to give up. Just as she clicked the key in the ignition, the tracker on the screen sprang to life. She spotted the Bronco as it glided through the gate, three souls inside, one a woman. Abbie ducked as the car sped by. Putting her Lexus in gear, she followed.

*

After zipping into the Bottoms Up parking lot, Barton turned to Nick in the back seat. Lyle was primed, his adrenaline kicking in. This is why he was still among the living, the only reason, to get to Martinelli and hunt down Gianni Fosselli. To see that justice was done for his wife and child. "Hand me that jacket."

"Happy to. The stench's making me sick."

Nick was still in a mood. They'd been quiet on the long way over, each lost in their own thoughts. Lyle slid his arms into the worn flak jacket. "This baby hasn't been washed in twenty years, my good luck charm. I keep it at the station. Steinmetz dropped it off. Picked up the rest of the costume at the Salvation Army." He motioned to the stained pants and grimy polo shirt. "Soaked it in whiskey for a day." Lyle fitted a faded Giants cap backwards on his head. "How do I look?"

"Like a vet who's seen too much action," Bree murmured, leaning across the seat to examine his face. "Those red blotches actually look like sores."

"Good." Lyle scratched his chest. "This tape itches like hell. I haven't worn a wire in years."

"Why don't you start talking as you walk away from the car, so we can adjust the volume." Bree grabbed the small transmitter on the console.

Climbing out of the car, Barton buttoned the jacket at an angle. He staggered across the parking lot. "Can you hear me?" he whispered.

At Nick's nod, Lyle lurched through the door, grabbing the doorframe to steady himself. He took a moment to let his eyes adjust to the dim lighting. A smoky haze settled over the central stage. Martinelli must've paid off the local cops, every John in the place puffing away. Strobe lights flashed. Three topless bimbos in G-strings clung to poles and gyrated to the music. Typical stripper fare with decent bodies.

The clientele was a motley group. Young and old. Tattoos and tank tops. Muscle men and derelicts and even a few suits. Lyle tried to picture his old partner Bushman hanging out here. This was where Bush had made his connection with Martinelli. Bush and his strippers and his hellish double life.

- 108 -

The bartender was out of shape, huge and bald. "Shot of gin with a chaser," Lyle said, taking a stool. "Got a match?" Goldfinger tossed him a pack with a single match in it. His derelict hands shaking, Lyle pulled a faded pack of unfiltered Camels from his pocket and lit up.

*

"Quick, there's Martinelli," Bree whispered, crouching in the front seat.

Sinking low, Nick watched the don emerge from the back of his limo. He entered Bottoms Up, and the limo coasted out of sight.

A sharp rap on Nick's window startled him. "Christ, it's Abbie."

"Abbie?"

"You met her opening night, Jessie's friend. A pain in my ass." Nick flipped the window down. "What the hell are you doing here?"

"That's a question for you, lover boy."

"Goddammit, get in." Nick unlocked the car door and Abbie slid in next to him on the back seat. She looked like a cat burglar, dressed all in black. "Start talking."

"You're the one who better start talking." Abbie looked pointedly at Bree.

Bree bolted up. "Nick?"

"You've been following me?"

"I'm so onto you, you and your affair with Ms. NEW YORK TIMES."

"This is bullshit!"

"Nick, calm down," Bree whispered. "Anyone in the parking lot can hear you."

"You're lucky I don't kill you," he hissed at Abbie. "But it would make too much noise."

"Look," Bree said, "I don't know where you got the idea Nick and … Wait, that's Barton. Shit!"

Barton's whisper filled the car on the one-way transmitter. "… pigeon arrived. Walked straight through to the back. Get over there!"

Scrambling into the front seat. Nick started the engine, whipping the Bronco through the parking lot.

"Would someone please tell me what's going on?"

Nick pulled around the rear of the joint.

"That's his game?" Bree murmured, "sneaking out the back?"

Scanning the alley behind the strip club, Nick could see several vehicles parked. A block down, a car's rear lights turned onto a side street. "Look. Might be a Honda."

"Follow him. It's worth a shot."

Nick sped after the car, two blocks ahead. A red light brought the Bronco to a screeching halt. Two drunken couples staggered across the street in front of him, laughing uproariously. "Dammit." Nick watched the taillights veer around the corner and disappear.

"Listen," Bree said, "on second thought I don't see Martinelli driving a Honda. It's beneath him."

"Martinelli?" Abbie asked.

"Which means it's the perfect cover." Nick slapped the steering wheel. "We've lost him. Happy, Abbie?"

"If you'd explain, maybe—"

"Maybe, hell." Nick spun the car around and headed back to Bottoms Up.

Barton's voice floated through the Bronco. "Just used the head to see the back of this place. A Do Not Disturb sign's on a door handle, looks like an office. Martinelli's either holed up in there, or he snuck out a back way. I'll stick around as planned. Hope you're following something."

"We're following shit," Nick muttered. He edged the car into the alley, berthing next to a dark brick wall. "Keep your eye on those back doors, Bree. Maybe he's still in there."

"Would someone please start talking?" Abbie's whisper was a soft shriek. "Why are you chasing Martinelli?"

Nick glanced over his shoulder at Abbie, her black turtleneck up to her chin, unruly hair pulled back in a ponytail. "You might've blown everything tonight. Those few seconds were critical."

"Please just tell me why you're investigating Martinelli, okay? Because of the matches?"

"No." Nick looked her in the eye. "Because Gianni's alive. Andrew's killer, my dear idiot, is alive."

*

Gianni, alive … As Abbie shrank into the back seat, Nick spelled it out for her. Bottom line, he finished grimly, Gianni was out there, waiting to exact his revenge. For the rest of the night, Abbie was quiet, trying to process the horror, while her companions' chatter merged into meaningless static. Idly, Abbie observed their body language. Nick was all business. Bree … Bree had a hard time keeping her hands off him.

The sun rose and Martinelli still hadn't left the back office. If that's where he was. Nick pulled around the entryway to meet Lyle, climbing out from behind the wheel. Barton did a double-take when he saw Abbie. "What the—"

"I'll explain later," Nick said. "Get in. You and Bree take the Bronco. I'll ride with Nancy Drew here." Abbie ducked out of the car, not looking Lyle in the eye.

"There's a diner on Route Twenty-four in Flanders," Bree said. "Eggstacy. A giant egg dancing with a slice of bacon on the roof. You can't miss it. If you get lost, call one of our cells."

Pointing out the Lexus to Nick, Abbie slipped into the driver's seat. Nick immediately spotted the tracker. "Nice. Barton will be thrilled to know his car's wearing a tracking device."

"Nick, I'm really sorry about this," Abbie croaked. "I don't know what to say."

"Try."

As Abbie followed the Bronco out of the parking lot she explained what it had looked like between Bree and him. "I'm sorry. I can see now you're just working partners. At least you are. But--"

"What does that mean?"

"Nothing. Forget it. When you lied to Jessie at the theater about lunch I--"

"You've been at this a long time, haven't you?" A pulse clicked in Nick's jaw. "Don't you know me better than to think I'd cheat on Jessie? You, of all people? After the hell we went through with Gianni?"

"I said I was sorry. But why are you keeping this from Jessie? She should know. I'm not trying to turn this around. I was wrong. But--"

"Shut up and listen to me. Jessie finally has her life back. You know what she's been through. I can't take the chance she'll backslide. Hiding in that house twenty-four, seven. Drinking, pills. I have it covered. Willie knows what's going on. Stay out of it, Abbie. And not a word to Jess. I want your promise."

A quick glance at Nick's face told Abbie his eyes weren't full of brotherly love. She quickly flicked her attention back to following the Bronco onto Interstate Ninety-Five. "Gianni sent me matches, too. He threatened me. And don't forget what happened last time you kept a secret from Jessie, when we investigated Gianni and pretended to hate each other. She went ballistic."

"Look," Nick said, his voice flat, "Gianni wants Anthony, not us. I'm Anthony's father, Jessie's fiance. I'll handle this. Now swear you won't say anything."

"Okay. I promise. But I have a bad feeling about this."

CHAPTER 12

Eggstacy was a Fifties diner. Formica tabletops, miniature juke boxes in the booths, waitresses wearing saddle shoes, bobby socks, and poodle skirts. Nick studied a menu, with Twenty-First Century prices. Fifteen bucks for a couple of fried eggs, ham, and toast.

The sleepy team rehashed the situation over breakfast, careful not to mention names. "I think our friend either has a babe stashed in his office," Nick said, dredging his toast through yolk, "or he was in that Honda. I think it was green."

"Something's going on, that's for sure," Bree took a bite of her cheese omelet. "Like I said, he overnights at Bottoms Up several times a week. Rarely two nights in a row. Every Saturday evening."

"Then we go back tomorrow and the day after," Nick said. "We go every night until we figure it out and get something on him."

"And just what are you going to tell Jessie?" Abbie asked. "How many times can you come up with an excuse to stay away overnight?"

"She's right." Lyle pointed his fork at Nick. "Since you insist on keeping this from Jessie you can't chance it. So this is the way it works. Bree calls my cell if the limo leaves Southampton at night, meaning it's a good bet he's going to the club. It's a half-hour drive to the Bronx. I'll be at Bottoms Up way before our pal shows up. I don't have to account for my whereabouts to … Uh, Abbie. Tell me about Gianni's shoes." Lyle reached for his coffee.

"His shoes. He wore shoes."

"Size? Italian made?"

"Nothing but. Expensive. And his feet were small for such a big man. We joked about his slippers almost fitting me. Maybe a size nine or ten. Why?"

Lyle explained his theory about the shoe they found floating in the water. "Unfortunately, it doesn't prove anything. The chain of evidence was broken after Fosselli's escape. It's--"

"I'm going." Nick shoved his plate away, still seething. He'd always been a free agent when it came to an investigation. He hated having his hands tied, an executive committee overseeing every move.

Dropping a twenty on the table, Nick said, "I'm getting some fresh air, Abbie. Meet you at the car."

*

The cell phone shrilled, drilling into Roberto's sleep. He glanced at the clock. Seven a.m. Couldn't the world leave him alone on a Sunday? Even God rested on the seventh day. Jersey City was supposed to be his haven. He grabbed his cell, whispering, "What?"

"Bad news," Aldo said. "Marcella's mother died yesterday. The two of you are flying to Genoa tomorrow. The funeral's Wednesday."

Being cooped up with his wife's family was like being trapped in a black and white foreign movie that droned on and on about nothing. Roberto felt a drop of guilt. He slipped out of bed and tiptoed into the living room. "How's Marcella?"

"A mess. She keeps asking for you. What time will you be home today?"

"When I get there."

"Another thing. Our friend called. He's meeting with Vaughn two nights before the wedding. I'll handle Vaughn on our end. Fosselli's plastic surgery's finished. He swears we won't recognize him."

"I'll be glad when this fucking mess is over."

"When that boy disappears, the cops will be all over us."

"I have an idea about that. We'll talk when I get back from Italy." Roberto hung up. He'd been thinking about Anthony Brady's kidnapping. And he'd come up with a sweet way to keep the NYPD and the Feds off his ass.

Returning to the master bedroom Roberto smiled down at the tiny creature in his bed. They'd been awake most of the night. She'd been sobbing, crying out for her mommy and daddy. It had taken him hours to calm her down. He finally bribed her with her favorite teddy bear, promising a new one just like it, the secret to making her compliant.

Roberto's trip to Italy meant he'd be away at least five days. A lifetime. He feared a setback after coming so far. After all his hard work, he couldn't afford to lose momentum.

*

By Tuesday morning Jessie's plan to catch Valentine in the act was set, James and Nora eager participants. Jessie would go about her normal routine, but nothing would be normal.

The torment had to end. In the shower that morning Jessie had noticed her hipbone still bruised from her Saturday-matinee fall. She needed to be able to walk onstage without fearing for her safety. And Valentine needed to be stopped

"Mom, we're home." Anthony swung into the kitchen with Zane Harwell in tow. Zane was sleeping over on a school night. Nick's agent Liz had scored ringside seats for the basketball game at Madison Square Garden. Zane handed Jessie a planter sprouting herbs, a gift from his mother. Jessie smiled, liking this kid with the spiky blond hair and clear gray eyes.

*

His mind in overdrive, Nick stared at the ceiling. Jessie was sleeping at his side, but he'd been awake for hours.

He'd hoped an evening with the boys at the Knicks game would be a diversion. Instead, he'd spent the game scanning the crowd, convinced Gianni was in the stands. Afterwards, Nick took the kids to the Knicks' locker room for two signed basketballs. How Liz accomplished this was a mystery, but Nick had learned over the years not to question his agent's methods.

Turning onto his side, Nick pummeled the pillow. This room was too damned hot.

Finding Gianni in the metropolitan area was like trying to find a molecule in a haystack. And how could he write the ending of his book if he didn't know how the story ended in real life?

The heat was smothering. Nick was dying to open a bedroom window, but cool air wasn't healthy for Jessie's vocal chords. Maybe the sitting room. Nick drifted into the other room and threw open one of the windows, breathing deeply. Better. He returned to bed and tucked the blankets up around Jessie's neck. If she missed a performance because of laryngitis there'd be hell to pay.

Maybe Fosselli was out on the Island somewhere, close to Queens. Nah. Nick was betting Gianni was right here in the city, maybe even--

It was freezing now. Shivering, Nick hustled into the other room and closed the window. The house was always too hot or too cold. Diving back into bed he pulled the covers up to his chin, chilled to the bone.

*

"Anthony?"

Anthony opened his eyes. The room was freezing. Anthony could see his breath. He sat up and looked at Zane. But his friend wasn't in the trundle bed. He was standing near the window.

"I saw him," Zane whispered, his teeth chattering. Zane eyed a framed photo of Andrew. "He was here, the guy in the picture."

His heart pounding, Anthony snapped on the bedside lamp. "You saw him? You saw my father? Andrew?"

"I thought I was dreaming." Zane shivered and crept to the bed, dropping down beside Anthony, "He was sitting over there." Zane nodded toward the easy chair. "He called to me and I came over. It wasn't scary. And it wasn't a dream. Honest." Zane wrapped his arms around himself.

Anthony didn't know what to say. He and Mom and Dad had all promised never to talk about Daddy's visits to anyone outside the family. They knew no one would understand. But if Daddy had shown himself to Zane ....

"Did I really see a ghost?"

"Listen, you have to promise, swear to me on-on the life of your dog that you'll never tell anyone what I'm going to tell you. Swear."

"I swear." Zane gulped.

"I'm sure my-- Andrew was here. But he's gone now." Anthony held out his palm. "Feel how much warmer the room is? I wonder why he talked to you and not me. What did he say?"

"He was glad you and I were friends. And he wants you to listen to your dad's instructions. What does that mean?"

Pulling his medallion out from under his T-shirt. Anthony said, "See this? It's made special for me. If anything happens to me, Dad can find me. It's like spy stuff. And Dad told me what to do if someone takes me. Or I get lost."

"Takes you? 'Cause your folks are famous?"

"Yeah. I wonder why Daddy let you see him? He only showed himself to me and my dad. And Mom once."

"And he said you and I would be friends a long time. How does he know that?"

"Remember, you can't tell anyone."

"I promise." Zane laughed. "Besides, who'd believe me?"

Wow. Anthony couldn't wait to tell his dad. But the next morning Dad was asleep. And he was locked in his office working when Anthony got home from school. Anthony was given strict orders not to bother Dad when his office door was closed. He had a deadline. Anthony wasn't sure what that meant, but Dad's lips tightened whenever he talked about it, and his eyes didn't look happy.

*

By Thursday night, Nick had a manuscript disaster on his hands. Due date was a month away and he didn't know how to end the damned book. THE SILVER LINING was the story of Andrew's murder. But Gianni was alive, a locust hiding in the earth waiting to hatch. There was no end to the story now. Nothing worked because the story wasn't over. Nick stared out the office window, the black night sky a sullen backdrop to his mood. He should've stuck to his original idea of counterspies in London.

Closing out the manuscript, Nick checked his e-mail. Bree had been writing daily. Martinelli hadn't gone back to Bottoms Up since last Saturday night. Had he spotted them? The man was keeping some kind of crazy secret.

When he figured out Roberto's soft spot, that's when the don would guarantee Nick's family's safety, part of the price Martinelli would pay for his secret to stay a secret. He could be stealing gold bars from Fort Knox or running a prostitution ring in the Senate. It didn't matter, not as long as Nick's silence guaranteed Jessie and Anthony's safety. And Martinelli would sever ties with Fosselli, Nick and Barton taking it from there. Fosselli must be stopped.

Abbie had called that afternoon, asking if there was any news, begging Nick to let her help. His anger ebbing, Nick had filled her in. Not that there was much to tell. But Abbie was resourceful and fearless, proving herself when they'd nailed Gianni the first time. Anyway, she was already in the club by virtue of her own set of matches.

It was Nick's tough luck Andrew was keeping a low profile this time. Just those silent warnings to Anthony, the little boy they both loved dearly.

*

Staring at the hockey game on his new flat-screen TV, Barton could swear he heard Barb yelling at him to turn down the volume. He rapidly flipped through the channels, desperately trying to silence the voices in his head. Lyle was bored. Boredom meant he thought too much. He had to avoid thinking. At least he finally had some television, the big screen and a postage-stamp TV in the bedroom, plus a recliner. The only furniture in the living room, all he needed.

Taking a swig of beer, Lyle wandered to the window, old-fashioned street lights illuminating rows of brownstones frozen in time. Only the cars lining the curb brought the street into the Twenty-First Century. This was where he lived now. In this cinematic neighborhood in this multi-million-dollar apartment. How the hell could a life change so drastically overnight?

His lip twisted into a bitter smile. His new life came with another new tail, this time an ugly female watching Jessie's brownstone day after day. She saw nothing but a broken-down cop head to a bar every few nights for all the good it did her.

Whirling at the sound of the back door opening, Lyle composed himself. Nick appeared in the archway, house key in hand. He didn't look happy. "I should be writing, but I had to take a break. Hope you don't mind, letting myself in …"

"I can use the company. What's up?"

"How the hell can I end this thing when Fosselli's still out there? Nothing's finished. Nothing." He washed a hand over his mouth. "Everything's going to hell."

"We'll get him. Write the ending."

"I can't." Nick eyed the television. "You think that screen's large enough?"

The man was in bad shape. And neither one of them could afford to let down, or Anthony would pay the price. "Hey, the Rangers are playing the Capitals. Want to take a look?"

"I'm a Rangers fan." Nick smiled faintly. "I hate the Capitals."

"Grab yourself the desk chair in the den. I'll get the booze and chips."

A few minutes later, the two men were parked in front of the television. "Jessie's going to be late tonight," Nick said, his eyes fastened to the screen. "Some party for the director after the show. Filled with everyone who's anyone. If Martinelli makes a move now, I could slip out unnoticed."

"He's way overdue." Lyle tore open the bag of chips. "I'm having trouble getting my hands on the new rentals and sales in Jersey City. Different state. Lots of red tape."

"Maybe Bree could talk to THE TIMES' real estate editor. The Sunday edition lists Jersey locales."

"Good idea."

*

As Max Callaban straightened the knot on his cranberry silk tie, he squared his shoulders, looking into the mirror. His new suit fit perfectly, a subtle cranberry herringbone on charcoal, the pattern faint. The new London tailor had done well with his measurements. The conservative English look was perfect. No more Italian designs. Not for Max.

He fingered his custom-designed blond toupee, ordered from an Internet site. But the look wasn't natural. No matter. The only thing that mattered was a blond Max Callaban making an appearance. He checked his Rolex. Time to leave the hotel. He had a date to keep.

Carlo chauffeured him through the heavy New York traffic, Max staring out the limo's dark-tinted window. He was surprised to realize how much he didn't miss New York. The lights, the sounds, the frenetic energy, it wasn't exciting anymore. Max had grown accustomed to quiet Ohio, where he could begin life over again with his son. Which was why tonight's test was so important. Max Callaban was about to face his first trial in public. Aldo and Roberto would never know he was here. Assuming everything went well.

Waiting for his moment, Max had been following TO HAVE AND TO HOLD. Finally, he'd spotted an item in the NEW YORK POST'S gossip column. A birthday party was being held for the play's director at Nordic Nirvana tonight. Max loathed the restaurant, its trademark vast quantities of bland Scandinavian food as tasty as whale blubber. According to the POST, the entire cast would be in attendance, including its famous leading lady, Jessica Kendle. Max was counting on the paparazzi coming out in full force.

With a call to an underworld connection, it hadn't been difficult for Carlo to provide Max with a fake ID. Tonight he was Oscar Fuentes, food critic for the fictitious THE CURIOUS EPICUREAN, which meant Max would get his table of choice. The one lovely thing about Nordic Nirvana was no private rooms. And Max wanted a front row seat for Jessica's new opening act, written and directed by Max Callaban. Jessica would improvise the new role he'd created for her.

Max tapped on the glass separating him from the driver's seat, telling Carlo to let him out a block from the restaurant. He wanted to stretch his legs. Carlo would join him later, wearing his own hairpiece and glasses. Max wasn't taking any chances Jessica would recall the fan that had accosted her a few months ago. He smiled, humming a melody from AIDA. No one who noticed his blond self tonight would recognize Max Callaban at the wedding. Meanwhile, he had time. The party hadn't yet begun.

Flustered by the food critic's surprise visit, the maitre d' was ridiculously eager to please. Max chose a table within a few feet of where the gala was being set up. He ordered a variety of dishes from the menu, making a show of wanting a sampler of food. "I'll keep the menus, of course," he added. He hid his irritation at the shrill music thrumming through the sound system.

Jessica finally swept into the party like royalty, Max surprised McDeare wasn't at her side. Already fornicating with another slut? Max had known Jessica could never keep the goat's libido satisfied. In his place was Jessica's leading man, Joshua Elliot. Max smiled, signaling the waiter for another drink.

The actor would do nicely. Elliot hovered over Jessica like a dragonfly during dinner. He had the look of a man who spent more time on his muscles than his walnut of a brain. Jessica was rarely in her seat, signing autographs and socializing with her grotesque clan of peers. The scene was set.

*

The party was in full bore, the piped-in music heavy on jazz and swing. Jessie was in a party mood, tapping her foot to the beat, careful not to trip the waiters cruising around her chair. Her shoe flipped off with "Boogie Woogie Bugle Boy," but she retrieved it quickly.

Day after day, Jessie's life was about the play and the wedding and the unceasing interviews and personal appearances. In between, she worried about Anthony, worried about Lyle, and watched her back at the theater. Jessie needed just one unscripted block of time to relax and breathe and enjoy the moment. Like tonight. It would be better with Nick at her side, but he was in a panic over his manuscript. Jessie knew what it was to be focused on your work.

Picking at a meatball, Jessie returned a famous director's smile from across the tables. She was wearing a slinky periwinkle sheath with a jeweled buckle clasp at the shoulder, the other shoulder bare. The dress was made of a sparkly stretchy fabric, the kind of material that made Jessie glad she'd been working out and watching what she ate.

It was a gathering of a hundred people, everyone near and dear to Quill in the theatrical world seated at tables for four. Quill was just back for the event unfortunately. He'd be gone tomorrow. Jessie was dining with Josh and the Rudolphs, Josh filling in as escort. She flashed Josh a thanks for a new drink, leaning over to tell Marcy her diamond choker was exquisite. Jessie didn't have a clue where Abbie was tonight, and she didn't ask. Last week, Abbie had admitted she didn't think Josh was that into her. Abbie had also mentioned an ex-lover was in town, an Italian artist.

Jessie was bombarded with autograph requests from other diners between courses, Josh ignored. He shrugged, joking he'd grown used to it. Jessie caught the Rudolphs' amused smile, but she couldn't say no. If it weren't for her fans, she wouldn't have her career. An elderly couple asked to have their picture taken with her. Jessie rose and posed with each of them in turn.

Out of the corner of her eye, Jessie caught sight of Valentine York, surprised to see her here. Squeezed into something crimson and nearly transparent, she was draped around an esteemed composer who had a hit musical running in London. Valentine rarely attended social gatherings, but when she did, she came alone, brushed up against every influential male in the room, and left alone. Eyeing Valentine, Jessie absently sipped another drink Josh delivered.

*

Josh studied Jessie over the rim of his martini. He was taking full advantage of his time with her tonight. In fact, this night wasn't going to end anytime soon. After the party there was no reason for Jessie to go home. A nightcap at his apartment sounded much better. He had a feeling Jessie would think so, too.

She just needed one night with him to realize what a mistake she was making with McDeare. He'd show her what a man was all about. Josh had never had one leading lady express her regrets about sleeping with him. In fact, they often swore their performances benefited. One actress who specialized in virginal roles was sure it won her the Tony.

But first, Josh needed to loosen Jessie up and make her forget her surly Hemingway. With single-minded focus, Josh played bartender, fetching Jessie drinks, slipping in more without her noticing. Nothing like double shots of vodka mixed with tonic water to get things rolling. He'd have to remember to thank his friend Hans for posing as a lipstick executive on the phone, luring Abbie to a dinner interview tonight for a brand new company. Of course, he'd never show up.

*

The party was at the dessert stage, everyone up and mingling. Max was delighted to see his waiter remove the remainder of the revolting Swedish meatball kebabs and gummy noodles. He lingered over watery coffee and a horrendous crème brulee, waiting for his moment. When the hulking Elliot journeyed to the bar after swiping Jessie's glass for another refill, Max palmed a tiny pill and grabbed his menu. He intercepted the actor on his way back, asking if Mr. Elliot would be kind enough to sign his menu. Joshua had taken off his sport coat, revealing a poorly tailored blue shirt over what Americans called a ripped torso.

"Here. Let me hold your drink for you." Max cast Joshua an accommodating smile and produced a pen from his pocket. The dolt handed Max his drink in return for the pen. He looked thrilled someone was asking for his autograph.

Carlo tapped Elliot on the shoulder, asking for an autograph, too. As the actor swung around to accommodate, Max dropped the pill into Jessica's vodka. The effects of the drug varied from person to person. Sometimes the woman passed out. Sometimes she became a sex kitten, lusting for the nearest man in sight. That was more Jessica's style.

No matter what the outcome, her behavior would ensure that Jessica was the headline in tomorrow's gossip columns. And with a man who was not her fiancé. Jessica's true great love in life was her image. Max was simply ensuring that that image would flood the tabloids. It may not be the picture Jessica fostered, but it would be the truth. Jessica Kendle was a tramp. The publicity would make her all the more famous. Everyone would be happy, no?

Handing Elliot's drink back to him, Max returned to his table. He thanked the maitre d' for the lovely meal and assured the man Max's review would be glowing. As Carlo disappeared to fetch the car, Max eyed Jessica's table. Ah, she was sipping her drink. Excellent.

It was time for the true test. Had Gianni Fosselli become Max Callaban? Max took deep breaths, relaxing himself. His son's future depended on this meeting. Rehearsing his lines one last time, Max glided to Jessica's table. "Excuse me, Miss Kendle," he said in precise English. "I admire you, both professionally and personally. You're an amazingly talented woman who has survived a horrible tragedy."

"Thank you for your kind words." Jessica donned a tragic smile and extended her hand.

"I wish you the best." Max folded his hand around hers. Glancing down, Max released her hand quickly and nodded. "Have a pleasant evening."

Perspiration sheathed his brow as Max walked briskly towards the front of the restaurant. *Mio Dio*, what a close call. If Jessica had looked down, she would have seen the scar circling the base of his thumb. A memento from the night he'd aimed his Ferrari at a roadside tree upon hearing that Jessica had married Andrew. A scar Jessica had once suggested he have sanded off. Gianni had preferred to keep it as a reminder of what he'd lost. He'd visit the plastic surgeon in Cleveland immediately. This had been a serious oversight.

As Max reached the revolving door he noticed Jessica's chauffeur standing a few feet away, his gaze fixed in the direction of the party. Was this man more than a driver, perhaps a bodyguard? Had he seen Max drop the pill into Jessica's drink, or even observed him watch her too closely? The man turned his dark stare on Max. Max smiled. The black giant nodded before returning his attention to Jessica.

Relieved, Max hurried to his waiting limo. Despite the near miss with the scar, tonight had been a resounding success.

Jessica had looked the enemy in the face and not recognized him.

And the show had just begun.

*

Staring mindlessly at Lyle's TV, Nick grunted as a flying puck almost took a goalie's head off. At his cell's buzz, he muted the sound. "It's Willie. I'm on my way home with Jessie. She, ah, we have a situation, Nick. It took three of us to get her in the car."

"What? What kind of situation?"

"We'll be home in a few minutes. Almost there. Meet me out front."

Willie clicked off, Nick bounding out of the chair. "It's Jessie," he told Barton. "Willie said something's wrong." Nick took off. Had Jessie collapsed from exhaustion? She never should've gone on that talk show last week. Or maybe it was the photo shoot the week before. It was his fault for letting her work too hard, not resting on her days off. Nick sprinted across the yards and through the brownstone, Mary calling out to him as he sped by.

The limo was approaching as Nick burst out the front door, Lyle at his heels. Willie leapt out and opened the back door. Jessie was sprawled across the seat, sound asleep, pale hair spangled across her face.

"A minute ago she was singing at the top of her lungs. I swear it."

"Jess?" Nick leaned over Jessie and shook her. "Come on, honey, wake up."

"Uh, Nick, we've got company." Lyle clapped a hand on his shoulder. As Nick looked up, a flash went off in his face. A slob of a photographer with a face like a grapefruit stood a few feet away, snapping photo after photo.

"Get out of my way, you fu--"

"I'll take care of this." Willie muscled the photographer away, grabbing his camera and ripping out its insides. "There you go. Sir." He shoved the camera back at him.

"That's destruction of private property!"

"You want to see destruction?" Willie asked, his voice dulcet. Keeping his eyes on the paparazzi, Willie whispered, "Get her in the house, Nick. More are on the way."

Scooping Jessie up, Nick strode into the brownstone, Jessie not stirring. Nick laid her on the couch in the living room. "Jess? Baby? Can you hear me?" Nick's heart was hammering. What the hell had happened to her?

"Is she drunk?" Lyle asked.

Willie entered the room. "I don't think so."

"Start talking, Willie." Nick looked down at Jessie, Sleeping Beauty, dead to the world. "Weren't you watching her?"

"Jessie was never out of my sight all night," Willie said quietly. "She was fine until about a half hour ago. Josh was refilling her drink. At first I thought she'd just had too much to drink, but … I don't know how to say this—"

"Tell me."

"Maybe he slipped something into her glass."

Mary stood in the doorway, her hand on her heart. "Slipped her what?"

"I don't know, Aunt Mary." Willie turned to Nick. "I'm thinking maybe a tranquilizer . A psychedelic drug."

"Describe her behavior." Lyle lifted Jessie's eyelids.

"She had trouble walking and then … Look, this is none of my business, but Josh was glued to Jessie's side tonight. She was a perfect lady until the end, when … Nick, she had her hands all over him."

CHAPTER 13

"She what?" Nick wasn't sure he heard Willie right.

"She was, um … shimmying up against Josh like some stripper on a pole. I've never seen Jessie act that way in all the years I've known her. She kept asking him to take her out of there. She wanted to go someplace private. Josh said he'd get a cab."

"I don't believe it." But Nick knew Willie wouldn't lie.

"I couldn't believe it either. I came over when she started acting, uh, strange. I was standing right behind them. I said I'd take her home. She turned into a wild woman. She yelled at me to leave her and Josh alone. It took Bill, the director, and me to force her into the limo. I pushed the security locks so she couldn't leap out on the way home. That's how much she scared me."

"Mary, call Jessie's doctor." Lyle straightened up. "We need to take a blood test ASAP and get it to a discreet lab."

"Blood test?" Mary asked, backing towards the kitchen.

"Sounds like a date-rape drug. We have a short window to prove it, or traces of the drug disappear from her system."

Nick swore under his breath.

He wished he had something to punch.

Like Josh Elliot's face.

*

Croquet. Someone was banging a ball with a mallet, stroke after pounding stroke. Her head was the ball. Jessie cracked one eye open … Nick snored lightly beside her. Sunlight peeked through the drapes. She was in bed? How did she get here?

The party … The last thing Jessie remembered was laughing with Josh about a drink she spilled on their table. Coming home, a blank.

A wave of nausea swept through her. Jessie sat up gingerly, her face hot, like someone had flipped on a sunlamp. She scrambled out of bed. Dizzy, she stumbled to the bathroom and kneeled in front of the toilet. Her stomach rebelled, black and yellow splotches blinking in front of her eyes with every heave. And then she felt Nick's arms fold hers as he slid to the floor behind her.

Her stomach finally empty, Jessie collapsed against Nick's chest. "I-I don't know what's wrong with me. Feel like … I drank a quart of vodka." She tried to focus on Nick's blurry face. "I only had two or three drinks." Nick handed her a tissue and she wiped off her mouth.

"Willie told me Josh kept refilling your glass." His expression tight, Nick studied her. "Maybe you didn't notice."

"What?" Was Nick angry? "I'm sorry." She choked on a sob. "I don't remember. I don't even remember coming home. I'm sorry. I--"

"You have nothing to apologize for." Nick brushed her tears away. "It was Josh's fault."

Had she gotten so drunk she couldn't remember getting drunk? "It wasn't Josh's--"

"Don't defend him," Nick said. "Never again."

"I don't understand." Another wave of nausea hit her. "God, I'm sick ..."

*

In Pennsylvania, Max and Carlo stopped off at a Christmas factory and toy outlet. They didn't arrive home until late afternoon. Max intended to decorate the living room for Anthony. This would be a Christmas the boy would never forget, a magical holiday with his father. The first of many family traditions Max would establish for them. He wanted Anthony to grow up with good memories of their times together. He was rescuing the boy just in time.

Max prepared a small antipasto of Italian meats and roasted peppers for dinner. Before he ate, he called his plastic surgeon at his home. Max arranged for the scar on his hand to be sanded off immediately. Now it was time to read the reviews from last night with his dinner. Had Jessica received the raves she so deserved?

To begin the evening, Max opened the NEW YORK POST'S gossip section, the tabloid with the dirt. One look at the headline and Max threw his head back and laughed out loud. Intoxicated Jessica Kendle Steps Out On Nick McDeare. A photo showed Jessica wrapped around Joshua Elliott like rabid ivy. Max bit into the Genoa salami in his salad, relishing it as much as the blurb under the photo:

Is the Kendle-McDeare romance already on the rocks? Falling down drunk, the bride-to-be was all over her leading man at Nordic Nirvana last night. Judging by Josh Elliot's smile for the cameras, he was enjoying himself. What must go on behind the curtains when it comes to rehearsing those red-hot love scenes the critics are raving about?

Losing his smile, Max realized he was shivering. He put the paper down and checked all the windows in the house, the furnace, and the thermostat. His eyes bulged. It was fifty degrees. *Che cosa l'inferno?*

*

After going ten rounds with Jessie, Nick trotted down the stairs to the kitchen. She'd woken up from a long nap, furious to discover the curtain had gone up an hour ago. Without her. And Anthony had been trying to talk to him all day. Nick had been too consumed with worry over Jessie to focus on the boy. Now Anthony was at Zane's for the weekend. More guilt. Mary had been so upset by everything he'd sent her to her sister's for some overnight R and R.

Lyle was waiting for Nick in the breakfast nook. He was wearing his finest, beat-up jeans, a Mets sweatshirt, and a Knicks cap. "How's Jessie?"

"On the mend and not happy she's missing the show tonight. She thinks it's because of a hangover. I have to tell her the truth," Nick said grimly. "She has to know what her golden boy did to her."

"Not until Leon calls from the lab."

"It's nine o'clock. Where the hell is he?"

"Cool your jets. The police lab's a zoo. Leon's doing me a special favor. He said he'd let us know today."

The doorbell rang. "Maybe Leon decided to hand-deliver them." Nick dashed down the hallway.

"I just got your message." Bundled up against the chilly weather, Abbie burst through the front door. "Has anyone told you your command of English goes to hell when you're mad? I could barely understand you. All I got was Jessie's sick, and Josh should be castrated."

"Where've you been all day?"

"I was with a friend in from Italy for a few days. Why?"

"Why weren't you with Josh last night?"

Looking at him like he was nuts, Abbie said, "What's the big deal? I was supposed to have dinner with a new lipstick exec last night. I waited an hour. The jerk stood me up."

"Your boyfriend's the jerk. Josh played bartender for Jessie at Quill's party last night. He slipped something into her drink. Barton thinks it was a date-rape drug."

"That's ridiculous."

"Tell me something. If you hadn't had dinner with a potential employer last night, would you've gone with Josh to the party?"

"I'd planned on it."

"When did you get the call about this dinner?"

"Monday afternoon."

"Monday morning I told Jessie I couldn't go to the party, that I had to work on the manuscript all week. Right before she left to meet Josh for an interview. Then you suddenly get a call about a business dinner Thursday night. The guy never shows up. You ever hear of this company?"

"It's, uh, brand new."

"Google it. I bet it doesn't exist."

"Are you saying …" Abbie's face dropped. "You think Josh got me out of the way to move in on Jessie?" Nick watched doubt creep across her face. "Does Jessie know what you suspect?"

"Barton insists we wait for the lab results. Jessie thinks she's hungover."

Lyle hurried down the hall towards them. "Abbie, hi. Hey, Bree just called. Martinelli's on the move. I'm heading to the Bronx."

"Damn." Nick's anxiety spiraled higher. "I belong there with you."

"You go with Lyle," Abbie said quickly. "I'll stay with Jessie and cover for you." She tugged a stocking cap off her head, minky hair springing loose.

"Thanks, Abbie." Nick snatched his trench coat from the closet, rapidly filling her in on Mary and Anthony's whereabouts.

"Wait. The GPS tracking system. It's in my car, still in your garage. I never got around to moving it." Abbie dug in her purse for the key. "If the Honda's in the alley, attach the tracker."

Nick and Lyle stared at each other.

Abbie grinned. "I guess you two don't know everything after all."

*

Roberto Martinelli lounged in the limo's backseat as it breezed across the Long Island Expressway, his cell pressed to his ear. Damn. Voice mail. "It's Roberto," he whispered." Just got back a couple of hours ago. I'm on my way to the Bronx right now. Should be in Jersey in a couple hours. Hope my absence didn't disrupt our progress. Tell … never mind. I'll tell her myself. I have a surprise for my girl, something soft and cuddly."

Smiling in anticipation, Roberto clicked off. Marcella had chosen to stay in Italy, closing out her mother's affairs, visiting with her adoring brothers and sisters. Roberto would be able to spend every night in Jersey City until his wife returned.

It had been five long, miserable days since he'd been part of the action in the Jersey City condo. It had become an addiction. A part of his life he couldn't live without.

*

After Nick and Lyle left, Abbie poured herself some brandy and made a beeline for the computer. She Googled Wet 'n Wicked Cosmetics, holding her breath. Nothing. Nick had been right. She'd been stupid not to check out the company when she'd gotten the call. Was she that desperate for a job? And Josh had played her for a fool.

Fuming, Abbie headed back to the kitchen for something to eat. She spotted the NEW YORK POST on the island, open to the gossip page. Abbie sank onto a stool and scanned the trash. Jessie looked like a lush, a slutty lush. What a vile piece of garbage.

"Oh my God." Jessie whispered over Abbie's shoulder. She grabbed the paper out of Abbie's hands. "Oh my God! No wonder Nick was angry."

"Listen, Nick's not angry." Abbie put a hand on Jessie's shoulder. "He knows how the press loves to make something out of nothing." Abbie looked down at the photo, Josh aiming a cheesy smile at the camera. She'd love to boil Josh in oil.

"I'll never live this down." Jessie tossed the paper across the kitchen. "I get drunk once, just once, and it makes the papers. I can only imagine Twitter. I might as well have invited the press to the watch-Jessie-Kendle-self-destruct marathon." Jessie pressed her fingers against her forehead.

"Jeremy will handle it," Abbie said calmly, working on keeping her fury in check. "He's an ace at damage control."

"Where is Nick anyway?"

"Uh," Abbie glanced out the window at Lyle's place, relieved to see lights on, "he's at Lyle's." Abbie spotted the satellite dish on Lyle's porch roof. "One of these satellite sports marathon things. Nick wants you to get some uninterrupted sleep. He said he'll see you in the morning."

Jessie moaned. "He's too sweet. After I made a spectacle of myself last night. Over a man he loathes."

If Jessie knew what Nick was really up to, would she feel the same way? Or would she want to tear Mr. Sweetness from limb to limb and call off the wedding? "Hey," she said brightly, "let's microwave some popcorn and watch an old movie. And then it's back to bed. Tomorrow's a matinee day. Can't let Valentine get too comfy in your role."

*

Zane's mom made spaghetti and meatballs for dinner. Zane's big sister Monica ignored Anthony and Zane, but his older brother Dylan played in a band and was cool and joked around with them. Best of all was Zane's dog, big and black and curly. Zane said his pedigreed name was too long to remember, but Zane called him Clumper. Clumper followed the two of them everywhere.

Mrs. Harwell let the two boys camp out in sleeping bags on the living room floor and watch TV all night, Clumper stretched out between the sleeping bags. Anthony stroked the dog's soft coat. "I want a dog like this. I've been begging my mom for a dog forever. I'm going to ask for Christmas."

"He's a Portuguese water dog," Zane said, playing with Clumper's ears. "Mom got him from a rescue place. The people who had him before were getting a divorce. Clumper's supposed to be the whole family's dog, but he's really mine. Mom says these dogs usually like one person the most."

"You're lucky. I'd give anything to have a dog love me more than anyone else."

*

Rubbing a palm over his chin, Nick waited for Martinelli to emerge from Bottoms Up like a cockroach out of a cabinet. Lyle had parked his Bronco behind a garbage dumpster fifty yards down the alley. A green Honda sat empty ahead of them, the GPS under its bumper.

His cell jangled, Nick scrambling to answer. Leon. "Miss Kendle was administered Rohypnol, a date-rape drug, Mr. McDeare. Mixed with the booze in her system, she's lucky she's not in a coma. Tell Barton I've got the paperwork for him, whenever he wants to swing by."

"Thanks." Nick clicked off and stared out the windshield. "You were right. Elliot gave Jessie a date-rape drug. Rohypnol." He turned to Barton "I want the son of a bitch arrested."

"Shhh. There's Martinelli. And turn off your damn cell." The don slid through a rear door of Bottoms Up and climbed behind the Honda's wheel. "We'll deal with Josh later. Focus on Martinelli."

Powering off his cell, Nick smothered his anger. He grabbed the GPS screen and watched the red blinking light partner the Honda down the alley. When the car turned onto the far street, Barton began to follow.

The two men were silent as they trailed Martinelli onto the Cross-Bronx Expressway. The Honda stayed on the highway into Manhattan, exiting onto the Henry Hudson Parkway. Martinelli was moving at a good clip, racing towards lower Manhattan.

"We got him." Nick kept his eyes on the GPS screen. "He's turning off …"

"The Holland Tunnel. Heading for Jersey City."

Nick held his breath as they glided through the tunnel. Tunnels gave him trouble, and this one was encased in the Hudson River. He focused on the GPS until they were out of the sardine can. Following the light, Nick directed Lyle through Jersey City's gritty streets, gradually morphing into gentrified brownstones, funky restaurants, boutiques, and massive condos. They tracked Martinelli to a luxury high-rise along the riverfront. Roberto was nowhere in sight when they pulled up.

Across the Hudson, the lights of lower Manhattan winked back at them, a zillion pinpoints soaring into the midnight sky. In the distance, Lady Liberty raised her torch over New York Harbor. One World Trade Center loomed over the skyline, a glistening monument. Beside them, sleek yachts bobbed on a private inlet. "Look at this joint," Lyle said, whistling. "The real estate has to be off the charts."

"According to the GPS he pulled into that private underground garage. Permit only."

Barton's brow kneaded. "It's pointless to talk to the doorman. Fosselli or Martinelli would be using an assumed name. And we risk tipping them off in any event."

"So we see how long he's in there." Nick peered up at the windows. Martinelli was behind one of those windows, with God knows whom. And every second Nick didn't know the answer to that question put Anthony in more danger.

"This could be a long night." Lyle backed into a vacant parking spot.

Slipping down into his seat, Nick folded his arms and closed his eyes. "You take the first watch."

Lyle was right. It was a long night. Martinelli never reappeared. Tired and hungry, Nick and Lyle gave up at seven in the morning, heading for a busy intersection and the nearest diner. Nick's clothing had more wrinkles than Methuselah, and he needed a shower. "Fosselli's not in that building," Nick said, rubbing his eyes. "Martinelli wouldn't spend the whole night with the SOB."

"Martinelli's got a babe stashed up there. Has to be it."

"Everything I've read about him says he's a straight arrow. No ladies on the side."

"That only means no one's caught him yet."

"But so what if he has a mistress? They all do."

"I don't know. Maybe she's someone in the public eye? Something's wacky here."

*

Jessie watched Nick trudge across the back yard, hair hanging in his eyes. His trench coat looked like he'd slept in it. She met him on the porch. "Where were you all morning? I've been worried. Mary got home from Violet's and didn't have a clue. When your cell kept going to voice mail I scouted out Lyle's place. You were gone."

"Sorry to worry you." Nick kissed her, his stubble scratchy. "You look much better."

"And you look terrible. So where were you?"

"Lyle and I had business to take care of."

"What kind of business?"

"Come on, honey. I need to talk to you." He headed for the den.

"Is this about the gossip columns?" Jessie said slowly. "It's not how it looked. There's nothing between Josh and me."

"I know there's not." After shrugging off his coat, Nick closed the den doors and led Jessie to the couch. He looked serious, the way ...

"Anthony!" Jessie cried. "Did something happen to Anthony?!"

"Anthony's fine. I'm sorry, didn't mean to scare you." Nick dropped down next to her. "Come here. I love you." Nick kissed the top of her head. He drew back, looking down at her. "Jess," he said gently, "answer a question for me, okay? When did you tell Josh I wouldn't be at the party?"

"Um, I think ... I think I told him before our interview Monday morning. He said Abbie wasn't coming either so we could look out for each other."

"Interesting. It seems Josh knew Abbie wouldn't be at the party before Abbie knew she wouldn't be at the party." Nick told Jessie about Abbie and a new lipstick company, the exec never showing up for an interview.

"So," she said impatiently, "what does this—"

"We need to fast-forward to the party. I don't know how to say this, so I'll just say it. Barton had a blood test run on you at the police lab. A drug was found in your system. It's called Rohypnol. It's ... a date-rape drug."

"A date--?"

"Willie told me Josh played bartender for you all night at Nirvana," Nick rasped. "He dropped a drug into your drink."

Jessie felt like she'd slipped into a nightmare. She was hearing the words, but they didn't compute. "This-this is ridiculous. There has to be a mistake."

"Think about it. Your behavior was more than being drunk. You wouldn't behave that way, not even drunk."

"Behave that-- You mean besides what's in the tabloids?"

"Willie," Nick said quietly, "was privy to everything that night. You, uh, you were all over Josh. That's what the tabloids picked up. But there's more. You don't remember attacking Willie when he told you it was time to go home?"

Numb, she shook her head.

"He needed Bill and Quill's help to force you into the limo. Willie had to lock all the doors to keep you from jumping out. You sang at the top of your voice. And then you fell dead asleep. A drugged sleep."

"I thought ..." Jessie buried her face in her hands. "You told me I was drunk."

"That's what it looked like to people who don't know you, what the tabloids reported. But you were drugged, not drunk." Nick's eyes narrowed. "Even though Josh made sure to loosen you up with plenty of alcohol. None of this is your fault."

Why didn't she feel better? There was more going on here, distorted, swirling undercurrents. "I don't understand. Why would—"

"Josh got rid of Abbie for the night. And he didn't have to worry about me being there either. He kept your drink full. He--"

"Listen to me." Jessie put a hand to her head, trying to keep the facts straight. Maybe she did ingest a drug. She could believe that, as bizarre as it sounded. But the rest— "What you're saying, it's not right. Josh would never do something like that to me. I've known him forever. He--"

"Your loyalty's admirable, but you have to pull your head out of the sand. The man's not who you think he is. He's a sick--"

"Stop it!" Jessie pushed herself off the couch and strode to the mantle. "Your hatred of Josh has gone over the top. Is this the business you were taking care of this morning? Having a drug test done on me so you could crucify Josh?"

Nick sprang to his feet. "You have to see--"

"Any number of people could've slipped something into my drink! Assuming it was intentional and assuming it was meant for me." She squeezed her eyes shut, trying to remember the party. Josh, being so considerate and bringing her drinks. Josh, filling her glass whenever it got low. Her glass. Jessie snapped her fingers. "My glass sat on the table for long stretches of time. What if--"

"Jessie, wake up. Josh sets Abbie up with a phony dinner interview. He knows she's hungry for work. He plies you with drinks. He wants you. Can't you see--"

"Stop shouting at me. I see a man blinded with jealousy! And it's not Josh. It's you, Nick, you. This has to stop!"

"Me? You're the one who's blind. And look who's shouting. Josh belongs behind bars. He--"

"Think of what you're saying. You have no proof. You'd try to ruin the man's career, all because--"

"I don't give a shit about his career." Nick waved his arms. "For God's sake, he intended to rape you!"

That dark light in Nick's eyes, the irrational anger. It frightened her. He had to get a handle on her career, her working with rugged male actors, or their life together would be impossible. Jessie poked a finger in his chest. "Quit wasting your time on Josh and find the real culprit, the person who hurt me. Stop this jealousy and get to the truth."

"This is about the truth." Nick forked a hand through his hair. "Do you remember how you never listened to me about Gianni either? You defended--"

"How dare you use Gianni?" Jessie fought for control, drawing a deep breath. "One thing has nothing to do with the other. This conversation's over, do you hear me? Josh is not Gianni. That's low, really low." Jessie headed for the door. "After the last few years I've learned how the law works. You can't do a thing if I refuse to press charges. And I refuse."

"Jessie--"

"I'm going to the theater early to talk to Josh. He must think his leading lady's a nut after the other night!" She threw the doors open and dashed upstairs.

When Willie arrived a half hour later, Jessie marched out the front door with him, Nick nowhere in sight. She waded through the paparazzi with a casual, "No comment." She wouldn't let the bloodsuckers make her cower. She'd done nothing wrong. At least Nick had told her that much she could believe.

But reality sank in on the drive to the theater. Jessie stared out the window, tears welling. According to Nick, someone had put a date-rape drug in her drink. Why? To rape her? Or to watch her make a fool of herself? She knew in her heart of hearts it wasn't Josh. But if not Josh, who hated her that much?

And then the fog lifted. How dense could she be?

She'd set a trap, but she'd miscalculated, never suspecting danger would strike outside the theater walls.

Valentine York hated her that much.

*

After getting nowhere with Jessie, Nick holed up in his office. He called Willie, cautioning him to stay backstage and watch Elliot. If Jessie was too stubborn to protect herself, Nick would do it for her. He phoned Lyle and nagged him to do something about Josh, but Barton reminded Nick there was no proof Josh drugged Jessie. It was pointless to work on his manuscript. The ending kept eluding him, and he was in no mood. He needed distance. He wished Anthony were home.

Nick dragged Martinelli's RICO file onto his desk. He'd already gone through it once. Now he scrutinized the thick document in minute detail, devouring it all over again. Nick flipped through page after page, scanning the bios and photos and federal agents' scribbles. More of the same, the history of a Mafia don and his machine in the making. Aldo Zappella. He knuckled his eyes, the words and pictures blurring. Remembering Aldo's lush of a brother-in-law Ian Wexley. He hated Jessie. Blamed Andrew for blackballing him from Broadway ...

Suddenly, Nick stopped, his finger on a black-and-white photo. It looked like it was taken through a telephoto lens, the image grainy. Martinelli sat in the front seat of a car with someone on his lap, his or her back to the camera.

Grabbing a magnifying glass, Nick took a closer look, scanning every inch of the photo. The location was Bottoms Up, the back alley. And they were sitting in the Honda. The unidentified person--someone small—had long dark curls. Martinelli's face was bent over ...

Nick's heart picked up speed. He checked the photo's date. Three months ago. RICO considered it nothing. The notes said it was probably some piece of ass Martinelli was banging, maybe a call girl.

RICO had gotten sloppy. Or bored.

The back of Nick's neck began to tingle, his fingers trembling.

This was no call girl on Martinelli's lap.

It was a child.

CHAPTER 14

Grabbing his jacket, the RICO photo, and the magnifying glass, Nick rushed across the back yard, shivering. He'd called ahead, Barton expecting him. The swirling wind kicked dead leaves into the air. Dark clouds scudded across an ominous sky. Snow was predicted.

Lyle was on the computer in his den. Nick tossed the picture and magnifying glass onto the desk. The detective looked like a dog with a juicy bone as he studied the photo. "RICO blew her off," Nick said. "Never looked twice. But it's a kid."

"This wouldn't mean a thing to RICO." Lyle examined the photo closely. "They're looking for narcotics, meetings with wise guys, hard evidence." Barton tossed the magnifying glass aside and stretched back in his chair, hands laced on his head. "A child?"

"Martinelli and his wife never had kids."

"So let's play with what we know." Barton straightened up. "This photo was taken in the alley behind Bottoms Up. Roberto Martinelli's sitting in a Honda parked behind a strip club with a child. We know he uses that car and Bottoms Up as a cover for his visits to Jersey City."

"He's working hard to keep whatever's going on in that high-rise a secret. The little girl may, or may not, be connected."

"We need to find out what's happening in Jersey and if it concerns the child."

"This could be it, Lyle. His Achilles heel."

Standing up, Barton stretched. "Got time for a drink?"

"I've got the whole day and night." Nick wasn't exactly on Jessie's list of favorites for the moment.

"Later we can order in Mexican from that new place on Lexington."

"I'm going to call Bree and tell her about the photo. She might have some ideas."

*

After the matinee, Josh stopped at Jessie's dressing room, hesitating, then knocked on the door and poked his head into the room. "Um, how're you feeling? I never got a chance to talk to you before the show, rushed in late. I called yesterday, left a message. I never thought having fun over a few drinks was going to turn into," he threw up his hands, "a circus. What happened?"

Jessie turned from her dressing-table mirror. "I wasn't in any shape to talk to anyone. I'd like to talk to you now though." She smiled. "Got a minute?"

Josh let out a breath. She didn't sound pissed off. Josh didn't worry about other people too often. It was a new feeling. He slipped into the room. "I have a meeting with my publicist in a few minutes. That guy can talk. As soon as he leaves, how about a bite between shows? My treat. I'll send in from the 2nd Avenue Deli."

"Great. Just a salad for me."

"Listen," Josh smothered a grin, "how did you like Valentine calling off for the matinee?"

"George says she had some kind of emergency at home."

"Broke a nail."

"A claw."

"Thank God you're back," Josh said fervently. "Valentine screws up the blocking. And she left my ass hanging out more than once."

"Nora mentioned the rumba number. Valentine's stepping down on the count of one instead of before the music begins?"

"And landing on my foot. The whole damn beat's thrown off."

"James told me she's off on the harmony, too."

"She missed the first note and ended up singing straight melody with me. Not exactly a dazzling finish."

"I'm sorry."

"Not your fault. I hate working with an understudy. And she ain't Jessie Kendle." Josh backed towards the door. "Ah, have you seen Abbie the last couple of days?"

"Sure, why?"

"Nothing. I can't reach her. Have to run. Be back soon." Josh sprinted for his dressing room. He'd tried calling Abbie all day yesterday, but he kept getting her voice mail. Josh was dying to hear her bitch about being stood up. Abbie was damned hot when she was angry. He wasn't about to dump her until it was Jessie's turn for some Josh action.

*

"No," Clint hissed into his cell, "I'm not in some bar, Aldo." He made his way down his apartment's stairwell. "But I'm not wasting another fucking Saturday. Barton's a recluse. There's nothing going on there. I'll check in enough to earn my pay. And I'm sick of Hinkie and her bitching."

"I wish I knew what Roberto sees in you."

"It's not my good looks? Listen, tell Martinelli I need a tux for this wedding. On his dime. There's only a couple more weeks till we take the kid. And I want detailed instructions. No surprises." Clint headed outside. Still afternoon and the street lamps were on. Clint hated winter with its muddy skies and filthy snow. Might as well park his ass in the Arctic and play with the penguins.

*

By the time Josh was back Jessie had the deli delivery set out on the side table, next to the couch. Jessie knew what she needed to say. The trick was how to say it. "Josh, um, about Nirvana." Jessie nibbled at her carrot salad, picking out a rasin. He

- 134 -

bit into his salami sandwich. "First, I want to say I'm sorry if I made things, well, look bad for you in the tabloids."

"Jessie, no. Don't even think about it. You weren't your--"

"There's more. I don't know how to-- It's like this. Lyle Barton had a blood test done on me that night. Someone slipped a date-rape drug into one of my drinks."

Staring at her, Josh froze mid-chew.

"I know you were refilling my drinks all night--"

"Jessie," he choked, "I hope you don't think," Josh swallowed the lump of sandwich, "that I'd ever--"

"Oh, God, no. I know. But, well, I was wondering if maybe you saw a stranger hanging around our table? Or ... did anyone else handle my drinks?"

"There were people around our table all night. I was the only one who touched your drinks. But wait, there was a guy ... A couple of fans actually asked me for an autograph." He chuckled. "It doesn't happen that often, so I remember. The one guy held your drink while I signed his menu."

"Do you remember what he looked like?"

"Mmm. Green eyes. Wearing a blond rug. Kind of striking."

"I know who you're talking about. He spoke to me briefly. Was he in plain sight the entire time?"

"I turned around for a few seconds to give another guy an autograph." Josh sat forward. "Uh, I hate to say this, but have you considered Valentine? She rarely goes to these things, but that night she shows up through dinner and afterwards? And you have to admit she had motive. She did go on in your place last night."

Setting her salad down, Jessie said, "You know all the problems I've been having. Now I'm drugged at the first party Valentine attends full-time since we began rehearsals?"

"Valentine York would drug her own mother to play Christine. We've both heard the stories."

Jessie thought about the trap she'd set for Valentine. She was about to tell Josh, but she shut her mouth at the last minute. The fewer people who knew, the better. There was one card she hadn't played yet. It would have to do until her trap was sprung. "I'm calling Bill."

A call to Bill Rudolph twenty minutes later produced immediate results. Valentine disappeared from the backstage area that night. Bill promised Valentine would be rendered all but invisible. And George Penfield remained in his booth, speaking to no one and glaring at Jessie. Jessie returned his stare, a small smile playing over her lips. She didn't like pulling rank. But sometimes being the star of the show meant more than a standing ovation.

Clapping her hands, Nora was ecstatic. "It's about time George realized you're not some gypsy off the bus from Iowa." Nora helped Jessie into her wedding gown. "You're Broadway's brightest star and Bill Rudolph's most profitable investment. That means something, Jessie."

*

"And so Zane's brother Dylan had to do a book report." Anthony stopped for a breath and finished the last of his strawberry pancake. Nick and Mary exchanged amused smiles. The boy hadn't stopped talking since he'd gotten home from Zane's an hour ago. "Only Dylan didn't want to read the book so he got the movie On Demand and we watched it with him. It was about a guy who escapes from prison and gets revenge on everyone who put him in jail. THE COUNT OF MONTY CRISCO."

"Monte Cristo," Nick corrected.

"Monty Crisco sounds better."

Jessie clipped down the back stairs. Nick hadn't seen her since their fight yesterday morning. He'd come home from Lyle's in the middle of the night and found Jessie asleep in a third-floor bedroom. Was she still furious with him, or was it a more ordinary mad?

"Mom, can I have a dog?" Anthony begged. "P-l-e-a-s-e? Zane has a Portuguese water dog. He'll protect the house. You said I could get a dog when I was older."

"A dog's a lot of work." Jessie poured a cup of coffee. "You're in school all day."

"Mary could take care of him when I'm at school."

"Who's going to take care of him?" Mary stopped stirring her pot of chili.

"Uh, Dad?" Anthony's eyes pleaded with Nick.

Nick had a mutt when he was growing up in Tokyo, a scruffy terrier named Haywire. "Sorry, Bongo, this one's up to your mother."

"No," Jessie said firmly. "You've got Hamlet."

"Cats are for girls." Anthony shoved his plate across the table. It sailed over the edge, cracking into pieces.

"Anthony, look what you've done," Jessie said. "Get the broom to clean that up."

"It's your fault! Why can't you be a normal mother like Mrs. Harwell?!" Anthony raced across the kitchen and up the stairs.

"I don't know what to do with him anymore." Jessie buried her face in her hands.

"Like mother, like son," Mary said, getting the broom and dustpan from the pantry. "Yesterday I could hear you shouting all the way down in the basement."

"Um, about that, could we talk, Nick, before we deal with Anthony?" Jessie peered at Nick over her coffee cup.

Nodding, Nick slowly followed Jessie to the back porch.

"First of all," Jessie said, "I'm sorry I yelled yesterday. But I talked to Josh about what happened. He remembered a man holding my drink while he signed some autographs."

"I'm not interested in Josh's lies."

"There's more, things going on you don't know about. Valentine Yor--"

"First a strange man, now your understudy. What's next, the butler? The problem's your leading man, but you refuse to see it."

"Enough!" Jessie whipped a hand through her hair. "This is about my work. I know what I'm talking about. You don't understand."

"Enlighten me."

"How? You won't listen to a word I say." Jessie took a deep breath. "I don't want to fight with you anymore. Christmas is around the corner. Anthony hasn't had a real Christmas since Andrew died. Neither have I."

Taking a step forward, Nick cupped Jessie's face with both hands. "I don't want to fight either," he said softly. "But I worry about your safety. That drug mixed with the alcohol could've put you in a coma. Will you at least tell Josh his services won't be needed at the wedding? The further apart he and I are the better. Will you do that for me?"

Her eyes haunted, Jessie searched Nick's face. "Sure," she said quietly. "I'll talk to Josh for you." Nick felt a continental divide opening between them he couldn't cross. Not with all his energy poured into finding Gianni. He couldn't focus on Josh at the same time and prove to Jessie this was more than Nick McDeare being a jealous fool.

*

Abbie was waiting in Josh's dressing room when he arrived for the Sunday matinee. Josh looped his arms around her waist, those sleepy blue eyes on her face. "Hey, stranger, where—"

"The good old days are over." Abbie pushed him away.

"What's wrong?"

"You can stand there with a straight face and ask that question?"

"You want to clue me in? What are we talking about?"

The bastard played dumb so well. Went with the peroxide. "You forget I'm a private investigator. I got my license in L.A." Abbie enjoyed the wary look creeping into Josh's eyes. "You set me up with that phony lipstick exec the night of the party, so you could make a move on Jessie. What I find revolting is that you had to drug her in order to lure her into your bed."

"You're nuts. I did not --"

"Doesn't say much for your sexual prowess, having to use a date-rape drug." Abbie laughed in his face. "Don't try to compete with Nick. You'll lose every time."

"Get out of here." Josh's face twisted. "I can have any woman I want. More women than McDeare can count."

"Yeah, yeah, yeah. Don't worry, I'm going. I'm meeting a world-renowned artist for lunch. Gorgeous. Sexy. And he doesn't need chemicals to seduce a lady." She sashayed to the door. "Ta."

*

After Jessie left for the matinee, Nick found Anthony at his desk, doing homework. "That was an ugly display of temper downstairs."

"I'm sorry, but Mom promises things and then she takes them back. It's the same as lying. She promised I could get a dog when I got older. Well, I'm older."

"I don't know about promises your mom made. But you and I had a deal. Good behavior in exchange for my silence on being called to school. So did you lie to me, too, when you broke our promise?"

"I forgot." Anthony put down his pencil. "But I want a dog. I don't have any brothers or sisters. A dog would be company."

Nick tended to agree with him. "Give me some time to work on your mom. Maybe I can get her to come around."

"By Christmas?"

"I'm not sure I can work my magic in that short a time. But I promise I'll try." That squeezed out a smile. "Now. What did you want to talk to me about last week? I'm sorry I've been so distracted."

Closing the door, Anthony hurried back to the desk. "Zane saw Daddy Andrew."

"You mean ... ?" Nick's breath caught. "When?"

"The night he slept over after the basketball game. Zane woke me up afterwards. The room was cold like when he visits."

The night after the game. Nick remembered. He'd been hot so he'd opened a window, and then it had turned bitterly cold. Had Andrew been trying to contact him? "Did Andrew say anything to Zane?"

"That I should follow your instructions. You know, about what I should do if-- Does this mean someone's going to try and take me?" Anthony's eyes widened.

"No," Nick lied, "of course not. Andrew just wants to make sure you're always extra careful," he soothed, a knot in his gut. Gianni must be close. Very close. "Let's keep it between us for now," Nick said lightly. "It might upset your mother."

"Okay. But you'll work on Mom about a dog?"

"Hmm? Yeah. It'll just take a while." Nick rose and headed for the door. "You know what to do about what happened downstairs, right?"

"Apologize to Mom. I know."

"And Mary. She ended up cleaning up the mess you made. It should've been you sweeping up that plate. This wasn't Mary's fault or your mom's. It was yours."

Making his way to his office, Nick dropped into a chair and fanned his fingers over his mouth. Andrew had shown himself to Zane. His powers were dimming, but he was still around. And he knew what was going down.

Andrew wasn't about to say goodbye until Gianni was gone.

*

The weeks before Christmas were a frenetic haze for Jessie. Eight performances a week plus special matinees for the drama students in the tri-state area. Last-minute decisions for the wedding. Final fittings for her gown. Dozens of scripts to be read. Offers from talk shows and prime-time television. Two days of taping a song for a Christmas special. And Jeremy had arranged an all-important NEW YORK TIMES interview, Jessie's chance to explain to her fans what had happened at Nordic Nirvana.

A week before Christmas, Jessie finally talked to Josh about not singing at the wedding. They met in her dressing room between shows. She told him they were trying to keep the ceremony simple.

"You're lying." Josh gave her a hard stare. "For him. You're trying not to hurt my feelings, and I love you for it. But this is about Nick. He thinks I drugged you."

"It doesn't matter what he thinks. What matters is what I think. I-I really don't want to get into this. It's bad enough with Nick ..."

"Bad enough? You want to explain that?" Josh flicked his head back, flinging the hair out of his eyes.

"Nick thinks the idea of Valentine drugging me is ridiculous." Jessie sighed. "He didn't want to hear it."

"Look," Josh took her hand, "I don't want to put you in an awkward position. I'll stay away from the wedding completely."

"No. You're my dear friend. I want you at my wedding. Please. For me."

"For you, I'll be there. And for the record," he leaned over and kissed her cheek, "I believe Valentine drugged you."

After Josh left, she felt better. It was comforting to have a handful of friends believe her, even if her fiancé wasn't one of them.

Focusing on Christmas, Jessie pushed the subject of Valentine out of her mind. An eight-foot Colorado blue spruce and a six-foot Douglas fir were sitting in buckets of water in the back yard. She and Nick were having a few close friends over for Christmas Eve. But the house was nowhere near ready for the holidays.

Over breakfast the next morning, Jessie suggested they hire a decorator.

Anthony objected so vociferously you would've thought she'd canceled Santa Claus. "Zane's mom and dad put up their tree and decorated their own apartment. Why can't we be a regular family?"

Jessie looked at Mary.

"I can't do it alone," Mary said.

"I'll help," Nick said, shoving a piece of bacon in his mouth.

"You?" Jessie asked. "Your manuscript's due in less than two weeks."

"It's almost finished. I sketched out the ending yesterday."

"You and I can decorate, Dad," Anthony chimed in. "It'll be fun. Zane's mom put popcorn and berries on their tree."

"Honey, Nick would eat the popcorn."

Nick leaned forward. "You don't think I can do this?"

"Hamlet would do a better job."

"You're on."

*

Pacing his apartment, Lyle restlessly flicked channels. He'd tried every which way he knew to get his hands on the tenants' list for Fifty-Five Washington Street in Jersey City. He called in favors, badgered every contact he knew, and tried to bribe a guy in the doorman's union. Every avenue led to a brick wall.

He shadowed Martinelli relentlessly, racking up useless mileage on endless trips to Jersey City. He knew it was idiotic to sit outside the Jersey building for long stretches, often overnight. But it was better than sitting home alone. Staring at Martinelli's apartment building and playing games on his iPhone kept his mind free of memories. Memories led Barton to a dark place that beckoned seductively, promising eternal peace if he found his service revolver.

But the price of peace was too high. Anthony Brady McDeare's life was at stake. Meanwhile, Martinelli's tail was still plastered on Jessie's street. He hoped the crone was bored silly.

Christmas was only a few days away. Barton clicked every TV channel on the guide. He should be buying a tree at the discount lot on Jewel Avenue in Flushing.

Marcos always saved him the best pine of the bunch. The house smelled of sugar cookies and fruitcake. Dina would search for hidden presents--

Flinging himself into the chair, Lyle slammed the door on the memory. He quickly punched in ESPN. January second couldn't come soon enough.

*

Max poured himself a grappa and pulled up the NEW YORK TIMES magazine on his laptop. Jessica was supposed to have an exclusive interview in the current issue. But he was freezing.

Leaping to his feet, Max jiggled the thermostat, cursing the moronic heating repairman who had sworn there was nothing wrong with his furnace. He woke up every night in a sweat after his recurring dream, only to freeze in a room that belonged in an igloo. And that dream, the same night after night. A dog. Anthony racing to McDeare, Barton, and Jessica behind the fence ...

Ridicolo!

Anthony didn't even have a dog.

Shrugging on a sweater, Max sat down, going back to his laptop. Ah, there it was. Bypassing Jessica's drivel about the play and her upcoming marriage, Max zapped to the good part. The reporter asked the big star about the "incident" at Nordic Nirvana and let Jessica Kendle speak for herself.

He read rapidly:

Marlene, I'm always very careful about how much I drink, because I eat sparingly. I didn't remember coming home. I didn't even remember the last hour of the party. How would I get drunk on two or three drinks? The answer is shocking. My fiancé had a blood test run on me, and it revealed I'd ingested a date-rape drug. Someone spiked my drink. The police are investigating.

Reading on was delightful. The reporter was shocked. She hoped Ms. Kendle found the perpetrator. Max sipped his grappa. It felt good to be the perpetrator. Jessica was mortified by her behavior that night? He laughed heartily. That was nothing compared to what was in store for her on New Year's Eve.

He couldn't wait to see Jessica's behavior after that.

CHAPTER 15

A couple of days before Christmas, Nick signed off on his novel. He detached THE SILVER LINING from real life, wrote the ending the story called for, and mailed the finished manuscript to his agent. Now it was time to get cracking on Christmas. The holiday took on a new meaning with a child in the house. Nick had been picking up gifts for weeks and stashing them away. Thanks to Abbie, everything was wrapped and stowed in his office closet. All that was left was the decorating.

Whistling "Jingle Bells," Nick went in search of Anthony.

*

By the time she dragged home from the theater, Jessie was exhausted. Today had been her final two performances before her three-week vacation, with the exception of a special benefit performance on the twenty-eighth for the Andrew Brady Foundation. Tomorrow was Christmas Eve. Then Christmas ... and the wedding.

The role of Christine Mackey would temporarily belong to Valentine York. Just as Bill had promised, Valentine had become invisible. There'd been no other incidents. And there were too many other things on her mind. Like decorating the house. Nick had been buried for the last few days, finishing his manuscript. Anthony had been whining this would be the worst Christmas ever.

Willie her escort, Jessie hurried to the front door. She thanked him and turned the locks, relieved to feel the home's warmth. The weather had turned frigid in the past few days, a major snowfall predicted.

The house smelled woodsy, reminding her of Christmases past. Jessie lifted her head, catching sight of the living room. She gasped, a hand going to her mouth. The blue spruce towered majestically between the two front windows, tiny white bulbs twinkling like so many stars. Sparkly gold trumpets, snowy white angels, and gold and white bows stunned the eye. The blanket at the base was a mesh of green and gold and white.

White poinsettias transformed the room into a magical kingdom. Fresh holly hung in the archway. Bayberry, spice, and vanilla candles in assorted sizes and shapes waited to be lit on the mantle, the coffee table, the grand piano, their fragrance nirvana. Jessie practically swayed under the sensory onslaught.

A smug smile on his face, Nick was planted in the middle of the room, waiting for her.

"Did you really do this?" she squeaked.

"You doubt me?"

"It's just--" Jessie waved a hand, looking around in awe.

"To be honest, Mary oversaw everything. She nixed the plastic reindeer for the front window. It lit up and its nose blinked. Come on. Let me show you the study." Nick guided her through the connecting door. "This is strictly Anthony's and my doing."

At one look, Jessie couldn't stop smiling. The room was a walk down Memory Lane. The Douglas fir was covered with old-fashioned multi-colored bulbs, the ornaments hand-made. A wooden reindeer Jessie had painted in first grade. A picture of her in pigtails, frozen on Santa's lap. Pottery masks of comedy and drama from Andrew's art class at Performing Arts High School. Hand-sewn bells and stars Jessie's mother had created. Lace doilies stitched by Jessie's grandmother. Cheap silver tinsel looped the branches, sparkling next to strings of popcorn and cranberries draping the boughs.

"Oh, Nick— It's magic. I don't know what to say."

"Mary dragged out the old boxes from the basement, and Anthony and I went to town. He had the best time. You should've seen him."

On the mantle was the Advent calendar Jessie had made in grade school. A mechanical Santa stood in front of the grate; a plastic Santa lit the window overlooking the back yard. Fiery poinsettias graced opposite ends of the coffee table. Gaily-wrapped presents were scattered on the blanket that had belonged to Mary's grandmother.

"Anthony tried to stay up to see your reaction, but he gave out around ten. Mary thinks he's warm, gave him some children's aspirin. Wipe that worried look off your face. Kids get sick, no big deal. So, you like?"

"I LOVE. I love you. So much."

She was the luckiest woman in the world.

*

The weathermen had been right this time. Nick stared at the winter spectacle outside his office window. The snow had begun at dawn. Christmas Eve.

The brownstone was humming, Mary and Violet working on the food for the small get-together that evening. Jessie was locked in the master bedroom, wrapping gifts. Anthony was feverish, taking a nap.

Nick fingered Lyle's gift. He'd placed a few calls to Barb's family in Boston, and a few days later an envelope had arrived. Nick hoped he'd done the right thing.

Swiveling around, he stared at a framed picture of Jeffrey on the bookcases. That photo had accompanied him all over the world. What would his son be like today? Nick ran a finger down his cheek, trapped eternally at nine, a wisdom in those eyes most children didn't have. Shouldn't have.

After Jeffrey's death Nick had turned his back on the holidays. He'd spent them alone, usually in a hotel room, drinking himself into oblivion. This Christmas he had Jessie and Anthony. And for the first time his memories of Jeffrey didn't kick him in the gut. He was grateful for the ten years he'd had with his little boy. There was nothing like the love of a child.

Picking up Lyle's gift, Nick took it downstairs, placing it under the tree in the study.

*

December twenty-fourth was just another day to Max this year. Christmas Eve wasn't tonight. It would be next weekend, when Anthony was here. Max planned to spend the coming days wrapping Anthony's presents and decorating the living room. One week from tonight, Max would get his son back.

If there was something Anthony wanted he hadn't already gotten, Max would move heaven and earth to get it for him. His son would have everything his heart desired. It was a whole new beginning for the two of them. Eventually, Anthony would meet his Aunt Luciana, Gianni's adored baby sister Luci. In mourning ever since her unworthy son Eduardo had met his maker, Luci was the only one besides Martinelli and Aldo who knew Max's true identity. She was making a scrapbook of Anthony's life, filling the pages with pictures Gianni had sent her, already doting on her nephew. She knew everything about him, marveling at how much he looked like his father as a young boy.

Shivering, Max turned up the electric heater he'd bought, one for every room in the house.

*

The Christmas Eve gathering at the brownstone was in full swing. Outside, the snow had been accumulating all day. New York would have its first white Christmas in a decade.

Out of deference to Lyle, the guest list had been shaved to the oldest and closest friends. Bill and Marcy Rudolph stopped by, dripping in furs, leaving a gift for Anthony under the tree. Jeremy and his wife Sarah arrived, covered in snow. Even Liz made an appearance. The agent swept in, kissed Nick dramatically, sampled the caviar, and swept out again. Willie and LeJeanne hit it off with Nora and her husband. Nora beamed at Bill, thanking him for seeing that she always had Christmas Eve and Christmas Day off.

Nick's mother had called that morning, wishing him a merry Christmas. She'd also broken the news they wouldn't be at the wedding after all. Charles had been called to Afghanistan to assist in limb transplants for children, his specialty. She hoped Nick understood. He did. They hadn't been at his first wedding either. He loved his parents dearly, but he'd always been an independent child and they'd nurtured his inclination to stand on his own.

In a rare moment alone, Nick and Lyle helped themselves at the hors d'oeuvres table in the dining room. "What you passed on to me, Bree's speculation about Martinelli and the girl," Barton said in a low voice, "... I did some research. Turns out one of the Genovese family was busted a few years back, same kind of operation she thinks Martinelli's into."

"Lots of money in that business."

"And Jersey City's perfect, out of Martinelli's territory, away from prying eyes. He can even," Lyle grimaced, "sample the goods privately. The deviate."

Dropping a tasteless prawn on his plate, Nick tried a scallop wrapped with bacon. Tasted like a leather glove. "Disgusting."

"The appetizer or Martinelli?"

"Both. Especially Martinelli. More especially if you're right on this."

"I got on the Net and took a look at his building's floor plans. Enormous places, the smallest four bedrooms. The choicest apartments have a waterfront view of the Manhattan skyline over the Hudson. Floor-to-ceiling sliding glass doors walk out onto huge decks. You won't catch Roberto Martinelli looking at the butt of Jersey."

Nick tried a crab-stuffed mushroom. "Needs seasoning."

"I think they're pretty good." Lyle popped two more in his mouth. "I got an idea. Why don't we get that telescope of Bree's, find a good view from lower Manhattan, and start watching those riverfront apartments? If astronomers can detect mountain ranges on the moon, we should be able to pick out Martinelli. I got a buddy who works in the local precinct. Isaac Mint. We worked together in Brooklyn when we made detective. Maybe he can set us up somewhere."

"Good idea, worth a shot." Nick set his unfinished plate on the tray of dirty dishes.

"Heard from Bree?"

"Talked to her this morning. Yves is on his way back."

"Nick," Jessie appeared at his side. "Feel Anthony's forehead."

Nick looked down at his son, pressing his hand to the top of Anthony's head. "He's hot again. Come on, Bongo. You need some sleep."

Upstairs, Nick got Anthony into bed and told him he could open his gifts tomorrow. Anthony turned onto his side, Hamlet snaked along his back. "All I want is a dog," he mumbled. "A Portuguese water dog." He was asleep a moment later. Nick turned out the bedside lamp and backed towards the door. The room looked cozy and inviting, lit by a snowman on the desk. It would be nice to creep into bed himself. But he couldn't be sick. Not this Christmas.

*

Roberto Martinelli was bored. He was hosting the traditional Christmas Eve dinner for his family, the capos, and their soldiers in a rented hall in Brooklyn. Tomorrow was Christmas dinner with his other family, his wife and her relatives. His cousins and his uncle. Their children. They'd explore his Southampton palace like termites in a mound and try to guess how much he was worth and be fearfully polite to his face. And all the while he'd long for Jersey City. He couldn't wait to get back to the one place that made him feel alive. Warm. Where he could indulge his most secret fantasy and make it come true.

The room fell silent, Aldo clinking on a goblet. Squaring his shoulders, Roberto rose and lifted his glass, making the traditional toast to the long lives of the Martinelli Family. "*La vostra salute!*"

*

Even the liquor tasted off tonight. Nick parked himself on the study couch, a bourbon in hand. The weather had chased almost everyone home early, thank God. The city was in the grip of a nor'easter, twelve to fourteen inches expected by morning. Ten inches had fallen already.

Staring out the windows at the falling snow, Lyle had been quiet for the last hour. "I'm heading home." He grabbed his jacket.

Nick snagged a gift under the tree and walked Barton to the porch. "Uh," Nick shoved the gift in Lyle's hands, "this isn't really a Christmas gift. It's just something I thought you could use. Not now. Later maybe. It got me through some dark days."

Staring at the package, Lyle nodded. Nick clapped him on the back and watched Barton forge across the yard, the snow up to his knees.

"Okay, guys," Jessie announced, emerging from the kitchen with Mary and Abbie. "Let's get rolling. Mary and I will stack the gifts under the tree. Abbie, you and Nick can hang Anthony's photographs. I can't wait to catch his face when he sees his work all over the hallway in the morning."

Where did she get the energy? Nick sloped against the porch doorway. All he wanted was to sleep for days.

*

Grabbing the bottle of scotch, Lyle left Nick's gift in the kitchen and drifted to the living room. He turned on the television, settling for CNN. He took a swig from the bottle, enjoying the burning sensation as it hit his gut. Pushing back in the recliner, he closed his eyes, taking another gulp.

Lyle awoke shortly after dawn, cramped from sleeping in the chair, his head thumping from the scotch. CNN was telling the world the entire east coast was buried under sixteen inches of snow, New York and Washington at a standstill. Subways had stopped running. The suburbs had massive power outages. The newspapers would be delayed. Cleveland, Pittsburgh, and Richmond were sending extra plows to help clear the roads.

Staggering to the front windows, Lyle saw no sidewalks, no curbs, no stoops or stairs to the brownstones. Everything was a mound of white, the tree limbs threatening to snap under the weight.

Time for aspirin. Lyle gobbled three for good measure. Waiting for his head to clear, he crept down the hallway to the kitchen. Christmas was almost over. Only one more day to survive. Lyle spotted Nick's gift on the island. Hesitating, he finally tore off the paper and lifted the lid. Three framed photos. A family portrait taken less than a year ago of Lyle, Barb, and Dina. A wedding picture of Lyle and Barb. And Dina's most recent school picture.

How …? Every photograph was destroyed in the fire. How the hell did McDeare do this? Lyle dabbed a finger over Dina's photo, her curly red hair …. Tears sprang to his eyes. What had Nick said last night? Not now. Later. Photos got him through his own dark days.

Shit. He would never get through this. Lyle dropped his head and the tears came. And came.

*

Clint hated Christmas. He hated everybody having to feel good and smile at each other and pretend to like fucking bells coming at you from all over. Christmas was for kids, and Clint kept his distance from anything under the age of eighteen. He'd grown up as fast as he could to get away from his father's heavy hand, leaving childhood in the dust. He was proud no brat had ever called him Dad. Clint had

- 145 -

never knocked a child around in his life and that's because he was careful never to have one.

Heading over to Hanratty's early on Christmas day, now that was a good Christmas. Thank the gods, the tavern never closed. He'd start with some chili fries and move on to a greasy burger with fried onions.

The bartender gifted him with a double scotch, the second shot on the house. "Merry Christmas," the idiot added. Where'd they get this banana? He must have turned twenty-one yesterday and Hanratty's hired him to temp.

The television was tuned to a tabloid news show, lapping up the pending McDeare-Kendle wedding. Clint guffawed as a young male reporter with too much hair drooled over McDeare, his bride-to-be, and Kendle's kid. The child Clint would help abduct on New Year's Eve. Footage followed of the perfect family in Central Park, captured by some dirtbag paparazzi with a long-distance lens. A little boy playing catch with McDeare.

After getting down to some serious drinking, Clint trudged home early, taking his food to go and a bottle. Ending up at his computer, he rehashed the grim history of Gianni Fosselli and his son, Anthony Brady.

When he finished reading, Clint shook his head and devoured the last of his greasy burger, licking his fingers. Fosselli wanted what he wanted and what he wanted was his biological kid. He'd go to any lengths to get him. No accounting for different tastes in this world. Clint sucked down more scotch.

Merry fucking Christmas.

*

After two days in bed, Nick and Anthony rebounded from the flu and fast-forwarded to their lost Christmas, gathering with everyone in the study. The sun had set an hour ago. Candles flickered from the mantle, the tree's lights bathing the room in a warm holiday glow. So what if it was December twenty-seventh?

"Only a couple left." Abbie pulled a gift from under the tree and handed Anthony a small flat box. "From your mom."

"That's not a dog."

"Open it," Mary urged.

Tearing off the paper, Anthony lifted out a note. "I owe you ..." Anthony jumped to his feet. "I can have a dog? Really?"

"Really." Jessie smiled at Nick. "Nick promised it will teach you responsibility. Now you need to follow through and not make your dad out to be a liar."

"You can pick him out," Nick added, "but it has to wait until we get back from London."

"A Portuguese water dog! I want a dog just like Zane's." Anthony threw his arms around Nick. "You did it, Dad. You said you'd convince Mom and you did."

*

A ring box? Bree accepted the small gift-wrapped box from Yves with hesitation. She dug deep for a smile and peeled off the paper. Damn. A ring box. She opened it with a gasp. Worse. It was Yves' mother's ring, something that meant a great deal to him. A treasured antique, in his family for generations.

"Not exactly a surprise," Yves murmured. "We've been talking about it for months."

Not long ago, Bree would have happily accepted his proposal. She and Yves were the same kind of people, bohemians with a love for adventure and travel. Their careers were on the same track. The sex was good. Not Fourth of July, but not Veteran's Day either. Bree knew what a catch Yves was.

There was only one problem. Yves wasn't Nick.

"Let me give it some thought. It's so, it's so important."

*

"Jessie, open your last three from Nick," Abbie urged.

"Uh, save this one for later," Nick said, grabbing a box from Jessie's hand.

Blushing, Jessie quickly began to unwrap another gift, carefully tearing the exquisite paper.

"That's not from me," Nick added.

"It came just before Christmas," Mary said. "I--"

Shocked speechless, Jessie lifted out a box of ... diapers? Nick grabbed the card on the box, rapidly scanning it. "I should've known."

"Don't tell me," Jessie said weakly. "Kristin Wallingford."

Anthony looked up. "Who's Kris--"

"Hey," Abbie said, leaping to her feet, "Let's research Portuguese Water dogs on my iPad."

"And I'll throw this stuff," Mary picked up the box and the card, "in the garbage."

"I'm so sorry," Nick rasped in their wake. "Kristin's pathological. She--"

"We're not wasting any more time on Kristin Wallingford." Jessie smiled brightly, quickly unwrapping the last present. She paused and looked up at Nick, at a loss all over again. Nestled in a wooden box was Nick's manuscript, the crisp white paper a stark contrast to the crimson satin lining. Kristin was forgotten. "Nick ..."

"I haven't been easy to live with while writing it," he explained, his eyes soft. "I dedicated it to you. You'll understand when you read it."

Jessie hugged Nick close. She knew what sharing his manuscript meant to a solitary man used to sharing nothing for so many years, including his feelings.

Racing back into the room, Anthony asked, "Can we eat now?"

"Not yet." Nick pulled a small flat package from under the couch. "We're official. You're Anthony McDeare. These are the adoption papers."

Letting out a whoop, Anthony pumped his fist into the air. "This is the best Christmas ever ... Dad!"

*

It was the perfect location, an empty apartment in lower Manhattan on a top floor. The problem was the snow swirling like polar bear fur outside the picture window, obscuring the view of Fifty-Five Washington Street from across the icy Hudson. Bree's telescope was useless. Lyle glanced up at Isaac Mint from the scope's eyepiece. "Can't see a damn thing."

"Look," Isaac said, "I got the space for your lookout. I can't control the weather."

- 147 -

"I know. Not your fault." Isaac was a towering mass of bronzed bulk, a scary figure to anyone who didn't know him. Lyle and Isaac went back a long way on the force. "It just pisses me off. I want results now."

"It don't always work that way, brother."

*

Roberto wasn't prepared for what greeted him when he finally returned to Jersey City, in the middle of a blizzard that made driving a nightmare. But he couldn't wait one more day to see his honey.

The condo's heat was turned way up. Dirty dishes and empty water bottles littered the tables. Mugs filled with dried-up tea bags cluttered the sink. A large pot of cold soup was on the stove.

A feverish child was shivering under a mound of blankets on a couch, her new blue teddy bear tucked under her arm.

Dropping his armload of presents, Roberto felt the girl's forehead. He murmured something soothing, kissed her cheek, and quickly went in search of the others. He found the older boy and girl in bed, piled with blankets, their eyes dull.

Furious, Roberto ran from room to room. He finally came across Celine in one of the bathrooms, slumped by the toilet. Her mane of shiny raven hair was greasy and in tangles. A towel was pressed to her mouth.

"What the hell happened here?" Roberto asked, his voice low.

"… Flu."

"Where's Candy?"

"Went … home … sick."

"Why didn't you let me know?"

"I was …" Celine hunched up, looking like she was going to be sick again, "afraid to call. Thought you'd get mad. And if you left and your wife got--"

Roberto strode down the hallway, cell in hand, punching in his private doctor's number.

Dammit all to hell, what a fuck-up!

CHAPTER 16

Sliding from bed, Nick threw on a robe. Jessie was asleep, hair a web of spun gold across her face. Nick had one last thing to do. He grabbed his cell and tiptoed down to his office.

Bree had texted him late tonight. She wanted to talk, in person. She also mentioned Yves was heading to Washington tomorrow for a few days.

Texting back, Nick suggested they meet tomorrow night when Jessie was at the theater. The new place Lyle had found in lower Manhattan. He'd call in the morning.

Catching movement out of the corner of his eye, Nick looked up. Jessie, standing in the doorway. "Didn't mean to wake you," he croaked, quickly punching the cell back to his home screen.

"I wasn't asleep." She drifted to his side. "You had to text someone in the middle of the night?"

"It's ... Barton. He--"

"Lyle?" Jessie glanced out the window. "I don't see any lights on over there. What's going on?"

" ... Lyle must be in the bedroom. He, uh, texted me. Rambling, sounded drunk. I don't think he realized what time it was."

"Nick ... is there something you're not telling me?"

"Of course not, honey ... We agreed to keep an eye on Lyle, remember? Let's go back to bed." Swinging Jessie into his arms and lifting her up, Nick grinned down at her. "Unless you want to check my cell and see Lyle's text for yourself?"

Nick held his breath.

*

"Don't be silly." Jessie laughed, dismissing an uneasy little voice inside her head. "Let's go back to bed."

"To sleep?"

"Um, do you have something else in mind?"

The sun was rising when they finally fell asleep, the texts forgotten along with the little voice. Jessie awoke mid-afternoon, feeling delicious.

Scrambling out of bed after looking at the clock, she got ready quickly, shoveling down a salad before the show that night. At five-thirty she rushed out of the house to the waiting car. After four days off she was rusty, needed extra time to warm up. Tonight was the benefit for The Andrew Brady Foundation, all proceeds going to gunshot victims and their families. This was a personal cause for Jessie. She wiped everything else from her mind.

Stepping into the theater with Willie, they both paused. Yusef, the stage door security guard, wasn't there. Gus, who manned the sign-in desk, looked frightened. "Something's going on, Ms. Kendle," he said in a low voice. "It's serious."

Exchanging a wary glance with Willie, Jessie entered the anteroom with him. Crew members and actors loitered, whispering. The door to the green room was closed. Yusef stood guard, muscular arms crossed.

Dabbing at her eyes, Valentine sat alone, off to the side. Nora and James were huddled at a table, staring at James' laptop. Jessie hurried over to them, trailed by Willie. "What's going on?"

"Your plan worked," James said.

*

Nick filled Barton in on last night's close call with Jessie as they cabbed down to meet Bree. "If she'd seen my text I would've been sleeping on your floor. Which reminds me ..." Nick quickly deleted all texts with Bree and Barton on his cell.

"You really think Jessie would snoop like that?"

"I'm not taking any chances."

"For God's sake," Lyle said wearily, "just tell her the truth about Fosselli."

"I know what I'm doing."

"Said the captain of the Titanic. George Custer. General George Pick--"

"Shut up."

*

Relief swept through Jessie. The nanny cam had worked. Concealed behind a fern in her dressing room it was set for vibration triggering, recording when there was movement. James had coordinated the camera with his laptop, examining the footage daily. "I'm almost afraid to ask but ...what did you catch her doing?"

"Him."

"What?"

"As in George. George Penfield."

Jessie opened her mouth. Nothing came out. George?

"He's locked in the Green Room until the cops get here," James said helpfully. He cued up the video as Jessie held her breath. "Take a look."

*

The doctor assured Roberto it was just the flu, the same strain going around the East Coast. Keep them hydrated and get a lot of rest. Roberto had spent the last twenty-four hours watching over the kids and Celine. He hired a private nurse, a housecleaning service, and a personal chef under his Jersey alias, one Robert Marsh. Only Celine knew his real identity.

Meanwhile, Roberto told Marcella he'd been called to a meeting in Cancun. Roberto intended to spend the next few days at the condo. He wouldn't leave his special girl's side until she was back to normal. He ordered her five new teddy bears online, all shades of blue, her favorite color.

Watching her sleep now, dark curls spread out on a pillow patterned with cartoon characters, triggered a childhood memory. When Roberto was nine, a case of the flu had morphed into pneumonia, leaving him deathly ill for days. His mother had never left his side. She prayed in Italian, put a silver charm under his mattress, a holy Good Shepherd medal under his pillow, and held his hand around the clock. Sophia Martinelli had been a saint, devoted to her only son.

Roberto vowed to stay here and take care of them all, especially his beauty. She was breathing easily, long eyelashes fluttering on rosy cheeks. Like a little princess out of a fairy tale.

*

"It's good, Lyle." Bree had lugged over the camera and tripod, set it up next to the telescope, and checked and double-checked all the equipment. Hands on her hips, Bree looked pleased. "Now we have to figure out which condo belongs to our friend. Train the telescope on the deck windows and wait to get lucky. When we find him I'll set the camera to shoot whenever there's movement."

"Forty-three units, twenty-one on the river side, plus the penthouse." Barton studied a paper, the building's vital stats. "It shouldn't take long."

"We're not going to see anything until the snow lets up." Nick cursed the weather. The last few days had been clear, the moon and stars neon vibrant. Tonight the snow had returned, big downy flakes dripping past the window like soapsuds.

"I'm going to grab a bite and head home." Barton shrugged on his coat. "Coming, Nick?"

"I'll hang around. Maybe the snow will stop."

"Suit yourself." Barton let himself out.

Nick paced to the window, squinting through the swirling flakes at the building across the Hudson. "Shitty time of year for surveillance."

"I think I'll move in here." Bree perched on the sill beside him. "This is going to be a twenty-four, seven job with the weather. And Martinelli could pop in any time, not just Saturday night."

"How will Yves feel about that?" Nick hadn't had a chance to talk to Bree about her message. He'd gotten her voice mail this morning, texted about tonight's meet.

"He's heading to Libya after your wedding."

Leaning against the window, Nick watched Bree sip her coffee. Zabars. Her favorite. She even traveled with it. "Sorry I couldn't call you back last night. What did you want to talk about?"

Inhaling slowly, Bree said. "Yves proposed on Christmas."

"Really? Congrats."

"I ... I'm not sure I'm going to accept."

"Why not?"

"Come on, Nick." She flashed him an amused smile. "You know exactly why I'm hesitating."

*

Jessie watched the nanny cam's footage in horror.

George Penfield entered Jessie's dressing room and tugged on rubber gloves, his eyes checking the door. Hands shaking, he pulled a prescription bottle from his pocket, removed the lid, and sprinkled something on Jessie's prop wedding bouquet. As he replaced the cap, the vial dropped, spilling some of the contents. Cursing, George ground the white powder into the carpet with his boot, kicking the residue from side to side. Quickly fitting the top back on the bottle, he slid it into his pocket and sidled from the room.

"What's in that bottle?" Jessie asked hoarsely.

"George won't tell us. After Yusef saw the video he caught up with George on the stage and held him at gunpoint. He used a handkerchief to take the vial from George's pocket, but the lid was loose. It spilled again."

"That's why he cleared the crew from the stage? He thinks it's some sort of …" her mouth went dry, "poison?"

"Yeah. And he locked the sicko in the Green Room."

"Where's the bottle now?"

"Yusef took it. The stage and your dressing room are off-limits to everyone until the cops get here."

If she hadn't set up the nanny cam … Jessie felt faint.

"We're not done. Take a look at this next part." James cued up his laptop. "Valentine ran into your dressing room to get her things out before you got here. George dropped in to hurry her along. Looks like they've been an item for a while."

"So we were right about Valentine."

"Watch. I'm starting from when George says he wants Valentine to come over after the show." The video sprang to life.

Valentine was throwing her things into a bag, looking distracted. "I told you. I need to be with my mother tonight."

"I'm so sick of this. People talk, Val. They want to know why you never show up for anything." George stood far from the spot where he'd dropped the vial, his eyes flicking back and forth. "When's the last time you had dinner with me? You ever think about that?"

"The doctor told me this morning the cancer's spread."

"Don't take this the wrong way. But maybe you'll have a life after she's gone."

"My mother's my last living relative! I need to be wih her. She sacrificed everything for me."

"You've sacrificed everything for HER. And when do I get some thanks? I did everything I could to get Kendle out of the show for you, honey."

A leotard in her hands, Valentine paused. "What …?"

"Truth be told, it was a double payback," George said. "For you and for someone else."

"What are you talking about?"

"The diva's heel breaking? The costume glitches? I was thinking of having a set piece come down on her head next." He chuckled. "But then I came up with a better idea."

"My God, what have you done?" Valentine dropped the leotard. "Who the hell are you, George?!" she shrieked.

Nora walked into the room, a shocked expression on her face.

James stopped the video. "Nora was trying to calm Valentine down when I got there. That's when I looked at the footage on the nanny cam and showed it to Yusef."

Glancing at Valentine weeping on Nora's shoulder, Jessie was flooded with guilt. She'd accused the woman of so many vile—

Four policemen pushed into the room, three uniforms and a detective, consulting in low voices with Yusef. The room hushed, everyone trying to hear the conversation. Splitting up, two cops headed towards the stage and dressing rooms.

The detective and a uniform approached James and Jessie.

*

"What are you talking about, Bree?" Nick said smoothly. "I don't have a clue why you wouldn't marry Yves."

"You're not being honest with me." Bree's smile widened. "Or yourself."

"This is ridiculous." Nick wandered towards the window. Real-life dialogue should come with a delete button. He didn't want to know where this was going.

"Is it?" Bree followed, blocking the window and facing him. "Let me ask you something. Does Jessie know you're here tonight?"

"Of course not."

"What are you going to tell her if she asks?"

"I'll think of something."

"You'll lie."

"To protect her." His lips thinned. "Bree, you're out of line."

"Lies are death to a relationship. What do you think they'll do to a marriage?"

Nick's brow rose. "You're an expert on marriage now?"

"Don't you see the pattern? Lying is second nature to you. You've lied to every woman you've ever known. And now Jessie. You don't want her to know we're working together, you lie. She can't know Gianni's alive, you lie. Is she so frail she needs all those lies?"

"You don't know Jessie," Nick said flatly. "You don't know anything about her."

"She's a woman. And none of us like to be lied to. For any reason. Trust me."

*

The theater was swarming with cops, more alighting by the minute. Even the Hazmat team was there. The police cleared the building of anyone not directly involved. The nanny cam and prop flowers were confiscated.

After being interviewed by a Detective Lally, all bulging muscles, Jessie huddled with James, Nora, and a weepy Valentine. Lally disappeared into the Green Room. Jessie couldn't believe this was happening, enveloped by a fog of confusion. George had said something about double payback. What did that mean? Valentine knew nothing, using tissue after tissue to sop up her tears and sniffle she was so sorry. Jessie put an arm around her, consoling her. Willie hovered nearby.

Two uniforms, guns bulging on their belts, finally emerged from the Green Room with Lally. "He's not telling us what's in the vial," Lally said to Yusef. "We're taking him downtown."

"Wait." Jessie approached the detective. "I need to talk to him. This was directed at me. I have to hear it from George. I deserve that much."

"Not a good idea."

"You're from Midtown North?"

At his nod, Jessie said, "Your boss is my close friend. Lyle Barton's going to be in my wedding. I'll call him. He'll okay my talking to George."

Lally's action-hero face puckered into a patient look. "The lieutenant's on leave, Ms. Kendle."

"Then I'll have Lyle call his stand-in. Or Sergeant Steinmetz. Please, Detective," Jessie pleaded, turning on the charm and looking into his eyes as if he were the only man in the room. "I have to find out why George wanted to hurt me like this!"

The cops exchanged guarded looks. Jessie held her breath, waiting.

"Okay," Lally said, his eyes turning human. "But we go with you."

"Me, too." Valentine joined them, a determined look on her face. Her hair was pulled back in a ponytail, no makeup. She looked like a little girl. "I deserve to hear this too." Jessie nodded.

Sighing, Lally said, "Let's go."

The five of them entered the Green Room. Lally nodded at Jessie, and he and the uniforms blended into the background. George Penfield slouched against the wall, cuffed. Looking from Jessie to Valentine, he laughed. "What? You two besties now?"

"Why, George?" Jessie asked. "What did I ever do to you? You thought Valentine would thank you for this?" Valentine pressed a tissue to her eyes. "Or was there more?"

"You really are everything Ian Wexley said you were."

Ian Wexley?

"Ian Wexley?" Valentine echoed. She looked from George to Jessie. "Didn't he used to be on a soap?"

"Used to be," Jessie said, starting to put the pieces together. If George was Ian's friend ... "He's dead now," she continued. "When he was alive, Ian Wexley was an alcoholic sociopath."

Straightening up, George turned to Valentine. "Ian was on the fast track to Broadway until Jessie Kendle and Andrew Brady ruined his life. He ended up dead. Because of them."

"Ian ended up dead because he got involved with the mob," Jessie snapped. "He helped kill Andrew."

"Ian wouldn't kill anyone," George retorted. "Aldo set him up, his own brother-in-law. But can you blame Ian for hating you, after Brady blackballed him with every producer out there? He used to be a great guy."

This was crazy. Ian had stalked Jessie after they broke up, threatened to reveal Gianni was Anthony's father, and helped set the stage to murder Andrew. The great guy had personally handed Eduardo Santangelo the gun used to kill Andrew.

"I lived next door to Ian for years," George choked, "before be became a big soap star. When my fiancée was killed in a street mugging, I lost everything, including my mind and my job. Ian got me through it, found me my first stage gig Off Broadway. He didn't have to do any of that." Eyeing Jessie, he hissed, "Then

Ian moved in with you, baby. He was obsessed with you. After you dumped him, he became another person."

"Enough pathetic memory lane," Lally said. "Take him away."

Rubbing a hand over her forehead, Jessie almost laughed. Ian Wexley, major soap star, had mesmerized naïve little actress Jessie Kendle. Until she found him in their bed with another woman. Who turned out to be one in a series of women, like a packaged set of dolls.

As the cops hauled him away, George yelled over his shoulder. "Did you know there were only three people at his funeral? All because of you and Brady!"

Crying softly, Valentine covered her face with her hand.

"Entitled shits like Jessie Kendle get all the breaks," George screamed, his voice fading. "What about the rest of us? It was Valentine's turn!"

Yusef poked his head in the door. "The Hazmat team wants the theater cleared. No show tonight. Not until they identify the substance used."

Josh rushed into the room behind him. "Would someone please tell me what the hell is going on in this place? I had to talk my way in here!"

*

"Bree, you don't care about Jessie," Nick said quietly. "Where's this coming from and what does any of it have to do with marrying Yves?"

Her expression softening, Bree crooned, "Neither one of us has changed over the years, Nick. Your tap dance with Jessie proves you're not the marrying type. Neither am I. We're two of a kind." She stepped closer and reached out, skating a finger over his jaw.

Her scent carried an elixir of spices, redolent of Hong Kong. Nick's tiny flat in Kowloon. The Harry Ape, their hang-out bar. Nick writing THE GREEN MONSTER. The two of them chasing down a story for the AP.

"You're remembering, aren't you?" That husky voice could charm secrets out of an informant or turn a strong man weak. "Hong Kong ... Renting a junk and making love against that backdrop of skyscrapers and mountains in the harbor."

Despite himself, Nick was seeing it. Those jade-flecked eyes wouldn't let him go, holding him in place.

"Skinny-dipping in that forbidden cove," Bree whispered, inching closer. "Make-up sex after a fight ..."

Close, too close, he searched her face, pausing at her lips.

*

Jessie collapsed against the limo's soft leather, relieved to be going home. Bill would compensate the audience and reschedule the benefit performance. Snow swirled around the limo, turning it into a cocoon.

Ian Wexley. In freefall the last third of his life. Married to Aldo Zappella's sister Paula, the woman who eventually turned him in for murdering Andrew. Aldo had set it all up so cleverly, manipulating Paula, manipulating Ian. Long ago, before he'd lost his humanity, Ian had been an exciting lover. Friends with her agent Jeremy. And apparently, George Penfield.

Jessie was about to get married. She was back on Broadway. She was starting over. But the ghosts of her past wouldn't leave her alone. She was still reliving her history, her bad decisions, her lack of judgment about the men in her life.

- 155 -

Could you ever shake free of your past, or was it there forever, a lethal sliver under the skin?

Mary met her at the door, in a panic. "It's all over the news, the theater shut down, some kind of toxic substance. Are you all right?"

"Where's Nick?"

"At Lyle's."

Jessie dug her cell out of her purse, the battery dead. She was going to charge it at the theater but ... "Be back in a minute."

Running to Lyle's back door, Jessie used her key to barge in. Lyle was parked in front of the TV, a basketball game blaring.

"Where's Nick?"

"Jesus. "Lyle jumped. "I didn't hear you come in."

"Sorry. I wasn't ... Is Nick here?"

"Nick's, uh," Lyle eyed the window, "he went for a walk."

"In the snow?"

"He didn't care ... Wedding jitters, big day coming up. The usual stuff for a guy. He won't be long. What are you doing home so early?"

Trying not to babble, Jessie explained the situation at the theater.

Lyle's solid response calmed her, his voice steady. After a hug, he told her he'd call Lally. "He's a good man. I'll see what I can find out for you."

"Thanks, Lyle." Jessie trudged across the backyard. Was Nick really out for a walk?

No. She had to shut up that little voice in her head. This was no way to start a marriage. She refused to spend the rest of her life worried Nick would cheat on her. Kristin Wallingford would not win.

*

"Hong Kong," Nick said gruffly, "was a long time ago, Bree."

"Not so long."

"Everything's changed."

"How?"

"You wouldn't understand."

"Try me."

Turning away, he finally broke the spell. "I lost my son. I lost my brother. I met Jessie."

"You'll tire of her."

"Like I tired of you in Hong Kong? That's what this is about, payback for how things ended?"

"I left you, remember?"

"I'm marrying Jessie." His face set, Nick eyed Bree, hoping she got the message.

She didn't. "It won't last."

His cell buzzed. Barton. Nick clicked on, going cold at his words. The theater. A toxin. Jessie looking for Nick. Pocketing his cell, Nick reached for his coat. "I have to go."

"Go. Run home and make up another lie. To 'protect' Jessie."

Hurling his coat to the floor, Nick gripped Bree by the shoulders. "Don't do this. Not now. Listen to me. I'm terrified I'm going to lose another son to that monster out there, and I can't let that happen. I'm desperate for your help. Nothing else matters. Just that."

"You're playing with fire, Nick. You're rushing into a doomed marriage. And you're obsessing about Gianni's son."

Stepping back, Nick angled her a stony look. "Anthony is my son. In the eyes of the law and in my heart. Don't you ever forget that." Grabbing his coat, he strode to the door.

"Wait." She was at his side in an instant. "I-I'm sorry. You're right. A child's life is at stake."

"My son's life, Bree."

"… Your son." Bree swallowed hard. She moved to the telescope, staring out at the snow.

Nick went to her, touching her arm. "Are we okay?"

"Does it matter?"

"Always."

Turning around, Bree looked up at him, a tear splashing her cheek "Then we're okay."

He quietly let himself out and hailed a cab.

The long ride uptown was a blur. Nick had the driver drop him a few blocks from home, and he walked the rest of the way.

CHAPTER 17

No one could stay out in this weather for long. Nick had to be home any minute. Where was he already? Jessie bit her lip, flicked the remote to another local news report. The theater shutdown was all over the place. Lyle had called with an update a few mintues ago. Unsettling information.

At last. The front door slammed, followed by footsteps to the study. Nick dropped down beside her, brushing the snow from his hair. "Jessie? Why are you home?"

"Why were you walking in the snow?"

"What happened with the benefit?"

Trying to still her anxiety, Jessie filled him in. She explained about George, Ian Wexley, the nanny cam, the theater shut down. "George hates me," she quavered, "because of Ian. A dead man from my past." She swallowed, her nerves shot. "When does it all end, Nick?"

Stroking a hand through her hair, Nick murmured, "It will stop. I promise you. It will."

Nodding, Jessie told him, "Barton made some calls, got a preliminary report. They think it might be," she gulped, "ricin. They'll know for sure in a day or so. They're not releasing any information to the press. And George didn't cook this up in his kitchen. They're not even sure he was acting alone."

"The ricin. He'd need money for access."

"Money or a connection with money ..." Jessie felt the blood drain from her face. "Aldo. Aldo Zappella. George hated him for setting up Ian but maybe they both hated me more and George went to Aldo for--"

Pulling her into his arms, Nick said, "Stop. Your imagination's working overtime. My God, to think what he's been doing to you ..."

"I've been telling you about these incidents for weeks. I thought my understudy was doing it."

"Your Eve Harrington?"

"Not funny."

"Sorry. I should've paid more attention to your situation." He pressed his lips to her forehead.

"I googled ricin," she said, her voice shaky. "It can do permanent lung damage. George put it on the prop flowers. He knows I sniff the bouquet before I toss it in the wedding scene. My career would've been over. He hates me that much."

"Thank God you installed that nanny cam."

"And he could've gotten to me anywhere before this. Like Nordic Nirvana."

"He admitted he spiked your drink?"

"It's obvious."

Releasing her, Nick said, "Jessie--"

"For God's sake, you don't still think it was Josh? It was George!"

Rising, Nick paced to the grate, warming his hands. "I don't want to argue about this anymore."

Neither did Jessie. Nick was too blinded by jealousy to ever see Josh objectively. "So why were you out walking?"

"I needed some time to think." He threw up his hands. "It's been a non-stop circus around here--my manuscript, Christmas, the wedding, you name it."

"You've been so secretive lately." She joined him in front of the fire. "More than usual."

"I'm okay. Really." He wouldn't look at her.

"Getting cold feet?" Jessie gently brushed back the snow-damp hair from his brow. "That's what Lyle said."

That got his attention. Nick's eyes lit. "No way. No cold feet except from the snow." He draped his arms around her. "Tomorrow's the twenty-ninth. Only two more days to live in sin. Let's make the most of it."

*

The twenty-ninth. The day had finally arrived. Max was ready.

"I put your bags in the car, Mr. Callaban." Carlo Nori appeared in Max's study. "I spoke to my contact. We switch cars at Emlenton, Pennsylvania."

Nodding, Max opened the top desk drawer and extracted the medical supplies he'd need, everything acquired from the physician who'd supplied the Rohypnol. Roberto Martinelli's reach extended far and wide. Like God Himself.

Max flipped the pages of his desk calendar from the twenty-ninth to January first, the day he'd return. He'd marked it with a red star months ago. They were driving overnight, arriving in Southampton early the next day.

Tomorrow morning he'd meet his associate, Clint Vaughn. The man arrived this evening.

*

"I'm busy right now," Clint snapped, pacing from one end of the cheesy box of a hotel room to another. "I don't punch a time card for you. Later." He clicked off and checked the cheap clock radio on the bedstand. Ten p.m. Doing time in the Southampton Holiday Inn was not Clint's idea of fun. Finally, a coded knock on the door. Clint opened it.

Aldo slunk into the room, opened his briefcase, and handed Clint a large manila envelope. "Everything's in there. Our friend arrives in the morning. We have two men in the Rudolph security detail. Their pictures are enclosed. They'll let you exit an isolated side door when you give them the high sign. There won't be a problem getting the boy out."

"I don't see any cash." Clint eyed the envelope.

"Greedy SOB." Aldo pulled out a smaller envelope.

"I'll let you know when I start doing charity cases."

"Fuck you, Vaughn." Aldo oozed out the door.

Dropping onto the bed, Clint emptied the large envelope. Wedding invitations. Parking permits. Pages of instructions. A map of Bill Rudolph's mansion and estate grounds, the McDeare/Brady bedrooms marked. Excellent.

And false ID's.

The picture on his passport was a classic. That sleazy photo booth on Times Square and Martinelli's London contact had done the job. A little facial putty, a mousy hairpiece, a skimpy mustache, and wire-rimmed glasses had changed Clint into a dour cellophane man no one would eye twice. Clint wasn't taking any chances on Barton recognizing him. The loser PI spinning his wheels on a cheating-husband case couldn't afford to be spotted as a guest at the society wedding of the year.

Clint studied Fosselli's British passport. Even the man's mother wouldn't recognize him. Fucking amazing.

*

George Penfield's allotted phone call after a night in a smelly jail was a no-brainer. There was only one person he wanted to talk to.

"Get me a lawyer," he said when his call was finally answered. "Someone better than a court-appointed hack. Thanks for not answering last night. My accommodations were not exactly spectacular."

"You deserved it, you idiot. When you said you needed big bucks for your latest stunt I didn't expect Armageddon."

Asshole. "Ricin's not cheap, not for my purposes. I needed a refined product."

"The Department for Public Health and the cops are crawling all over the theater. It's on the fucking news. If anyone--"

"Do I get my attorney?"

"Why should I help you now?"

"Because the George Penfield canary starts singing if you don't. And it won't be a Broadway melody."

*

As the morning sun filtered into Nick's suite, he shucked on gray slacks and a black turtleneck. He reached for the matching gray jacket, the lone item hanging in the closet. Stuffing his pockets with his wallet, loose change, and his pocket watch, he scanned the room.

Was this how it had looked when he'd first arrived at the brownstone last April? It was pristine, the clutter gone. Mary had finished transferring his belongings to the master bedroom yesterday. Jessie and Nick had spent last night making love up here one last time, putting the havoc at the theater behind them. When they arrived in Southampton this afternoon, they'd be sleeping apart until after the wedding.

Wedding. Honeymoon. Nick looked down at his left hand's ring finger and all it would symbolize. Jessie and Anthony. They were his life.

Downstairs, the front hallway was chaos. Willie and Lyle were hauling bags out to the car. Abbie hugged the wedding attire sheathed in thick plastic to her chest. Mary handed a cat carrier to Gertie Skolnik, Hamlet yowling. Anthony was snapping photographs with that old camera Nick had given him. The boy treasured it. Jessie slipped into her sable coat.

A curious group of refugees, born in grief, united by a ghost, and about to seal the future with vows of love and commitment.

*

"Mr. Vaughn? I'm Max Callaban." Max extended his hand. The dreary hotel room was an abode suitable only for those who didn't know better. He and Carlo were at the Inn at Windmill Lane, a hotel in Amagansett.

"Sure you are. And I'm John Gotti." Clint shook.

Gianni sized up the man, weathered planes and angles and eyes that reflected the ice within. What Americans called a hard ass. Exactly what he needed. "Actually, I'm Jeremiah Hawthorne. And you're my brother Winston. Let's grow accustomed to addressing each other by those names, yes? I understand you have a packet of information for me."

"Your ID and instructions are inside." Vaughn handed him an envelope. "I suggest you memorize it."

"You're not dealing with a fool, Winston."

"No shit, Jeremiah."

*

As the limo swept up a winding tree-covered driveway, the Rudolph mansion slowly materialized, a vision from the Magic Kingdom. A three-story stone mansion with thirty bedrooms. Jessie hadn't seen it in years, not since she and Andrew had hidden from the press in the solarium during a party. The reception would be held in that glass-enclosed solarium, a luscious oasis with towering trees, a running brook, and dense foliage.

Bill and Marcy appeared as the car coasted to a stop under a massive portico. Like a scene out of MASTERPIECE THEATRE, servants supervised by a butler hurried to the trunk and began unloading luggage.

"It's about time," Liz Scott said, marching through the portico. She was followed by Sabrina, the wedding planner. In the end, Jessie had left the final plans to Sabrina. She instilled confidence. At six feet, Sabrina was a big woman, with a voice as calm as a mountain stream. Jessie had immediately taken to the consultant when Liz introduced them months ago, after interviewing ten wedding planners and declaring this one was the best. Surprisingly, Jessie had agreed. She hoped Sabrina's cool presence would counter balance Liz and Jeremy, two piranhas gleefully feeding on the publicity coming their clients' way.

As they entered the outer vestibule, Jessie grasped Nick's hand. Even accustomed to her share of wealth and theatrical grandeur, it was hard not to be overwhelmed. Ten feet wide, the vestibule ran the entire length of the front of the house. Liz pushed open double carved wooden doors leading into the Great Hall.

Jeremy approached, clipboard in hand. "You'll enter here, Jessie, through these doors. And there's your aisle."

"God," Jessie whispered. The aisle, approximately eight feet wide, rolled ahead of her for miles, culminating in a set of stairs that fanned out from the landing.

"The ceremony will take place on the landing." Jeremy pointed.

Jessie hoped she'd make it without tripping. Large cushioned mahogany church benches lined the aisle. Mahogany newels, Liz jabbered, crowned with a white candles under glass, would light Jessie's way to the landing. By tomorrow, Sabrina added, each post would be covered with fragrant layers of lilies and white roses. In serene tones, she assured Jessie it would be magnificent, the flowers adding a mystical aura the florist had been working on for months.

"Look up there," Liz warbled, looping her arm through Nick's and pointing up three stories to an enormous skylight. "You'll get married under the stars. Flowers and candles will line the staircase along with those crystal chandeliers and the balconies. Amazing what two agents and a wedding planner can arrange, huh?"

Leaning into Nick, Jessie whispered, "Is it too late to elope?"

*

The minister was an hour late for the rehearsal. Barton was edgy, worried about security in the massive house. Anthony was cranky, pouting because Zane wouldn't arrive until tomorrow. He dropped the cushion holding the rings halfway down the aisle, and Jeremy barked at him. Nick told the agent to lay off the kid. Liz and Jeremy argued about every inconsequential detail.

Sabrina floated about the palace, languidly conferring with the florist and her lighting director and the caterer about the flowers, the candles, the lights, the tables, the decorations, the wedding cake, the guest book, the presents, the sound system, and the orchestra. Nick smiled sourly. It might as well be a Broadway play. They just needed Jerome Robbins and dancers. Should've rented out Radio City.

By the time they sat down to a small dinner, Nick was in a foul mood. Anthony and Mary quarreled about what he had to eat, Abbie kept tossing a feathered boa in Lyle's face and making him sneeze, and Bill and Marcy had to deal with the paparazzi flying overhead in helicopters. The stuffed trout whipped up the acids in his stomach, the small talk was giving him a headache, and the server spilled red wine on Jessie's lavender gown.

Worst of all, Nick hadn't had a moment alone with Jessie. They were housed in opposite wings of the mansion. You needed a golf cart to journey from one end to the other.

Jessie was smiling and saying all the appropriate words, but he could see her facial muscles were as taut as violin strings. Nick grabbed her hand and whispered, "Come on. Maybe we can steal a minute alone."

"Um, excuse us for a minute--" Jessie began as she followed Nick into the Great Hall. Nick helped her into her coat and they ducked out the front door.

"Sorry, I just had to get out of there."

"Gosh, it's cold." Jessie nuzzled against Nick.

Nick pulled her into his arms, trying to warm her. "What's wrong with this picture? We're outside freezing our asses off, our first moment alone since this morning." Jessie shivered again. "This is ridiculous. Let's find a room and lock ourselves in."

Tittering, Jessie ran for the door, tugging on it. "Um, looks like we locked ourselves out."

*

Barton caught up with Nick and Jessie as they climbed the stairs to their rooms. He hated to intrude, but they needed to hear this. Pulling them into a maid's closet he whispered, "I got a call from Lally, the Penfield investigation. It's confirmed. It was ricin."

Jessie's hand flew to her mouth. "My God, Lyle, this is sick."

"Bill Rudolph wants us to keep the poison angle quiet, afraid it'll kill business. So does the department. We don't need any copycats. Only Bill, a handful of detectives and the three of us know. HazMat is taking care of the theater. The play will be up and running next week. One more thing. Penfield's suddenly got himself a fancy Park Avenue attorney. The kind that charges a retainer fee the size of a stage manager's salary. Does Penfield have that kind of independent income, Jessie?"

"I don't know anything about him," Jessie said, looking shaken. "Just that he and Ian Wexley went back a long way, and he felt a crazy loyalty to the man. He hates me."

Ian Wexley. Barton exchanged a subtle look with Nick. He had to be thinking what Lyle was thinking. The lawyer changed everything. Barton and Nick had spoken privately this morning. They'd agreed George was a lone crazy nursing a grudge, wanting to impress his honey on the side. But a high-priced attorney representing an ordinary schlub—that was a signature Mafia move to protect someone they were in bed with. And George had a link with Aldo Zappella, a common object of hatred: Jessie.

They'd deal with this after the wedding.

*

Later that night, Jessie couldn't sleep. The room was too big, the bed was too big, and she was too alone. This time tomorrow night she'd be on her way to London as Nick's wife. Mrs. Nick McDeare. She had everything she could ever want. A thriving career, especially now with George gone. A beautiful son. Nick.

If only the adrenaline would give it a rest and let her sleep.

*

The limo headed towards the Rudolph estate the next day, Gianni glancing out the window. Even the weather was cooperating for Jessica's union with the devil. The clouds had cleared, snow predicted for later tonight. A pearly moon and a million stars were swirling in the early evening sky.

Tensing, Gianni watched as Carlo Nori handed the Hawthornes' invitations and ID to the security detail at the gate of the Rudolph mansion. The guards peered at the two brothers in the back seat, their eyes flitting back down to the passports. Vaughn was pasted in place beside him, as steady as a tank. They were waved through, only to go through the same inspection at the front door. The wedding was under lock and key.

Clint Vaughn never missed a beat, today a colorless British paper pusher with a mustache and glasses. Martinelli had picked the right man for this job.

It was just a matter of hours before he was reunited with his beloved son, his *quello piccolo*. Gianni fought to steady his breathing.

*

It was impossible that the moment had arrived, but here it was. Jessie willed herself not to perspire. The hairdresser and makeup artist and manicurist had gone. Jessie had shooed out Abbie and Mary and Sabrina. She was alone.

Taking a breath, Jessie studied her reflection in the full-length mirror. Her wedding gown was a strapless soft satin, the bodice fitted, the skirt flared. The back dipped to her waist. An embroidered lace coat covered the dress, a train drifting behind for several feet. The stiff collar buttoned from the neck to below her breasts and flared out into an elegant arc. A diamond headpiece entwined her French twist and dropped to a V over her forehead. Florentine, Jessie's personal designer, had outdone himself.

She was wearing Andrew's solitaire on her right hand. Something old. The strapless teddy was something new. The dusty rose nail polish on her fingers and toes was Abbie's. Something borrowed. Her mother's simple strand of sapphires on her wrist was something blue.

Jessie couldn't shake the memory of Andrew. She loved Nick and wanted to marry him more than anything in the world, but Andrew keep slicing his way into her brain. She looked into the mirror ... and her mind imagined Andrew staring back at her.

Well, it was only natural. She was marrying Andrew's brother after all, due to his matchmaking. Why shouldn't he be hovering?

*

Bree and Yves were seated in the second row, directly behind the Rudolphs. Bree took in the opulence, plastic people with plastic smiles from plastic surgeons. This kind of thing was usually reserved for kings and queens. Hollywood's rich and shallow. Movies. This was not Nick McDeare. It reeked of Jessica Kendle. How had he been brainwashed into this circus?

*

As Lyle helped seat over four hundred guests in the Great Hall, he examined each celebrity, luminary, politician, actor, writer, and friend. Including the mayor and the governor and a senator. He'd spent the day checking out every door and window in the mansion. All locked and impossible to penetrate.

Lyle was alert but satisfied. Gianni would be a fool to try to pull something tonight. The security was at presidential level.

*

"This is so cool," Zane whispered to his mom as they were led down the aisle to the front row. "It's like a castle. We get to sit with Anthony's family."

"Your friend must think an awful lot of you."

"Anthony's the best friend I ever had." Zane sat down and eyed the skylight. "He's normal, not like the other rich kids at school. And his parents are cool."

Zane had never told his mother about his encounter with a ghost. It was a secret.

*

Nick fastened the last notch of his waistcoat and checked himself in the mirror. The black tails fit well. The white shirt, tie, and waistcoat looked good. Not bad for a human penguin.

Moving to the window, Nick gazed out at the silvery surf. A half moon was suspended in the blue velvet sky, its reflection bouncing off the inky ocean. He was on edge, but it wasn't about marrying Jessie. They should've eloped, putting a stop to this Olympic event months ago.

His diamond studs and cuff links winked at him in the light. Andrew had worn them at his-- A frigid blast slammed into him, icy and menacing.

Andrew.

Dashing for the door, Nick collided with Lyle as he entered the room. "Anthony," Nick gasped. "Is he--"

"He's fine. I just left him. He's with Bill, waiting for Jessie. Sabrina said it's time."

"Give me a minute, okay?"

*

Jessie stood at the window. Gentle waves lapped up on the beach, the candy-colored lights from the solarium spilling out onto the sand. The ebb and flow of the surf cast a net of tranquility over her. Things changed, but life--

A jolt of icy air punched Jessie like a car's air bag sprung loose. Goose bumps scaled her arms and legs. Jessie started at her cell's jangle, rushing to answer. "It's me," Nick said.

"Nick, the cold! I just felt a frigid blast."

"Me, too."

"Do you think Andrew, uh, changed his mind about our marrying each other?" Jessie giggled nervously. This couldn't be serious. Not now. Not today. Her nerves were getting to her, that's all.

"I think he's … just letting us know he's here." Nick was right. That's what it was.

Abbie poked her head in the doorway. "Time to go, bride. Sabrina's orders."

"I hear Abbie," Nick said. "I love you. Okay, let's get this dog-and-pony show over with."

That's the Nick she knew and loved.

Everything was right with the world.

*

Bree's heart melted at the sight of Nick getting into place on the staircase. He was movie-star gorgeous as he scanned the crowd, too handsome for his own good. What tails did for a man.

Nick spotted her and smiled. Bree smiled back.

He'd tire of Jessie within a year. Wouldn't he?

*

Standing quietly behind closed doors at the back of the Great Hall, Anthony Brady held a white satin pillow, his parents' rings resting on top. What if he dropped it again? Everybody would laugh. Dad had said to focus on him as he marched towards the landing. That's what he'd do.

Sabrina gently told Anthony to get ready. The ceremony was beginning. Anthony heard the music change from a violin to something else. Pretty music. Dad said it was harps and flutes.

He'd focus on his dad and --

A brittle wind hit Anthony, his hair blowing off his face, the lace on the pillow lifting. Daddy Andrew. Daddy was here and … he wasn't happy. Anthony didn't know how he knew that, but he knew. "My dad," he told the big lady. "I need to talk to—"

"Sshh, honey." Sabrina signaled two maids to open the doors. Anthony was suddenly facing a great big hall full of people. But then he saw his dad standing way down at the end of the aisle, at the bottom of the landing. Dad smiled at him, and Anthony knew everything would be okay.

*

Dio, Anthony was no longer a baby. Seated on the aisle, Gianni watched his son perform his duty, so handsome in his miniature tails. He was a young man, almost eight. And that beatific smile on his face. Following his son's line of vision, Gianni realized with disgust the boy was smiling at McDeare. And the degenerate was looking at Anthony the way a real father--

Gianni stifled the red hot rage sweeping through him. McDeare wouldn't be smiling much longer. Gianni would die before he'd let that cretin raise Anthony. And he'd proven to be a man hard to kill.

*

Stoic in his tails, a vision in her black beaded gown, Lyle and Abbie walked towards Nick at the landing.

And then, my God. Jessie.

An angel kissed by a cloud of lace. Jessie glided down the aisle on Bill's arm, glowing. Her eyes were locked on Nick, a hint of a smile on her face, eyes shining. As she approached the stairs, Nick reached for her. He felt her relax at his touch and covered her small hand with his. Together they climbed to the landing and turned to face each other. Every second was magnified, every sound heightened, every color brightened.

The minister began his recitation. And then it was all a background blur, Jessie Nick's sole focus. Her crystal blue eyes on his-- He snapped back to attention as the minister said, "Do you, Nicholas Patrick McDeare, take this woman …"

*

More fucking jewels in here than Tiffany's. Clint shifted in his seat. The place smelled like a perfume factory. He didn't get McDeare. Why get married when he didn't have to? He was already living with Kendle and he had plenty of his own money. And why the big deal over raising another man's son? The kid wasn't even his own.

*

How could Jessie marry this boor? Josh was witnessing a travesty. Jessie deserved a man to worship her, share her passion for the theater. A man who knew how to make love to a woman and savor every morsel of that exquisite body. Someone like … Josh.

*

"And do you, Jessica Kendle Brady, take this man …"

Lyle tried to tune out the words, the images of the day he'd married Barb flashing through his mind like a torturous collage.

Forcing himself to scan the guests, he searched for the face of a dead man.

CHAPTER 18

Her own ring catching the candlelight, Jessie slid the wide gold band onto Nick's finger, her hand trembling a tiny bit. "I now pronounce you man and wife." Nick drew Jessie into his arms and kissed her. There was no crowd watching, no minister, no Abbie and Lyle. There was just Nick. Her husband. Her future.

Anthony joined them, beaming. Nick tousled his hair, put Anthony between them, and hand-in-hand the trio headed down the long aisle to the sweetest applause Jessie had ever heard.

*

"Look, if you haven't gotten the photo by now, you're never going to," Nick growled at the photographers. The wedding party had been posing for an hour for their official pictures. The press was still out in force, not banished until the bride and groom retired to the dinner reception. Most of the actors were loving it, but he'd noticed De Niro slink out the back way. Nick was tired and hot and thirsty. "My son probably got better pictures in five minutes than you're going to get."

"Nick, please." Jessie turned to Nick and stroked his lapels.

"This is bullshit, Jess."

"Hey, Mom and Dad." Nick looked at Anthony, clicking pictures rapidly. The boy danced over to them. "These will be the best!"

"You heard the official photographer," Nick declared to the press corps over their snapping lights. "We're finished here."

*

"We have plenty of time," Gianni whispered to Clint. "The happy couple won't be leaving until after midnight." Gianni smirked as Nick and Jessie waltzed their traditional first dance around the glittery dance floor under a pink spotlight, the orchestra playing a song more fit for a gaudy Broadway musical than a spiritual union.

"I say we look for our best opportunity and grab it," Clint grunted, downing a scotch. "I don't want to fuck around."

"I'll decide that."

*

Anthony dashed from one end of the reception to the other, snapping pictures. Zane stuck by his side, scribbling notes for the school paper. "We're going to be famous," Zane crowed, high-fiving him. "I bet our article makes the front page."

- 169 -

"Come on. Let's get more cake and the strawberry and chocolate things."
Turning, Anthony collided with a tall bald man. Anthony backed away. The man
gave him the creeps, the way he smiled down at him with those weird green eyes,
like the stones Mom had on a bracelet. Emeralds.

*

Yves had taken shot after shot of the wedding, trying to capture the unusual
aspects of the ceremony and guests. It was a study in contrasts, the juxtaposition of
Jessie's ivory beauty to Nick's exotic looks only part of it. There were guests who
were giddy and drunk. Guests who looked annoyed. Stimulated. Bored. Thrilled.
Celebrities, strangers, friends, and family.

The photos would be a wedding present from Bree and himself.

*

"Let's duck the rest of this party," Nick whispered in Jessie's ear.

"We have to stay until midnight."

"Listen, Bill's jet is gassed up and waiting. We've toasted. We've danced.
We've gorged ourselves. We've cut the cake. Let's get the hell out of here and
celebrate the New Year somewhere over the North Atlantic. I'm dying to see you in
your Christmas present."

"We can't ... can we?"

"Sure we can."

To leave their own reception ... Oh, why not? They'd gone along with every
other part of the scripted ceremony. Time to put a little McDeare adventure into it.
She was a McDeare now ... Jessica McDeare.

Jessie slipped her hand into Nick's. "Let's go."

"I'll tell Mary. You tell Anthony."

*

Mary had been talking to Nora and her husband Chester for hours. Old friends,
people with a great sense of humor. At the same time Mary kept an eye on Anthony,
dutifully checking in every ten minutes or so.

"Mary, we're leaving early," Nick whispered in her ear. "Keep a close eye on
Anthony, okay? Promise?"

"You bet."

*

"They're leaving now," Clint whispered to Gianni. "Hours early."

Gianni cursed under his breath. He'd wanted to stop the joyous celebration in
its tracks, wipe the faces of the bride and groom clean of all joy, like raking a trowel
over wet cement. But if Nicholas and Jessica were halfway to England by the time
they heard, they'd be frantic in their scramble to return. Imagine their horror, their
sense of helplessness suspended in mid-air. Yes, this might work even better.

"All right. We wait for our moment."

*

Scrambling through the crowd, Anthony caught up with his parents at the
door.

"There you are!" His mom hugged him tightly.

"We'll call you every day, Bongo," Dad ran his fingers through Anthony's
hair. "Remember our deal and don't give Mary any trouble."

"Can Zane stay with me next weekend?"

"If it's okay with Mary, sure." His mom kissed him. "Love you."

"Love you." Dad folded Anthony in his arms. "See you soon."

Anthony hung onto his dad for a moment, whispered, "Love you, too, Dad."

He watched his parents run for the limo, waving over their shoulders and disappearing into the lightly whirling snow.

After that, Anthony stood in the Great Hall, snapping pictures of guests as they left the party. One lady had on a crazy zebra coat. Another lady's hat looked like a bird was sitting on her head. He made a face at Zane, flapping his arms like wings. They both started to laugh.

Mrs. Harwell joined them. "Zane, time for bed. The party's breaking up."

"You said I could stay up till midnight. It's New Year's!"

"I'll go, too," Anthony said. "Can we watch New Year's on TV in my room?"

"Mmm, I guess so. But be sure to ask Mary. Zane and I will wait for you upstairs."

"I'll get cookies and stuff from the buffet and knock on your door." Anthony rushed towards the solarium, the camera swinging from his neck. Mary was still talking to the lady who dressed his mom. Out of breath, he begged Mary to let him watch TV with Zane. "Okay? Please?"

Mary smiled. "Okay, if it's okay with Mrs. Harwell. Tell me when you're ready to go upstairs."

"Thanks! I'll get dessert first." Anthony kissed Mary and dashed towards the dessert buffet. He stacked towers of cookies into a napkin, and a nice waiter got him four cans of soda from the kitchen. Anthony piled them in his arms, but one slipped and cracked open, spraying his face, hair, and suit. Anthony remembered to protect his camera.

The waiter threw a napkin over the can and laughed. He told Anthony to wash himself off, and he'd get him a bag to carry everything. Anthony handed the waiter his stash and trotted towards the hallway with the big guest bathroom.

*

His coat slung over his arm, Gianni trailed Anthony down the deserted corridor, Clint a few steps behind. Gianni's pulse soared, his joy almost impossible to contain. Martinelli's two security guards in their navy blazers were positioned at a nearby side door, waiting for them.

Gianni and Clint entered the bathroom. The fates were with them. Anthony was alone and brushing his suit with a wet paper towel, his camera on the sink. Gianni smiled warmly at the boy. He set his coat on the adjoining sink and began to wash his hands. Clint entered a stall and closed the door.

*

The bald man with the weird green eyes gave Anthony the creeps. Tossing the paper towel in the trash, Anthony grabbed his camera. He hurried to the door and heard a noise. Anthony looked over his shoulder. The guy who'd been in the stall lunged for him!

Panicked, Anthony swung the door open. The man grabbed him with strong arms, covering his mouth and nose with a cloth. It smelled sickly sweet, icky. Anthony struggled, kicking and squirming, but … his arms felt heavy and … he was

... so weak... Something heavy was wrapped around him, and he felt himself lifted into the air. His camera dropped ... He heard it hit the floor ...

Anthony floated into darkness.

*

Pausing at the side door, Clint withdrew a piece of paper from his breast pocket with a handkerchief. He dropped it onto the stoop while Martinelli's men checked the outer perimeter. The limo was idling a few yards away, lights off, the back door open. The boy was unconscious in Fosselli's arms, wrapped in the man's coat.

The men nodded and Clint and Gianni strode for the limo, Fosselli's man driving. They climbed in and Fosselli set the kid on the seat across from them, the coat a perfect camouflage across his small body. The car coasted away, blending into the traffic leaving the estate. No security check on the way out. The idiots.

As the limo sped towards the Holiday Inn, Fosselli moved to the other seat and slid the coat off, kissing the boy's forehead and running his fingers through his hair. He opened a small bag on the floor and withdrew a medical packet. Clint watched as Gianni carefully injected his son with a sedative. The kid would be out for hours.

Clint felt a prickle of pity for Anthony, for the way he'd surprised him like that in the bathroom. There was something about him. Clint had watched Anthony tonight. He seemed older than his age, smart and undemanding. What would his life be like with a cold fish like Fosselli?

The limo dropped Clint in front of his hotel. He watched the car bullet into the night, destination unknown. Mission accomplished. Job over. Hinkie would be thrilled her watch was done.

Climbing behind the wheel of his Chevy, Clint began the long drive back into Manhattan. He wished he'd brought some scotch for the ride home. His stomach was queasy, nothing a good shot of scotch wouldn't squelch. He'd stop in the first town and find the nearest bottle.

*

"We've reached our cruising altitude," the flight attendant told Nick and Jessie. "Feel free to move about the plane. I'm Ruby. Can I get you anything?"

Nick ignored the attendant's sexy smile and reached for Jessie's hand. "I think my wife and I will catch some sleep."

"Um," Ruby's smile faded, "there's some champagne in the bedroom, compliments of Mr. Rudolph. Our flight time's seven hours, ten minutes. I'll call you a half hour out of London."

*

Aldo Zappella hated New Year's Eve. Who gave a shit when one year ended and another began? Every day was the same, full of threats and snitches and cops.

Still no word from Vaughn about Fosselli and the kid. He was sick of the whole Gianni Fosselli mess and its endless tentacles. His sister Paula was making him nuts, calling constantly, whining and wailing. Ian Wexley had ruined her life. No man would ever want her again. She blamed Aldo. He'd been too hard on Ian. Aldo cursed the day he involved Wexley in the Andrew Brady extermination, and he cursed Nick McDeare for exposing the scam.

But most of all, he cursed Jessie Kendle for turning Ian Wexley into the bitter, twisted alcoholic who married star-struck Paula Zappella and started this whole thing.

*

Mary looked at her watch. Anthony should've checked in with her by now. She bet he was still loading up on sweets and needed some help. Excusing herself, Mary said good night to Nora and Chester. As she headed for the Great Hall, a waiter approached. "Excuse me. You're the McDeare boy's nanny, right?"

Swallowing her dislike for the word nanny, Mary nodded.

"He went to the men's room and was supposed to come back for this." He showed Mary a bag of cookies and soda. "I figure he probably grabbed some cake and forgot about it."

Squashing a jolt of anxiety, Mary thanked him. The waiter was probably right. Anthony packed up cake instead and got distracted. She hurried towards the Great Hall, carefully scanning the mass of people waiting for their cars to be brought around. No Anthony. Trying to stay calm, Mary made her way to the stairway. She spotted Lyle chatting with a member of the security detail by the door, the guard easy to pick out in his navy blazer.

Making her way upstairs, Mary entered their suite, calling out to Anthony as she opened the adjoining door to his room. He must've forgotten she'd told him to let her know before he went upstairs.

The room was empty.

Zane's room. They had to be in Zane's room. Mary felt her heart flutter. She knocked on his door, Mrs. Harwell appearing. She said Anthony had never shown up. Zane had fallen asleep waiting, watching TV.

Panicking, Mary flew down the stairs and found Lyle and the security guard. "Anthony, I can't find him." Gasping for breath, she told Lyle about Zane and the bag of cookies.

"Maybe he's with Abbie?" Lyle's face blanched.

"I haven't seen her for a while either."

"You find Abbie. I'll search the house."

"I'll get my men and help you." The security guard pulled out his short-wave radio and broke into a run.

*

Bree and Yves were at the door, waiting for their car. Bree spotted Lyle and a guard jogging across the Great Hall. "Something's wrong. Wait here." She hurried after Lyle, the cop heading towards the side hallway and the bathrooms. "Lyle, hold up! What's going on?"

Stopping, he shot her a look. "Anthony's missing." The man's face was ashen, his eyes as hollow as a skull's sockets. He turned down the hallway and halted abruptly.

An old-fashioned camera lay on the tile floor outside the men's room. Lyle scooped it up, examining it.

"Is it--"

"It's Anthony's. Nick put his initials on it." He looked sick.

"Oh, my God. Fosselli."

*

Abbie was tired of arguing with Josh. They'd taken their quarrel into the family study, far from the party. The man continued to claim he had nothing to do with drugging Jessie. And he had the nerve to invite Abbie upstairs to his room to make nice and apologize to him. Was he insane?

"Abbie." Mary stood in the doorway, looking distraught. "Have-have you seen Anthony?"

"No. Why?"

"He's," Mary patted her heart, "he's gone." She started to sob, crumbling in front of Abbie's eyes.

"Dear God." Had Gianni ...? No. Please, no. Abbie helped Mary up, mouthing words of comfort and asking Josh to watch her. Abbie dashed towards the hallway.

*

Gianni cradled Anthony in his arms. Tucked in a soft blanket, the boy looked serene and beautiful lying in the back seat next to him, an angel. They'd make the change back to his car at Emlenton. Anthony would sleep through it all until he was safe in his new bed. Gianni kissed his forehead and pulled his son closer.

His son. Anthony was finally his. They'd nestle into their haven in Ohio until the furor in New York died down. Nicholas and Jessica would call on the FBI and the police to find Anthony. There would be a nationwide search for the kidnappers, but Anthony would never be found. Gianni Fosselli was officially dead. If Nicholas and Barton searched on their own, their hunt would be fruitless. Max Callaban had no connection to Gianni Fosselli.

In the meantime, Gianni and Anthony would be self-sufficient for months, up to a year. He had freezers full of meat and prepared dishes. Carlo would fetch anything they'd need. Gianni was prepared to tutor the boy on his own, having meticulously researched the proper curriculum for a seven-year-old. And his son would learn Italian with tapes and his father's help. Gianni had planned ahead, taking every detail into consideration.

Eventually, Gianni and his son would travel the world. Max Callaban would take his boy Bryce to Italy and teach him about his proud heritage and introduce him to his real family. Luciana would be thrilled. She couldn't wait to meet Anthony, calling Gianni constantly for the smallest details.

The dark days were finally over. The loneliness was behind him.

Life was glorious.

*

Lyle met the local police in the vestibule and quickly filled them in. Chief Slutsky was tall and lank with floppy dark hair, thick glasses, and intelligent tan eyes. He immediately sent his men to search the grounds. "Calm down, Lieutenant, we'll find him. Word is this place was as secure as Rikers tonight. He's around here somewhere. You know kids."

At war with himself, Lyle desperately tried to think like a cop and shove his emotions out of the way. He'd failed to protect another child on his watch. Another sweet child— Lyle swallowed, his mouth parched. He should've kept his eyes glued to Anthony every minute. How was he going to tell Nick? And Jessie. She had no idea Fosselli was out there. He cursed himself for letting Nick convince him to keep the man a secret. Jessie was going to see this as the ultimate betrayal. Nick had no idea.

Huddled on the stairs, Mary was crying, Abbie trying to comfort her. Abbie met Lyle's eyes, her brown eyes moist. Lyle read her perfectly, Gianni Fosselli haunting them both.

Bree sidled over to him and whispered, "Did you tell the cops about Fosselli?"

"Are you kidding? I need their cooperation, not a trip to Bellevue." Telling the authorities a dead man was alive would make Lyle part of the problem. It would end his ability to influence the investigation more quickly than ... a child vanishing into the night.

*

In the cozy bedroom aboard the Rudolph jet, Jessie emerged from the bathroom. She was wearing Nick's Christmas present and feeling sexy. Nick lounged against the bed's pillows, watching as she swayed towards him. The lacy lilac negligee was as sheer as glass.

"You're stunning." Nick's eyes devoured her from head to toe, making her grow warm. "You're also blushing." His lip quirked as he pulled back the sheet.

"It fits like a second skin." Jessie slid into bed beside him. "How did you do that?"

"I've memorized every delicious inch of you." He pulled her down into his arms, combing his fingers through her hair.

"I love you, Nick."

"Ditto, Mrs. McDeare."

"Mrs. McDeare. I like hearing that."

"I like saying that."

"Nick McDeare, bachelor at large no more."

Nick chuckled, a throaty laugh that made Jessie tingle. He pressed his lips to her collarbone. His tongue moved down, tickling the hollow between her breasts, teasing her nipples, sending ripples down her body and igniting every pleasure point on every nerve until she quivered with wanting him.

*

A bottle of scotch tucked under his arm, Clint returned to his car. Convenient that liquor stores stayed open late on New Year's Eve. He had a powerful thirst. As he headed for the ramp of the Long Island Expressway, he speed-dialed Aldo. "It's done."

"I'll let him know."

"I expect the rest of the money ASAP." He clicked off.

Clint took a swig of scotch, the liquid burning going down. The second one was smoother. The image of a drugged Anthony McDeare began to blur.

A few more swallows, and it was forgotten.

*

"Lieutenant Barton? The side door was unlocked. This was on the stoop." His face grim, Chief Slutksy used his plastic-gloved hand to show Lyle a note. The letters were cut from magazines and newspapers and pasted on a plain sheet of white paper: HAVE THE KID. WANT 3 MILLION IN UNMARKED BILLS. WILL BE IN TOUCH.

This was bullshit. Fosselli or a surrogate had been here tonight and taken Anthony. And no amount of millions would get him back.

The grandfather clock began to gong. Midnight.

Happy New Year.

*

The news was good. Roberto Martinelli clicked off his cell and stared out the window of his Jersey condo, a happy man. Gianni had the kid. The police had found the phony ransom note. And Roberto had a dunce in place to pick up the money in a few days. The guy was so far removed from the Martinelli family he wouldn't be able to give the cops anything more than his name. Roberto was in the clear. The security guards would never talk, their families well provided for, an attorney a phone call away. He could call off the brownstone watch. It was over.

The New Year was beginning perfectly.

Time to get back to his princess and the little party in the bedroom.

*

Gianni pulled a chilled bottle of Dom Perignon from the sterling silver ice bucket. He covered it with a towel and popped the cork. Filling a flute, he toasted to his sleeping son. "Happy New Year, Anthony. Here's to all our future years together. I love you."

Sipping, he gazed out the window. They were already deep into Pennsylvania's rolling hills. What a wonderful New Year's Eve. Gianni's mind flitted to Jessica and her demon. This would be a New Year's she'd never forget.

Welcome to hell, Jessica. Your turn.

*

"You're sure?" Bill Rudolph stared at Lyle. "Maybe we should consider giving Nick and Jessie a few more hours of happiness?"

"Your call," Chief Slutsky said, pushing his glasses up his nose. "I've sealed the estate and called in the feds. We're done here."

Lyle dropped his head, the pressure building. The cops were running in circles, the ransom note the perfect misdirection. The minutes were ticking away, Nick and Jessie somewhere over the North Atlantic. Fuck the honeymoon. He needed Nick back ASAP. "Turn the plane around, Mr. Rudolph." Lyle turned to Chief Slutksy. "Make sure they have immediate clearance when they land at Islip. Do whatever you have to."

Pulling out his cell phone, Bill nodded. The chief hurried away, on his own phone. Lyle said a silent prayer Fosselli was within a hundred miles of the city. In range of the medallion.

*

Nick collapsed onto his back, brushing the damp hair from his eyes as his breathing leveled off. Jessie smiled at him, her eyes smoky, cheeks flushed from making love. Gravity suddenly rolled them towards the edge of the bed, the plane banking sharply to the right. Were they already heading south towards London from the Irish coast? Impossible.

It was only one in the morning. Nick pushed his anxiety away, not about to waste his honeymoon worrying about flight patterns. "Hey," Jessie purred, "we missed--"

The bedside phone buzzed, breaking the spell. Caption Arnold. Nick turned numb at his words, a message from the tower at MacArthur Airport on Long Island ordering them to return to New York. The captain said he didn't know why they were turning around. The order came directly from Mr. Rudolph.

"We're going back to New York," Nick told Jessie. "Bill's request."

"Why?"

Shrugging, Nick tried to stay cool. "Maybe he needs the plane for something." Bill wouldn't order the jet back on their honeymoon flight for anything but an emergency. Nick's stomach lurched.

"Nick, I'm scared."

"It could be weather up ahead or-- anything. Try not to worry." Nick draped his arm around Jessie and kissed her softly. But his gut was roiling.

*

Hanratty's was crowded. New Year's Fucking Eve. Clint cursed holidays and signaled the bartender for a double scotch, his eyes drawn to the overhead television. Rockin' New Year's Eve was interrupted with breaking news.

A female reporter stood in front of the Rudolph estate, her face as animated as a plastic doll's. "We've just learned that Anthony Brady McDeare, the son of Nick McDeare and Jessica Kendle, has been kidnapped. As everyone in the metropolitan area knows, McDeare and Kendle were married here at Bill Rudolph's mansion this evening in a lavish ceremony. Shortly after the newlyweds left for their honeymoon, the child disappeared. There's talk of a ransom note, but we haven't been able to confirm that. We do know the McDeares are on their way back to New York."

So the Keystone Kops found the decoy note. The image of a drugged Anthony McDeare bolted into his brain, Clint grabbing the kid and shoving that cloth over his face ... Clint pushed it away, downing his drink and ordering another.

*

Willie pulled the limo onto the private terminal tarmac at Islip's MacArthur Airport. Lyle Barton sat in the back seat, as still as stone. Lyle only allowed the facts into his brain. No emotions or he'd bust his fist through the window and start a scream that would never stop. He could see the press jamming the terminal, their faces and lenses pressed to the glass. Thank God the Long Island police had ringed the tarmac with cops.

The Rudolph jet roared towards them, cutting its engines and coasting to a stop. Lyle and Willie got out of the car and waited. The cabin door opened and the stairway was dropped. A moment later, Nick and Jessie descended.

*

As she and Nick clattered down the stairs, Jessie saw Lyle approaching. She glanced at Nick, his eyes planted on the cop. Lyle looked like a slab of granite, avoiding her gaze.

"What's wrong?" Jessie cried. Anthony, this was about Anthony. She knew it with every breath she drew.

"Come on," Lyle said. "I'll tell you in the car. The press's up there, watching."

Jessie spotted the vultures in the terminal. Nick grabbed her hand and they ran for the safety of the tinted car glass. Once inside, she turned to Lyle, forcing out the dread words. "It's Anthony, isn't it?"

"I don't know how to say this." Lyle looked at Nick and cleared his throat. "I'm so sorry. He-he's been kidnapped."

All the oxygen was suddenly sucked out of the car, leaving an airless vacuum. Jessie couldn't catch her breath. This wasn't happening. She looked at Nick, the color draining from his face. He stared wordlessly at Lyle, his arm encircling her.

Collapsing against him, Jessie heaved broken sobs.

*

The car pulled away from the airport, Nick listening as Lyle explained what had happened. No mention of Gianni. Nick knew the ransom note was a joke. Fosselli had done the impossible and bridged the estate's security. He'd taken Anthony, like some supernatural force from beyond the grave. How? Nick cursed the man, his utter fear for the boy at war with his hatred for the monster who'd murdered his brother.

Jessie was weeping on Nick's shoulder. He kept his arm around her and pressed his lips to her forehead. Paparazzi trailed the car, Willie trying to outmaneuver them. Nick glared over his shoulder at the maggots.

"We're going to pull a switch when we get to the Rudolph estate," Lyle said in his cop voice. "Abbie, Josh, and Mary will leave the property in this car. The press will follow. You two go home in Bill's limo."

"Go home?" Jessie murmured. "But--"

"Nothing more to be done at the mansion. Every inch of the estate's been searched. Sealed as a crime scene."

Still reeling, Nick met Lyle's eyes. Lyle looked down at Nick's chest and back up again. What ... He got it. The medallion.

Nick casually slid his hand into his pocket, finding his key chain. He fingered the gizmo that turned on the homing chip in Anthony's necklace, pressing it. He waited anxiously for his own medallion to vibrate. Please. Please, dear God, let Anthony be near.

Nothing. His medallion was still.

Fighting tears, Nick shook his head at Lyle.

Anthony was ... lost.

CHAPTER 19

Falling snow made the drive across Pennsylvania tedious. Gianni nodded off for long stretches, rousing before dawn when they hit the Ohio border. From there it was only an hour's ride home.

He carried his sleeping son up to his new bedroom and changed his clothes. The pajamas were snug, the boy growing quickly. Gianni made a mental note to order a new array of clothes for Anthony immediately.

Never again would he be separated from his precious son. Gianni ran his hand across Anthony's dark locks. A ring on Anthony's finger caught his attention, an expensive piece of jewelry with a radiant diamond in the middle. Anthony had never worn jewelry before. It looked like his son had inherited Gianni's passion for exquisite things. Blood always told. And a medallion—Gianni studied it closely—stating Anthony was allergic to sulfa drugs. Eventually, he would take Anthony to a pediatrician for regular check-ups, but that was in the future.

It was seven-thirty. Dr. Greenglass said the sedative would wear off within ten hours. Anthony should be awake soon. They'd have breakfast together and begin to get to know each other again. The scent of sweet Italian sausage and vegetable strata was sure to rouse Anthony. He'd be hungry.

Downstairs, Gianni checked the front door. He'd installed locks on both doors that required a key on the inside. He kept the keys with him at all times. The only phones in the house were his two cells, both always in his pocket. His supply of prepaid phones was stored in Carlo's cottage.

In a few days Anthony could venture outside, once he felt safe and loved. The estate was isolated. The high wrought iron fence would prevent him from leaving the property. No electronic security, no need to involve a second party with the installation of an elaborate alarm system and camera, which would invite unwanted attention. McDeare and Barton might suspect he was alive, but they would never find him. No one else had a clue he existed. Gianni had considered every conceivable scenario.

*

Ten hours after the kidnapping and the new day dawned, gray and sullen. The press had moved onto the block in force, reminding Nick of the night Andrew died, the night he'd stood vigil. The brownstone was ringed by police keeping the horde at bay. Barton's ruse with the limos had worked, Nick and Jessie speeding home before the press had a clue. The FBI had arrived simultaneously, taking up residence on the first floor and waiting for a ransom call that would never come.

The agents were buff and wholesome, straight from J. Edgar Hoover Central Casting. Agents Holstrom and Coleman. They'd grilled Nick and Jessie about any encounters with strangers. Did they sense they'd been followed or watched in recent months? Had Roberto Martinelli threatened them, going back to Nick's accusation about criminal dealings with Gianni Fosselli? Nick had choked on his lies, silently cursing Gianni. How did you tell the feds you were being stalked by a dead man?

They were advised to call their attorney to arrange for the ransom money. Another sham. Hold onto hope, the agents advised. Chances were good both Anthony and the money would be returned safely. They had years of experience in kidnappings. Nick had made the ridiculous phone call, Jessie in no shape to do anything.

Mary did what she always did in a crisis, retreating to the kitchen and making coffee, baking muffins for the agents. Nick knew she blamed herself for Anthony's kidnapping, but he was too consumed with his own guilt to help. Everyone was locked in their own shell of misery.

Barton had slipped off to his apartment with Abbie. Nick should be with them, working the case. But he couldn't leave Jessie, as bereft as a lost child herself. Nick McDeare knew too well what losing a child could do to a parent. When he'd stared into the murky Potomac after Jeffrey died, no mythical siren could have been more seductive.

Abbie's departure had left the idiot Elliot behind at the brownstone. The actor had arrived without being asked and attached himself to the feds, pestering them with questions. When he'd started to hover over Jessie, Nick had hustled her upstairs to their bedroom and told him to leave. Night had finally turned to dawn.

Now Jessie was curled into a ball on the bed, her eyes closed. She'd finally fallen asleep, thank God. Her grief devoured Nick like a flame eating through tinder. His fault. He'd failed to stop Fosselli.

He couldn't lose another son.

Leaving the room, Nick closed the door quietly, ignoring his cell's buzz, in no mood for any calls. He paused in the hallway, staring into Anthony's darkened room. Empty. Anthony must be terrified. A ghoul had taken him, the dark creature that lurked under every child's bed.

"Andrew," he begged, "if you can hear me, take care of our son. I know you can't talk to me. You said your goodbyes. That's over. But if you have any earthly power left at all, please make this right. Please."

*

"Hell, Abbie, Anthony could be on a plane or a slow boat to Italy by now." Lyle gulped his fifth cup of coffee and poured Abbie her third. They'd been at his place awake around the clock, the door left unlocked for Nick. He rubbed his eyes.

"I don't think so." Abbie twirled a lock of hair around her finger. "Anyway, the Long Island cops moved fast and sealed the airports and seaways."

"They thought I was nuts. Maybe I should've told them about Fosselli. If--"

"If what?" Nick stood in the doorway. "They never would've believed you."

"It always comes back to that, doesn't it?"

Nick told them Jessie was sleeping. "Any news?"

"Slutsky's kept me up to date. The FBI spent the night questioning the security detail. Someone unlocked that unused side door, the same area where the ransom note was found. That was the escape route, close to where I found Anthony's camera. Two guards failed polygraphs. Recent hires, clean records. They're being held, not talking, lawyered up. Martinelli's people never talk. They're useless."

"Anthony's camera, it uses film. Where's--"

"The police lab. No prints except Anthony's, yours, and mine. They're developing the film."

*

Bree awoke from a yummy dream. She and Nick were back in Hong Kong, making love. Bree smiled, the memory of Nick's naked body entwined with hers making her tingle. Guilt crept in when she looked over at Yves' side of the bed. Empty.

Last night hurtled back. Anthony's abduction. Poor Yves not understanding why she was so frantic to help, blindly going along with her insistence they hide his camera in his carryall. It wouldn't be the first time he'd used a secret compartment to conceal forbidden film. She'd seen the feds confiscating the guests' cameras and cell phones, hoping someone caught the kidnappers in the act. Yves' photos might provide an invaluable key to Gianni, a dead man no cop would be looking for.

As they'd left the Rudolph mansion, Bree had asked Yves to drive back into Manhattan instead of her mother's house. She wanted to print out the film on her work computer. Yves had complied, but he'd demanded to know what was going on. Bree promised to explain everything tomorrow, the rest of the ride home silent. She'd gone through the photos quickly, after Yves went to sleep. Nothing.

Now it was tomorrow. She called Nick on his cell again, no answer.

Throwing on a terry robe, Bree hurried into the living room. Yves was slumped on the couch, a mug of coffee in his hand, his eyes ringed with circles. He motioned towards the large stack of color photos on the table she'd printed out. "Start talking. What's this about?"

"I owe you." Bree dropped down beside him. "When you know the reason, you'll understand. I hope." Yves offered her his coffee. She sipped, calling on the caffeine for strength. "I've been working with Nick and Lyle Barton. It's complicated."

*

Anthony's head hurt. He cracked his eyes open. Did he have the flu again? Everything looked fuzzy. He struggled to sit up.

Where was he? How did he ...? A memory surfaced. The guys in the bathroom. His heart began to thump.

Panicked, Anthony threw back the covers and staggered up. The room started to spin, and he gripped the bedpost, taking shaky steps towards the window, looking out. This wasn't New York. It wasn't where his dad and mom got married either. There weren't any houses. All he saw was a barn and lots of trees and snow.

Opening the door, Anthony inched into the hallway, looking around. Empty. He dashed for the staircase, creeping downstairs quietly. He had to find his mom and dad! The front door was ahead of him. He ran for it and yanked on the knob. It wouldn't open. There was a lock, but it needed a key.

"What are you doing?" a soft voice asked.

Startled, Anthony swung around. The man with the weird green eyes! Anthony ran blindly, looking for an escape route. He circled through room after room, the man his shadow. In the kitchen, he spotted the back door and tugged on it. Locked. He started to cry.

"Anthony, don't be afraid." The man came closer. "I'm Gianni. Your father."

*

Clint lurched to the bathroom. He had a blinding headache and an acid stomach. He needed food. Food and-- He grabbed the toilet and tossed last night's scotch.

Anthony McDeare popped into his brain. Clint heaved again. Why was his brain stuck on the repeat key with that kid? Straightening up, he turned on the sink, slurping water from his cupped hand. Better. He glanced at his image in the mirror. He saw Anthony staring back at him.

Cursing, Clint shuffled back to the bedroom and threw on some clothes. Hanratty's was the answer. Hanratty's and a double scotch.

*

"So we need these pictures to try to identify Fosselli," Bree concluded. "And I have to get back to that telescope and try to uncover whatever Martinelli's hiding in Jersey City. That's our leverage, all we have. And now it's more important than ever."

As usual, Bree didn't have a clue what he was thinking. Yves hadn't said a word during her detailed explanation. He'd stared at the floor in that quiet manner of his. "Why didn't you tell me this long ago?" he finally asked.

There it was. The million-dollar question. "Because ... well, because of Nick. I was afraid you'd think ... something was starting up between us again."

Yves seemed to find this amusing. "The man's crazy in love with Jessie Kendle. Anyone can see that."

A searing pain slashed through Bree. She used to think Nick would be no more satisfied with Jessie than an orchestra maestro with one violin. So sure. Now, now she didn't know what to think anymore. "So ... you're not mad about last night?"

"I knew you were troubled, ma cherie. You were wearing your work face I find so irresistible. I just wish you'd told me the truth sooner." He curled his fingers through hers. "I'm touched you thought I'd be jealous."

Bree felt like a shit.

"Come." Yves sprang up. "Let's get these photos to Nick and Barton. Then you and I will take up residence in that vacant apartment on the waterfront until I have to leave for Libya."

*

Pondering last night's events, Josh sat in his kitchen chugging down a cup of coffee. He'd left the brownstone after the ogre dragged Jessie upstairs. Josh's heart ached for her. How much more could the woman take? Jessie would never recover if anything happened to Anthony. She adored her son.

- 182 -

And Abbie. Her behavior was bizarre last night, weird for weeks now. She was hiding something. Was she sleeping with McDeare? Look how she'd embraced the bastard's accusations that Josh drugged Jessie. Was that when they started banging each other?

Whatever was going on, Josh intended to uncover it. He'd be there for Jessie when she discovered the truth about her husband and needed a warm shoulder. The more Jessie turned to Josh, the more she'd appreciate how right he was for her.

*

"We have to think," Nick said. Abbie and Lyle looked like wrecks. He knew he looked worse. Nick rubbed the back of his neck. "Where do we begin looking?" His cell jangled. He checked the screen. Agent Coleman.

"We don't want you leaving the premises. If the kidnappers phone--"

"I'll be back shortly." Punching off, he said, "What a joke. The Feebies want me hanging around to answer a call that's never going to come." Playing games was a waste of time. "Let's continue this in my office. Keep the feds happy."

Barton stared at him. "It's time for the truth. Tell Jessie about Gianni before it's too late."

"Not now. She's dealing with enough." His cell buzzed. "What?" Nick snapped.

"Coleman again. The family should make some kind of statement. Entreat the kidnappers to return the boy safely. Maybe Mrs. McDeare could--"

"Mrs. McDeare's speaking to no one. And neither am I." He clicked off. "They want us to plead with the kidnappers. Make a statement."

"I'll do it." Abbie's eyes darkened. "I'd love to deliver a message to Gianni. And think about what Lyle said, Nick. Tell Jessie before it's too late. Things have changed. You can't keep this from her anymore."

*

"Get away from me," Anthony whimpered. He breathed harder as the man stared at him with those glassy eyes.

The face crumbled. "You're my son. I love you. It's me. Gianni. Listen to me," he rushed on. "I had a doctor change my face so no one would recognize me. I'm alive."

"You're lying!"

"I can prove it, *quello piccolo*. I gave you ships for your birthday and Christmas. I brought you amaretto cookies from Oceano. I taught you the proper Italian greeting, a kiss on both cheeks. And that talk we had on my terrace, when I told you the truth, that I'm your real father--"

"You're dead. You died when the boat exploded. It was on TV! I saw it!"

The Gianni-man looked hurt. "It wasn't me on that ship. It was someone who looked like me."

Anthony covered his ears. "I want to go home. I want my mom and my dad--"

"Never say that again," the Gianni-man shouted. "That man is not your father."

Crying like a baby, Anthony ran for the hallway. He collapsed at the foot of the stairs, hugging the medallion under his pajamas. "Find me, Dad," he begged. "I know you can find me. You said this had special powers, like magic. Please."

- 183 -

*

Aldo called as Roberto parked the Honda behind Bottoms Up, back from his haven in Jersey.

"Fosselli and the kid arrived safely. He's grateful."

"And the other business? The ransom?"

"The cops found the first note. The follow-up's being mailed from Brooklyn. But we got a problem."

There was always a problem. His drug dealers were getting busted—Washington Heights, Brooklyn, the Bronx, one raid after another. They were going after his clubs, lounges, private transactions, shipments, even foreign ports. If only he could disappear into his Jersey City penthouse forever.

How did Churchill handle the generals who screwed up, the enemy that never let him sleep? Roberto crossed the alley and entered his office, the cell pressed to his ear. "What now?"

"The schmuck supposed to pick up the ransom money disappeared. He must've figured it out and ran. I'll get somebody else if we don't find him in time."

Roberto popped an antacid as he strode through the bar. Two broads were pole-dancing. Not a single john in the place. The bartender was reading a betting form. What the fuck was he doing here on New Year's Day? If he didn't need the cover for Jersey, he'd shut the place down.

Pushing through the front door, he climbed into his waiting limo. "Roberto? You there?"

"Forget finding a replacement. Just let the money sit while the cops watch the place. They'll think the kidnapper got scared off. It'll drag out and the mess will go away. One more lost kid. And when you find our disappearing act, make sure he disappears for good."

*

Clint inhaled enough scotch at Hanratty's to squash his hangover. The overhead television was tuned to an all-news station, Anthony McDeare the lead story. Colorful images of the boy and his parents chased each other over the screen, rehashing Andrew Brady's murder and Gianni Fosselli's death. Fosselli was like some monster in those Greek myths you couldn't kill. He kept growing another head or whatever they did back in the day.

Enough. He bought a bottle from the bartender and got a bacon cheeseburger and chili fries to go. At home, Clint sat at the kitchen table, wolfing down the food, guzzling scotch, and trying to forget the past twenty-four hours.

In hindsight, he should've said no to Martinelli and stayed out of this mess. That little kid wrapped in a coat, drugged. That sick control-freak psycho fawning all over him. Clint wished he'd never heard of Nick McDeare.

*

"Nick?" Jessie opened her eyes, scanning the empty bedroom. She jerked up. Instantly, she remembered everything, her gut clenching.

Her little boy, gone. Impossible. How could you lose a part of yourself?

Lyle saying the words that had changed her life forever. Words that made her die inside and split into broken pieces. Where was Nick? Robotically, Jessie left the bedroom, her legs moving like wooden stumps. Jessie paused in the hallway. Anthony's bedroom door was closed.

Jessie's heart leapt with hope. Had Anthony been found? It was open earlier. The medallion! She'd forgotten about Anthony and Nick's medallions. The police found Anthony and he was back in his own bed. She blessed Nick for having such foresight. Nick was with him, trying to calm him after what he'd been through. Her little boy was safe!

Throwing open the door, Jessie rushed into the room.

Empty.

Dear God. Jessie collapsed onto the bed. She hugged Anthony's pillow, smelling of shampoo and his sweet skin. She rocked back and forth, squeezing the soft pillow, the tears flowing. She wanted her baby back. She wanted to hold her son in her arms and hear him laugh and never let go.

*

While Abbie prepared to make a statement in front of the brownstone, Nick checked on Jessie. Seeing her asleep on Anthony's bed clutching a pillow shattered him all over again. He covered Jessie with a quilt and tiptoed out, leaning against the door and looking back. Anthony's baseball and bat were in the corner, tossed there after Nick had worked with him at the batting cage in the basement. A new photo Anthony took at Christmas was on the bookcase waiting to be framed, his schoolbooks scattered on the desk.

Only cold, hard thinking would work to get his son back. No giving into his emotions. He fingered his medallion, willing it to spring into life. Nothing.

Returning to his office, Nick joined Lyle. The TV was tuned to a national news network covering Anthony's abduction. Abbie stepped to a bank of microphones, the regional FBI director introducing her as a close family friend. Abbie cleared her throat. "Nick and Jessica McDeare have asked me to thank the public for your thoughts and prayers in this trying time. They appreciate it more than you'll ever know. Now I'd like to speak to the person who has taken Anthony."

Abbie looked directly into the camera. "I'm sure you're watching right now, enjoying your moment. Your victory will be short-lived." Agent Coleman cast Abbie a look of surprise. "Anthony will be brought home safely. We will hunt you down and put an end to the misery you've caused this family. That's a promise."

Coleman began to yammer about steps being taken to apprehend the kidnapper as Abbie hurried up the front steps.

Punching a button on the remote, Nick shut off the image.

"She said too much," Lyle said tonelessly. "The feds can't suspect we know more than we're telling them."

"She didn't say enough. She should've said we'll find Gianni and kill him. That's what she should've said."

*

Shivering, Gianni threw on his cardigan sweater. He'd have to make sure Anthony dressed warmly in this house of ice. He flicked off the television, laughed at Abigail's empty rhetoric, and tossed the remote. The TV snapped back on. *Che cosa l'inferno?* He clicked it off. The screen popped back up. Frustrated, Gianni unplugged the set.

The television jumped back on, Abigail's statement replayed.

Stumbling over his own feet, Gianni hurried to the kitchen, trying to focus on fixing Anthony a plate of sausages and strata. But the television ... A short in the set. Or maybe the batteries kicked in. Did televisions have backup batteries?

Anthony's terrified face crept into his mind. He'd looked so small, hovering at the bottom of the staircase, crying to the maniac he called his father. Gianni had swallowed his disgust and tried to comfort Anthony. But the boy had fled to his room, slamming the door. He'd take him a plate of food and leave him alone.

It would take time for his son to adjust. It was to be expected. Gianni had read books about children who'd been abducted by their rightful parent. Eventually the children bonded with the parent and led happy lives. Luci had assured him everything would be splendid, given time.

Something nagged at Gianni. Anthony's words, so soft and pleading.

"Find me, Dad. I know you can find me. You said this had special powers, like magic. Please."

The small television in the kitchen suddenly popped on, Abigail filling the screen and repeating her statement. Gianni gasped. The ring! The ring on Anthony's finger. Perhaps it housed a homing chip, the police zeroing in on Anthony right now. Had Nicholas planned ahead, suspecting this day would come?

Striding to his locked desk drawer, Gianni removed a pill from a vial. He rushed to the kitchen and placed the food on a tray and poured a glass of cold milk. Dropping the pill into the glass, he stirred. It was only a mild sedative, but it guaranteed Anthony would sleep through the afternoon.

Long enough for Gianni to remove the ring from his finger and dispose of it.

CHAPTER 20

The intercom on Nick's desk buzzed. "This is Agent Holstrom. There's a Brianna Fontaine and Yves Leveaux to see you."

"Send them up." Nick glanced at Lyle and Abbie as he opened the door for the visitors.

"Bree told me everything." Yves hefted his camera bag onto the desk and dug out a thick stack of photos. "Maybe you'll find Fosselli in here."

"Wait a minute." Lyle eyed the photos. "The police confiscated everyone's cameras."

"Bree told me to hide mine. My carryall has a secret compartment for similar ... situations."

"So as not to compromise your journalistic integrity," Nick said dryly.

"Something like that."

"Thank you." Nick nodded at Bree. She shot him a crooked little smile. Nick, Lyle and Abbie grabbed handfuls of photos to study. The first one made Nick swallow hard. Post ceremony, Nick and Jessie coming down the aisle with Anthony between them, beaming at Nick.

"Yves and I are heading downtown to the telescope." Bree fanned through several pictures.

The intercom sounded again. Holstrom. "Josh Elliot's here to see Mrs. McDeare."

"Mrs. McDeare's seeing no one." The jerk never gave up.

"Who's this guy?" Abbie handed Nick a picture of a man with a mustache and wire-rimmed glasses. Looked like he was wearing a rug.

"Never saw him before. Or the bald guy standing next to him. There were tons of guests Jessie and I didn't know. A circus."

"Everyone was vetted and scrutinized for credentials at the gate." Lyle grimaced, staring at another picture. "How the hell did Fosselli breach security?"

"Wait a minute. Look at this guest." Barton passed Nick a photo. "The face looks Italian. With a little makeup and a rug--"

"That's my attorney, Grady. And he's Irish. With his own hair."

"What about this?" Bree handed Nick a picture from the reception. Nick and Jessie, dancing their first dance. Bree pointed to a man seated at a large table in the background. "He looks familiar. An actor?"

"I think--" Nick studied the picture. "That's George Penfield, the show's stage manager." He gave a short laugh. "Former stage manager. Currently under arrest."

"Yeah," Bree said. "The theater thing. It's all over the news. You know, with that kind of grudge against Jessie ... maybe he helped Gianni take Anthony?"

"Getting past security would be easy," Lyle said thoughtfully, "an invited guest. And he knows Zappella has no love for Jessie either ..." He took the photo from Nick. "I'll notify the FBI and Lally. Penfield has motive."

Frustrated, Nick rubbed his eyes. "It doesn't matter. Fosselli would be a fool to let George know Anthony's final destination. He'd keep that to himself no matter who helped him."

"If Fosselli was there he drastically altered his appearance." Lyle dumped the photos onto the desk. "We have to study every face under a magnifying glass. Look at hands, height, facial structure."

"Fosselli would relish taking Anthony right in front of our eyes." Nick's expression hardened. "He was there."

*

When Gianni took the tray of food to Anthony, the boy refused to acknowledge his presence. He lay in bed, staring at the ceiling. Gianni left the tray and returned to the kitchen, watching the clock.

An hour later, Gianni looked in on Anthony. His food was untouched, but the glass was empty. Anthony was asleep, the sedative working.

Gianni carefully slipped the ring from the boy's finger. Anthony stirred and his eyelids fluttered. Hurrying back downstairs, Gianni phoned Carlo's cottage at the rear of the property. "Come quickly. I have a job for you."

*

Someone had just been here, touching his hand. Anthony's eyes blinked open. He felt for his ring.

His ring! Someone took his ring. Gianni. Anthony knew he was really Gianni. Everything he said to him— It was real. The bald man was Gianni Fosselli. His blood father. A bad man. Why did he want his ring?

Leaping out of bed, Anthony gripped the bedpost, dizzy. Shaking it off, he dashed downstairs. Gianni was in the kitchen, talking to a big guy. "Get rid of this," Gianni said to the man, holding up the ring.

"No!" Anthony did a cannonball into Gianni's stomach. Gianni collapsed against the sink, the ring dropping to the floor. Anthony scrambled for it, but the other man snatched it. Jumping to his feet, Anthony pounded the stranger with his fists. "I. Want. My. Ring!"

"Stop it, do you hear me?" Gianni grabbed Anthony's arms hard. "This behavior stops now."

"I want my ring," Anthony sobbed.

"What do I do with it, Mr. C?" The guy pocketed the ring. He acted like Anthony wasn't even in the room.

"Drop it in Lake Erie, Carlo."

Struggling to escape Gianni's grasp, Anthony shrieked as the man left. "I want my ring. Dad gave--"

"Nicholas is not your father." Gianni held him back, pinching his arms until it hurt. "Never mention him in my presence again. He's a disgusting—"

"Don't talk about my dad like that." Anthony twisted free and backed away from Gianni. "I hate you!"

"What's happened to you?" Gianni looked mad. "You're disrespectful and rude--" The light over the sink exploded. Shards of glass sprayed Gianni, cutting his skin like razors. Thin lines of blood ran down his face.

Galloping for the stairs, Anthony heard Gianni's Italian curses echoing behind him. But he heard something else, something that made him stop and gasp. A laugh.

Daddy Andrew.

That was his laugh. Daddy was in this house!

*

After Bree and Yves left, Lyle made some calls, relaying his speculation about George Penfield. Penfield hadn't been arraigned yet. The FBI met Lally at Manhattan North to question the stage manager.

While he waited for news from Lally, Lyle sifted through the photos with Nick and Abbie. His eyes burning from lack of sleep, he scrutinized each face. Hundreds of people. This would take days. Steinmetz delivered the developed pictures from Anthony's camera, back from the police lab. Lyle added them to Yves' collection. No Gianni.

Tossing the photos aside, Nick paced to the window. "I need to do something. We're sitting around waiting for a phone call that means shit."

"I've been thinking," Barton said, rubbing the back of his neck. "Let's start looking for Anthony in Buffalo. That's where Jessie's opening night flowers came from."

"And my matches," Abbie added.

"Okay, we start there," Nick said. "Let's go."

Lyle reminded Nick he couldn't go anywhere with the feds all over the place and Jessie in the dark. "I'll go in the morning with Abbie."

"This is my--" Nick shut his mouth as the door opened. Jessie floated to Nick's side, deathly pale, eyes red and puffy. Lyle looked away, her pain too palpable to watch.

"What are ...?" Jessie quavered. "Are those wedding photos?"

"Uh, yeah." Nick glanced at the pictures in his hand. "Anthony's and hundreds of photos from Yves. He and Bree just swung by for a few minutes. Bree thought maybe ... I don't know what she thought. Are you okay, honey?" Nick put his arm around Jessie. "Can I get you--"

"The medallions. I remembered this morning. Did you turn yours on?"

Lyle watched grimly as Nick said, "Yeah. There's ... nothing."

"Oh, God." Jessie wept against Nick's shoulder. "Anthony's far away, isn't he? He's just a little boy. He has to be so scared." She went limp, wracked with sobs as Nick enfolded her in his arms.

*

Carlo stopped at a Marathon gas station in Akron and filled the Corvette's tank. He went inside to take a leak and paid a pimply kid behind the counter with cash.

An hour later, he arrived in Cleveland. Parking along a deserted stretch of Lake Erie, Carlo reached into his pocket for the ring. And reached again. Gone. He checked the other pockets. No ring. Retracing his steps, he scanned every inch of ground before searching inside the Corvette. Nothing.

Racing back to the Marathon station, Carlo asked the attendant at the cash register if he'd seen a ring. The idiot shook his head, not looking up from playing on his cell phone. Cursing, Carlo searched the bathroom, a few steps away. One scared mouse, hiding behind the toilet. No fucking ring. He stalked out of the room. From the window he saw a van driver detach the pump and walk towards the station to pay for his gas.

Okay, he could beat the hell out of the punk once the van was gone, scare him shitless, and get the ring back—if he had it. And draw attention to himself. Exactly what he was paid not to do.

When he got home, Carlo casually told Gianni he'd disposed of the ring. It was the truth. He just didn't know where.

*

By the time Lally called Barton back, Nick was on his third bourbon. Lyle listened and clicked off, his voice strained. "Penfield swore he only went after Jessie at the theater. That's what it was all about for him, getting her where it hurts. He offered to take a polygraph. Passed with flying colors."

"I'm not surprised." Nick drained his glass. "It was a long shot."

"Lally made sure Penfield was asked about Nordic Nirvana during the test."

"Why?" Nick slammed his glass down on the desk. "George didn't drug Jessie. Josh Elliott did."

"We can't prove that. But we can pretty much eliminate Penfield."

"Nick's right," Abbie chimed in. "Josh did it."

*

Harvey Spittel finished his shift at the Marathon gas station and drove to Contessa Jewelers in downtown Akron. The old man behind the counter examined the gold and diamond ring with his loupe. "I'll give you a hundred. Not many people will pay much for a child's ring. Two sets of initials inside. J.N.M. and A.B.M. Relatives?"

"Yeah. Dead for years." Harvey filled out a receipt, signed it, and stuffed the money into the pocket of his Marathon overalls.

*

"Have you slept at all since this began?" Jessie and Nick were in bed, watching the lights from the news trucks and reporters reflected on the bedroom ceiling. Voices drifted up from the street, jumbled and unintelligible. Too reminiscent of when Andrew died, when she'd curled up under the covers hopeless and empty and full of tears. She fought the heavy feeling. "Nick?"

"The answer is no. I can't sleep."

"You should try."

Nick shrugged.

"You're too quiet." She remembered the Nick McDeare who'd alighted on her doorstep last spring. A few short months ago and a lifetime ago, but one thing was the same. That Nick McDeare was a man who'd gone through life alone. Shut down.

"What's there to say? I failed Anthony."

"This isn't your fault. You weren't even there when it happened."

"Right. I wasn't there."

"Stop beating yourself up. You did everything you could to protect him. The medallions--"

"Useless." Nick looked away.

Jessie gently turned his face to hers and stroked his cheek. Nick's eyes filled with tears. Jessie put her arms around him and hugged him tightly. He'd been a tower of strength since this happened. And what had she been doing? Weeping and falling apart. The same Jessie who fell apart when Andrew was killed. For two lifeless years.

She couldn't let that happen again. She had to be whole for Anthony when he returned. And strong for Nick before he slipped away. "I'm sorry you've had to take care of everything," she whispered. "I haven't been any help. But that changes tomorrow. We're in this together from now on."

"I'll get him back," Nick said, his voice hoarse. "I swear to God, I'll get him back."

*

Lasagna and garlic bread. Anthony only liked Mary's lasagna. He set his untouched dinner tray outside his bedroom door.

The snow outside lit up his room like day. Anthony climbed into bed, trying to fall asleep, but he ended up thinking about everything instead. Daddy Andrew's laugh made him feel better, but worse, too. His laugh was so much like Dad's. It made Anthony miss Dad even more.

The room suddenly got cold. Really cold, like refrigerator air. Anthony could see his breath.

Sitting up, he looked around.

Daddy Andrew stood a few feet away. "Hey, Bongo."

*

Lyle had been poring over Yves' photos for hours. He kept coming back to one face. A man with wire-rimmed glasses, a mustache, and a hairpiece. Sour smile. He couldn't place him. Not yet. Maybe he was an actor, a character actor who played the nondescript everyman. The place had been crawling with actors and celebrities.

Dropping his head in his hands, Barton gave in. Time to get a little sleep before the shuffle to Buffalo in the morning.

*

This house was a menace. Gianni was freezing. The bedroom window had sagged open. Every time he fought to shut it, the window fought back. He wondered if Anthony was cold. Maybe he needed another blanket. Wrapping himself in his thick terry robe, Gianni strode down the hallway.

As he neared Anthony's door, he heard his son's voice. He couldn't be on a phone. The only phones in the house were Gianni's cells, locked in the safe overnight.

"I forgot about the rules," Anthony bubbled. "But I remember them now …"

Panicked, Gianni lunged for the door, slamming into the hard wood. Wincing in pain, he turned the knob again and pushed. It didn't budge. But there was no lock inside the door, just outside. Had Anthony jammed it? "Anthony, open up."

"I love you, too," Anthony piped.

"Anthony, open this door right now, or I'll break it down!" Gianni pushed against the aging wood, ramming the weight of his body against it. The door was like steel.

Stepping back, Gianni lifted his foot, aiming for the knob. As he thrust forward, the door swung open. Losing his balance, Gianni fell forward, his chest coming down hard on his bent knee. He toppled onto his side, a searing pain shooting through his shoulder.

Grunting, he sat up and scanned the room. Anthony was alone, asleep in bed. "I remember," the boy murmured, before rolling over. Gianni crawled to the bed. Anthony's breathing was steady, in the deepest state of relaxation. The child must be talking in his sleep.

But how to explain the door? Maybe the old house shifted slightly with the strong wind outside. Did houses shift? They must, especially with the wet ground. His own bedroom door had done the same thing a few months ago.

Struggling to his feet, Gianni rotated his shoulder. The room was frigid, worse than his own bedroom. He grabbed a handmade quilt on the rocker and covered Anthony, stroking the boy's silky hair.

Limping from the room, Gianni left Anthony's door open, just in case.

As he headed down the hallway, Gianni flinched at a hollow laugh. How many times had he heard that insane cackle since he moved into this drafty old house? Awake or asleep, it haunted him.

Gianni glanced back at Anthony's room.

The door closed slowly, whining on its hinges.

*

The next morning Nick slumped across from Jessie in the breakfast nook, Mary's cheddar and mushroom omelet untouched. Lyle and Abbie should be nearing Buffalo by now. Was the medallion vibrating?

His cell warbled again, ringing all morning. Glancing at the screen, Nick let his editor go to voice mail with the other inconsequential calls. He looked over at Jessie, miles away and staring out the window. Reaching for her hand, he squeezed it. His heart lurched at the brave little smile back that did nothing to hide her grief. Nick wanted to take Jessie in his arms and comfort her, reassure her everything would be okay.

But Anthony had been gone for thirty-six hours. And Lyle's silence meant the news from Buffalo was not good.

*

A knock on his bedroom door. Anthony didn't answer. Gianni barged in anyway.

"You must be hungry after not eating yesterday."

"These clothes are too small." Anthony fidgeted in his black slacks and gray sweater.

"I ordered clothes in a larger size yesterday. Overnight express."

"Jeans and T-shirts?"

"No. Jeans aren't--

"I like jeans." Anthony looked away, remembering Dad's rules and what Daddy Andrew had told him.

"I made some minestrone soup for lunch. And there's tiramisu for dessert."

Anthony made a face. "Got any peanut butter or strawberry ice cream? I like strawberry."

"Um, no."

"Hot dogs?"

"No."

"I'm not hungry then." Anthony turned his back on Gianni and went to the window. "Where are we?"

"You have to eat something. Why don't you try my soup?"

"We're in the country, right? Are there any roosters? I never saw a chicken."

"How about a hamburger? I have some excellent Black Angus beef in the freezer. And I'll put it on a fresh Kaiser bun."

Turning around, Anthony stared at the man. "With ketchup?"

"If that's ... what you want. But you have to come to the table and eat."

Anthony pretended to think about it. "Can I have french fries?"

"French fries take a long time--"

"I'm not hungry then."

"I guess I could make some. If you come to the table."

Taking his time, Anthony finally nodded.

Smiling, Gianni practically skipped from the room.

Anthony took a deep breath. He didn't feel as scared as before.

*

Another ransom letter had arrived in the mail, postmarked Brooklyn. Nick and Jessie were summoned to the living room.

Nick eyed the paper skeptically: TUESDAY. 10 AM. CRUISE SHIP TERMINAL # 3. GARBAGE CAN - ROOFTOP PARKING. NO COPS OR HES DEAD.

"That takes balls," said Agent Coleman. "Where Andrew Brady was mur-- Oh, sorry, Mrs. McDeare."

Jessie was shaking. Nick clasped her hand, trying to contain his rage. Gianni was taunting the feds, screaming out he was alive. With that bastard Martinelli's— Lyle called, his name popping up on the cell phone's screen. "Uh, have to take this," Nick told Holstrom.

"Mr. McDeare," the man said, his fair skin reddening, "this isn't the time for--"

"I'll be right back." Nick hurried from the room, vaulting the stairs two at a time. He bolted for the bedroom and closed the door. "What's up?"

"I'm sorry, Nick. No vibration. Anthony isn't within a hundred miles of Buffalo."

"Then we've got nothing."

"Hang in there. We'll get him if we have to visit every corner of the world. I swear it."

As Nick began to tell Barton about the ransom note, there was a knock at the door. "What?"

Agent Holstrom barged into the room, his face red. "Mrs. McDeare said you have a medallion that can help us find your son. Why didn't you turn it over to us?"

"Because it's ... an amateur gizmo. It ended up being useless."

"That's not for you to decide. I want it now."

"I threw it away."

"Enough of the games." Holstrom glared at Nick.

"What are you talking about?"

"I don't sense you're very anxious to help us. I know all about your reputation. Think you can find your son all on your own? The famous Nick McDeare pops another case?"

"I don't have the medallion anymore," Nick said coolly. He unbuttoned his shirt and pulled it open, turned his pockets inside out. "See? Search the house if you want."

"I'll do that." Holstrom stalked from the room, closing the door hard.

Seething, Nick switched back to his cell. "You hear that?"

"I'll hide the medallion and keychain. In the meantime, play nice with the feds even if it kills you. We don't need them looking over our shoulders. Do the money drop tomorrow and let them worry about it."

No sooner had Nick clicked off than his cell buzzed again. His editor. "What, Alex?"

"I know this is bad timing, your son missing. Any word? I'm sorry--"

"I can't talk about it. Just tell me what's so important."

"Okay. We have a problem with the manuscript. Linden hates the ending. Where's that classic McDeare dark twist? Linden wants it released on schedule ... You there?"

"Tell Linden I'll get to it. After I find my son."

CHAPTER 21

Sipping the last of his soup, Gianni eyed his son with satisfaction. Anthony was wolfing down his hamburger and fries. At last, he had an appetite. His palate would improve with time. For now he'd placate his appalling taste.

"I have a surprise for you." Gianni smiled at Anthony. "Today is Christmas."

"No, it's not." Anthony dredged his last fry through ketchup. "It's in December."

"Christmas isn't just a day. It's a feeling. Family coming together and showing their love by giving gifts. I have dozens of presents for you under the tree in the living room. Come and see."

Progress. Anthony looked curious. Gianni led him into the living room and lit the towering spruce. Tiny white bulbs made the antique ornaments spring to life.

"That's like the tree Mary made Dad and me put in the living room. We liked the one in the study better. It was really cool with--"

"How about some soothing opera after lunch?"

"Like what Mary watches?"

Gianni stifled a curse. Anthony was almost eight, old enough to know opera. This was the devil's influence. "It's a story told by music." He went to the DVD system and inserted LA BOHEME.

"Why can't they sing in English?"

"It's so beautiful in Italian. And it's time you learned your father's native language." Anthony turned away, eyeing the gifts under the tree.

"Here." Gianni lifted a present wrapped in exquisite silver paper. He'd ordered it long ago, anticipating this moment. "Open this." He watched as Anthony unwrapped a stunning Waterford sculpture of a pointer hunting dog on the scent, frozen in motion.

Tears welled in the boy's eyes. Anthony looked from the dog to Gianni.

"What's the matter?" Gianni asked, alarmed. "Don't you like--"

"I don't want a glass dog." Anthony pitched the sculpture onto the couch. "Don't you know anything about kids? If I was home I'd have a real dog!" Anthony ran for the stairs. A moment later his bedroom door slammed.

How could he have made such a mistake? He should have asked Luci what to buy a seven-year-old boy. But this was McDeare's fault. Animals over opera. Base tastes over intellect and the arts.

The lights on the tree flickered and went out. Annoyed, Gianni unplugged the cord. A jolt of electricity sizzled through his body. *Merde!* He dropped the cord with a yelp.

This house was cursed. It was always too cold. The electricity was defective. Doors jammed and swung closed on their own. And that laugh. That maniacal laugh.

*

"I'm sorry, Mrs. McDeare, but your husband's fighting us every step of the way." Holstrom's eyes were bullets as he glared at Jessie. "If I didn't know better, I'd think he was the one who'd taken the boy."

"How dare you--" A hot rage bubbled up. "Your snide insinuations are-- You're a guest in my home!"

"Then why did Mr. McDeare toss the medallion out? If, in fact, he did."

"Where-where did you get that idea?"

Nick stepped into the room. "It's true. I threw it away."

"Nick, why would you ... I don't under--"

"It was a piece of junk," he said calmly, his face opaque. "It's gone. Forget about it." Nick turned to Holstrom. "Now, how do we go about delivering the ransom money?"

It was true the medallion hadn't worked, but that was because Anthony was outside the hundred-mile range. At least, that's what Nick said. Why would he get rid of it? If, in fact, he did.

*

"I'm sorry I made you cry." Gianni sat beside Anthony on the bed.

"I want my dog." Anthony avoided Gianni's creepy Zombie eyes. "A Portuguese water dog like Zane's."

"Zane?"

"My best friend."

"Anthony ... dogs are a huge responsibility. They have to be trained. They're messy creatures."

"They love you no matter what."

"I love you no matter what."

Anthony bit his lip. He wanted Dad, Mom, and his dog to love him. Monty. He'd name his dog Monty Crisco.

"Why don't you come back downstairs and open your other presents? I'm sure you'll find something just as good as a dog."

"Leave me alone, okay?" Anthony buried his face in the pillow, crying. When he heard the door close, he sat up and wiped his eyes with his sleeve.

He wanted to be home with Monty. He wanted to work on his camera with Dad and toss balls and practice his swing. He wanted Mom to kiss him goodnight on her nights off and tell him funny stories about the actors at work. He wanted Mary's peanut butter cookies. And he wanted to see Zane.

Wandering to the window, Anthony pressed his hands against the icy glass. His empty ring finger looked naked. The ring had been Jeffrey's, Dad's son who died. Dad gave it to Anthony because he loved him so much. Now it was gone, and it was Anthony's fault.

*

"Jessie, please. I don't want to talk about it anymore." Nick stared out the bedroom window, the back garden crusted with snow.

"There's something going on with you. I don't believe you threw away that medallion. You're trying to find Anthony on your own, aren't you?"

"Barton and I have been trying to come up with ideas."

"And you still have the medallion?"

"Barton has it. Not a word to the feds, okay? They don't like anyone meddling."

"Not even the great Nick McDeare?"

"Especially not him." Nick turned around and pulled Jessie into his arms, closing his eyes. He'd never felt so tired in his life.

"I won't say anything," Jessie whispered. "I know how much you love Anthony. You know what you're doing. I trust you."

The guilt spiraled. Nick cleared his throat. "You okay?"

"Yeah. Uh, I think I'll take my shower now. I never took one this morning."

*

Quietly closing the bathroom suite's door, Jessie sank to the bench, staring at the marble floor. She turned on the faucets. And then she wept uncontrollably as the water poured out. Was Anthony eating? Did he brush his teeth? Did he think they'd forgotten him?

Afraid Nick would hear her sobs, she drew in a shuddering breath. Jessie started the shower and stepped in. She threw her head back, a kaleidoscope of memories flashing through her head. "Oh, God, my baby," she cried, the water cascading over her body like needles. "If anything happens to you, I'll die."

The water mingled with her tears until there were no more left, her insides dry. Jessie stepped out and splashed her swollen eyes and blotched cheeks over and over with cold water. She carefully applied layers of base and powder and concealer, eyeliner and mascara. Nick couldn't see her ravaged face.

*

Gianni tried repeatedly to lure Anthony back downstairs. The boy had gone silent. They'd made progress today, until the Waterford dog. Now Gianni paced the kitchen, determined to find a way to bring Anthony around. He would do anything for his son.

First, Gianni had Carlo take the rest of the gifts to Anthony's room. Maybe the child would find something he liked. Then he dispatched Carlo to the supermarket with a list of items to purchase.

Late that afternoon, Gianni set about making Anthony the dinner of his dreams, arranging everything on a tray. Grilled frankfurters on toasted buns, not the cuisine of kings, but the passion of little American boys. Sizzling french fries, golden brown on the outside, tender on the inside. Corn on the cob, dripping with sweet butter, flash-frozen last summer. Chocolate milk with cocoa syrup and sprinkled with cinnamon. And for dessert, homemade double-chocolate brownies with walnuts and strawberry ice cream. Gianni remembered now how much Anthony loved strawberry. He finished off the tray with jars of ketchup and relish. Also a puzzle book and sharpened pencils.

When Gianni took Anthony's dinner up to his room, he found the boy staring out the window, silent. Gianni left the tray and returned to the kitchen, his heart heavy. He had to find a way to put a smile on his son's face. He was afraid he was left with only one choice. He called Luciana, and she not only agreed, but urged him to do it immediately.

At his computer, Gianni researched Portuguese water dogs. A fairly rare breed, loyal, intelligent, and obedient. Breeders weren't abundant and most only sold puppies, but there was a private rare-breed rescue group in Erie, Pennsylvania, only a couple of hours away. They took in dogs that needed a new home. An older trained dog would be best, no accidents on the priceless oriental rugs. He decided to avoid the official Portuguese rescue association—a private organization would be easier and faster.

He placed a call to Erie, Pennsylvania.

*

Zane Harwell turned out his light and patted the bed. Clumper jumped up. Zane stroked the dog's thick coat. Mr. Yablonski had said reporters were hanging around, wanting to talk to him, so Zane hadn't gone back to school since Anthony's kidnapping. Zane wasn't going back without Anthony, and Yablonski and his parents weren't making him.

But earlier today Zane overheard his mom and dad whisper to each other about how some kidnapped children--he swallowed over the lump in his throat— disappeared forever. Zane hugged Clumper and closed his eyes, trying not to cry.

In the middle of the night, Clumper's whining woke him. The room was freezing, and Zane shivered, turning on the lamp. Clumper was standing by the desk, barking at something on the rug.

His book on Portuguese water dogs was open on the floor, the pages fluttering back and forth as if an invisible hand were flipping through them. Zane's heart started to pound.

*

Cracking his eyes open, Anthony heard voices from outside. Sitting up, he looked towards the window. It was still dark, but he could see a little morning light along the ground. Why would people be outside so early? He gasped. Maybe Dad had found him!

Leaping out of bed, Anthony ran to the window. There was a car that looked like Lyle's. Anthony laughed and clasped his medallion. It had worked. They found him! But then he saw Gianni behind the wheel. The mean guy—Carlo--came out of the garage and put a blanket in the back seat. Gianni drove away and Carlo came into the house.

Where was Gianni going? And why was he leaving him alone with that man? Terrified, Anthony dove under the covers and prayed for Daddy Andrew's help.

*

The piers were deserted at this time of year, ships migrating south to warmer waters. Willie coasted the limo to a stop in front of the Cruise Ship Terminal. It was ten a.m. Nick grabbed the canvas satchel and stepped out of the car. Somewhere out there, the FBI was watching.

Nick strode into the terminal. He paused and stared at the row of chairs where his brother had been shot. Above it was a plaque, dedicated in Andrew's memory. This wretched building held horrible memories for Nick's family. Now it was the scene of a twisted joke.

Riding the elevator up one flight, Nick emerged onto the deserted rooftop parking. The wind whipped his hair in the frigid morning. Yellow-eyed gulls perched on the railing, blending into the choppy Hudson's gray backdrop. New Jersey was an ashy haze, its features indistinguishable.

The trashcan was a few feet away. Nick dumped in the satchel and headed back to the car. Maybe the feds would get off his back now. They could spend their time watching a garbage can, waiting for a kidnapper who would never come.

*

When Anthony woke up, he found two trays in his room, breakfast and lunch. He must've slept through the morning. He'd had a hard time going back to sleep after Gianni left. After that Daddy had visited and made him feel better.

Anthony approached the trays. The eggs and muffins were cold and rubbery. The lunch tray had a hot dog and potato chips. Anthony tore open the bag of chips and tossed some in his mouth the way Dad did.

Was Gianni back? Maybe Carlo was gone and he was alone in the house. Anthony crept downstairs and peeked in the living room. No one. He moved on to the kitchen. The big man was sitting at the table playing with his iPad. Anthony tiptoed back upstairs.

Maybe he could escape while Gianni was gone. He knew the windows in his room were locked with a key. He'd thrown a chair at one, but it had bounced off the glass. Maybe there were other windows that weren't locked.

Creeping down the hallway, Anthony peeked over his shoulder in case the guy appeared. He ducked into several rooms, checking the windows. Locked. The last room was Gianni's. The bed was made, a robe folded on top and slippers lined up perfectly underneath. There was perfume on the dresser and little sculptures and framed pictures, many of Anthony, all in straight lines. It didn't look like a guy's room. Dad's side of the bedroom had clothes piled all over the floor and junk on the dresser.

Time to check the windows. One was cracked at the top! Anthony climbed on a chair and tugged on it, stuck.

"What the hell are you doing?"

Startled, Anthony lost his balance and fell off the chair. Carlo stood a few feet away, looking mad. Anthony jumped to his feet and ran for the stairs, but the man grabbed him halfway down, his big hands like monster claws. "You can't get out, kid. Everything's locked, so just give it up."

Anthony squirmed out of his grasp and sprinted for his bedroom, terrified.

*

Staring at the back gate, Jessie had taken refuge on the porch. The press hadn't discovered their back yard escape, thank God. Nick had slipped out almost two hours ago to deliver the ransom. She knew the FBI would have his back. Still, she worried.

Just when she couldn't wait one more minute, Nick appeared, trudging across the back yard to the porch. Jessie threw her arms around him. "Thank God. I've been so worried. How'd it go?"

"Fine." Nick tossed his coat on the divan, looking exhausted and drawn.

"Abbie's still upstairs," Jessie said. "She says she's not going home until Anthony comes home. I don't know what time she came in last night. Or where she disappeared all day yesterday. Do you?"

"Mr. McDeare?" An agent stood in the doorway. "There's someone here to see you, a boy. Says his name is Zane and he's your son's friend."

Jessie told the agent they'd see him. After the man left the room, Jessie said, "Why do you think he wants to see you?"

"I, uh, threw a few balls with the kids." Nick looked distracted. "Took them to that basketball game. You know boys."

They hurried into the hallway. Zane and his mother looked small and intimidated, flanked by the FBI agents. Jessie motioned Zane and Mrs. Harwell into the kitchen.

"Zane insisted on coming over," Jane Harwell explained. "He wouldn't tell me what it was about."

Zane cradled a book in his arms. "Can I talk to you alone, Mr. McDeare?"

*

Lyle answered his cell as he sat at his desk, studying Yves' photos.

"It's Bree, your friendly Peeping Tom."

"Did you spot Martinelli?" Lyle's adrenaline sped up.

"Not yet. But I've been able to cross most of the riverfront apartments off my list—got a good look at the occupants through those sliding glass doors onto the deck area. A few others never open their blinds or drapes. But I think I'm getting warm. I spotted some kids in the penthouse during the day. A penthouse is more Martinelli's style. I've also seen a couple of women there and a man, maybe in his thirties. I'm focusing on those windows now."

"We need a break." Lyle rubbed his eyes, shards of glass growing on his eyeballs. "Buffalo was a bust."

"Yves set up a new camera for me. High-powered telephoto lens with a fine degree of color resolution."

"Keep me posted. I'll give Nick the update." Lyle hung up, feeling helpless. No matter where they turned, Martinelli and Fosselli were two steps ahead of them.

*

"McDeare made the drop, and the feds are watching." Aldo lit one of Roberto's cigars and parked himself in a tub chair. "Fosselli has the kid, and the cops are running in circles. It's over."

"It's never over." Roberto puffed on his Cuban and stared out the study windows. He'd spent the last two days putting out brush fires in his organization. A robbery down at the Seaport. A skirmish between two capos out in Brooklyn. A dealer arrested during another raid, the second in a month. Why couldn't he have just one week without a problem?

"You going to Jersey tonight? They're predicting more snow."

"Too much shit going on. Marcella's birthday's tomorrow. And the meeting with Tony Amato. Fucker wants too big a piece of the pie."

What he wouldn't give to disappear into that penthouse on the Jersey Shore forever. His princess was a better tonic than all the heart pills in the world.

*

"So this book was on the floor, and the pages were flipping back and forth all by themselves." Zane looked up at Nick. "I know Anthony told you about me seeing his dad, uh, his first dad. I figured I better tell you."

The boy was spooked, but he'd thought rationally and come to Nick. Impressive. "You did the right thing." Nick thumbed through the book. "Anything like this ever happen before you met Anthony?"

"You mean, seeing ghosts?"

Nick smiled. "Yeah. Anything out of the ordinary?"

"Kind of, little things. My grandma told me I have a gift. Like the time I knew Mom left the iron on, even though I was in my room. What does it mean, the pages moving all by themselves?"

"I'm not sure. But I think Andrew's trying to communicate with you." Nick looked down at the book. "You know, Anthony wanted a Portuguese water dog. I promised I'd get him one. You mind if I keep this?"

"I was going to give it to Anthony that night. You think he's okay?"

"I think ... he has Andrew watching over him. The best news I've had yet. Let's keep this between us. If anything else happens, let me know. You're welcome here anytime, buddy."

*

Did Gianni think hot dogs and french fries and strawberry ice cream would make Anthony like him? Anthony had been stuck in his bedroom all day. He hated this room and he hated this house and he hated Gianni. He hoped wherever Gianni went he'd never come back.

At the sound of a car, Anthony didn't go to the window. What good was looking outside if you could never go out?

A moment later Gianni stuck his head in the door. "I have a surprise for you." He pushed the door open. A big black dog bounded into the room, straining on its leash, wearing a silver collar. It was a Portuguese water dog, his fur curly and shiny! Gianni released him and the dog ran to Anthony, jumping on the bed and licking his face all over.

"Monty!" Anthony laughed and hugged the dog, lifting up his chin as it licked his face. He looked up at Gianni. "He's mine? Really?"

Gianni nodded. "He's two years old. He was a show dog, but never took to it. He's highly trained and very friendly."

"I love him." Anthony hugged Monty tighter. "Hi, Monty. I'm Anthony."

"Monty?"

"Yeah. From THE COUNT OF MONTY CRISCO. You know. About the guy who escaped from prison?" Anthony hid his smile, burying his face in Monty's soft coat.

*

George Penfield followed the guard to the small spare room with the telephone. What did his lawyer want now? He'd spent two hours with Jason W. Burberry IV that morning. The jerk was a pompous ass, but he was one of the best criminal attorneys in New York City.

Penfield picked up the phone, glaring at the guard standing a few feet away. "Do you mind? Attorney-client privilege."

Finally alone in the airless room, George grabbed the phone. "What's up, Mr. Burberry?"

"It's not Burberry."

Wha--?" Shit. "You."

"Is that any way to talk to your benefactor?"

"What do you want?"

"You like your attorney?"

"No. But he'll do."

"If you want to keep him, listen closely. Accept the plea bargain. No trial."

"Why would— Look, you're in this as deep as I am. I kept quiet so far, but remember what--"

"Mention my name and take your chances with a court-appointed attorney, a kid so green you'll end up behind bars for life. Ricin, George. That's a big deal in this country. Makes you sound like a terrorist."

"I'll be sharing a cell with you."

"Go ahead. Tell the cops about me. It won't amount to a thing."

"You think nobody can touch you?"

"Not only can I afford Mr. Burberry, but my fingerprints aren't anywhere in this scenario. There's no proof. He said, he said."

Perspiration broke out on George's forehead as he flashed back over their history. A cash transaction. Private meetings. Wait-- "We're talking on the phone now. And I called you the other--"

"You called a prepaid cell, unidentified number. Trashed after this chat. So. Take the plea bargain. Nice and simple. I might even throw you a bone when you get out. Not easy for an ex-con to get work ... Agreed?"

"Screw you."

"And you. Deal?"

"Deal."

George buried his face in his hands. He was fucked but good.

CHAPTER 22

The hours after the drop ticked by, Nick's frustration escalating like a stairway to nowhere. On his fourth bourbon, he prayed for the numbness to settle in. How many damn drinks would it take, the entire bottle? He sat on the window seat, watching Jessie pace the sitting room.

"Why hasn't someone picked up the money yet?" Jessie paused to drain her wine glass. "It's been over six hours."

"They probably know the feds are watching."

Jessie stared at Nick. "Why are you so calm?"

"I'm as anxious about Anthony as you are, and you know it." Nick went to the bar and poured another shot of bourbon. He took a large gulp.

"You don't believe the FBI will find Anthony, do you?"

If anyone had the right to be distraught, it was Jessie. Nick took a deep breath, holding his temper in check. He took another swallow.

"I see. The old Nick is back, the zipped-up version."

"Enough, okay? First Anthony, then the book."

"Why did Zane have to see you alone about a book anyway?"

"Not that book. THE SILVER LINING. My editor hates the ending. I have to do a major rewrite. One day."

"When-when did this happen?"

"Yesterday."

"Why didn't you tell me?"

"I never got a chance. Anyway, it doesn't matter, does it? Not important."

"I'm sorry, Nick." Jessie moved to his side and kissed his shoulder. "And I'm sorry I've been on your case all day."

"I need to get out of here for a while." Nick swigged down the last of his drink. "See Barton. Watch a basketball game or something. You mind?"

"Go ahead. I know how you feel. I'm ... thinking of going back to work when the play resumes production. I can't stand sitting here, waiting for— I'm going out of my mind. Bill called a little while ago to see how we're doing. He said the role's waiting for me. Anything to keep from going crazy, you know?"

"I think it's a good idea." Nick kissed her lightly. "Maybe we should both get busy, you with the play, me with my rewrite." He set his glass on the bar. "See you later."

Nick zipped downstairs, his conscience plaguing him. He'd given LINING a happy ending, a first for him. Jessie had no idea the authentic ending was being written in real life right now.

*

"Great," Josh said into his cell, trying to hear over the traffic noise, his spirits soaring at Jessie's news about coming back to the show. He kept his tone even. "Going back to work will be good for you. I've been trying to come by, but I can't get past Nick."

"Really? He, um, he's just trying to protect me, you know?"

"Yeah." He knew. Josh swallowed his bile. "Listen, I'm on the street, on my way to meet my agent for drinks and an early dinner. Maybe I could drop by afterwards, if that's okay?"

"… Sure. Nick's out for the evening. I was planning to look at my script."

"We'll run lines. See you later." Josh clicked off. The tabloids were all over the kidnapping. One article said a high percentage of marriages didn't survive that kind of trauma. What were the chances of mismatched newlyweds making it?

Whistling, Josh flagged down a cab.

*

"I used my key to let myself in. Hope you don't mind."

Lyle looked up from his desk at Nick's voice. His friend looked like hell, a bottle of bourbon in one hand, a glass in another, a book tucked under his arm. "I don't."

"It's snowing."

"It's winter."

"I'm helping myself to your bourbon." Nick waved the bottle.

"Go ahead." He'd obviously already had a few. Who could blame him? Lyle went back to studying one of Yves' photos.

Pouring the snifter full, Nick took a hefty swallow.

"Bree called." Lyle gulped his cold coffee. "She thinks Martinelli's in the penthouse. Spotted some kids up there. She'll keep us posted." Nick seemed a million miles away. "You okay?"

"Anthony's friend came by today. He gave me this book," Nick nodded at the paperback, "on Portuguese water dogs. Got me thinking. Anthony wanted a dog more than anything. And I promised him one."

"So?"

"So I figure Gianni will do anything to make Anthony happy, including getting him a dog. And not just any dog. A Portuguese water dog."

"You think we can track Gianni through a dog?" Lyle cast him a grim smile.

"These canines aren't your everyday mutt. Fairly rare. I looked into them before we decided to get one for Anthony."

"It's more than a long shot. About as easy as picking out Gianni in Yves' photos." Lyle went back to studying a picture.

"Any luck?"

"This one character's driving me crazy. The guy with the wire rims Abbie pointed out. I know him from somewhere." He handed Nick the photo.

"Looks like someone trying to look like no one."

Grabbing the photo, Barton stared hard at the face. "Shit, Vaughn!"

"What?"

"Clint Vaughn, that two-bit PI I told you about? I caught him watching your street when this whole thing began with the matches. Paid him a visit."

Quickly typing in a computer search of Vaughn, the man's photo took shape on the screen. Lyle put the wedding shot next to it. "Take a look. A little putty, glasses, a toupee ..."

Nick looked over Lyle's shoulder. "Son of a bitch."

"First he's on the street, chumming for a gonif who can't keep it zipped. Then he shows up at your wedding in disguise? He's been sitting on the street all this time. How could I've been so stupid?"

"Martinelli knew you'd never guess he'd send the same tail twice." Nick grabbed his jacket. "What are you waiting for?"

*

Stretched across the bed, Jessie went over her script. She knew it inside out, but it always helped to visualize the entire play in her head.

Abbie had returned an hour ago and immediately gone across the back yard to Lyle's. She'd come back within minutes, covered with snow, saying Nick and Lyle had gone out. Abbie declared she was taking a long soak in the tub and tromped up to her room.

Were Nick and Lyle really out, tossing back a few at a bar and trying to relax? Or were they chasing down a lead on Anthony? Jessie pushed it from her mind. She trusted Nick to tell her about any consequential leads.

Yawning, Jessie closed the script. Their luggage was strewn across the room, the bags open but unpacked. What did it matter, until Anthony-- Jessie spotted Nick's manuscript nestled among her lingerie. She'd intended to read it on their honeymoon. Picking it up, she wandered into the sitting room.

THE SILVER LINING. She turned to the first page. The inscription was simple, so Nick: "For Jessie, my beloved wife, my best friend, my muse."

Curling into a corner of the couch she began to read.

*

"Not now, honey." Clint turned away from the pathetic middle-aged woman, pancake makeup so thick you could pour syrup on it. Hanratty's was a dive tonight. It was a sad day when Clint had to settle for a grandma in heat. He tossed some bills on the bar and headed home. It was snowing, the flakes fattening by the minute.

Pushing into his building's vestibule, Clint unlocked the front door, cursing women. Two men burst out of nowhere and bookended him, slamming the door behind them. Clint had inhaled a lot of scotch over dinner, but he sobered up quickly. Batman and Robin. His adrenaline started racing.

"Remember me?" Barton politely brushed snow from Clint's coat.

McDeare got in Clint's face. "Where's my son?"

"You're that writer, the one--"

"Where's my son?!" McDeare moved closer, his eyes full of rage. Clint could smell the bourbon on his breath.

"How the hell would I know?"

Producing a photo, Barton held it up. "Why were you at this wedding?"

"That's bullshit."

"Why were you at my wedding?" McDeare pressed.

"You think that's me? Look, you got the wrong guy."

Clawing at his arm, McDeare banged him against the wall. "I want my son," he hissed.

Clint tried to yank his arm free, but McDeare had a solid lock on him. "This is harassment," Clint bit out. "I know my rights."

"Rights," Barton shot back, "you gave up when you got into bed with Fosselli and Martinelli."

Squirming under McDeare's grip, Clint tried to wrench away, but the man upped the pressure, twisting his arm. "Get out of my face or I start yelling police brutality."

"Your buddy Martinelli blew up my house with my wife and kid in it." Clint felt the barrel of a gun shoved up hard against his belly. "You think you know police brutality?" A click as the gun cocked. "Outside, my car. You pull anything, I shatter your kneecap and move up from there, body part by body part. Guess what's next?"

The cop was psycho. And McDeare? Clint hadn't seen that deranged expression since Nam.

Barton gave him a shove towards the door, the gun planted in his back. Outside, Clint scanned West Seventy-First Street. An old hag walking her dog trotted by, both wearing fur coats. A well-dressed dude and his fashionably anorexic wife shuffled towards them in the snow, careful of their footing. "Lyle? Is that you?" The yoyo halted a few feet away.

"... Uh ... yes, sir."

Sir? Clint glanced over his shoulder. Barton was staring at the stranger.

"I've been meaning to call you," the man continued, "to see how you're doing since your house-- uh ..." Hubby turned to his wife. "Eloise, you remember Lieutenant Barton--"

"Excuse me," she interrupted, "aren't you Nick McDeare?"

His glance ping-ponging from face to face, McDeare settled on Barton's with a question.

Barton croaked, "Nick, this is Deputy Inspector Morris."

Holy fucking shit. The NYPD cavalry had shown up to save Clint's ass. "Look, I have to go," Clint said amiably. He swung away from Barton, grinning as the cop fumbled to hide the gun. "What a great time," he said with relish. "Let's do it again real soon, okay?"

Striding away, Clint knew his window for escape was short, the slippery sidewalk making a run perilous. At Broadway, the well-traveled walkway was clear. He broke into a mad sprint, weaving around pedestrians like Tiki Barber through the Eagles.

At Ninety-Sixth Street Clint dove into the subway, hopping the first train into the station. Changing trains three times, he finally emerged on the lower East Side, wiping the sweat from his brow. He jerked out his cell and speed-dialed Aldo. "You tell the boss we got a big mother-fucking problem."

*

Patting the bed, Anthony called Monty up and wrestled with him, the dog licking his face like crazy. "Don't worry, Monty," he whispered. "Dad will get us out of here soon. He can do anything. You'll see."

Anthony heard Gianni climb the stairs and braced himself. They'd been making a lot of noise, rocking the bed. The door opened. "Anthony, what is that dog doing on your bed? Dogs don't belong on the furniture."

"He's scared. Like ... like I was when I first got here, remember?" Anthony was sticking to Dad's rules. It was time to make Gianni trust him. "Please, Uncle Gianni? He won't hurt anything. Please?"

"All right, Anthony." Gianni sighed. "I'll be up later, before bedtime."

"Great. And ... thank you for Monty. I love him."

"You're welcome, Anthony. I love you."

Forcing a smile, Anthony watched the door close. He wrapped his arms around Monty and stared into the dog's soft brown eyes. "Listen. We're partners now. So you need to know the truth. I hate Gianni! He killed Daddy, and he stole me from Mom and Dad. But we have to pretend to like whoever took me. That's what Dad told me. To keep us safe."

Monty wagged his tail as if he understood. What an awesome dog. Tomorrow would be better with Monty here. And Gianni said he and Monty could go outside. Maybe they could escape, dig a tunnel like the Count of Monty Crisco.

*

"Son of a bitch!" Nick took a gulp of bourbon from the bottle and paced Barton's den. "If I hadn't hit that fucking patch of ice, I'd have gotten the bastard." He fingered his swelling brow. He'd gone down hard, belly flopping and bouncing his head on the ice. His knee was killing him.

"A cockroach like Vaughn knows how to disappear into the cracks."

"Goddammit to hell!" Another swig of bourbon.

"Stop it. I'm as frustrated as you are." Lyle snatched the bottle. "No more booze. We need to think before this fiasco gets us all flushed into the toilet."

"I want my son back!"

"Listen to me. Vaughn was on his cell to Martinelli the minute he was out of sight. They have a contract out on us by now. They know we put it together. This is Roberto Martinelli we're dealing with, Nick."

Slowing down, Nick sobered. Barton was right. If the two of them ended up at the bottom of New York Sound, where did that leave Anthony?

"I want the bastards as much as you. But we have to be careful. Now they know we're coming after them. Everything's changed."

A new fear punched Nick in the gut. "Jessie wants to go back to work--"

"Jessie stays home until this is over. Martinelli won't try anything with the feds camped out at your house. She'll be safe at least."

"But how-- What do I tell her?"

"The truth."

*

It hadn't taken Jessie long to realize Nick's secret. She slammed the manuscript down. After reading only five pages she'd jumped ahead, scanning the book. Why hadn't he told her? He had to know how she'd feel about this!

A cell phone went off. Nick's ring tone, on the window seat. In his hurry to get out of here, he'd forgotten his cell.

Anger propelled her to the phone. She glanced at the screen.

Brianna Fontaine ...?

The phone went silent, then buzzed again and again. Silent, and then yet again. *Brianna* ...

Why would she be calling him so incessantly? Jessie was rooted in place, an argument raging in her head.

She shouldn't snoop... Bree was a former lover ... *It would be invading Nick's privacy* ... Nick had offered to show her Lyle's text that night ... *She'd be letting Kristin Wallingford manipulate her* ... If Nick had anything to hide why would he give Jessie his cell code, Andrew's birthday? And she was so damned mad ... After another silence, the phone jangled again, and again and again. *Brianna.*

That did it. This would be the one and only time. Jessie reached for the cell.

Punching in the passcode, she went to Nick's texts. No Bree, no bimbos at all. In fact, there were almost no texts, period. And none from Lyle. But Nick had said Lyle texted him ...

Okay ... Jessie tapped the call records. Scanning the long list a hot rage swept through her.

Dozens of calls to and from Brianna Fontaine, literally dozens. Including before and after the wedding. Calls this morning. The flurry a few minutes ago.

Shoving the cell in her pocket, Jessie grabbed the manuscript, her down coat, and the key to Lyle's place. She'd wait all night for them to return if she had to.

Jessie let herself into Lyle's darkened kitchen. Voices. So they were back. Taking a step towards the den, she halted, going cold at what she heard. Lyle ...

"... kept this from Jessie too long, made Abbie and me your accomplices. Put a stop to it now, or I'll tell Jessie myself." Jessie put a hand to her mouth.

"Stay out of this. It's between Jessie and me."

"Martinelli murdered my wife and daughter. You think he won't kill Jessie to shut you down before you expose his part in this? We made Vaughn and his connection to Martinelli and the kidnapping. We threatened him!"

Her heart hammering, Jessie inched closer to the den.

"Jess is devastated by Anthony's kidnapping. She won't survive knowing Gianni has him. Much less ..."

Going numb, Jessie heard nothing more. Even her heart was silenced. The manuscript slipped from her hand to the tile floor.

*

Nick whirled around at a sound ... Jessie, standing in the doorway, the color leached from her face.

"Is it true?" she whispered.

A house of cards. His world began collapsing all around him like a proverbial house of cards. Nick couldn't find his voice.

"Is it true?" Jessie turned to Barton.

About to answer, Lyle clamped his mouth shut. He looked at Nick. "Like you said, this is between the two of you. Tell her." He touched Jessie on the arm and headed out of the room.

Cutting to the window, Nick turned around, willing the words to come. Except words couldn't make this right. Not all the words in the world.

"Nick?"

" … Let me start at the beginning."

"Is Gianni alive?" Her eyes dilated. "That's all I want to know. Is the man alive?"

"Yes. But there's--"

"You're sure?"

"Yes."

"How … is this possible?"

Drained, Nick threaded a hand through his hair. He had no choice. Jessie had heard too much. "It was a look-alike on the Milano," he said dully. "Not Gianni."

Silent for a moment, Jessie stared at the floor. "A look-- Where is Gianni now?"

"We don't know. We're trying to figure it out—"

"He has Anthony?"

"That's what Barton and I believe."

"And the FBI?"

"We couldn't tell them. A dead man rises from the grave, steals a little boy in front of hundreds of witnesses? And even if they did believe us, their investigation would tip off Gianni. Martinelli has eyes everywhere. It would drive Fosselli further underground."

"How did you realize Gianni was alive in the first place? When?"

Jessie's eyes pinning him in place like a butterfly on velvet, Nick started at the beginning. The matches, the flowers in her dressing room, Abbie's matches. The Milano officer, Martinelli and Zappella's reactions, the shoe. Anthony's sense of being watched. The hit on Lyle that killed his wife and daughter. Andrew's visit to Zane. His lips tightened. "There's new danger now. To all of us. Another disaster." He told her about Clint Vaughn and Martinelli.

"I don't care about me!" Jessie flared. "I care about my little boy. You knew Gianni was alive for months. You knew Anthony was in danger. But you didn't tell me? You couldn't tell me this?"

"Honey, I did everything possible to keep you and Anthony safe. The medallions. That's—"

"The medallions. My God. The lies … All this time, nothing but lies …"

"We took extra precautions, hired Willy as a bodyguard. Heightened security at the wedding--"

"Security that didn't work." Her eyes hardened into blue chips. "You knew Gianni wanted revenge. Wanted his son. How could you keep me out of the loop? I'm your wife. Anthony's mother. I deserved to know more than anyone!"

"I was trying to protect you. I—"

"Don't you know I'd rip Gianni apart to protect my son? You had no right! You put Anthony in danger with your silence. You should've come to me and the police with this information. If you had, maybe Anthony would be asleep in his own bed right now instead of out there with that monster. You failed me and you failed our son, Nick!"

"Don't say that. Don't you ever say that again!" Nick's cell jangled, the tone muffled. He fingered his pocket, not there. "I'd give my life for Anthony. Everything I've done has been for you and Anthony." His cell went silent, then buzzed again.

"When I think of the times you were away on 'business,' doing 'research,' every time you and Lyle and Abbie were together, lying to me--"

"Where the hell is my phone?"

*

Yanking his cell from her pocket, Jessie glanced at the screen and slammed it into Nick's chest. "Here. Talk to your lover."

"My--?" He glanced at the screen. "Let me explain--"

"Forget it. I saw your call list. You forgot to erase the calls when you deleted all the texts."

Staring at her, Nick rasped, "... You-you looked at my phone records?"

"Don't you dare turn this around on me. This is about you and Brianna Fontaine."

"You've got it all wrong. Bree's been helping us. That call could--"

My God. Jessie stumbled backwards. "She knows? Bree knows, too? What in God's name is wrong with you? You keep secrets that could get us killed, that got my son kidnapped. You're in a conspiracy with my friends. You screw around with some whore while you're marrying me."

"That's not—"

"Shut up! You'll never change, never. Nick McDeare and his bimbos, part two. Kristin Wallingford had your number. Oh, and one more thing." Jessie snatched the manuscript from the floor. "You take Andrew's life with me, your life with me, and you turn it into fiction? Out there for everyone to see? What the hell were you thinking?"

"I-I thought you'd be happy. It's my tribute to you and Andrew. And I'm not screwing around with Bree!"

"No more lies. No more! Leave me alone. I can't even look at you. *And if I never see my son again it will be your fault, Nick!*"

"You don't mean that--"

"I'll never forgive you." Jessie threw the manuscript at him. "Never!"

"Jessie—"

Jessie ran for the brownstone, tears streaking her face. Bursting through the kitchen door, she collided with Josh Elliot.

*

It was hours before Clint felt safe enough to make his way back across town, slipping and sliding in the snow. Keeping to the shadows on his street, he saw no sign of Barton and McDeare. Clint ducked into his nearby parking garage, grabbed a metal box from his car's trunk, and slid behind the wheel. Unlocking the box, he lifted out the pistol.

Attaching the silencer, Clint slid the gun into his boot and started the car.

He crossed Central Park at Seventy-Ninth Street and drove south a few blocks, looking for a parking space.

As he inched across East Seventy-Sixth Street, Clint was stunned to see McDeare vault out of a residence directly behind the Brady home, Barton on his heels. Like viewing a scene from a silent movie, Clint watched the cop grab McDeare's arm and say something, but McDeare jerked away and cannonballed down the icy street, slipping every other step. Barton shook his head and trudged back inside.

What the hell? And then it hit Clint. This was how the two heroes had been coming and going all this time without being seen. Brilliant. A secret hole out of their burrow.

It was child's play to follow McDeare at a safe distance. The man was wandering up one slick street and down another, going nowhere. He was making this too easy. Clint pulled the gun from his boot.

Martinelli had given the order less than an hour ago. First McDeare, then Barton.

CHAPTER 23

Head down, Nick trudged through a snow globe, the white stuff swirling all around him. His head pounded. His knee ached. Worse, images sliced through his mind like a hot laser. Gianni and Anthony. The book. Letting Vaughn slip through his fingers.

Jessie's rage. *And if I never see my son again it will be your fault, Nick!*

Twisting south on Lexington, Nick tried to shake the slide show, passing an endless row of boutiques, jewelry stores, and restaurants. The busy street was buzzing with pedestrians.

Pausing in front of an antique store, he eyed a collection of shiny pocket watches arranged on a Louis Quatorze coffee table. Nick tugged his own timepiece from his pocket. A gift from his birth mother, handed down through the generations to the first born, to him, not Andrew. Seven o'clock.

Damn, it was cold. The snow was picking up in intensity, damp flakes stinging his eyes.

Nick ducked his head and plodded on, his boots crunching on the packed powder.

*

It was getting dicey, the streets a mess, drifts piling up. Clint trailed McDeare from a distance, inching his car down Lexington. An irate cabbie on his tail laid on his horn. The cab swerved around him, barely missing his bumper and spinning out of control. More horns as the taxi ricocheted off a gypsy cab. Both drivers leapt out of their vehicles, cursing, slipping in the slush.

The clamor broke McDeare's stride. The man halted, glancing back at the commotion. Clint slid down in his seat to avoid recognition.

This was bullshit. McDeare might be intent on freezing his ass off, but not Clint. He dug a pint of scotch from the glove compartment. Liquid heat.

*

"My God, what's wrong, Jessie?" Josh caught her as she collapsed against him, sobbing. Gasping for breath, she clung to him.

One of the feds approached, asking if he could help.

"I've got it." Shielding Jessie from the man's prying eyes, Josh hustled her into the kitchen and sat her in the breakfast nook. He grabbed a box of tissues and dropped down beside her while she cried, her face in her hands. Lifting her head, Jessie reached for a tissue, her breath catching. She looked at Josh as if seeing him for the first time. "Josh …?"

"Yeah."

"I … I forgot you--"

"What happened?" Josh looked into her eyes, starry with tears. "Tell me how I can help."

"Nothing. There's nothing … It's all been a lie."

"What has?"

"Nick … My friends …" Her voice strained, she whispered, "I've been such a fool."

Lies. Had Jessie caught McDeare with another woman? Her friends knew about it?

*

Slurping his cold coffee, Lyle watched the whiteout from his den window. He hoped Nick was tucked into a neighborhood bar and not out walking in it. The man was a wreck. Lyle had heard their fight from the bedroom, every harsh word. He never should've let it get this far, should've told Jessie about Gianni a long time ago.

But he wasn't the same man he used to be. He was empty. The only thing that kept his engine running was the thought of stopping Martinelli and seeing Fosselli pay for Barb and Dina. Saving Anthony.

He was starved for a solid lead. They had nothing but a high-rise in Jersey City. A grainy picture of a child on Martinelli's lap in the Honda. Two lawyered-up security guards who couldn't pass a polygraph and wouldn't say a word except two: not guilty. Clint Vaughn at the wedding, Martinelli's man. So what? Where did that get him? He mashed a hand over his face, as frustrated as hell. At his cell's buzz, he picked up. Bree.

"Why isn't Nick taking my calls?"

"He …"

"Is he with you?"

"He, uh, he went for a walk."

" … What? In the storm from hell? What's going on, Lyle?"

Exhaling, Barton filled Bree in on the confrontation with Clint Vaughn, the probability of a hit out on them.

"My God. Lyle."

"There's more." He told her about Jessie finding out about Gianni, her anger. He hesitated.

"There's something you're not telling me."

He'd never liked dealing with reporters. He liked it less now. "Listen, I have to go."

"And do what? Walk the dog? You're hiding some-- Wait. Nick's blowup with Jessie tonight. From what you just told me it happened in the same timeframe as my last call … A connection?"

Swearing to himself, Lyle said, "Your imagination's working overtime."

"Maybe she realized I was calling him? Jessie thinks there's something going on. Just like Abbie."

Nothing like putting two and two together and getting four. Lyle sighed into the phone.

"I'm right aren't I?"

"Why were you trying to reach Nick anyway?"

"My question first."

"Was it Martinelli? You got something? For God's sake, Bree--we're desperate."

A little laugh. "Okay, yeah. It's big. I finally got a picture of him—he's in that penthouse, shot through the glass deck doors. And it gets better. He's with a little girl, the prettiest thing, maybe three, four years old. They're sitting on a thick area rug; she's on on his lap. And Martinelli, he's showing her something on an iPad. God knows what. A video of them playing doctor? He's rubbing her back, his hand under her top—I got that in the shot. I wanted more, but they left the room."

"Goddamn."

"It's so creepy. I wanted Nick to know right away. A child porn ring—this is huge. Even for Martinelli. We need more evidence, but even this--maybe you can use the picture to neutralize him. Get some leverage."

"Good work."

"Maybe you can use it to make Martinelli tell you where Gianni's hiding."

"Or he'll laugh at us and send Gianni further underground. It's not enough. But maybe we can use it later. Send it to me."

"Will do."

"I have to go--"

"Lyle, wait! Am I right? Jessie knew it was me calling Nick tonight?"

"Actually," Lyle grimaced, "she knows about all your calls, back and forth. She looked at his cell records." Barton rubbed his pounding forehead.

"Holy shit. And she thinks Nick and I are sleeping together?"

"You're the reporter. Figure it out. Keep me updated on Martinelli. And thanks for your help." He clicked off, stared at the computer on his desk, searched his mind for a lead, any lead. Drew a blank. His eyes dropped to the book about a dog breed Nick had left. What did he have to lose?

Lyle Googled Portuguese water dogs.

*

The temperature had dropped, the snow feather-pillow thick. Passing block after block of ritzy shops, Nick moved on, heading west across Fifty-Ninth Street, past the landmark Plaza Hotel.

He was so damned tired.

Shuffling down Fifth Avenue, his legs took on a life of their own. At Fifty-First Street Nick tripped over a mound of blankets. Landing hard on his hip he skated down the sidewalk, a glass bus shelter finally breaking his momentum.

Dazed, Nick looked up to see the pile of blankets rise and rush towards him like something from a horror movie. It was a man, filthy from head to toe, hair and beard matted, a pink mouth yelling, "My sign. Give me my sign!" Nick rolled away as the man clawed at him. The primitive life form waved a hand-made cardboard sign that read HOMELESS. Nick's sled. "You ruined it!"

"Sorry," Nick muttered, struggling to his feet. He pulled out his wallet and gave the guy a twenty. His thanks was a curse.

*

Clint watched McDeare schlep across Fifty-Ninth, a one-way street heading east. Damn the man. He'd have to either double-park and continue on foot or drive blocks out of his way, circling one-way streets and hoping to spot him. His car would be towed or booted if he abandoned it. Clint had too many unpaid parking tickets to risk it.

Shooting across Fifty-Seventh Street, Clint paused at each avenue and peered north. With all the pedestrian traffic and that damned floating curtain of snow it was impossible to spot anyone.

*

"I-I don't know who to trust anymore." Jessie felt drained, her senses dulled. Too much had happened too fast.

"You can trust me." Josh squeezed her hand, his eyes warm.

Could she? Jessie flashed back to Nick stubbornly accusing Josh of drugging her at Nordic Nirvana. Nick spitefully keeping Josh from singing at the wedding. But Josh had coolly let Nick's jealousy roll off his back, always on Jessie's side. Everyone else had betrayed her, allied with Nick ...

Nick had known about Gianni, alive. Gianni Fosselli, a demon come back into her life. Her trusted husband had kept the information from her, snaring Lyle and Abbie in his conspiracy. His lover, Bree Fontaine, that snotty reporter--even she'd known about Gianni. Had Nick and Bree laughed at her, snug in bed after making love?

And stupid fool Jessie Kendle, believing Nick every time he slipped out the door to do God knows what with God knows whom. Trusting him.

In the end, her hero Nick had been an illusion, as fleeting as any character in a play.

Meeting Josh's eyes, Jessie whispered, "You're the only one I can trust."

Josh pulled her close, pressing his lips to her forehead. "We go back a long way. They say old friends are the only friends."

Not all of them. Not Abbie.

*

Staring across the Hudson, Bree sipped her coffee. Her conversation with Barton gnawed at her. Nick and Lyle were in mortal danger. Snow swirled outside, surveillance difficult to impossible. At least she wasn't glued to the telescope anymore. With the camera focused on Martinelli's window now, she'd set it to snap photos every ten seconds if movement occurred.

After Yves' left for Libya that morning, she'd called Nick before the ransom drop, a time-wasting sham. His frustration had come through in his voice. The man was on the ropes, his pain at losing another son eating him alive. Now the Clint Vaughn debacle, then Jessie-gate. Damn the petty woman for making things worse. Grabbing her cell, Bree speed-dialed Nick again, holding her breath. Answer.

"Yeah?"

Thank God. "Where are you?"

"... Somewhere in Midtown."

"I-I talked to Barton. I know what happened tonight. Everything. Are you okay? About Martinelli, I got a--"

"I have to go."

"Look ... Jessie's anger about Gianni. She'll get over it. Give her time."

A hollow laugh. "You were right. Everyone was. The lies. They all blew up in my face."

"Where are you? I'll come--"

"Forget it."

"Nick, I got a pic—"

He clicked off.

Bree's heart sank. Grabbing her coat, she knew what she had to do.

*

Just as the lines in front of the theaters were queuing up, Nick found himself in the heart of Times Square, hordes of people bottle-necking the sidewalks. Might as well be in a pinball machine. His right knee was killing him, his left hip throbbed, and his brow was swollen and sore.

Taking cover under a corner awning, he avoided the logjam. The gaudy store advertised authentic New York memorabilia. Authentic? The Yankee baseballs were plastic and their logo would wash off in a drizzle.

Blinking at his reflection in the glass Nick realized why no one had recognized him all night. He looked more like the homeless man than a successful international author. He just needed a beard.

Spinning around, Nick collapsed against the glass. What the hell was he doing alone in the middle of New York City on a Saturday night? How had his life changed so drastically, transformed from a man with a family and a home and a future to ... this?

And then he saw it, across the street. The Rodgers and Hammerstein Theater. In the chaos he hadn't realized which corner he'd chosen for refuge. The marquee lights were dimmed, yellow police tape across the lobby doors. TO HAVE AND TO HOLD. Starring Jessica Kendle.

His wife. Jessie's fury at his betrayal had come from deep within. The look in her eyes ...

Nick shivered, but it wasn't from the cold.

*

Throwing away her crumbled-up tissues, Josh brought Jessie a glass of water. She was grateful he wasn't pushing her to talk. She peeked up at him, his blue eyes soft with concern.

Andrew had adored Josh, even brought him to Bill Rudolph's attention. Andrew had great instincts when it came to people, something Jessie sorely lacked. He always said Jessie was attracted to the wrong men, and she'd proven him right repeatedly.

"Where's Mary tonight?"

"Around." Jessie shrugged. "We don't talk much these days." A house of secrets, she thought bitterly. Was Mary a co-conspirator? "Abbie's here somewhere, too." Speaking of conspirators.

"Mrs. McDeare?" An FBI agent approached her. "There's a Brianna Fontaine here to see you."

*

Clint Vaughn had lost McDeare back when the target crossed Fifty-Ninth Street. Now he was stuck in Times Square theater traffic. Martinelli wasn't paying him enough to put up with this kind of crap.

By now McDeare could be anywhere in the naked city. There was nothing to do but head back to East Seventy-Sixth and hope McDeare hadn't gone home while Clint was wasting his time. Nah. From what he'd seen, the idiot was crazy enough to still be out in this weather, making like Frosty the Snowman.

Someone would be waiting for him when he returned home. The street would be deserted in this shit. No one would hear a shot fired through a silencer.

And Frosty would be no more.

*

Nick headed west on Forty-Seventh Street, veering south at Tenth Avenue. The snow was coming down harder, wet flakes fusing his lashes together. At Forty-Fourth he ducked into a local bar, far off the tourist path. The place was doing a decent business. Nick slid onto a bar stool and ordered a double bourbon.

The bartender sized him up and hesitated. "I need cash or a credit card up front."

This was a first. Nick tossed his Amex on the bar.

The guy studied it. He looked up in disbelief. "Nick McDeare? Come on, buddy. You don't look like--"

Nick offered his driver's license.

"Jesus. What happened to you?"

*

Jessie flew into the hallway, Josh trailing. Brianna Fontaine stood a few feet away. She flicked back the hood on her down coat, dark hair tousled. Two agents lurked nearby.

"What are you doing here?" Jessie didn't bother to hide her swelling rage.

"We need to talk."

"Get out of my house!"

Brianna didn't move. When one of the agents stepped in, the woman angled him a chilly smile. "I'm a reporter, NEW YORK TIMES, friends with Mr. McDeare. Unless you want a front page expose regarding the Bureau's fuck up on a missing virus at NIH six weeks ago, stay out of this." She turned back to Jessie. "I have a few things to say, and you're going to listen."

The agents watched, speechless, as Bree sailed into the kitchen and planted herself by the island.

Swearing to herself Jessie followed, Josh at her side.

"Want me to get her out of here, Jessie?" he asked.

"I'm not going anywhere." Crossing her arms, Bree eyed Jessie. "Always performing. You want to do this in front of your co-star, fine."

"Josh, it's okay. Stay." Jessie returned Bree's stare, trying hard not to betray the crack in her heart. *Her husband's lover.* "I can't imagine what you have to say to me," Jessie managed, hating that quaver in her voice, "but say it and get out."

"Someone has to set you straight. You wouldn't listen to Nick."

"So he's already told you. Is he waiting in your bed right now?"

"Nick is walking the streets, trying to hold it together over another lost son and," her eyes darted to Josh, "everything going wrong." Josh put a comforting hand on Jessie's shoulder.

Pulling in a deep breath, Jessie said, "Don't you talk to me about losing a child. What do you really want, my blessing? You can have him."

"Jessie," Josh murmured.

"It's okay," she said. "I changed my mind. Let her chatter. It's amusing."

"Nick doesn't want me," Bree said flatly. "Or anyone else, for that matter. He wants you. We're not sleeping together. But you're right about me." Bree tipped up her chin. "I tried. I pulled every trick in the book to get him back. Nothing worked. He loves you. He's faithful to you. I can't imagine why."

Her knees wobbly, Jessie felt weak. This night would never end.

*

Downing his first bourbon in one gulp, Nick slid the glass to the bartender for a refill.

"So what happened to you?" The throaty female voice came from the next stool.

"Too long a story." Nick's eyes never left his glass.

"Try me. I've had a pretty shitty night myself."

The liquor seeped through Nick's body, a welcome tingling that numbed his senses. He took another gulp and closed his eyes, enjoying the anesthesia.

"That abrasion on your forehead looks bad."

"Abrasion?" Nick chuckled. "My father's favorite word for a scrape."

"He's a doctor?"

Nick nodded.

"So am I."

A sideways look revealed a mane of auburn curls. Long, angular face. Pale hazel eyes. Late thirties. A half-empty bottle of white wine in front of her.

"I'll tell you mine if you tell me yours." She refilled her glass and sipped, her full lips caressing the glass.

"You first." Nick was content to thaw for a while and listen to someone else's problems. The liquor was working its magic.

*

Bree pushed on. The blond hunk never left Jessie's side. The fragile ice princess, teary eyes and all, captured the male of the species even now. Bree chose her words carefully, keeping Gianni's name out of the dialogue. "It wasn't easy, coming here. Nick's in a dark place. Cut him a break for God's sake. Yeah, he was wrong not to tell you about … what he knew. He thought he was protecting you. His motives were pure. His method was wrong."

Hoping she was getting through to the diva, Bree's voice softened. "I was around when Jeffrey was sick," she continued. "I saw what it did to Nick. Anthony being abducted—Nick knows he wouldn't survive losing another son."

Stepping closer, she forced Jessie to look at her. "Call him. Tell him to come home. He needs to be safe. He needs to be with you."

*

"Let's see." The doc set the glass down and ran her finger around its rim. "Tonight I got held up in the ER. Again. When I got home my fiancee was gone. Amanda. She was tired of taking second place to my job. I found the ring in the toilet." She looked over at him. "How's that compared to your saga?"

Reaching for his bourbon, Nick took another swallow. "Doesn't come close."

"So tell me."

"You're an ER doctor?"

"At Roosevelt. Six years now."

"A few years ago a man was brought into the ER. A famous Broadway actor."

"Gunshot wound to the head. I remember. He was young. Tragic."

"He was my brother." Nick drained his glass and signaled for another.

"Brady. Andrew Brady ... Your brother? I'm sorry. The bartender said your name was Mc-something."

"McDeare. Nick McDeare."

"Different fathers? I'm Maggie McWhorter. Fellow Irishmen."

"Not exactly. I was adopted."

"You're an actor too?"

Nick was intrigued. "You don't know who I am?"

"Should I?"

"You read books?"

"My job owns me." She chuckled, a husky laugh. Sexy, even if she was gay. "Any leftover time is for the fiancée. Or used to be. The hell with Amanda. She knew my hours when we got engaged." She shook the mood off and turned her pale eyes on him. "You write? Are you well known? "

"Doesn't matter." Nick focused on his drink again.

"Okay, your turn. Make me forget my troubles."

"It would take too long."

"I'm not going anywhere." She swiveled to face him, crossing her long legs. "And just for the record, I'm not gay. I'm bi." She licked her lips, staring into his eyes. Maggie McWhorter was a tease. And available.

Nick smiled at her.

*

Stumbling to the breakfast nook after Bree was gone, Jessie sat down hard, her knees giving out.

He loves you. He's faithful to you.

"You didn't buy that woman's song and dance?" Josh slid into the seat across from her. "She was covering for him."

Tell him to come home. He needs to be safe.

Safe ...Everything Nick had said tonight rushed back. A problem with a man named Clint, new danger from Martinelli. Too much to process all at once. What were they going to do? The FBI was in the brownstone. She was safe, for now. But Nick was out there, a target ...

"Jessie?"

"I—I can't to talk about this now, Josh. Let's talk about something else. Anything else, okay?"

"Sorry." Josh lifted his hands in surrender. "We'll switch the subject. Hey, Bill says we can reopen in a couple of days. The benefit ..."

While Josh prattled on, Jessie made all the appropriate responses, her eyes on him, her mind on Bree. Nick. Lyle. Anthony.

"Did you see George on the front page of the POST?" Josh continued. "I can't believe how wrong we were about Valentine. But Georgie's going away for a long time. Ricin's--"

"What did you say?" Jessie attention snapped back to Josh with a vengeance. She suddenly had no trouble focusing on him at all.

"I said ..." He stopped, mouth open.

"You said ricin."

"It's been all over the news." Josh shrugged

"The police didn't release information about ricin to the press. They didn't release it on purpose."

Jessie looked at Josh with new eyes. "How did you know it was ricin, Josh?"

CHAPTER 24

"Josh ... ? How do you know about the ricin?" Jessie repeated.

"You know," Josh wrinkled his forehead, "if it wasn't in the news I really don't remember. Maybe one of the stagehands wandering around? They hear everything."

Her heart starting to jackhammer, Jessie said, "Try again. The truth this time. I've had enough lies to last a lifetime."

"Are you accusing me of something?" Josh leapt up, managing to look outraged.

"Stop lying!" Jessie sprang to her feet. "There's no way you can know about this!"

Suddenly deflating, Josh looked away. "It's not, it's not what you think."

Jessie didn't know what to think. She felt dizzy, stuck in a funhouse of distorted mirrors, one uglier than another. "Tell me now," she croaked. "Or I swear to God I'll call Detective Lally this minute and press charges."

Staring at the floor, Josh said hoarsely, "I caught George fiddling with your costumes before opening night. When I confronted him, he moaned he was in love with Valentine. He wanted to give her a little stage time, get you to, uh, take a day off—"

"By killing me?"

"No! Just take time to regroup after a few minor mishaps, that's all. Not that I wanted to work with Valentine. I despise her. She's--"

If it weren't for the agents on the first floor, Jessie would've shrieked out her next words. Instead, she dropped her voice to a whispered scream. "And that was okay with you!?"

"Of course not. But, see, I-I understood how he felt," Josh mumbled, rubbing his forehead, " ... because that's how I feel about you." He raised his head, looking at her with puppy-dog eyes. "I saw the chance to prove I can protect you, be there for you. Jessie, you and I belong together!"

It was so absurd, Jessie started to laugh. "You encouraged a nut case like George to sabotage my career so you could be my hero? This is how you protect me? My God." She covered her mouth, on the verge of hysteria.

"I saw a woman who needs someone to understand her, support her, like Andrew did. Like Nick never could. What's so funny about that?"

"Ricin is a POISON." She stepped closer. "How could you do that?"

"I didn't know anything about it, I swear. I thought the man was lovesick. Our agreement was he wouldn't do anything to hurt you."

"So you just kept your mouth shut?" She shook her head. "Or was there more?"

Swallowing, he muttered, " ... Your schedule. I let him know when your dressing room would be empty, where you'd be when. That's all."

"Uh huh. Who paid for the ricin?"

"He asked for money later. But I had no idea--"

"You could have killed me!"

*

Parked down the block from McDeare's home away from home, Clint was bored. He was also invisible, sandwiched between two monster SUV's. His cell buzzed. Aldo. "Stop calling me. When McDeare shows, I'll blow smoke up your ass."

"The boss--"

He punched the end button, sick of Aldo. He hadn't told him about McDeare's secret refuge. Aldo didn't need to know everything Clint knew, and Clint knew a lot. More than Aldo and Roberto could begin to imagine. As far as McDeare, all Aldo knew was that McDeare had taken off before Clint had gotten a shot.

Clint fingered the .45-caliber pistol under the seat. It had been with him since Nam, reported stolen and hidden in a safe place when he was de-commed. The only holdover from years in the service, the weapon had saved his life a dozen times deep in the jungle of that God-forsaken country.

He'd used it on occasion for Martinelli since coming home for good. The hits were emotionless. He did the job and moved on, a fresh bottle of scotch erasing the deed. It always worked.

*

"I had no idea that's what he was up to," Josh insisted. "I'd never hurt you, never."

"But you did hurt me. More than—Oh my God. You used ricin, a poison. And at Nordic Nirvana you--"

"No! Absolutely not. I swear I did not put that drug in your drink. I wanted you in my arms because you wanted me back. Me. Not because you were stoned senseless."

Sucking in a breath, Jessie believed him. The man's ego was too big for anything else. If he couldn't win her on charm, he wanted her vulnerable, turning to him for support. Jessie just needed to fill in one more piece of the puzzle. "Are you paying for George's attorney?"

Guilt washed across Josh's face.

"He's blackmailing you."

"Something like that, or he tells the cops I knew about it." Flushing, Josh said, "Look, the right person's behind bars. I had nothing to do with the ricin. And I'm sorry for playing any part in this. So sorry." Reaching over, he brushed her cheek with his knuckles. "Can't we just forget about--"

Reeling, Jessie backed away from the stranger in front of her. How could she be so consistently wrong about everyone in her life? Valentine. Josh. Abbie. Nick. Was it something genetic? Neurological? Could you find it on an MRI?

"Jessie, please," he pleaded, raising his hands. "Tell me how to make things right. Please don't go to the cops."

Running her hands through her hair, Jessie paced the kitchen, her mind racing. She'd keep quiet, but for her own reasons. Not for Josh's sake. She stopped and faced him. "Here's how it's going to work," she said icily. "You give your two-week notice to Bill Rudolph immediately. Make up an excuse, a good one."

"But my contract—"

"You have an attorney. Use him." Eerily calm, she approached Josh. "And you will never be in another Rudolph production again. Do you understand? As soon as my life returns to normal, I'll make sure of that."

" … You're joking. You'd--"

"You pull out of the show now, or you and George share a cell. Do we have an understanding?"

"Yeah." Josh's sparkle and charm melted away like dirty snow in a heat wave. "We've got an understanding." He strode from the room without another word.

Her hands shaking, Jessie sank into the breakfast nook. Josh. It had been Josh all this time. How could she have been so blind?

*

Abbie heard the front door slam. Hopefully, Josh had finally slunk home. Tiptoeing down to her favorite hiding spot at the top of the steps, she peeked around the corner. Jessie was alone in the breakfast nook, her head in her hands.

"Is the meatball gone?"

"My God." Jessie's head shot up, her hand flying to her heart. "You." Her expression hardening, she dropped her head back in her hands.

"I, um, eavesdropped tonight." Abbie sat across from her.

"So you know about Josh?"

"Bree. I went back to my room after she left. Why? Did I miss something good?" No comment. Abbie forged on. "I, um, gathered from what I heard with Bree, you know about Gianni."

"And you." Jessie's eyes glittered with tears. "Sneaking behind my back with Nick and Lyle."

"It killed me, Jessie. But I didn't think I had a choice."

"You, no choice?" Jessie let out a mirthless laugh. "You're a big girl with a big mouth. You could've told me what was going on any time of any day."

Feeling her face grow warm, Abbie said, "Nick swore us all to secrecy. He was frantic about Gianni, out of his mind with worry. We all were. We were trying to protect you."

"More heroes in my life," Jessie whispered. "Protecting me. God save me."

"What does that mean?"

"Never mind. You're my best friend. My oldest friend. You hurt me, Abbie, so much."

Crestfallen, Abbie stared at Jessie, seeing the pain in her face. Her heart sank. She should've told Jessie about Gianni right away. She'd made a terrible mistake. If only you could turn back time and do it all over. If only. But you couldn't.

"Nick was so sure you'd freak if you knew Gianni was alive," Abbie said in a little voice, blinking back tears. "He was so positive. I-I believed him. I'm sorry. I should've told you."

"I don't know any of you anymore." Jessie wiped her eyes. "I feel like I'm locked in that mask class of Pierre's at Juilliard. Everyone's wearing a mask and I'm watching a charade."

Leaning forward, Abbie whispered, "Except this isn't make-believe. We're all human. Fallible. The mistakes Nick made—we all made—they came from love. Don't throw that away. Please. Be mad about everything else, but not that." Reaching across the table Abbie took her friend's hand. "I really am sorry. And I swear on Andrew's grave I'll never keep anything from you again. Never. Forgive me?"

Relief swept through Abbie as Jessie squeezed her hand back. "Okay," Abbie said quietly, "tell me what happened tonight with Nick."

*

Nick held up his glass for a refill, the booze doing its job. He saluted the first Stone-Age man with the brilliant idea of fermenting a few grains to take his troubles away. Genius. The bar was hopping, every stool taken. A jukebox blared, the buzz of conversation reaching a new decibel.

Maggie McWhorter lifted her wine glass to him. "To new friends."

To Neolithic man and a still. Staring into her hazel eyes, Nick clinked glasses and drank.

"You know," Maggie cooed in his ear. "We could take this party to my place. Only a couple blocks away. I'd like to see what you look like when you clean up a little."

*

Her anger fading, Jessie told Abbie about her disastrous night. The manuscript, Gianni, Nick, Bree. A man named Clint and new danger.

"What about Josh?" Abbie went to the refrigerator for water.

" … He, uh, confessed his undying love for me tonight."

"Oh that." Abbie waved an arm. "Everyone knows he has the hots for you. What a jerk. You and Nick have a fight, he makes a move. Disgusting."

If Abbie only knew how disgusting.

Sitting back down, Abbie took a slurp of water. "Okay. Let's start with Bree. For what it's worth, I thought Nick and Lois Lane were having an affair, too, at first."

"What changed your mind?"

"Seeing Nick with her and knowing the situation from the inside." Abbie explained how she'd bumbled into the secret. "Nick's not into Bree. He loves you. She's useful, helping with Martinelli and Gianni. So cross that off your worry list. Now, about Clint and Martinelli. Go to Lyle's. If Nick's back, work things out. If he's not, call him. Get him home. With the FBI all over the place we're secure here."

Swallowing, Jessie knew Abbie was right. Nick needed to be safe at home. He needed to find Anthony. They could deal with everything else afterwards.

*

Slipping out of bed, Roberto Martinelli drifted towards the living room. He poured a hefty shot of Courvoisier and drank it in one gulp. He poured another. His ulcer was kicking, the brandy igniting a fire in his belly. He didn't care.

He stared across the Hudson at Manhattan, still aglow at this late hour, the craggy rooftops an artist's shimmering fantasy. The city that never slept. Roberto couldn't sleep either. Somewhere over on that island was the cause of his insomnia. McDeare and Barton.

It was a risk, but he had to take care of the problem. If he let it go and McDeare unearthed Fosselli, the media would be all over it, Roberto and his involvement exposed to the world. McDeare would have evidence. Proof, with Barton to back him up. People were murdered all the time, but back from the dead? Roberto Martinelli would be the main attraction in a media circus.

It would never reach a trial, but that sensational kind of press he could not afford. You couldn't buy off the public, the pressure on the authorities to do something. His vital contacts—the cops, the politicians, the DA, the judges, the press, the bankers—they'd all disappear if McDeare produced Fosselli in the flesh. Better to answer questions from the cops about quiet hits on two men who each had a habit of making enemies. He'd skated before. He would again.

After making the arrangements with Vaughn, Aldo had updated Gianni, not concerned by the news. Fosselli was a remade man, so sure he was untouchable.

*

Seeing lights in his apartment, Jessie knocked on Lyle's back door. The cop swung it open, surprise on his face. She stepped inside, brushing snow from her hair and coat. "Is Nick back?"

"I was just about to call him."

"Do you think," Jessie gulped, "something happened?"

Leading her into the den, Lyle looked at her in that steady way of his. He'd worn the same unshakable gaze over two years ago when he promised Jessie he'd find Andrew's killer. And he did, Nick his partner. Eduardo Santangelo. Roberto Martinelli. Gianni Fosselli. A trio of killers. Deep down, Jessie knew she could trust Lyle, even though he'd kept Gianni a secret. That was Nick's doing, not Lyle's.

"I won't sugarcoat this," Lyle said evenly. "We've got a problem. But Nick's a survivor." Tossing a sweatshirt into a duffel, he added, "I'm sure he's fine." Lyle grabbed a small knapsack, quickly closing it.

The place was a shambles. Canvas bags, rope, blankets, and assorted tools were piled on the floor. "Are you going somewhere, a lead on Anthony?"

"It's a long shot, but we're taking it. I need Nick back here."

"I was thinking of calling him. Asking him to come home."

"Do it now."

*

Sliding off the bar stool, Nick turned away from Maggie to answer his cell when he saw who was calling. "Jess?"

"I-I … wanted to make sure you were okay, that Marti--"

- 227 -

Maggie laughed uproariously at something the bartender said, drowning out Jessie's words.

"I'm having trouble hearing you."

"Where are you?"

"A bar."

"Hey, cutie," a drunk Maggie draped herself around Nick, "who's so importan' you can' talk to me?"

Jerking away from her, Nick croaked, "Jessie, you still there? ... Jess?"

"You make me sick." She clicked off.

"Party's over," he said to Maggie, beginning to sober up. "Got to go." Grabbing his coat, Nick limped to the street, ignoring Maggie's pleas to stay. As he searched for a cab his cell buzzed again. Barton.

"Where are you?"

"Trying to get a cab."

"Get the hell off the street and call Willie."

A cab stopped. Nick crosschecked the cabbie's face with the license and picture on the console. Satisfied he wasn't Martinelli's idea of a taxi driver, he climbed in and gave Lyle's address. "Jessie just called."

"She's here."

"Let me talk to her."

A long pause filled with muffled voices. "She, uh, doesn't want to talk right now. Look, get home ASAP. I have news. And be careful."

*

A cold calm descended over Jessie as Lyle talked to Nick. Nick McDeare would never change. Never. All that mattered now was finding Anthony. Nothing else.

"He's on his way home." Lyle clicked off.

Jessie eyed the duffels on the floor. "I'm going with you."

"Not a good idea. It's dangerous out there now. I don't know what we're heading into. And it could be one day or it could be more."

"I'm Anthony's mother. I'm going." She locked eyes with Lyle. "You and Nick will not leave me out of anything concerning my son ever again. Understood? I want your word on this. You've never let me down until now, Lyle. Make it up to me."

" ... Pack a bag. We leave in a couple hours."

*

"Hey, I'm your goldmine," Clint barked into his cell. "You should be kissing my ass." Draining the pint of scotch, he tossed the bottle on the car's floor mat. "I got some shit going on, but I have something for you." Leaning over, Clint rummaged through the glove compartment, pulling out a small notebook. Flipping through the pages he straightened up. "Works out of a mom-and-pop bodega in East Harlem--" Headlights down the street caught his eye.

McDeare emerged from a cab and limped up the stairs to Barton's place. "Got to go." Tossing the cell, he reached under the seat, snatching the .45.

Too late. Barton opened the door and both men disappeared inside.

Fuck.

*

Barton had a fresh pot of coffee waiting when Nick stumbled through the door. "Where is she?" Nick looked around, snow dropping from his coat and puddling on the floor.

"Home."

"I have to explain--"

"There'll be time for that. Sit down before you fall down. How much have you had to drink?"

Struggling out of his coat, Nick collapsed into the desk chair, gripping his knee.

"You look like shit." Handing him a steaming mug, Lyle ordered, "Drink." As Nick drank, Barton continued, "No more booze. You need to be clear-headed until this is over." Barton brought the coffee pot from the kitchen, filling a mug for himself. "Keep drinking."

Casting him a dirty look, Nick took another sip.

"Listen to me. While you were putting mileage on your boots, I did some research." Invigorated, Barton began to pace. "I got to thinking about what you said, that Gianni would give Anthony anything he wanted to make him happy. Meaning a dog."

"You said it was a long shot."

"The longest. But you were right about those dogs--Portuguese water dogs. They're fairly rare. And knowing Gianni's fastidious tastes, he'd want an adult, housebroken, right?"

"Go on."

"Okay. Breeders sell puppies. Adults don't turn up in a city pound, too valuable. They're usually found in a rescue shelter. The Portuguese Rescue and Relocation program is in Florida. But official channels aren't for our boy. You should see their online questionnaire. He'll look for a private operation, cut through the red tape."

Confident Nick was listening, Barton paused, pouring more coffee. "I found three private rescue groups specializing in rare breeds within a two-hundred mile radius of Buffalo. Erie, Pennsylvania, Rochester, New York, and Cleveland. They work out of their homes, take calls any time. I called them tonight. Now, no one's come looking for a Portie in recent weeks in Cleveland. Rochester doesn't have any available. But someone picked up a Portie in Erie this morning. Ninety-three miles from Buffalo."

Lyle saw some life in Nick's face.

"I talked to the director, said I was NYPD looking into a case. He wasn't buying it over the phone. Needs to see my badge in person, which I had to turn in with my gun."

"Dammit, what--"

"Wait. Steinmetz brought me my badge." Lyle grinned. "Don't ask. And there's more. I've been studying that wedding picture of Vaughn between phone calls, and it hit me. How stupid could we be? If we know Vaughn was at your wedding that means we also know who he was with." Lyle dug into his briefcase and held up the photo. "Take a look at our recast Gianni Fosselli. The bald guy talking to Vaughn."

Nick grabbed the photo. "Doesn't look anything like him. Not even the bone structure."

"Plastic surgery. We knew he'd alter his appearance; we just didn't figure going under the knife to do it. But he left nothing to chance. Fosselli had extensive work, the kind that turns Dr. Jekyll into Mr. Hyde. It ensured he could show up at the wedding unrecognized, give him total freedom of movement."

"So we head to Erie and show the rescue director this photo."

"If he showed up there, we'll know it." Lyle put the photo back in the briefcase and snapped it shut. "It's a start."

"A start." Nick washed a hand over his face. "This never should've happened in the first place. Anthony has to be frightened out of his mind. It's my fault he was taken. We both know it. Now Jessie does, too."

"It's Gianni's fault. We're going to get Anthony back if it kills me. You gave him instructions on how to behave if he was kidnapped. He'll be fine." Lyle hesitated. "Speaking of Jessie ... she insists on going with us. We can't cut her out of this anymore. She has the right."

"It could put her in danger." Pushing himself out of the chair, Nick drifted to the window, his eyes glued to the brownstone.

"We set ground rules. She listens, or she stays behind."

"You set them. I doubt she'll listen to anything I say right now."

Glancing at his watch, Barton said, "I have more to tell you. Bree came through for us."

"The camera? Tell me."

"Later. It takes about seven hours to get to Erie. It's almost eleven. Shower and sober up before we leave. We'll get there in the morning, right after the kennel opens. We leave from here and avoid Martinelli's men. They'll be watching the brownstone. And, Nick," Lyle drew in a breath, "pack a bag. If we get a positive ID in Erie, we're going to track the SOB down from there. Steinmetz brought me supplies."

Giving the room a quick glance, Nick said, "That explains enough shit around here to storm Omaha Beach."

"Plus this." Reaching into one of the gym bags, Lyle held up the medallion with the tracking device in one hand, Nick's keychain with the compass arrow in the other. "They didn't help in Buffalo. Maybe they'll come in handy this time around."

"Any other tricks in those bags of goodies?"

"As a matter of fact, yeah. A few things I've been working on the last few days, waiting for our break. Including another gift from Steinmetz." Lyle pulled a revolver out of a small knapsack. "Untraceable."

*

Trapped in the middle of his nightmare, Gianni writhed. He yelled at Anthony to call his dog!

As Anthony finally complied, Gianni smiled warmly at his son. He thanked him in front of McDeare and Jessica, wanting them to understand at last how blood told. McDeare was an outsider here, no relation to Anthony Fosselli.

Cocking the gun, Gianni willed his trembling hand still, his moment approaching. He instructed his son to take the frenzied creature into the house. Now. He waited for Anthony to retreat so his father could do what was necessary. The boy played dumb. Gianni shrieked at him to run to the house!

Snarling, the dog leapt for Gianni's throat. The gun fired, a bright flash--

His heart running a race, sweat trickling down his brow, Gianni jerked out of his nightmare. Throwing off the blankets, he hurried to Anthony's room. The boy was sleeping peacefully, the dog at the foot of the bed.

Before returning to bed, Gianni waited for his heartbeat to return to normal. Aldo's call had spurred the dream this time. Amazing how the psyche could conjure up demons in the dark of night. But the dog was as gentle as an *agnello* and McDeare was far from here. There were no breadcrumbs leading from New York City to Canton, Ohio. He was safe.

The chill in this house was relentless. He pulled the covers up around his ears, closed his eyes, and willed himself back to sleep.

Wait … a soft laugh, the howl of a dog. What now?

Gianni trailed the sound to Anthony's room. Monty was in the middle of the room, howling. Anthony sat on the edge of the bed, muttering something. He smiled up at Gianni, his eyes open but unseeing.

CHAPTER 25

Nick limped into the master bedroom. Dressed in jeans and a sweater, face scrubbed free of makeup, Jessie was throwing a Knicks cap into her suitcase. "Jess? Can we talk?"

"There's nothing to say. Cutie." She zipped the suitcase with a swift yank and grabbed her down coat and a fur-lined hat from the bed.

"The bar. It's not what you think."

Picking up her bag, Jessie stalked to the door. "You'll never change."

"Hear me out--"

"I won't spend my life wondering if you're cheating or lying. Or if I should believe you when you say you're not cheating or lying. I deserve better."

"You can believe me. I wasn't cheating. The--" He was talking to the air, her footsteps fading down the hallway. Only her lilac scent lingered.

*

One a.m. Clint Vaughn debated calling Aldo with an update. It would serve the prick right to be yanked from sleep. He'd done it to Clint often enough. As he reached for his cell, Barton hatched from his hideout and jogged towards Lexington.

Curling his fingers around the gun, Clint waited for McDeare. Martinelli wanted him first. Ten minutes later a black SUV double-parked in front of the cop's place, and Barton climbed out and loped back inside.

On impulse, Clint grabbed his tracking device from the trunk. Sprinting across the street, he attached the gizmo under the SUV and dashed back to his car. If McDeare and Barton were going somewhere together and the cop was packing, too risky to do this here. Barton reemerged a second later with McDeare and Kendle. Clint swore at the clown car parade. What next, a juggler? They made several trips, packing the cargo space.

So the trio was going on the run. But you couldn't hide from Roberto Martinelli.

After they got into the car and took off, Clint turned on the tracking screen. A red blip blinked back at him, showing the SUV cruising across Seventy-Sixth Street and turning onto Lexington. He'd update Aldo later, when he knew more.

*

Barton drove, Nick staring out the windshield at the dark landscape of I-80. Jessie curled up in the back seat, silent.

"You okay back there, Jessie?" Barton guided the car across the George Washington Bridge, traffic skimpy.

"Fine. About to have one of the sandwiches Mary packed. Want one?"

"Sure."

Before Jessie handed it to Lyle over the car seat, Nick heard her unwrap the sandwich's crinkly paper, smelled the delicious aroma set free. His stomach growling, he peeked sideways at Barton digging into ham and smoked mozzarella piled high on a Kaiser roll. He couldn't remember the last time he'd eaten. The saliva almost drooled out of his mouth. "I'll take one, too."

Silence.

This was ridiculous. He revised the dialogue. *"How about you, Nick? Would you like one, too?"*

"Yeah, honey, that sounds—"

A sandwich sailed over his head and landed on the floor. "Special delivery," he said acidly. "Thanks." Not bothering with the niceties, Nick ripped off the wrapping and devoured the food in a few bites.

The silent car ate up more miles as Nick pulled Bree's Jersey penthouse photo from his pocket. He'd swiped it from Barton's desk right before they left the house. As he studied the don and the little girl, the sandwich turned leaden in his stomach. So little and innocent ...

Kiddie porn was not your typical Mafia business. And Martinelli seemed to be enjoying the merchandise himself. This went beyond the bounds, even for a monster. The skeleton in Martinelli's closet—*children.*

Slicing a hand through his hair, Nick grimaced. In exchange for Nick's silence after they rescued Anthony, Martinelli would pay. He'd pull his goons off Nick, his family, and Barton. He'd remove himself from the child-porn business and swear he'd leave this little girl alone. For starters. But the confrontation had to wait. They couldn't risk--

"There's a car back there." Lyle's voice shook Nick from his reverie. "Been following us since we got on 80. Hanging back, but he's keeping up with us." Barton fixed his eyes on his rear-view mirror. "Forget it. He's getting off at this exit."

*

Clint was forced to gas up, running on air. With the tracker he'd catch up later and figure it out then. Besides, they were the only two cars on the interstate for the last forty miles. Who else would be dumb enough to drive around at two in the morning on a freezing January night but a wolf after a rabbit? He couldn't afford to clue Barton into the hunt.

*

After her night from hell, Jessie was relieved to burrow into the back seat, draped in mute shadows. The SUV sped over the highway as they chased Lyle's long shot, making one stop at a rest area. She didn't know what the long shot was, and she didn't have the energy to ask. But she had to be there when Anthony was found. She tried not to think about anything else. Tried.

The rhythmic hum of tires on the interstate lulled her to sleep. A dream crept in. *Nick, Lyle, and Jessie, outside. Night, an owl hooting. Gianni loomed into focus, his eyes flashing. One hand gripped Anthony, the other a gun. He fired. Someone went down. Nick! Was it Nick?*

Awaking with a gasp, Jessie found both men staring at her from the front seat. "Bad dream?" Nick asked.

Swallowing hard, Jessie didn't trust her voice. The nightmare, Nick … But there he was, staring at her from the front seat. Alive and unhurt, eyes ringed with lines of exhaustion. She hated him for invading her dream.

And making her realize how much she loved him.

Straightening, Jessie tightened her ponytail and looked around. Sunlight streamed into the SUV. They were parked in front of a rambling three-story house in a rural area, kennels in the back, dogs barking.

Lyle grabbed his briefcase from the back seat. "You'll have to stay here, Jessie. This man thinks Nick is my partner. I'll fill you in when we get back."

*

"Can I take Monty for a walk before breakfast? You said I could go outside today." Anthony was dressed in the winter gear he'd found in his closet. He'd even wrapped the scarf around his neck to make Gianni happy. Monty sat at his side, tail beating the floor.

"First, I have to ask you a question." Gianni was washing green stuff and setting it next to a bowl of yellow stuff. "Last night, I think you were talking in your sleep. It's not the first time. Did this ever happen before you came here?"

Last night, Daddy had visited. They'd talked a lot. "No," Anthony said. "I never talked in my sleep before. What was I saying?"

"Never mind. Don't stay out long. We'll eat soon. Vegetable frittata and Italian sausage."

Whatever that was. Anthony had a plan. But first he needed to know something. "Where's that guy who was here before? He's mean. I'm glad he's gone."

"Carlo has his own cottage in the back of the property. I asked him to leave us alone for a few weeks so we could get reacquainted."

"Can you tell him to stay away for good?"

Chuckling, Gianni said, "He works for me. He protects us."

"From what?"

"From people who might want to hurt us."

"You mean like—" Anthony almost said Dad. "… Uncle Nick?"

"I don't worry about Nicholas." Gianni gazed out the window. "He can't find us. But I want to make sure you're safe. That's why Carlo's here." Gianni turned to Anthony. He looked angry. "It's time you stopped thinking about Nicholas. Maybe you've been talking to him in your sleep. I'm your father, Anthony. Do you understand? You--"

With a loud bang, the water in the sink started spraying everywhere. Anthony and Monty darted out of the way. Gianni tried to plug it, but the water soaked him each time he bent over, squirting him in the face. Finally he threw three towels over the spigot, cursing in Italian. Anthony tried not to laugh.

The water stopped. Gianni looked from the sink to Anthony, his bald head dripping wet. He lifted the towel and played with the knob. The water came out the way it was supposed to.

"Be back in time for breakfast." Anthony ran for the door with his dog. Out in the snow Anthony couldn't stop laughing. "I bet Daddy Andrew did that, Monty. He likes to play tricks on Gianni."

Look for an escape. That's what the Count of Monty Crisco would do. Anthony clasped the medallion around his neck. "This medal is magic, Monty. Dad gave it to me. I can't wait for you to meet him."

Monty trotted after Anthony, heading for the front gate. He rattled the lock. Solid. Moving on, Monty at his side, Anthony followed the iron fence around the property, looking for an opening. He avoided Carlo's cottage.

Anthony tried fitting himself sideways through the fence slats, but he was too big. Monty wouldn't fit through either. Anthony would never leave Monty. The fence was too tall to climb over even without a dog. And there were sharp spikes at the top, like knives.

Blinking back tears, Anthony clutched his medal.

There was no way out of his prison.

*

"Mr. Weinstein, I'm Lieutenant Lyle Barton, NYPD." Lyle showed the man his badge. "We spoke on the phone last night. This is my partner, Detective McDeare."

Nodding, Nick let Barton take the lead. Weinstein was mid-fifties, Norman-Rockwell face. He wore jeans and a plaid shirt.

Weinstein examined the badge, then looked at Lyle. Satisfied, he let them into the old house, the front parlor an office. Weinstein introduced a skinny young woman with a slash of red lipstick as his assistant director. She sat at a computer behind the desk.

A large dog with a black curly coat was curled on an overstuffed pillow next to the desk. Nick recognized a Portuguese water dog. She thumped her tail and opened an eye. "That's Athena. Nancy, these are the policemen from New York asking about that Portie we recently placed with Mr., uh …"

"Silva," Nancy supplied. "Such a nice man. He wanted the dog for his son."

Nick tried to stifle his grimace.

Looking from Nick to Lyle, Nancy asked, "Is there a problem?"

"Nothing serious," Barton said smoothly. "Mr … Silva is a crucial witness in a case. We need to find him. We're hoping you can help us out."

"Sure. Here's his information." Nancy pulled a file from the cabinet.

Taking the folder, Barton scanned it. "Rudolph Silva. Seven twenty-eight East Sixty-Eighth Street. NYC." He snorted, looking at Nick.

Swearing to himself, Nick clenched his fists. That address put Mr. Silva in the middle of the East River. Which was exactly where Nick wanted him. Face down.

"I see he listed references," Lyle mused, reading over the form. "Did you call them?"

"We, uh, didn't feel the need," Nancy said. "See, Mr. Silva was all about his family. He researched the breed so thoroughly. And he answered every question about his living conditions and the care of the dog in minute detail. You can see it all there."

"So," Lyle pressed, "you let him have the dog the same day he showed up? Isn't that irregular, not checking him out?"

"Uh," Weinstein said, "normally there's a short wait."

"But no normal for Mr. Silva?" Nick pushed. "Why was he special?"

Nancy and Weinstein looked at each other. "It's like this," Nancy finally confided. "Mr. Silva's a widower. His wife just died in this terrible boating accident on vacation in the Virgin Islands--the gas tank exploded--and his little boy's grieving, devastated. Crying every day for his mother."

Choking, Nick bit back an obscenity. Barton quickly put a hand on his arm.

"Are you okay? Nancy asked. "Can I get you a glass of water?"

"He's fine," Lyle said, tightening his hold on Nick. "He has asthma. Needs his inhaler."

"Anyway," Nancy continued, "It was so sad. His little boy was begging for a Portuguese water dog—that's the only thing that would make him smile. Getting a dog. And only that kind of dog. So we bent the rules and made an exception."

"And he gave the RBRA--Rare Breed Rescue Association--a generous donation," Weinstein added. "Far more than we usually suggest."

Of course he did. Stuffing his fists in his pockets, Nick looked away.

Lyle pulled the wedding photo of Vaughn and his accomplice from his briefcase and showed it to Weinstein, pointing to Vaughn's companion. "Is this the man who adopted the dog?"

"That's him. Exotic looking. The most unusual green eyes."

"Is there anything else you can remember about this man?" Nick asked tightly. "What kind of car was he driving?"

"A fancy one," Weinstein said. "A Porsche SUV. Big and roomy, silver. It had Ohio plates, and I asked him about that, since he was from New York. Mr. Silva said he was visiting family in Ohio and used their car. It was good for his little boy to see his aunt and uncle. And he was sure this dog was ideal for his son. After everything he told us, we knew it was meant to be."

Ohio. Nick met Barton's eyes. They both began to smile.

"Thank you, Mr. Weinstein." Barton shook the man's hand. "I'm sure it was meant to be as well. By the way, did he mention a town in Ohio?"

"Not that I recall."

"How close are we to the Ohio border?"

"Oh, only about a half hour away. Get on I-90 West and you're there."

As they walked back to the car Barton fished the medallion out of his briefcase and handed it to Nick. "Put this thing on. I have a feeling we're going to need it."

*

Parked behind a clump of bushes down the road from the kennel, Clint watched the door through binoculars. What the hell was going on in there—stocking the brownstone with Dobermans?

McDeare and Barton reappeared. Minus mutts. They sped off, hooking onto I-90W, heading for Ohio. Clint followed, cursing the state. Land of crappy sports teams and cow dung.

*

"Where are we going now?" Jessie asked. "What happened back there? You're both smiling."

Meeting Jessie's eyes in the rearview mirror, Lyle explained their theory about Gianni and the dog. "We just hit pay dirt. The guy back there gave a positive ID on the new Gianni Fosselli. He picked up a Portie yesterday and headed back to Ohio. Which is where we're headed."

"A new Gianni?"

"See for yourself. The picture's in that briefcase next to you. Yves snapped it at the wedding."

Digging out the photo, Jessie examined it. It meant nothing to her. "One of these men is Gianni?"

"The bald guy. Extensive plastic surgery. The other's our friend Clint Vaughn."

Jessie stared at the bald man with the startling marble green eyes. Wait. She'd seen this face before, but with a ... "My God."

"What?" Nick glanced over his shoulder at her.

"This ... this is the man who talked to me at Nordic Nirvana. Sought me out and said he was so sorry for all the tragedy in my life. It was Gianni!" Her heart started to thump the kind of beat that would leap off an EKG.

"Nordic Nirvana?" Nick said.

"He-he's the one who spiked my drink that night!"

"Jesus," Barton exclaimed. "Fosselli went public--dared you to recognize him?"

Turning away, Nick muttered, "Josh had reason and opportunity, too."

"Gianni wanted to humiliate me, and he succeeded!" Jessie bolted forward, furious, feeling like pounding Nick on his thick head. "For God's sake, why is it so hard for you to ever admit you're wrong?"

"We don't know I'm wrong, do we?"

"How pathetic. I knew it wasn't Josh."

"Your loyalty's misplaced. As usual."

Opening her mouth, Jessie clamped it shut. Unfortunately, Nick was right. Which was why she wouldn't tell him about Josh and George. He'd immediately pounce on Josh for drugging her and fling her bad judgment in her face. But now she knew the truth. *Gianni.* He'd even changed his voice, his accent. Frustrated, Jessie stared out the window, muttering under her breath, "You and your colossal ego."

Nick's response was a snort.

*

No sleep in days, not enough grub. Clint was wiped out. Worse, he'd run out of scotch while he was vegetating on East Seventy-Sixth Street. When the cop stopped for gas, Clint swung off the same exit and hit a convenience store. He bought three six-packs of beer and some chips. Comfort food.

Back on the interstate, Clint stayed a mile behind, tracking the SUV's progress on the display screen.

They crossed the state line. Welcome to Ohio. The Buckeye State.

What the hell was a buckeye?

*

Nothing on the road but a wintry landscape out of DOCTOR ZHIVAGO and billboards dripping ice. Nick yawned. They passed a town called Conneaut. Another blip in the white landscape. He desperately needed a hint Anthony was near. Nick touched the medallion on his neck, maddeningly quiet.

Jessie had been mute since the exchange about Nordic Nirvana. Nick peered over his shoulder. Two ice chips met his gaze before turning away.

Okay. He'd research Ohio's cities and towns. Nick tugged out his cell. Fosselli had lived in Genoa, Italy, and New York City, hubs of sophistication and cosmopolitan tastes. In Ohio terms that would translate into … Nick keyed in the search engine, coming up with Cleveland, Columbus, Toledo, and Cincinnati.

They were seventy miles from Cleveland, so cross that off. The medallion would be vibrating if Anthony was in Cleveland.

Toledo, or maybe a smaller city? Nick checked out Youngstown. Interesting. Youngstown had a rep for mob connections. Did Martinelli--

The medallion vibrated. Nick jumped.

The quiver faded.

Nick stilled, waiting. Barton glanced at him, eyebrows raised.

"What?" Jessie asked. "Is it the medallion?"

There it was again. The signal faint, but there. Nick eyed Barton, the relief overwhelming. He glanced over the seat at Jessie. "It's the medallion. Anthony's within a hundred miles. We're close."

"Thank God," she breathed, wiping a tear from her eye.

"What about the keychain," Barton asked, "the arrow? Which direction is it pointing?"

Nick quickly jerked it out of his pocket. The arrow was as dead as the hand on a broken clock. He shook it from side to side. "Damn, nothing."

*

B-o-r-i-n-g. Gianni was teaching Anthony Italian from a book. Anthony slumped at the kitchen table. He knew English good enough. He got an "A" on his last composition.

Gianni didn't look happy.

"Can I take Monty outside now, Uncle Gianni? I think he has to--"

"Just a half hour more. It's important to speak your native language."

"My native language is English."

"This is your true native language, Anthony, Italian, the language of your ancestors. The dominant side of your heritage. One day I'll take you to Italy. You'll forget everything about your life here when you see Rome, Genoa, Naples. We'll visit my--"

The TV on the wall blasted on. It hurt Anthony's ears. Gianni sprang up and turned it off. It popped back on. Gianni tried to turn it off. It kept playing, rapidly switching channels. A football game. A PBS cartoon for kids. A cooking show. A movie about Italian gangsters. Gianni banged on the screen and yelled in Italian.

Anthony's glass of juice tipped over. All by itself. It spilled all over the book. Anthony leaped up.

"What did you do?" Gianni glared at him.

- 239 -

"Nothing. Honest."

"Don't lie to me. Such a mess. You must learn to sit still, Anthony."

Backing away from those goblin eyes, Anthony hurriedly said Monty had to pee. "Really bad. Look at him. If I don't take him now he'll—"

"Yes, yes. Go already." A spot twitched on Gianni's bald head.

"Come on, Monty." Anthony grabbed his coat and galloped for the door.

Outside, Anthony took off running. He stopped at the fence, panting. "Daddy Andrew spilled the juice, Monty. He knew I didn't want to talk Italian."

The clouds hid the sun and made the house look creepy. Anthony suddenly felt cold. Gianni was so mad.

A killer. That's what everyone called Gianni. He killed Daddy Andrew. He was big. Anthony bet he could kill anyone if he got angry enough. Even him.

*

"*Madone de mia! Sta Migna!*" Gianni tossed the soaked paper towels into the garbage can. He looked at the book. The pages were soaked. At least the television had shut up.

Stumbling to a chair at the table, Gianni dropped down, forcing himself to take deep breaths. The television taking on a life of its own, the glass spilling by itself, if Anthony was telling the truth. The cold spots, the water spigot …

The wiring in the house must be faulty. The house needed new windows; the sink was useless. He'd done too much remodeling himself, an amateur. Anthony had spilled the juice. Anyway, none of that was important.

What mattered was that he was safe, yes? Even if Nicholas knew Gianni had Anthony, what did it matter? No one would recognize Gianni Fosselli anymore. Gianni Fosselli was non-existent. He was safe.

Gianni phoned Aldo, just to be sure. "Everything quiet?"

"McDeare took a walk and never came home. If we're lucky, he walked straight into the Hudson."

"Keep me updated." Hanging up, Gianni felt sick. McDeare had too much ego to leave this earth willingly.

If McDeare was missing, there was only one reason. The imbecile was on the hunt, looking for Anthony against all odds.

Let him. McDeare could search the world over and never find him. Determined to feel better, Gianni began to prepare dinner. He inserted a New York Philharmonic CD, the lush music filling the quaint old house.

But there was another sound … laughter. Gianni sprang up, determined to silence the pestilent noise once and for all. First, he had to find to find the source. He examined the house top to bottom, tearing apart the sound system, searching the insides of the stove exhaust fan, the air conditioning vents, the bathroom exhaust fans, the utility room, the furnace. He climbed into the attic and scoured the eaves, home to who knew what kind of primitive Midwest wildlife. But the laughter bubbled up from everywhere. And nowhere. He wiped his forehead, coated with sweat.

The sun dripped behind the clouds, casting the rooms in shadow. It would be dark soon.

A chill went through Gianni. This is what ancient man must have felt living in his cave, at the mercy of the creatures of the night.

*

The medallion's pulsing grew stronger as they neared Cleveland, more powerful the farther they drove. But the arrow remained as still as a stone. "Maybe Toledo," Nick muttered, ready to punch a fist through the windshield.

"Let me know if it starts to work." Lyle's lips thinned. "Meantime, we keep going west and see what happens." They continued on I-90, through Cleveland and beyond. It was getting dark. The quiver remained constant.

"Maybe we should head south," Jessie suggested.

Rubbing his eyes, Lyle stared at the endless ribbon of road. "Let's continue west for now. We'll change direction if the vibration fades."

At Elyria, I-90 merged with I-80 and the medallion was barely moving. Ten miles later it fell into a coma. Nick swore.

"Okay, time to grab something to eat," Barton said. "We'll buy a map and mark the boundaries where the vibration disappears."

They ate at a truck stop. Greasy food, formica tables, metal napkin dispensers, and waitresses old enough to have known Herbert Hoover, Ohio's claim to fame. No one bothered them, truck drivers in plaid flannel shirts and caps drinking pots of coffee and heading for their rigs. Jessie had stuck her Knicks cap over her ponytail and kept her head down. In this place, it worked. Nick hoped it still worked out of truck-driver land.

Over a stringy pot roast dinner Nick and Lyle plotted their route. Jessie picked at her food, remaining silent. Nick drew a grid using east-west roads. The western boundary was Huron; the eastern boundary ten miles this side of Conneaut. They'd continue to crisscross that grid, moving a little further south with each leg.

And wait for the arrow to wake up.

*

When Barton got off the highway to eat, Clint went through a McDonald's drive-up across the street and devoured three Big Macs in three minutes. Stuffed, he stopped at a liquor store up the road for liquid dessert and stocked up on scotch.

After a hefty swig from a bottle of Dewar's, Clint wiped his mouth on his wrist. Okay, now that he was feeling better, he considered his options du jour. He rejected taking out McDeare in front of Kendle. Call him a pussy, but he didn't like it. Likewise, he nixed going back to New York and hoping McDeare and Barton would head back home one of these days. Zappella would be up his ass.

But Clint had a new option. Something that could pay huge dividends if his hunch paid off. So he waited right where he was.

When Barton and McDeare got back on the road, Clint followed. They were heading east this time, veering onto I-80.

His gut was right. He knew it. They had a lead from the kennel. They were looking for the kid and Fosselli.

Reaching for his cell, Clint speed-dialed a number. Voice mail. "I have something for you. Something big. I'll be in touch."

- 241 -

CHAPTER 26

The farther they inched south, the stronger the medallion's vibration. Lyle swung back and forth across the state, turning around whenever the quiver began to fade. The damned arrow remained stapled in place.

It was almost midnight when the SUV neared Youngstown. The pulsing weakened as they entered the former steel mecca. Doggedly, Lyle swung around and headed west again. The vibration was stronger in the central part of the grid with each southerly swath, breaking the monotony of the dark icy landscape. That jiggle was the only thing keeping Nick sane.

As they entered downtown Akron the vibration grew stronger but the arrow refused to budge. Nick felt an irrational spurt of hated for a twig of metal. He flexed his fingers, trying to hold it together.

"Let's get some shut-eye," Barton said, yawning. "Start fresh in the morning. Try going straight south from here like Jessie suggested and see what happens."

"I'll drive. You sleep."

"Nick," Lyle said patiently, "we don't know what we'll find when we get to Anthony. We're stopping to recharge. Agreed, Jessie?" Lyle glanced into the rear-view mirror. "Jessie?"

Nick glanced over his shoulder at the darkened back seat. Jessie was snailed into the corner, her head resting on a blanket. "She's asleep." Kneading a hand over his eyes, Nick sank back in his seat. Lyle was right. He wasn't fit to take on a kitten at this point. They were all exhausted.

Barton pulled into a nondescript chain hotel on the next block and parked in the adjoining lot.

While Lyle and a sleepy Jessie went to the lobby desk and paid for one night, Nick picked up a pamphlet about Akron. Population two hundred thousand. Fifth largest city in Ohio, county seat of government. An airport for Akron and Canton farther south. The University of Akron and the Akron Civic. The Akron Aeros, a subdivision of the Cleveland Indians. Restaurants with a wide variety of ethnic foods. Hmmm.

"You onto something?" Lyle asked as they headed outside to their rooms.

"Akron's cultural. Diverse. Just big enough to suit Gianni Fosselli, at least, temporarily. He's close. I can feel it."

"We need that damned arrow to feel it."

They reached their rooms, two doors side by side. Jessie said good night to Lyle, sliding the keycard into a door's lock. She opened it, slipped inside, and closed the door in Nick's face.

Barton pushed the other door open. Glancing at Nick's expression, he said, "Hang in there. She'll come around."

*

Pulling up across the street, Clint watched the trio register, then slip into two rooms and hunker down for the night. Looked like McDeare was in the doghouse with the wife.

This shithole burg looked like a ghost town. Buildings dark and locked. No pedestrians. No nightlife. No sirens or horns or garbage or bums on the street. Even the rats were sleeping. If hell ever did freeze over, this is what it would look like. Clint pulled into the hotel lot and killed the engine.

Grabbing a flashlight from the trunk, he crept to the SUV. The windows were tinted, but Clint could make out what was in the back. Gym bags. Blankets. Rope. An axe. Tools.

McDeare and Barton had come prepared.

He bet a loaded gun was packed somewhere in that car, too.

*

It was nighttime. Anthony was outside, running towards someone with all his might, his legs pumping. There was a loud bang!

Gasping, Anthony jerked awake. His heart was pounding, just like after his old nightmares about Gianni chasing him. *Gianni was chasing him in this dream, too. With a gun.*

This time Anthony was even more afraid. Was Gianni going to shoot him? Gianni never acted like a real father. He didn't know anything about being a dad. Anthony was all alone, except for Monty. He didn't even have his magic ring anymore. Anthony started to cry.

"I'm here, Anthony." Daddy's voice.

Wiping his tears, Anthony looked around. "Where are you? I can't see you."

"You need to be brave, Anthony. Braver than you've ever been."

*

Showered, Nick was ready to go at nine the next morning. He and Barton had decided not to shave, using facial scruff for disguise. Barton was still out, snoring. Too revved up to wait in this cube one more minute, Nick left the hotel. Jessie's curtains were drawn, still asleep.

He took off on foot, the sidewalks clear and shoveled. The temperature had risen, the sun beginning to melt the leftover snow into slush.

Taking in the cityscape, Nick meandered through the streets, trying to imagine Gianni here. The university area was brimming with diners, bookshops, antique stores.

Nick moved farther into the heart of downtown. Name-brand department stores and quaint cafes mingled with chain restaurants. He checked out menus, particularly Italian cuisine. Maybe Fosselli would open another restaurant. He'd put nothing past the egomaniac.

Striding on, Nick scanned a jewelry store window. A sign in the window offered fair prices for family jewelry and advertised estate sale heirlooms. The window collection was a mix of precious gems and antique pieces. A silver tea service. Diamonds. Wristwatches--

Stopping, Nick stared at one piece of jewelry.

A ring. A boy's gold ring with a large diamond.

From Africa.

*

After a restless night, Jessie had risen early, showered, and grabbed a cup of strong coffee and a stale pastry from the hotel cafe. She'd felt numb, achy, full of a dread anticipation. When they found Anthony, they would also find Gianni. Then what? She swallowed. She couldn't bear thinking beyond that. Wouldn't. As she paid the cashier, she spotted Nick leaving the hotel, setting off on foot. On impulse, she followed him.

Tucking her hair under her hat and slipping on sunglasses, Jessie had stayed a half block behind her husband. He seemed to be sightseeing, perusing menus and store windows. Something caught his eye in a jewelry store. When he went in, Jessie whipped behind a pillar and watched what was going on inside, a clear view through the window.

*

An austere man with silver hair and wire-rimmed glasses greeted Nick as he dashed into Contessa Jewelers. "May I help you?"

"That ring in the window. The one with the large diamond. I need to see it. Are you the manager?"

"I'm the owner, Lionel Tibbets. Hold on a minute." Tibbets unlocked the window and lifted the ring from the display.

Nick tried to snatch it from the man's hand, but Tibbets was too fast for him. "What's going on here?"

"That ring is my son's. It was stolen," he said grimly.

"That's some accusation." Tibbets stiffened. "I don't buy stolen goods. Do you have a receipt or an insurance policy with the description to prove it?"

"I can do better than that. On the inside of that ring are two sets of initials. J.N.M. and A.B.M." Jeffrey Nicholas McDeare and Anthony Brady McDeare.

Taking out a loupe, Tibbets examined the inside of the ring. He looked up at Nick. "That proves nothing. You could have come in here and looked at it when my assistant was filling in yesterday."

"Are you kidding me?" Nick yanked out the contents of his pockets and spilled them onto the glass counter, digging for his wallet. "Look, how much do you want for it?" He'd pay anything.

The man fingered Nick's gold pocket watch. "A beautiful piece. I'll ask you the same question you asked me. How much do you want for this?"

"It's not for sale." Nick grabbed the watch, stuffing it back in his pocket, along with everything else. "The ring?"

"... Tell you what. Since you want it so badly I'll make you an even trade. The ring for the pocket watch."

"I'll give you three hundred cash for the ring."

"The pocket watch or no deal."

This was crazy. Nick pulled out the pocket watch, turning it over in his hand. A gift from Chelsea, all he had from his mother, handed down through the generations to the eldest son. He'd planned on giving it to Anthony one day.

But the ring. When Jeffrey was dying he'd gone out of his way to make sure Nick got the ring back, the beloved ring Nick had given him from South Africa. Anthony had treasured the ring as a talisman, its roots going back to Jeffrey. Now it had suddenly transformed itself into a vital clue to Anthony's location.

"Well?" Tibbets prompted.

"Deal." Nick ran his thumb across the pocket watch one last time and placed it on the counter.

As the man reached for the watch, Nick slammed his hand over it. "I need to know how you got the ring."

Tibbets thought for a minute. "A young man brought it in."

"His name?"

The man shrugged.

"A receipt? You have one, don't you?"

"It'll take some time to find it."

"Take the time."

The man slid Anthony's ring into his pocket and went to a file cabinet in the corner. Under Nick's stare he found the receipt in five minutes. He handed it to Nick. Harvey Spittel. An Akron address.

"Anything in particular you remember about this kid?"

"He was wearing a service uniform with a company logo. Sears? Maybe it was a gas station. That's it. He was wearing a gas station uniform."

"What gas station?"

"I don't remember. Maybe BP or Shell. Marathon."

"The ring." Nick tucked the receipt into his pocket.

"The pocket watch."

Nick slid the watch across the counter, fingers lingering on it for a moment. The man pushed the ring box his way. Nick grabbed the box and opened it, staring at the familiar ring, the diamond winking at him.

How did Anthony's ring end up here? Anthony would never give it up. Not willingly.

*

Whirling around, Jessie dashed into a drug store as Nick left the jewelers. He clipped past her, staring straight ahead, his lips set in a tight line. Jessie watched her husband through the window until he turned the corner.

His pocket watch. Nick had given the man his pocket watch in exchange for … what? The jeweler had plucked an item from the opposite window, too far away for Jessie to get a good look. But there had been no mistaking that big shiny gold watch.

Hurrying into the jewelry store, Jessie asked breathlessly, "The man who was just here, he gave you a watch. What did you give him in exchange?"

"I'm sorry, ma'am," the clerk said, drawing his face into a dignified mask. "All business transactions are private."

Gathering her wits about her, Jessie told herself there was another way ... Tugging off her hat, she shook out her hair, running her fingers through the silky curtain. She angled the man a soft look, her eyes wide. "I'm so sorry. Please let me explain, Mr....?"

"Tibbets. I own the store."

"Mr. Tibbets," she murmured, leaning over the counter and gazing up into his eyes. "That man is my husband. The watch he gave you—it's a treasured family heirloom. He wouldn't give that watch up for just anything. Please, sir. I need to know."

Leaning yet closer, she was glad she'd dabbed on perfume after her shower. Lilacs. Tibbets was staring at her, his eyes glazing over behind his glasses.

"Mr. Tibbets, sir ...?"

Blinking, he said, "Uh ... it was a ring. A boy's ring with a diamond."

My God. "A ring," she whispered. "Our son's ring."

"He said it was his son's."

Tears sprang to Jessie's eyes. Anthony was close. But he would never part with that ring willingly. Never. Gripping the counter she felt dizzy.

"Are you all right?" Tibbets came around the counter and grabbed a stool for her. "Please sit down. You don't look well."

"I'm sorry." Jessie dropped onto the stool. "I've just been going through-- I don't understand something. Why didn't my husband just pay you for the ring?"

Looking away, Tibbets said, "Now I'm sorry. I-I wanted the watch. I didn't know. Your son, is he ..."

"I'll pay you for the watch. Anything. Name your price."

"I, uh ..." Tibbets looked from the watch to Jessie." The calculating businessman shrank under her desperate gaze. "A hundred dollars. That's what I paid the kid for the ring."

Weak with relief, Jessie rose, pulling two hundred dollars from her wallet. "For your trouble, Mr. Tibbets." She thanked the man profusely and jogged back to the hotel, the watch tucked in her purse. Nick and Lyle were waiting for her in the lobby, their bags on the ground. Lyle leaned against the wall, slurping coffee. Nick paced, his hands deep in his pockets. The minute he saw her, he erupted, waving an arm in the air. "Where the hell have you been? Don't we have enough to worry about without your--"

"Calm down," Lyle said, "and lower your voice. Nick was worried about you, Jessie. We both were. We had no idea what happened to you. Don't disappear on us again."

"I'm sorry. I was--"

"We have a lead," Nick said shortly. "Get your things and meet us at the car." He strode out to the street. Jessie shook her head, wiping an eye.

"I'll tell you what I told Nick," Lyle said softly. "Give him time. He's anxious about Anthony, obsessed with making this right. That's all he can think about. When he found out you were missing, too, he went nuts." He touched her shoulder. "Hurry, okay? I'll explain in the car."

"I-- Just give me a minute." Jessie sprinted to her room. Nick would be furious if he knew she'd trailed him to the jewelry store. Time to deal with the watch later. Grabbing her bag, she dashed for the car.

As soon as she climbed into the back seat, Lyle headed out into the early morning traffic. "So what's the lead?" Jessie asked blandly.

"I found Anthony's ring in a jewelry store back there." Nick stared straight ahead. "We're going to talk to the kid who sold it to the jeweler."

"The ring," she said, her worry boiling over with it out in the open. "Anthony loved that ring. How would Gianni--"

"I got the ring back. I'm as upset as you are. Enough with the questions, okay?"

They rode the rest of the way in silence.

*

The kid who sold the ring lived in a neighborhood as decayed as a bad tooth. Boarded-up houses with roof shingles missing and shutters askew littered the street. Rusted junkers clogged his driveway. Fast-food wrappers and paper cups poked through the dirty blanket of melting snow.

Nick and Lyle climbed out of the car, Lyle asking Jessie to stay behind. She'd scared Nick silly with her vanishing act. When he'd returned to the hotel and Lyle said she was nowhere to be found, Nick had lost his mind. Swearing. Kicking the ice machine in the hall until it vomited out a waterfall of cubes up to their ankles and wouldn't shut off. Before he'd headed to the front desk to report the trouble, Barton had looked at Nick like he a needed a straitjacket. Nick still didn't trust himself to speak to her.

Leaping over the sagging stairs, Nick pounded on the screen door, Barton a few steps behind.

The inner door creaked open. A Pillsbury Doughboy of a woman stared at them over puffy eye pouches. She was wearing a faded robe, pink flesh pushing its way out at the seams. A cigarette dangled from her lips. She gripped a walker. "What?" she wheezed. "You the big bad wolf trying to knock the house down?"

"Sorry." Nick tried to collect himself. "Where's Harvey Spittel? Ma'am." Nick felt like ripping the screen door off its hinges.

"Who wants to know?"

"New York police." Lyle produced his badge.

"New York? My Harvey ain't never been to New York. Ain't never been nowhere."

"We need to speak with him." Lyle was the voice of authority. "He's an important witness in a case we're pursuing. Just tell us where he is please."

"Where he always is. At work." The woman started to hack. The cigarette remained clamped in place, ashes flying.

"Where's work, ma'am?" Nick fought the urge to shake her until she coughed up a lung.

"Marathon Station, south of town. Off Seventy-Seven."

"Where on I-77?" Lyle pressed.

- 248 -

The woman sighed, bringing on a fresh coughing attack. "First exit. Get on the highway--" Hack. Wheeze. "—three blocks down that way." The door closed in their faces.

As Nick climbed back into the SUV Mary called. The feds had returned the bag of ransom money. The FBI would continue to follow leads, but there was no longer a need for their presence in the brownstone. Nick hung up and filled in Jessie and Lyle.

"The case has officially gone cold." Lyle put the car into gear.

Staring out the window, Nick focused on finding his son, blanking out everything else. The case would never go cold. Not as long as he was alive.

*

Draining his coffee cup, Lyle tossed it on the seat. "We'll find him."

"What happened back there?" Jessie asked. "And where are we going now?"

"Nick?" Lyle glanced at him, miles away.

"What?"

"Where are you, man? Did you hear Jessie?"

"No." He looked back at Jessie. "What did you say?"

A long silence. "Never mind."

Lyle told Jessie about Harvey and the gas station. Steering the car onto I-77, Barton kept glancing at Nick. The man was on a tightrope. When he'd found out Jessie was missing, Lyle thought he was going to need a tranquilizer gun to calm him down.

*

The Marathon Gas Station wasn't hard to find. Before the SUV was in park, Nick leaped out of the car. Harvey Spittel was slouched behind the counter chewing gum and reading CAR & TRACK. Nick grabbed the kid by his coveralls and backed him against the wall by the throat. Flipping the lid of the ring box open with his thumb, he snapped, "Where did you get this, Harvey?"

Stunned, Harvey choked on his gum. Nick kept his grip as the kid coughed and gagged. Like mother, like son.

"Where, Harvey?"

"I-I can't breath--"

"Nick." Lyle came up behind him. "Take it easy. He can't talk if he's unconscious."

Nick loosened his grip. "This ring is my son's. How did it turn up at Contessa Jewelers in Akron?"

Lyle flashed his badge.

Harvey turned pale. "A-a guy dropped it in the men's room."

"What guy?" Nick hissed. "Who?"

"I don't know. He paid with cash."

"Keep talking," Lyle said.

"Please. Let me go and I'll tell you everything. I swear."

Breathing hard, Nick released Harvey.

"I-I found the ring in the bathroom after the guy left." Harvey's eyes darted from one man to the other. "When he came back about an hour later, he was pissed, scared the crap out of me. I told him I didn't know nothing about any ring. He went to the john, tore the room apart, cursing. He took off when a dude came in to pay for his gas. I decided to get rid of the ring fast."

"What did he look like?" Lyle grated. "What was he driving?"

"He was big, muscles. Dark, looked Italian, maybe Spanish. He was driving a red Corvette. A beaut."

"Where'd he come from?"

"I don't know. I swear to God I don't know. But when he left he headed south."

Nick pushed his face into Harvey's. He could smell the kid's peppermint gum. "If I find out you're lying, you're going to wish you were dead before I get back to you." Turning on his heel, Nick was surprised to see Jessie hanging back outside the entrance, her face drained of color. She spun on her heel and rushed to the car. Pushing through the door, Nick stalked to the SUV.

*

"Has to be one of Martinelli's goons," Barton said, getting behind the wheel, telling Jessie about Harvey's story. "Hired to protect Fosselli. Gianni had him get rid of the ring."

"Anthony would never give up that ring," Jessie said heavily, dropping her head into her hands. What had Gianni done to Anthony to get that ring off his finger? She felt sick at the thought of her little boy at the mercy of one of Martinelli's thugs. And spying Nick through the window with that attendant just now … For the first time Jessie allowed herself to wonder what was really going to happen when they found Anthony. She stifled a shudder. Lyle must have a gun. Maybe Nick did, too …

"She's right." Nick rasped. "Fosselli would have to rip that ring from him first."

Barton headed back to I-77 South. "Once he knew that ring was from you, it was history. It had to go."

"But Gianni didn't take the medallion," Jessie said. "Thank God for that."

"It's got his sulfa allergy on it. Fosselli would respect that."

Nick fingered his locket. "It's stronger here than Akron. We're getting closer."

*

Too much scotch and a killer of a hangover—he'd overslept. Clint Vaughn had pried his eyes open and managed to pop two aspirin just as the three stooges had taken off from the hotel in the SUV. The morning traffic had been thick and slow moving, the tracking device taking him where he needed to go.

Parked far back from the Akron house and the gas station, Clint had watched both confrontations through binoculars. McDeare had waved a ring around in the Marathon station. Judging from the terror on the kid's pimple face, McDeare was close to losing it.

Now they were heading south. A town called Green flew by. Ironic, considering there was nothing to see but white.

Aldo called, having no idea Clint wasn't keeping watch on the brownstone. "No sign of our targets?"

"Nope."

"Keep an eye out for Barton. You see him, take him. Maybe McDeare packed it up and quit the Big Apple. He could be anywhere." He hung up.

Clint snorted. McDeare had wormed his way out of the Apple all right. But only Clint needed to know that for now.

McDeare was going to lead him straight to the kid and Fosselli. Foxy would pay big for this. Clint had his cover story for Martinelli all worked out. As long as he eliminated McDeare and Barton, Martinelli would be happy, not check the plot holes.

And when it was all over, Clint would be a very rich man.

CHAPTER 27

The medallion started thumping full tilt as Lyle sped south and approached Canton. Fighting claustrophobia, Nick had to restrain himself from leaping out of the car and screaming Anthony's name.

"It's a fairly large city." Lyle veered off a downtown exit. "This could take some time, unless that arrow resurrects itself. Let's grab a bite, figure out what's next." Barton parked in a city lot, and they took off on foot. The snow was beginning to melt into runny mounds of slush, the temperature rising every hour.

The trio ducked into Benders, a busy seafood pub across from City Hall. Sliding into a wooden booth, they were surrounded by businessmen and lawyer types at the tables, another crowd at the bar. Barton's cop eyes imprinted everything at a glance.

"Better keep our voices down." Lyle grabbed a menu. "We don't need anyone to remember us. God knows what will happen when we find Anthony. This scruff on our faces and Jessie's cap aren't the best disguises in the world."

While Nick and Lyle ate fish and chips and drank a local beer, Jessie picked at a seafood salad. Without the arrow, Nick and Lyle agreed their best plan was to show Fosselli's picture around town and hope they got lucky. Jessie nodded, her eyes veiled. Nick had no idea what she was thinking.

After lunch their first stop was the Convention and Visitor's Bureau, a few blocks away. Nick took the lead, asking the young woman behind the counter where he might look to buy a home in the area. Someplace remote. Quiet. But upscale. Miss Simone Perdue was a font of information, marking a county map, pointing out neighborhoods he might want to consider.

"You look familiar," she warbled, flicking a hand through her hair and smiling up at him through her lashes. This was not the kind of conversation Nick was looking for. Her gaze drifted to Jessie. "So do you, even more. Have you been here before?"

*

"Uh, no," Jessie said quickly. She recognized that look on Simone Perdue's face. She was trying to place Jessie--TV, online, a tabloid? Or maybe she remembered her and Nick from the kidnapping, the media all over it. "It's our first time here," she added, stepping back.

"I'm sure I know you," Simone insisted. "You're somebody. Do I know you from--"

"We're late." Lyle clapped his arms around Nick and Jessie's shoulders. "My wife's expecting us. Thanks a lot."

Back on the street, Barton said, "Another thirty seconds she'd have made you two. Let me do the talking from now on. Hang back, both of you."

"I wasn't thinking," Nick said, looking chagrined.

"You both wear your sunglasses inside from now on. And we need a hat for Nick, too. Jessie, stuff your hair up into your cap. A couple of suits in that restaurant were staring at you."

"Sorry," she said quietly, her heart beating too fast. "It won't happen again." Jessie tangled her hair up into a bun under her Knicks cap and popped her sunglasses back on.

*

Stopping at a CVS, Nick dashed in and bought a Cleveland Browns cap. Jamming it on his head, he ambled into downtown Canton with Lyle and Jessie, three casual tourists out for a good time. The area was in rehab, staging a comeback. The arts district was packed with galleries, small theaters, clubs and restaurants. Flashing Fosselli's picture, they visited every joint. Lyle talked while Nick and Jessie lurked.

No one had seen the bald man with the strange green eyes.

Back in the car Lyle drove to an enormous shopping mall, Belden Village. He showed Gianni's photo in every store and restaurant. Nothing.

"He's holed up on some big estate," Nick said, more frustrated by the minute as the light faded. "Self-sufficient. Ordering from catalogs, using Martinelli's man to do his bidding locally. Living under a new name."

"We need the damned arrow." Lyle looked defeated. "Let's pack it in for the night."

"At least we know he's close," Jessie said in a little voice.

"Right." Lyle smiled. "We'll get a fresh start in the morning, grow more beard for me and Nick. And maybe get you a pair of plain glasses, Jessie. People have been eyeing you. Maybe those sunglasses are too Hollywood."

Rolling his eyes, Nick looked away. How could anyone not look twice at Jessie Kendle? Glasses weren't going to hide that famous face or body. Neither was a cap. Better a nun's habit. Or a burqa.

After Jessie ducked into a drug store for tortoise-shell reading glasses, Burritos at Chipotle passed for dinner. They checked into a motel near the mall.

By the time Barton turned on Sports Center and rolled into bed. Nick needed a drink, too hyped to sleep. He grabbed Barton's keys and his cap. The fresh air was invigorating. Stopping at the hotel desk, Nick inquired about local bars. He followed the clerk's hand-drawn map and drove to John's Bar.

Anything to keep from going out of his mind.

*

Idly flipping through the cable stations, Jessie's mind had been on anything but entertainment. She'd kept picturing her son with Gianni. The man's jeweled eyes, the gleaming bald head. To a little boy he must look like an evil genie out of a bottle. Anthony must be terrified. Thank God he had a dog to keep him company. Thank God for that.

Hearing a nearby door whap open and close, Jessie had dashed to the window and peeked through the curtain. Nick stood staring off in the distance before striding around the corner towards the hotel lobby. A moment later he reappeared, climbed into the SUV, and sped out of the parking lot.

She paced, a prisoner in the solitary confinement of her own mind.

*

Dimly lit and quiet, John's Bar suited Nick's grim mood. He sat on a stool at the far end of the counter, watching men in sports caps and T-shirts staring mindlessly at a mounted television while sipping their drafts. He fit right in.

Nick ordered a bourbon from the lone barmaid, friendly and happy to talk to someone not glued to a TV. When Donetta asked if he was new in town, Nick blandly told her he was here looking for someone. A bald man with vibrant green eyes.

Two hours later when the bar closed, he was still talking to her.

*

Clint had parked himself in the East of Chicago Pizza lot, across the street from John's Bar. The bottle of scotch cut the chill, and the all-meat pizza filled his hungry gut.

He'd followed the three Musketeers all damned day as they showed Fosselli's picture around. When they hit the Holiday Inn they looked like beaten dogs. Leave it to Gianni Fosselli to find the perfect hiding place in the middle of nowhere. Which meant Clint was sentenced to more pizzas and cold nights in his car. Paper-towel and soap-dispenser baths on road stops in Ohio.

The only thing worse than Ohio was Kansas. You could hear a fucking pin drop on the Canton sidewalk when the sun went down. What did the natives do for excitement, play hopscotch? Go to church? Pull a chair up on the sidewalk and watch traffic?

It would be so easy to take out McDeare when he left the bar. No one around to see or hear a thing.

But he needed McDeare alive until he led him to the boy.

And until he talked to Foxy and made his deal. He'd take out McDeare and Barton one way if he had an agreement. Another way if he didn't.

*

Anthony jolted awake in the dark. He had a hard time staying asleep. His mind wouldn't stop talking. He wanted Daddy to explain why he had to be braver than ever. He'd do anything for Daddy, but he was afraid.

Stretched beside him, Monty rested his head on Anthony's arm. The dog's eyes darted everywhere. Anthony liked the way Monty did that, looking around without ever moving his head.

Sighing, Anthony rolled out of bed and trotted to the window. The moon was big and bright tonight, but it had weird wispy clouds floating across it. Like ghosts.

Missing his ring, Anthony rubbed his empty finger. His ring had made him feel safe, like Dad was always with him. But he still had his locket, the special one Dad had made for him.

"Dad, please find Monty and me," Anthony prayed, looking up at the moon and clasping his medallion. "I want to go home so bad." He hated it here. He hated Gianni. He hated talking in Italian. He hated salads.

"Can you hear me, Dad?"

*

Five bourbons chasing away the chill, Nick wove his way to the SUV under a shimmering moon. He might even be able to sleep tonight. If he could shut down his brain.

The barmaid had ended up being useful. Donetta had worked at a convenience store out on Wales Road before she got a steady gig at John's a month ago. She remembered a man dropping by several times last September or October and flirting with her, foreign and exotic. He'd said he was new in town. She remembered his stunning green eyes. He always paid cash and bought basic supplies like milk.

When she'd tried to get to know him better, asking where he lived and what he did for a living, he'd been evasive and never returned. Donetta gave Nick the address of the store. Remote. A lot of farms and big estates set far back from the road.

Something to pursue tomorrow. A solid lead.

Nick fumbled for the car keys, the booze making him clumsy. The contents of his pocket took a hard bounce to the ground. Swearing, he crouched down and gathered his keys and spare change. His cell was okay. The ring box! Nick snapped it open. Safe and sound. What else was missing?

There, under the SUV, the key chain with the arrow. Nick crawled beneath the vehicle, cursing. Nick McDeare, underneath a car at one in the morning in Canton, Ohio, groping for a worthless piece of junk. Driving a car that housed an unregistered gun and enough questionable equipment to get him arrested.

*

Sleep eluded Jessie. She felt like she might never sleep again, a forgotten skill. Could that really happen? She'd read you could die from lack of sleep. Pulling the thin blanket up around her neck in the chilly room, she waited to hear Nick return.

There was nothing else to do.

Moonlight seeped through the frayed curtains, creating shadow figures on the walls. A movement on the ceiling caught her eye. A spider. It stopped moving when she spotted it. She hoped it didn't drop down to look back at her. Eight eyes. One to match each leg? She shuddered.

Rolling over, she fluffed the skimpy pillow. Here she was in a cracker box of a hotel room in Canton, Ohio, wondering where her husband was. Worried sick about her son. How had fate tossed her here?

This whole Gianni saga had been set in motion by a fatal choice Andrew made years ago to save her from Gianni. A choice made with the best of intentions that set off a chain reaction. The dominoes fell and the body count grew. Andrew. Ian Wexley. Eduardo Santangelo. Steve Bushman. Barb and Dina Barton. Lives scarred, trusts betrayed.

More dominoes would fall before this story drew to a close. The worst part was nothing Jessie could imagine was going to be as bad as what was coming. She knew it with a certainty that gave new meaning to feeling sick to your stomach.

When she let herself dwell on it: *Petrified.* She could feel every beat of her heart. Instead of counting sheep, she tried counting the deep breaths she inhaled, then exhaled to mask her terror.

It was almost three when she spied Nick's shadow pass her window. His hotel door opened and closed. And she had no idea where he'd been.

*

"What's this?"

Groggy with sleep, Nick cracked an eye open to see Barton staring at him, the morning sun filtering into the room.

Lyle waved a piece of paper at Nick. "Where were you last night?"

Sitting up, Nick fingered the hair out of his eyes and told Lyle about Donetta and the convenience store on Wales Road. "That," he pointed to the paper, "is the address. We begin there today." Nick headed for the shower.

"I'll call Jessie and update her."

Twenty minutes later Jessie joined them, bag in hand. She looked crumbled up and tired, glasses not hiding the circles under her eyes. She avoided Nick's glance, not answering his good morning.

How much longer was this going to go on? Nick gave up and snatched his things from the bedside table, stuffing his pockets and turning on his medallion. He scooped up the keychain arrow. "Worthless piece of shit." And then his heart leapt. "It's moving," he said in disbelief. "The damned thing's moving."

"You're kidding." Jessie roused from her lethargy.

"I dropped it last night when I was getting into the car. It must have jarred the arrow loose."

"Well, well." Lyle's eyes lit. "We're back on the Yellow Brick Road. Let's go."

Hurtling across Stark County, Nick dictated directions according to the arrow as Lyle drove. Traffic was heavy in the heart of the business district, thinning at the city limits.

The sun was bright, melting the snow into dirty gray mounds soaking in wells of water. Patches of brown grass dotted the landscape like Swiss cheese. A bank's neon sign posted forty-one degrees.

At Wales Road the arrow took them north. "Wales Road," Nick mused. "The street Donetta told me about. There's the convenience store."

"Donetta?" Jessie's third word that morning.

"The barmaid last night," Nick said shortly.

The further they drove, the more remote the landscape. Guided by the arrow through a sharp turn onto a rustic country dirt road, the area was desolate. The SUV passed pitted dirt tracks, farmhouses and barns scattered in the distance. Planes rumbled overhead, taking off or landing at the nearby Akron-Canton Airport. "Talk about godforsaken," Nick muttered.

"All the easier to disappear," Lyle said.

Bumping along the rutted path, they sped on, surrounded by uncultivated fields. "Look, over there, to the left." Barton slowed up and stopped on the side of the road, his foot on the brake. "Oz." The arrow pointed to a high black wrought-iron gate. Set back about twenty yards from the road, it peeked out from rows of tall spruce trees.

"Anthony's somewhere behind that gate?" Jessie faltered, her voice thick with emotion.

Nick reached for the door handle.

"Wait," Barton hissed.

*

Clint had followed the SUV across town and into the country, staying out of sight and watching the blinking red blip on his tracking screen. Seeing the car halt on a remote road, he stopped about a hundred yards behind them, pausing to see if it moved again. It did, but only a few feet, probably parking off the road. Clint pulled behind a clump of bushes and flipped off the engine.

Grabbing some items from his car, he took off on foot. Clint avoided the road, hugging the line of pines and watching for his targets. Vietnam had taught Clint Vaughn how to become one with the landscape, something city cops and writers didn't know from shit. He clutched his cell. Time to contact Foxy.

Tucked into his boot was the gun.

*

Parked behind a mass of bramble, Lyle said, "I'm going to check out the entrance for hidden cameras. Alone."

"The hell you are." Nick threw his door open.

"You're too close to the situation. Take the time to cool down. I'll be right back." Grabbing a pair of binoculars from one of the gym bags, Barton took off for the gate.

One foot out the door to follow him, Nick glanced over his shoulder at Jessie. She'd taken off her glasses and was staring down into her lap. Her eyes darted up to his and away again. "What?"

"It doesn't matter. The only thing that matters is Anthony." She reached over the top of the front seat, careful not to touch his arm, and flicked on the car radio, turning the volume down. An oldies station, Ray Charles. "I Can't Stop Loving You" floated through the car.

"Never mind. Turn it off," she said.

"Happy to."

"Thank you."

"You're ticked off at me again."

"You were out till three in the morning."

Staring at her incredulously, Nick said, "You're keeping track of what time I walk in the door?"

"You weren't happy when I disappeared. But it's okay for you?"

"That was different."

"How? And you haven't told me about Donetta. Or anything else. Lyle only said you got a lead at a bar."

"What are you insinuating?"

"Don't put words in my mouth--"

"Enough!" Lyle's whisper startled both of them. He slid into the driver's seat, his face red. "I've had a bellyful of listening to the two of you go at it. What's

- 258 -

important is your son." He scrubbed a hand over his face and looked away, his voice gruff. "Do you know how lucky you are? That I'd give anything to trade places with you? You have each other. Soon, you'll have your son back. Anthony's going to need you both. Together. Not chipping away at each other over nothing."

Feeling like a shit, Nick looked back at Jessie. Her eyes were glimmering with tears.

"Now." Lyle got down to business. "About the gate. No cameras. No alarm system. Just that fence. The putz felt damned secure when he set this up."

Clearing his throat, Nick said, "He was concerned with Anthony getting out, not anyone getting in. Besides, when he set this up, Fosselli never imagined we'd figure out he was alive, much less track him down."

"Let's go." Lyle eyed Jessie. "I hate to do this to you again, but I want you to stay here until we've checked out the grounds. We'll come back for you. I promise."

"I understand. Go."

Following the fence, Nick and Lyle picked their way around the property. Tall fir trees shielded them from sight. As they moved, the arrow zoomed in on the center of the estate. A sprawling home rolled into view.

From their hiding place Nick and Lyle studied the old white Victorian house, taking turns with the binoculars. Three wedding cake stories with pale blue shutters. A sweeping roof with cupolas. The veranda was wide and spacious. A state-of-the-art attached greenhouse, a four-car garage about twenty yards behind the residence. A vast hill loomed between the front of the house and the entrance from the road.

Nick's eyes drifted to the upper floors. Probably five or six bedrooms, maybe more. Which one was Anthony's?

The property was expansive and hilly, covered with trees and shrubs hiding the main house, the only open area inside the gate. They moved on, following the fence around the estate, circling wide when they came across a caretaker's cottage in the rear.

Back at the front, standing behind a fir, Barton pointed to the gate's lock. "It's electronic," he said quietly. "Opens with a remote."

"The car drives in here." Nick gazed out at the road. "The remote swings the gate open. You drive around to the garage in the back." Nick eyed the eight-foot tall wrought-iron fence posts, each topped with a dagger of a spike. Three or four inches between the bars. "We need to get that gate open. Even if we can climb in, climbing out with Anthony on my back is close to impossible. Not to mention a dog."

"Remember I said I've been working on a few things waiting for our break?" Lyle smiled. "I have an electronic gate decoder, courtesy of our medallion wizard. Along with devices to disable an alarm system and a camera. He wrote out diagrams for me."

"You're shitting me."

"Lots of wires on the decoder. Like a bomb."

*

Tomato was Anthony's favorite soup. Not this watery stuff in front of him with things floating in it. He missed Mary's thick soups, the kind you ate with crackers.

Gianni watched him, waiting for him to finish his icky lunch. He felt like puking. Anthony forced down the last spoonful and carried his plate to the sink. "Can I take Monty out and play?"

"'May I take Monty out.' May is proper English."

"You talk Italian. How do you know what's good English?"

"Proper English."

"Whatever. May I take Monty?"

"Anthony, the use of the word whatever is disrespectful. You must learn to speak like a gentleman."

Anthony waited silently.

"Yes, you may take Monty out."

Grabbing his coat, Anthony zoomed out the door, Monty at his side. He headed to his open spot by the front gate, behind the big hill. Gianni couldn't see him here.

Anthony snatched a stick on the ground and threw it as far as he could. Monty galloped after it and brought it back. "Good boy, Monty." Anthony tossed it again.

*

"Christ." Nick sucked in his breath. "It's Anthony."

Before he could take a step forward, Barton yanked Nick back farther behind the firs. "Don't let him see you. Not yet. He could yell out for you. Accidentally alert Gianni."

Through the foliage Nick watched Anthony and the dog. It was hard to swallow the lump in his throat. Blinking, he focused on the boy, shaking off the emotion. Physically, Anthony looked fine. He wore a down winter jacket and a scarf. But how was he deep inside? What had Gianni done to him?

"Listen, I have another idea," Barton whispered, "a way to get Anthony out of here that doesn't depend on figuring out that decoder or making like mountain sheep. But we'll need Anthony's help."

Barton sketched out the plan for Nick. They finessed the details, Nick's enthusiasm growing. Nick moved into the open, wrapping his fingers around the gate's bars, as Lyle went for Jessie. That hill blocked the view from the house. It was safe.

He watched Anthony and waited …

*

Anthony hurled the stick high into the air. Instead of chasing his prize, Monty whirled to the fence and growled. A low guttural grind. Anthony had never heard the dog do that before. "What's the matter, boy?"

Spinning around, Anthony gasped. His dad was on the other side of the gate! Dad put his finger to his lips, signaling Anthony to be quiet.

"It's Dad, Monty," he whispered, starting to cry. "It's Dad."

Anthony ran to his father, tears streaming down his face.

CHAPTER 28

Nick kept his finger on his lips until Anthony reached him. "Where's Gianni?" he whispered.

"Inside."

It was impossible to wait a moment longer. Nick crouched down, grabbed Anthony through the bars, and hugged him close. He kissed his cheek, ran his hand through the boy's thick hair, and hugged him again. Nick's eyes blurred with tears.

"I knew you'd find me," Anthony sniffled.

"Are you okay?"

Nodding, Anthony's eyes widened as Jessie and Barton rushed up. "Mom!"

Jessie flew to her son, kneeling and reaching for him through the bars, smothering him with kisses. "I love you," she gasped. "Are you all right?" Her cheeks were wet, her smile blinding. Rising, Nick put a palm on her shoulder. Reaching up, she squeezed his hand.

"Get me out of here," Anthony pleaded. "Please."

"We will, honey, we will," Jessie said fervently.

"That's a promise," Lyle added. He ruffled Anthony's hair. "That's why we're here."

"Right." Pulling himself together, Nick looked Anthony in the eye. "Listen carefully. We have a plan, but we need your help. You have to be strong for us. And brave."

"That's what Daddy Andrew said," Anthony quavered. "I had to be braver than ever."

"Andrew's here?"

"He talks to me at night."

Clapping a hand to her mouth, Jessie stifled a gasp. Lyle looked at her sharply.

Thank God for Andrew, still on watch. "Looks like you got your dog," Nick said gruffly. "What's his name?" The dog looked up at Nick under furry eyebrows.

"Monty Crisco."

"Of course." Nick grinned. "I should've remembered." Nick rubbed Monty's head.

*

"Thanks for taking good care of Anthony, Monty." Jessie rose, stroked the dog's soft coat. Monty licked her hand. She felt as if her heart had been sprung from a trap. Now it threatened to beat out of her chest with joy ... and terror.

Jessie watched Lyle crouch in front of Anthony, all business, their rock when they needed it most. "Anthony, I need to ask you some questions," Lyle said matter-of-factly. "Things we need to know so we can get you out of here, okay?"

Anthony nodded.

"Will Gianni come looking for you?"

"If I'm gone too long."

"How many people are in the house?"

"Just Gianni and me. Carlo lives in his own place in the back."

"The caretaker's cottage. And Carlo is ...?"

"A big scary guy who works for Gianni."

"No other servants? No cook or maid?"

"Gianni cooks. Icky stuff."

Jessie smiled through her tears.

"Only two people on the entire property," Barton said, glancing up at Nick before turning back to Anthony. "Okay, a few more questions. Does Gianni let you come and go from the house freely?"

"Not at first. But I did what Dad said and got Gianni to trust me. I can take Monty out now by myself."

"Are the doors locked?"

"Not the back. So I can take Monty out if he needs to go."

"Have you ever been off the property?"

"The gate's always locked. I tried to get out once, but I couldn't."

"Does Gianni go anywhere?"

Thinking about that, Anthony said, "Well, he got Monty for me. But he hasn't gone anywhere since."

"Anthony," Nick said, taking over and kneeling in front of him, "we need your help to get you out of here. But if you don't think you can do it, just say so, okay? We'll find another way. No matter what, you're a brave boy." Speaking slowly, Nick gave Anthony detailed instructions. What the boy needed to bring them. What to say in case he got caught. Jessie cast Anthony a reassuring smile, hiding her nerves.

"If you can't get right back to us," Nick said quietly, "come to the gate the first chance you get. We'll wait here no matter how long, even days. We aren't going anywhere without you. The most important thing is you come back to this gate without Gianni knowing."

"I can do it," Anthony said fiercely.

"Hey, you've got what it takes to wear a badge," Lyle said. "I'm proud of you."

His eyes lighting up, Jessie could swear her son stood taller. "We love you," she whispered,

"You'll be home in no time," Nick rasped, his knuckles white as he grasped the bars. "Be careful. Your mom's right. We all love you."

"I will. Love you, too." Anthony took off, glancing back one final time before disappearing over the hill, Monty a running shadow at his side.

*

Hunkering down along the fence line, Clint had stared through his binoculars at the Brady Bunch reunion, especially McDeare and the boy. His own father had been a drunk and a bully. Good days, he left Clint alone. Bad days, Clint was in for it no matter what he did.

His brow had creased watching father and son. The little kid idolized his hero, couldn't keep his eyes off him. And McDeare, Clint had pressed the glasses closer to his eyes, trying to figure it out by looking harder. McDeare looked like he was ready to scale the fence to get the boy back. Not even his. Not really.

The kid didn't deserve any of this. Clint felt a surprising wave of pity for Kendle's son, stuck with Fosselli ever since the wedding. Wait … What the— Anthony was rocketing back over the hill, the black dog matching his stride. Something was up. Things were moving too quickly, getting out of control.

Grabbing his phone, Clint speed-dialed Foxy again. Same result. No reception in the woods. Shitty satellite. Might as well be in fucking Afghanistan.

He was on his own. No deal.

*

Monty at his side, Anthony edged towards the garage's side door. He turned the handle, breathing a sigh of relief when it opened. "Come on, Monty."

There were three cars in the old garage. One was the big silver SUV that brought Monty here. Anthony checked its doors. Locked.

He moved on to the shiny red car. It said Corvette on the back end. Locked too.

The fancy black sports car looked new. He'd never seen anyone drive this one. It was locked, but the front window was rolled down a little. Anthony found a crate against the wall and dragged it to the car. Climbing on top he squeezed his arm through the gap in the window on the driver's side. He pushed all the buttons inside the door until he heard a click. Got it!

Pushing the crate away, Anthony opened the door. He slid into the driver's seat and looked for the remote Dad had described. He said it might be smaller than the TV clicker. He didn't see it anywhere. Panicking, Anthony looked up at the windshield flap you pulled down when it got sunny. There it was, the remote clipped to it. He stretched up and slid it off. Climbing out of the car, Anthony closed the door and got back on the crate. He reached his arm in and carefully locked the car door again.

Stepping back, Anthony inspected the car. It looked just like it did before Anthony got into it. Those were Dad's instructions. Put everything back just the way you found it. Anthony slid the clicker into his pocket and pushed the crate back against the wall.

Looking around the dark garage, he saw tools. A lot of junk. In the corner he spotted an old dirty tennis ball. Dad had said to find something in the garage Monty would want to play with. He picked it up.

"What are you doing in here?" Gianni stood in the open doorway.

*

Dropping the ball, Anthony quickly retrieved it. "I-I was looking for a toy for Monty." Anthony held up the ball. "Can I have it?"

Stepping into the garage, Gianni surveyed each car and jiggled the doors. All were secure. The window on the driver's side of the Ferrari was down exactly five inches, just the way he'd left it. Before Anthony arrived, Gianni had liked to smoke Cubans and drive the car for recreation. When he'd first moved in, he'd go into town and flirt with the pretty girls at their cash registers, until he realized it would raise his profile. After that, he just drove and kept the window down afterwards to air it out. Nothing seemed disturbed.

But Anthony looked guilty. "Why did you really come in here?"

"I told you," Anthony said, trying to look him in the eye. "To find something Monty can play with. He's tired of chasing sticks."

Gianni stared the boy down. He had never ventured in here before. Anthony stared back, all inocence. But there was a flicker behind his eyes. Guilt? "You're telling me the truth, Anthony?"

"Why do you always sneak up behind me anyway?"

"We're talking about you right now, not me."

"I am talking about me," he said in a little voice, looking away. "You scared me ... Dad."

Gianni held his breath. In his fear, Anthony's real feelings had finally surfaced. He did love him, as a son should love his father. Gianni smiled warmly at Anthony, feeling a rush of emotion. Blood told.

"This is a dangerous place for a young boy," Gianni said, his voice husky. "You could cut yourself or step on a rusty nail. I don't want you ever to come in here again without me."

"How did you know I was here?" he said, eyes wide.

There it was again. His mother had used those same guileless eyes to deceive. "I was washing dishes and saw you through the kitchen window."

"Can Monty have the ball?"

"Yes."

"Come on, Monty." Anthony ran for the door.

"Wait. We must scrub it first. It's filthy. And it's time for your Italian lesson. Then I'll teach you how to make lasagna. You can play ball with your dog tomorrow. I promise."

Anthony looked crushed. Gianni would keep a close eye on him for the rest of the day.

*

Tucked behind the firs near the front gate, Nick, Lyle and Jessie sat against a huge pine, hidden from sight if Gianni or Carlo walked the property. But Nick had a clear view of the estate through a gap in the branches.

"He's been gone hours. It's getting dark." Jessie's soft voice pierced the twilight.

"Anthony's a smart kid." Barton was reading the decoder diagram with a penlight. "If he got caught, he covered his tracks. Nick told him what to do."

"If you're not worried, why are you playing with that thing?" Nick's stomach growled.

"Backup. If Anthony doesn't show up tomorrow we use the decoder and go in for the boy at night."

"Even if he finds the remote," Jessie said, "what if it opens the garage, not the gate?"

"A house this old and a purist like Gianni?" Lyle chuckled. "I'm betting that garage door opens the old-fashioned way, by hand. Anyway, Gianni has to open the gate from the car to drive on or off the grounds."

Jessie nibbled on a cuticle. "I hope you're right."

"He is," Nick said, masking his own high anxiety. He draped an arm around her back, Jessie snuggling into him.

"By the way," Barton said, a faint smile on his face, "what's with Andrew being here? You guys believe in ghosts?"

"Would you believe us," Nick asked, "if we told you Andrew has visited us on occasion?"

"No."

"It's true, Lyle," Jessie said lightly.

Barton snorted. "And in my past life I was Julius Caesar."

Springing to his feet, Nick, said, "Anything to eat in the car? I'm starving."

"Apples. Peanut butter crackers. Bottled water du jour."

"Yummy," Jessie said dryly. "Bring me something, too, please."

Hiking back to the SUV, Nick had just enough light to make out the car. He opened the hatchback and scrounged for food, trying to squelch the gnawing fear Anthony had been caught and Gianni was setting a trap for them.

After snagging the crackers and grabbing some water, Nick found a blanket for Jessie. The temperature was dropping. His eye fell on a small canvas knapsack in the corner. Barton hadn't touched that bag since they left New York.

Unzipping it, Nick reached inside, coiling his fingers around the cold metal. He tucked the gun into his belt, his coat camouflaging the weapon.

*

Hunching his shoulders together, Anthony felt itchy. Gianni was watching him every minute, never leaving him alone, not even when Monty went out before dinner. "In the spring we'll build a pool," Gianni had said, waving an arm at the estate. "And a tennis court."

Anthony didn't want a pool or tennis court. He wanted to go home.

Fidgeting through dinner, Anthony picked at his lasagna. Gianni kept looking at him, staring like he knew Anthony was hiding something. Like he could read his mind with secret powers.

Glancing at his coat hanging on the wall hook, Anthony hoped Dad, Mom, and Lyle weren't worried he didn't come right back. If he could just get that remote to Dad, he could go home!

*

The boy seemed distracted, a poor appetite tonight. Teaching Anthony how to make lasagna had been a lesson in futility. By the time they were finished Anthony had gravy all over the kitchen and himself. The cleanup had taken an hour. Anthony's bath and change of clothes had taken another hour.

"Let's take Monty out. It's past your bedtime." Gianni glanced under the table. No Monty. Usually the dog took up residence at Anthony's feet during meals, eager to sweep up crumbs. "Where is he?"

"Maybe he went to bed without me."

"Come. Let's look for him."

They found Monty in the living room. He was pacing from window to window, whimpering.

Gianni looked out into the darkness. A clear night with a bright moon, the trees and brush in silhouette on the hill. "He senses something out there, Anthony."

"Maybe a cat," Anthony said too quickly. "We saw one this afternoon and Monty went crazy chasing it."

The boy was hiding something. Gianni pulled out his cell and speed-dialed Carlo. "Check the property. Report back to me. The dog is agitated."

*

On watch, Nick leaned against the base of a pine, hoping to see the dark shapes of a boy and a dog running down the hill towards the gate. But it was late. He told himself Anthony was in bed by now.

A sound. By the fence … Nick spotted Carlo before the thug got near the front gate. The caveman lumbered across the property with a flashlight, peering into bushes and behind trees.

Lurching to their feet, the trio tiptoed to the road, avoiding branches sticking out under the melting snow. They used a stick to blur any patch of snow holding their footprints. Safely out of sight, they watched Carlo's flashlight sweep the area where they'd just been squatting. The light inched down the fence and disappeared.

"Gianni suspects something," Jessie whispered.

"Maybe," Barton muttered. "Or this is routine. Checked every night."

Returning to their hiding spot they settled in for the long night. Jessie crept under the blanket and closed her eyes.

Nick exchanged a worried look with Barton before he focused on the property again, searching. His eyes were as dry as sand, sore with the strain of watching for a little boy running over the hill.

*

In the moonlight Clint could make out Gianni's man, his chauffeur at the wedding. The moron stomped around the property like the Green Giant, a cigar clenched in his teeth. Keeping away from the open areas of snow, Clint glided from the fence as the flashlight beamed his way.

The goon got so close Clint could smell the garlic he had for dinner over the cigar. The light bounced on up the fence and out of sight.

*

What if he threw up from being so afraid? Anthony didn't feel brave anymore. He was terrified Gianni was going to catch Dad and Mom and Lyle. And even more scared about what Gianni would do to them after he caught them.

While Gianni was staring out the living-room window, his cell rang. Eavesdropping, Anthony fingered ornaments on the Christmas tree. "You checked everywhere? … You're sure? … *Grazie*. Stay alert tonight." Gianni hung up.

Maybe Carlo hadn't found them. Or maybe they'd given up and left. No. Dad said he'd wait no matter what. Mom would never leave him, or Lyle. Anthony plucked needles from the fir tree, crushing them in his hand.

"Anthony, what is wrong with you? Stop that. You'll make a mess. And why is your dog behaving like this?" Monty was pacing from window to window, whining.

"I told you. That cat is probably out there. I'll take Monty to bed."

"He needs to go out first."

- 266 -

Anthony had an idea. He'd go to bed, wait for Gianni to fall asleep, then sneak out with Monty and the remote. "Monty was already out," he said. "Come on, boy, let's go upstairs."

*

"Anthony, the dog needs to go out one more time." Gianni called Carlo again.

"Okay. I'll take him." Anthony patted his leg, chirping for Monty. He trotted for the back door, Monty's nails clicking on the wood behind him.

"Wait. Don't go out there without me."

"Sir?" Carlo answered on the first ring.

Anthony and Monty headed to the kitchen. Gianni followed. "Anthony, stop."

"… Mr. C?"

"Carlo, I think someone--"

Throwing on his coat and scarf, Anthony opened the back door. Gianni felt a thrum of anger. "Anthony, not another step! Do you hear me?" The dog burst out of the door, followed by Anthony. Gianni swore. "Anthony!"

Dashing outside, Gianni was just in time to glimpse Anthony and the dog whip around the corner of the house.

"I'm coming, Monty. I'm coming!" A primitive fear clutched Gianni's gut. Anthony's elation—that's how he used to sound when his beloved Uncle Gianni would bring him a hand-carved ship on his birthday. Thrilled.

His heart thumping, Gianni shot inside. Before hanging up, he snapped at Carlo to meet him at the front gate. Gianni quickly pocketed the phone, unlocked a kitchen drawer, and snatched the loaded gun.

Now he knew exactly where his son was running, and he knew who was waiting for him.

His dream. It was happening. And he knew how to give it the proper ending.

McDeare had done the impossible and tracked him down.

Gianni sprinted for the door, cackling baritone laughter chasing him out of the house.

*

At the faint sound of Anthony's voice, Nick leapt up. He hurtled to the gate, Barton on his heels. His son appeared on the horizon, a white scarf whipping behind him as he bounded to the fence. Racing ahead of him, the dog's silver collar glinted in the moonlight.

Gasping for breath, his chest heaving, Anthony yanked the remote from his pocket as he ran the race of his life. Nick stuck his hand through the iron bars. "Come on, Anthony. Come on!"

Wide awake, Jessie stumbled to the gate. "My God. Anthony!"

"You can do it!" Lyle rasped.

Slipping in the slush, Anthony's feet flew out from under him, the clicker sliding from his hand. Monty stopped in his tracks and snatched up the remote like a stick, another toy to fetch. He eyed Nick, wagging his tail.

"Here, Monty." Nick's whisper was hoarse. "Bring it here, boy." Please, God, bring it here. The dog pranced to the gate, presenting his treasure to Nick. Sucking in a breath, praying to a slab of plastic, Nick punched the open button.

The gates swung inward.

"We're in," Lyle said, bolting through the gap after Nick and Jessie. Jessie darted towards Anthony, heedless of danger. "Jessie, wait," Nick said, scanning the hill. My God. "Jessie, no!" As the boy scrambled to his feet, it was too late. Nick stared helplessly at the apparition looming above his son.

The man in the wedding photo came alive in the moonlight, a bold face materializing as if steam were peeling off a mirror. Shaven head. Glittering green eyes. A shelf of new cheekbones.

Gianni Fosselli in the flesh. Armed.

Seizing the boy with one hand, Gianni pointed a gun at Jessie with the other. She skidded to an abrupt halt. "Stay where you are. All of you."

If Nick reached for his weapon, he risked hitting the struggling boy in Gianni's grip. Or Jessie.

Lyle cursed next to him, grabbing for Monty's collar. He missed, the dog dancing in circles, barking at Gianni.

"You're hurting me!" Anthony cried, kicking and flailing.

"Please, please. Let him go," Jessie pleaded, holding out her hands.

*

"Back up," Gianni ordered Jessica, tightening his lock on the boy. She froze, did an awkward backwards stumble. Gianni's lip twisted, seeing the fear on her face. Delicious. Monty was barking at him, growling. He needed to be silenced.

"Anthony, call your dog," Gianni said. "I don't want to hurt him." Anthony struggled in Gianni's grip. No time for patience. "Call him!"

"... M-Monty ..." Anthony whimpered. "Come here, boy." Monty sat down, tongue lolling, looking unsure. "Monty, come here. Please."

Tail dragging, the dog trotted to Anthony, growling sidewise at Gianni.

Gianni smiled. "Thank you, son."

"I'm not your son. I'm Nick McDeare's son. I'm Anthony McDeare!"

"You're Anthony Fosselli!" Gianni eyed his adversaries. The stupid detective out of a comic book. The whore mother, defiled and depraved. Nicholas McDeare, the idiot who thought he could raise Gianni's son as his own. Making the same fatal mistake as his brother.

A roll of laughter bubbled up in the darkness. *Che cazzo*? Outside. That maniacal laughter--it had followed him out of the house, tracking him. The back of Gianni's neck prickled.

"It's Daddy," Anthony gasped. "He's here."

A gust of wind stirred the trees, whistling through the bare silver branches. The moon paled behind a wisp of cloud. In the distance, an owl hooted. Gianni could feel the sweat beading on his forehead. "I'M here, Anthony. I'm your father. Not some wind in the trees."

"Daddy hates you."

A shudder shook him. "Go back to the house, Anthony. Take Monty with you. Now!"

"No." A low growl from the dog, his hackles raised, head lowered.

"Do it!" Gianni cocked the gun.

"I-I can't. You're ... holding ... me too tight."

Gianni's grip on Anthony had cramped his hand. He uncurled his fingers with an effort, releasing the boy. He had to get him out of here. He didn't want his son to witness what he had to do to stop the madness.

*

Time had gone haywire, everything happening in slow motion. Gianni let Anthony go, the boy looking dazed and falling limply to the ground. Nick felt the revolver press against his waist under the coat, his hands damp with sweat. He had to do something ...

Anthony lay still, eyes closed.

"Anthony," Jessie cried, "are you--"

"Get up," Gianni roared. "Stop this nonsense and take your dog to the house!"

With a snarl, Monty leapt at Gianni, fangs bared. Gianni fell back, arms flailing. The gun went off, a spark of light.

Nick watched in horror.

Jessie lunged for Anthony, covering him with her body.

Gianni toppled to the ground under Monty's weight, springing free with a vicious kick to the dog's belly. Yelping, the dog rebounded and crouched, ready to launch himself at Gianni again.

Barton slumped to the ground, clutching his chest.

Without thinking, Nick finally moved, ripping the gun from his belt and firing.

CHAPTER 29

Gianni clapped a hand to his heart. He looked confused. As if this wasn't supposed to happen. The gun slipped from his hand. Opening his mouth, he tried to speak. No words, just a trickle of blood. He staggered and fell to the ground, a look of surprise stamped on his face.

His gun in hand, Nick crept towards Gianni. The man stared blankly up at the moon, his mouth open. Nick put a hand to his carotid artery. Nothing.

McDeare's dark twist of an ending.

No time to think. Jumping to his feet, Nick ran to Jessie and Anthony, Monty quietly guarding them. The boy was prone on the ground, his head in Jessie's lap. "Is he okay?" Nick darted a quick glance at Barton.

"I think he fainted." Jessie tenderly stroked her son's cheek. "Take care of Lyle. Go." Tears streamed down her face as she looked in Lyle's direction. Barton lay where he'd fallen, hands clutching his chest.

Dashing back to Lyle, Nick dropped to the ground and clasped his wrist, the pulse rapid. Barton was in bad shape, coughing up clotted blood, short of breath. Nick had been an embedded reporter in more than one war. He knew bullet wounds. Fosselli's wild shot must've penetrated a lung, possibly both. A distant part of his brain coolly calculated Barton's condition even as his grief threatened to overwhelm him. Lyle was drowning in his own blood, slipping into shock in front of his eyes. Save him. He had to save him.

Yanking out his cell, Nick punched in nine-one-one. The inner gate area was an open space, away from the trees. He fervently prayed for reception. When Nick got an answer, he sagged with relief, reporting a shooting and requesting help ASAP.

*

Her son cradled in her arms, Jessie rocked him. Monty licked the boy's face. Anthony moved his lips, murmuring something …

Spotting movement out of the corner of her eye, Jessie glanced up. On the horizon, a goliath of a dark shape. Waving a gun, he sprinted around the hill towards Nick. Frozen with horror, she tried to call out twice, squeaked, finally found her voice. "Nick," Jessie shrieked, pointing, "watch out!"

*

Carlo. Fosselli must've called him before he ran out of the house-- Fumbling for the gun in the snow, cursing his clumsiness, Nick raised the weapon. Before he could fire, a bullet popped over his head from behind. Carlo halted mid-run, blood spurting from his neck. Balancing on one foot, his face contorted. He executed a half pirouette and collapsed into the slush.

Numb with shock, Nick glanced over his shoulder.

Clint Vaughn.

His weapon in hand, the PI ambled to the gate. Weathered and lean, as impassive as one of the fence posts, he glanced at Nick.

*

Ignoring McDeare, Clint strode to Fosselli. He knelt, feeling for a pulse. Nice and dead. Frisking Gianni, he found two cell phones. He pocketed them and jogged to Carlo, adding the goon's cell to his collection of artifacts from the dead.

Now to the next item on his to-do list.

Clint stalked towards McDeare.

*

If Vaughn wanted to kill him, he would've done it already. Throwing his gun down, Nick frantically ripped off his coat and pressed it against Lyle's chest, trying to staunch the flow of blood. Barton's breathing was rapid and shallow, his eyes dull.

"Hang in there." Please, God, hang in there. Sirens wailed in the distance. "Help's on the way. Hang on."

Barton's eyes slid to Nick. "Gianni ...?"

"Dead."

"... Stop ... Martinelli ... For me ... you."

"I will. I promise." Nick's coat was soaked with Barton's blood.

"You ..." Barton gulped for air, drowning, a fine mist of blood pumping out of his mouth, "... best partner ...friend ... I ..."

A lump lodged in Nick's throat. He didn't have friends. Not until Lyle Barton.

"You ... were right. Andrew ..." Barton's eyes drifted upwards.

*

Her son limp in her arms, Jessie stared at Nick and Lyle. At the lean stranger looming over them, a gun clasped in his hand. All her worst fears, the dread of what was to come. It was here. Happening in front of her eyes. A surreal nightmare and no chance of waking up. She shivered in the night air. Gulping for air, Jessie fought to keep calm for her son.

"Mom?" Anthony stared up at her.

Jessie gasped. "Thank God. You're back."

"Can we go home now?"

"Soon, sweetie. Soon." She buried his face against her breast. "Close your eyes, baby. Keep them closed for me, okay?" She didn't know what else to do.

*

"What about Andrew?" Nick swallowed hard.

His breathing labored, Lyle rasped, "He's ... here."

A sob welled from Nick's gut, a silent heave of anguish as he watched helplessly.

" … Barb." Lyle Barton's face went slack and his body relaxed, a remnant of a smile tracing his lips. He was gone. His best friend was gone.

*

"McDeare," Clint said urgently.

The man looked up at him, that stunned look when death paid a surprise visit. It took Clint back to Nam, buddies dying in a rice paddy. It never left you.

Shaking it off, Clint said, "Listen to me." He squatted beside McDeare. "I don't have much time." The sirens' whine grew louder, only a mile or so away. He had to move. "Dammit, look at me," he said sharply. He waited for McDeare's eyes to focus. "What did Barton mean about stopping Martinelli? How?"

McDeare's eyes cleared, taking Clint's measure. "He's running a porn ring," he rasped. "kids, in Jersey City."

"Porn …?" Clint finally put the pieces together. He laughed heartily. This was too good. "Oh, I have something much better for you than porn in Jersey City."

"What's the catch?" McDeare said dully. "Why are you helping me?"

"Beats me." Clint rubbed a hand over his jaw. "I must be going soft."

"You can do better than that."

The sirens shrilled, reaching the grounds. "I have to go. When the cops get here you don't mention Martinelli. You don't mention me. Not if you want to find out what's really going on in Jersey. I'll explain later. Trust me."

"Do I have a choice?"

"Not if you want to live and keep the boy and your pretty wife safe. I'll be in touch."

Clint sprang up. With one last look at the woman and the kid, he slipped through the gate and blended into the darkness, following the line of pines down the road. Invisible to two police cruisers and an ambulance racing past him in a swirl of red and blue lights, Clint jogged to his car, pointing it in the direction of New York City and civilization.

*

Jessie desperately wanted to go to Nick. He needed her. But she couldn't leave Anthony, the carnage all around them. As cars sped towards the gate, lights flashing, Nick pushed himself to his feet and ran to her side. He said, "This is what we tell the police." Nick explained their cover quickly, making her repeat it.

"Why," she licked her lips, "why do you trust this Clint Vaughn? What's this all about?"

"I don't know yet. But he saved our lives. Carlo would've killed us all."

"Nick, Lyle, is he—"

Nick shook his head, letting out a harsh sob.

"Oh, God." She threw her arms around him.

"How's Anthony?"

"Awake, but I didn't want him to see--"

"Dad …?"

Pulling back, Nick said, "You're safe now, Anthony."

"Nick, you're shivering, your coat …"

The cars screeched to a stop. Training a powerful flashlight on them, two cops approached, weapons in hand.

"We're not armed." Nick slowly stood up, raising both hands. "My gun's over there by—in the snow. I'm Nick McDeare. This is my wife Jessica Kendle and our son Anthony."

"You're—?" The older cop, a face that had seen it all, thinning hair cropped close, stared at Nick, then Jessie. He nodded, recognition in his eyes. "Detective Isikoff." He jerked his head towards the other man. "My partner, Sheen. This is the boy who was kidnapped in New York?"

"Yes," Jessie said. "He's my son."

"And they are ...?" He looked at the three bodies strewn over the yard.

"Lieutenant Lyle Barton, NYPD." Nick's voice cracked. He took a second, continued, "Gianni Fosselli. The man who kidnapped Anthony. And his ... associate."

His eyes narrowing, Isikoff said, "Try again. Gianni Fosselli's dead."

"He is now," Nick said flatly.

Springing up, Jessie interrupted, pushing her distress aside. "Detective, could we please get our son out of here? This isn't-- We need to get him to a hospital. We have a car across the road." She had to get Anthony away from this cursed place.

"In a minute," he said. "Where's your coat?" Isikoff asked Nick.

"Someone else needed it more," he said blankly.

The detective flagged down one of the EMT's. "Get this man a blanket." Isikoff told Sheen to take Jessie and Anthony to the ambulance while he talked to Nick.

Scrambling to his feet, Anthony eyed the yard. "Monty! Where's Monty?"

"He's right here." Nick patted his thigh, and the dog glided to him, a black shape in the moonlight.

"Listen to me, Anthony," Jessie said, steadying her voice, "I want you to hold my hand and look straight ahead. We're going to follow this man. He's a policeman. You're safe. We're all safe now."

Nodding, Anthony took Jessie's hand. Monty trotted at their side.

*

After a shitty day, Roberto had driven to Jersey City. He needed a diversion, something to make him forget the business rivals, the DEA, McDeare. He needed golden time with his Sophie.

Awakened by his cell at one a.m., he cursed. What now? Throwing on his robe and hurrying into the living room he listened to Aldo's urgent tone. "Turn on the TV. You're not going to believe this. I'll hold on."

The breaking story was on every twenty-four hour news station. Nick and Jessica McDeare had rescued their son in Canton, Ohio. How, dammit? How? The kidnapper, one undead Gianni Fosselli, was now really dead. So was an NYPD detective, Lyle Barton, and a third unidentified body. According to news sources, Barton had gotten an anonymous tip about the boy from someone in the Canton area. Martinelli swore under his breath. Gianni Fosselli's history was rehashed, but no mention of Roberto Martinelli.

"Son of a bitch," he grated. "What's McDeare up to?"

"Maybe he wants to let it go."

"Bullshit."

"So what's next?"

Feeling a tightening in his chest, Martinelli opened a window. The cold river wind filled the room. Roberto inhaled deeply and paced, his mind in overdrive. "We wait until we know what McDeare knows. Then we make our move. An accident. A hit and run on him and his wife. She knows everything he knows."

"What about Vaughn? He let McDeare and Barton slip through his fingers."

"Forget Vaughn. He fucked up. So what? McDeare's our problem. Contact Brezinski, our undercover cop at Midtown North. Have him call that precinct in Ohio and make like he's concerned about Barton, his beloved boss. See if he can get any info on what's going down and get back to me. Tell him to report every contact McDeare makes with Barton's people once he gets back here. Get a hold of our reporter friend Friedman, from the POST. We want to know if McDeare leaks anything to the press in the next two weeks."

Clicking off, Marinelli breathed in the brisk air and popped a heart pill. McDeare had outfoxed them all. But there had to be an angle to keeping Martinelli's name out of it. Everyone over the age of ten had an angle.

Sweat broke out on Roberto's forehead, his stomach churning acid. McDeare was coming for him. He knew it. He had to find out what he knew, who else knew what he knew, and what he was doing about it. Then he could block it.

Sophie's tiny voice called for him from the bedroom. Mopping his brow with his sleeve, he called, "Coming, sweetheart."

*

Clint sped across the dark Pennsylvania landscape, a fresh bottle of scotch beside him, an oldies station blaring. "Can't Get No Satisfaction" pounded through the car. Ain't that the truth. Lifting the bottle to his lips, Clint took a deep suck. If he wasn't driving, he'd get stinking drunk. The sweetest deal in the world ... up in smoke. Shit, shit, and more shit.

Wiping the back of his hand over his mouth, Clint stared down the black highway. He cursed fate, cursed cell phones, cursed satellites, cursed his own hide. He cursed Foxy Foxwell for good measure. Clint had been working for Foxy ever since he'd been cleared for taking out a drug lord trespassing on Martinellli's territory. Except for a reduced sentence, even Martinelli hadn't been able to help him out of that one, Clint caught with his ass in the cookie jar.

But then salvation in the form of an ambitious DEA agent wanting info on Roberto. In exchange for Foxy working the system and getting him out of the can, Clint had turned into his snitch. He'd been feeding Foxy inside info on Martinelli's drug operations for years. It paid well. He'd been happy. Foxy had been happy. Even Martinelli had been happy. Clint had served him faithfully every other way. Big deal if he was missing some drug revenue.

But this missed opportunity ... Clint banged a fist on the steering wheel. If Foxy had been able to act on Clint's tip and rescue Anthony McDeare, expose Gianni Fosselli, it would've meant major PR, a leap up into the big leagues. And big bucks for his prized confidential informant. The kind of wad to make Midas drool. But the fucking woods had blocked reception. When Clint saw Carlo bounding over that hill like a circus horse, he knew the goon was going to take out McDeare. The wife. The kid.

And what had he done? Clint smacked a fist against his forehead. Clint Vaughn had turned to jello and acted like a fucking hero. An object of his own scorn. Clint loathed heroes. And the story wasn't over yet. What was it Clint's unsainted mother used to say in rare moments of sobriety? In for a dime, in for a dollar. Great. Just great. Now he was quoting Ma.

Hanging a right into a closed gas station, Clint tried to check Gianni and Carlo's cell phones' records, couldn't get through the passwords. No problem. He knew someone who could hack in back home. Clint scanned the radio stations for hard news. He found a breathless report on Anthony McDeare's rescue, Barton's tragic demise, and Gianni Fosselli and an associate's death. Had McDeare held up his end? The report ended without a mention of Roberto Martinelli or Clint Vaughn. Clint took a deep chug of scotch. McDeare had played it smart.

In return, Clint would feed the man Martinelli's deepest secret. What Martinelli never imagined anyone knew except for Aldo. Clint had come too far to let the kid lose his father now.

*

Nick was separated from Jessie for hours. Endless questioning in separate rooms at Mercy Hospital while Anthony was examined by a doctor and a comforting nurse. Routine in a homicide case, seeing if their stories held up individually. Slowly, he regrouped. Empty inside, but functioning.

Blood covered his turtleneck beneath the blanket he kept wrapped around him. It was caked on his fingers, a constant reminder. Lyle …

Finally satisfied with his answers, Isikoff led Nick to a bathroom so he could wash up, then to a closed-off waiting room. They were free to go. The SUV was confiscated for now; he'd get a new coat to travel home. "We'll escort you to the airport if you want," Isikoff said. "The lobby's packed with media. You're the biggest thing to hit this town in years."

"Good to know," Nick said tonelessly.

"Bill sent his jet for us." Jessie stood in the doorway, dark crescents lining her eyes, her cell in her hand. "It's probably at the airport by now." She shuffled to Nick. Reaching for her, she came into his arms, small and wan.

"An autopsy's been ordered for Lieutenant Barton," the detective continued. "Then we can release his body to the family. Who do we contact, Mr. McDeare?"

"… Uh, he …"

"He has no family," Jessie finished. "Contact us."

"And Gianni Fosselli?"

"If no one claims the body, cremate him," Nick said shortly. "He wanted to be dead and invisible … grant him his wish. Jessie and I don't know anything about the other one."

A short man, black hair going gray, hurried into the room, a medical chart in hand. "I'm Dr. Wang, Anthony's doctor. First, your son's doing well, his vitals good."

"Thank God," Jessie, whispered. Nick squeezed her arm.

Peering at them over his spectacles, the doctor said, "My guess is Anthony fainted from shock, the body's way of protecting us from too much stress. He seems fine now, anxious to go home. He says he doesn't remember anything that took place after the deceased let go of him."

"We'd like to talk to the boy," Isikoff said.

"We'll call our doctor as soon as we get home," Jessie said firmly. "And we'll be in the room with our son if you come to New York to interview him. After he's been checked out."

"Where's Monty?" Nick asked. "His dog."

"With your son," the doctor said. "It was impossible to separate them."

*

Jessie squeezed into the back of the police cruiser with Nick, Anthony, and Monty. Behind them was a string of cars, the local press in pursuit, CNN already on the scene.

Anthony was quiet on the ride to the airport, his only words to Monty. "We're going home, boy. Just like I promised." Jessie wondered why he hadn't asked about Lyle. Maybe he didn't remember the detective being there. She kept looking around, expecting to hear his calm measured voice taking charge … She blinked back her tears, hands curled into tight fists. She couldn't break down in front of her son. It was one of the hardest things she'd ever done, to squeeze in her grief and hold it close.

The sun was peeking over the horizon when Jessie and Nick stepped onto the tarmac, holding Anthony's hand. Monty bounced out of the car and up the jet's stairs, trotting past the flight attendant as if this were routine.

The hungry press was cordoned off behind the glass of the small airport, cameras clicking away. Jessie knew it would be worse in New York, media Mecca.

Following the dog, Jessie was relieved when the jet's door slammed shut. She and Nick immediately took Anthony to the bedroom, ignoring the flight attendant's pleas to buckle up. Anthony stretched out on the bed with Monty while Nick sat on the small divan. Jessie stayed behind in the cabin to call Mary.

*

As soon as the attendant closed the bedroom door, Anthony sat up. "I have something to tell you and Mom, but Daddy Andrew said I had to wait until we were alone. Nobody but us and Mom can know." He lowered his voice. "Daddy came and got me when Gianni let go of me."

"What?"

"Daddy told me not to worry. He took me somewhere else."

Drawing a deep breath, Nick asked, "Where?"

"It was a feeling, not a place," Anthony said, his eyes big. "I slept there. Daddy said I was safe, that Gianni couldn't hurt me anymore. He was going to help Lyle find Barb. Who's that?"

Keeping his face impassive, Nick pushed a hand through his hair. Andrew had protected Anthony from seeing what a young boy should never see. He'd been there for Lyle in the end, for all of them. "Barb," Nick's voice caught, "is Lyle's wife."

Digesting that, Anthony's eyes filled. "But she was killed with his little girl. If he found her—Dad, is Lyle dead?"

Unable to speak, Nick nodded. He moved to the edge of the bed, grabbed Anthony's hand and clasped it.

- 277 -

"I'm going to miss him," Anthony said, wiping his eyes, his voice trembling. He looked up at the ceiling. "I have something else to tell you, Dad. You're going to be so mad at me."

"Anthony," Nick said, his voice thick, "I swear I won't be mad at you. I promise."

"I ... my ring's gone. Gianni got rid of it. It's all my fault!" The tears overflowed.

"Shhh. It's okay." Reaching into his pants' pocket, Nick pulled out the ring box and flipped it open. "Look. I got it back for you."

Gasping, Anthony said, "How did you do that?"

"It was important to you. To both of us."

*

Opening the door to the cabin, Jessie gazed at father and son as Anthony's breathing eased into the measured rhythm of sleep. They sat on the couch, Nick filling her in on Anthony and Andrew as the jet raced across Pennsylvania.

"Andrew," she said softly, taking it in, "Always watching over us."

A quiet fell as she and Nick watched Anthony sleep. There were no more words.

Nick broke the silence. "Jess ... I'm, I'm ... sorry for everything."

"Me, too." Reaching up, she turned his face to hers. "We'll talk more at home. I'm grateful we're together. Alive. With our little boy safe."

Do you know how lucky you are? That I'd give anything to trade places with you? You have each other. Soon, you'll have your son back.

Lyle had been their anchor. He would live in her heart forever. Jessie reached into her pocket. Opening Nick's hand she placed the pocket watch on his palm.

"That's where you were that morning in Akron?" Nick stared at it a long time before looking up at her. "You followed me and got the watch back?"

"Yes."

"I--" Nick put his arm around her and pulled her close. She rested her head against his chest and closed her eyes. "Is it finally over, Nick? Or is this just a lull?"

She felt his slow intake and release of breath. "There's still Martinelli to deal with. Then it's over."

*

Once Sophie had fallen back asleep, clutching three blue teddy bears, Roberto made himself a pot of coffee. He had a long day ahead of him. Parking himself in a club chair by the deck window he watched the sun rise over Manhattan. Beautiful.

On the first ring, he answered Aldo's call.

"Our man says Gianni and Carlo's cells are missing. The cops searched the estate. The good news is, no link to you. Officially. The bad news is--"

"McDeare has them. Damn the man. This isn't over."

CHAPTER 30

His eyes hidden behind sunglasses, Nick stood with Jessie, Mary, Abbie, and Bree under a canopy in front of the flag-draped rosewood casket. Nick and seven officers had carried it from the hearse. Chins up, hands stiff at their sides, Lyle's comrades lined the cemetery in dress-blue uniforms and white gloves. Bagpipes filled the air. Anthony was at home with Zane and his mother. After enduring Andrew's funeral, the last thing he needed was another service for someone he loved.

It had been a week home, a week without Lyle, a week in limbo. Nick raised his eyes to the sky while the commissioner cleared this throat and began to speak. Police helicopters buzzed above. He and Jessie had already said goodbye to Lyle, back in a blood-soaked yard in the middle-of-nowhere Ohio. They said goodbye to Andrew a few days ago. Jessie had found Nick in Andrew's old boyhood room on the fourth floor, a room untouched by time.

"What are you reading?"

He passed the book to her.

"A book of poems? Where did you find it?"

"On the desk, open to the highlighted section."

"Mary was cleaning the room?"

"Or ... read it."

Reading the passage, Jessie whispered, "'Where you used to be, there is a hole in the world, which I find myself walking around in the daytime, and falling into at night. I miss you like hell.' Edna St. Vincent Millay." She studied the ceiling. "One of Andrew's favorites." Closing the book, she nestled her head against Nick's shoulder.

Nick missed Andrew like hell, too.

Anthony was making progress, Monty his shadow. He was less withdrawn. More prone to crack a smile. But he never mentioned Gianni or what happened to him in Ohio. His spirits had soared after Zane paid a visit.

When the two Ohio detectives flew in for an interview, Anthony's halting response to their questions were Nick and Jessie's first insight into their son's life with Gianni. The man's rules. Italian lessons. English lessons. Bad food. But Anthony's recall halted the moment Gianni set him free to run to the house. He remembered nothing about the bloodbath, nothing about Clint Vaughn. Andrew had sheltered him well.

Dr. Logan recommended therapy, starting at home if possible. Nick had a friend who specialized in childhood trauma. When Jerry Kaufman showed up at the brownstone with a baseball signed by the Mets roster, he was an instant hit with Anthony.

*

Jessie blinked back tears as the service droned on. The entire NYPD seemed to be in attendance, along with the commissioner and the mayor. The press and the networks came out in droves, their vans ringing the cemetery. Lyle Barton would've hated this spectacle.

So did Nick, his face so taut she could see a pulse beat in his jaw. She squeezed his hand, their conversation last night playing in her head.

"I'm so sorry, Jessie. For the secrets I kept from you. Gianni. Getting your friends involved, Bree. The book."

"Don't, Nick--"

"My ego couldn't even admit you were right about Gianni drugging you at Nordic Nirvana."

"You believed me?"

A short laugh. "Of course he did it. I just couldn't admit it."

"I, uh, I have my own secret." She couldn't look him in the eye. "You-you were right about Josh all along." She recounted what Josh had told her about his collusion with George, his obsession with her. Every word, holding back nothing.

"My God, you should've gone to the police. He could've--"

"I hit him where it hurt most. His career. He's done with the play and Bill Rudolph forever. I'll see to it."

They promised no more secrets.

When he was with Anthony, Nick roused, his spirits high. They played video games, watched TV, honed their baseball skills in the basement batting cage. Mary catered to them, especially Anthony, making his favorite foods. But when she surprised Anthony with lasagna one night, he shrieked he hated lasagna and burst into tears. All Italian dishes were deleted from Mary's recipe file until further notice.

Jessie knew Dr. Kaufman would help. But it would take time.

And Martinelli's shadow hovered, a blot on the future.

*

Trying to block out the flag-draped coffin, the bagpipes playing "Amazing Grace," Nick reached back, thought of Clint Vaughn's last words. He'd be in touch. When, next Christmas? Nick and Bree had devised a plan, a way to catch Martinelli off guard. But he needed Vaughn's information first. Clint Vaughn, a man who might be setting him up, a man he had no reason to trust.

Except one. Nick was still alive.

When the service wound down, there was a white-gloved salute and the coffin's flag was folded and handed to Nick by the commissioner. The gesture stunned him, the flag usually reserved for family. As the cemetery began to empty, Nick caught sight of a cop standing alone near the coffin, ramrod straight, tears streaming down his immobile face. Cupping Jessie's hand, Nick approached quietly, handing the flag to Sergeant Harry Steinmetz.

As they headed to the car, Nick heard the mass of press thrumming like an agitated bee colony, calling out, demanding a quote, a photo. His arm around Jessie, Nick veered away from them as the police pushed the mob back, the reporters finally dispersing.

Another voice quietly called Nick's name from another direction. He glanced over his shoulder.

Clint Vaughn, standing under a grove of trees, a cap pulled low on his brow. Nodding at Nick, Vaughn effortlessly melted back into the woods surrounding the cemetery.

Nick asked Jessie to wait for him with Mary and Abbie in the limo, calmed her fears, assured her Vaughn was on the level. He wished he believed it. He found Vaughn leaning against a tree, lazy blue eyes slits in a craggy face. Nick dug his hands in his pockets, eyeing the PI, hoping he wasn't about to join Lyle in the hereafter. "What took you so long?"

"You wanted me to knock on the front door selling Girl Scout cookies?"

"It's been a week."

"I'm a busy man."

"We're here now."

"Nice attitude."

"I just buried my best friend."

*

Clint knew all about burying friends. He'd done it a dozen times in the steaming jungles of Vietnam.

Glancing around, making sure they were alone, he hissed, "Okay, you wanted the real deal on Martinelli and Jersey City. Listen carefully ..."

As McDeare listened, a stony smile flickered on the man's face. As a bonus, Clint handed him the three cell phones he'd confiscated in Ohio, explaining what he'd discovered on them.

"Okay, we're through here." Clint backed up, scanning the area.

"Wait." Nick closed the distance between them. "Why? I'm more useful to you dead than alive. You have a vendetta against Martinelli?"

A chuckle. "I have nothing against Roberto. No love for you. It's for the kid. By the way, move quickly on this. Martinelli's in the process of digging, figuring out what's going down so he can do damage control. Once he's sure he has the upper hand ..." Vaughn sliced a hand across his throat.

Turning, he headed deeper into the woods. "If you stay alive and we meet again, McDeare, pretend you don't know me."

*

Two nights after the funeral, the temperature dropped, snow beginning to fall. Rubbing his gloved hands together, Nick turned up the collar on his coat. A typical balmy January in New York. Bree was bundled in a down coat, woolen cap, and scarf. This was their second night on the stakeout, the first a dud. But tonight was a Saturday, their chances better.

Huddling along the back alley, they blended into Bottoms Up's shadows, keeping out of the moonlight. Willie had parked the car a few blocks away, obscured by an overhang. He was carrying, leaning against a telephone pole within sight.

Nick's own gun was tucked into his belt. He wasn't licensed to carry in New York. But when you planned to startle a Mafia don late at night, a weapon wasn't a bad idea. Martinelli's mind would be on a little girl waiting for him in Jersey City. He wouldn't see them coming. But Nick's real ammunition wasn't a bullet. That camera trained on the Jersey City penthouse window had snapped some beauties.

Peering around the corner of the building, Nick eyed the front parking lot. Business was scanty on this frigid night. "Dammit, where the hell is he?"

"He's been known to skip a Saturday every so often." Bree wrapped her arms around herself, shivering. "This may take days."

Gravel crunched as a limo turned into the parking lot, slowing as it approached the entrance, out of Nick's view. "That's got to be him."

*

"Be here at ten a.m." The driver opened the limo door and Roberto slid out, a gift-wrapped package in his arms. Sophie loved peeling off the paper. He eyed Bottoms Up with disgust as the limo sped off. The dive was lifeless. If there was any other way he could sneak off to Jersey, he'd set fire to the place and collect the insurance.

He clipped through the smoky interior and near-naked bodies writhing around poles into his office. Locking the door behind him, Roberto fished the Honda's keys from the desk drawer. He grabbed a fedora, shoved it on his head, and pushed out into the alley, eager to get going. The night air was icy, wisps of snow drifting silently to the ground.

Ducking his head, Roberto hustled towards the Honda, the moon lighting his way. Sophie would love the new princess doll. He had video games for the boy and the-- A pair of female boots came into view. He looked up.

Brianna Fontaine lounged against the Honda, a crooked smile on her face. "Nice night for a drive. Neighbor."

His Southampton journalist neighbor from the Pilgrim WASP family. Ties to McDeare. Here. Roberto halted. "What are you doing here, Ms. Fontaine?"

"Actually, Mr. Martinelli, I came with a friend. I think you know him."

"Hello, Roberto." Spinning around, Roberto looked at Nick McDeare, emerging from the gloom like a wraith. He fumbled the package, almost dropped it. Caught his breath, cursing to himself. Trapped like a fucking deer in the headlights. McDeare glanced over his shoulder in the direction of a dark hulk of a man slouched against a pole. "Don't bother going for your gun. He's keeping watch. Besides, once you hear what I have to say you'll agree it's in your best interests to keep me alive."

Relaxing, Roberto knew what this was about now. "You want to bargain. I know you have the cell phones."

"Oh, that," McDeare said, a glint of amusement in his eyes. He waved a dismissive hand. "Sure, we can talk about the cells if you want. One has a whole list of dated phone calls from a dead man to you. One belongs to your goon. And there's a third. Prepaid, one of several bought in bulk from a wholesale house in

- 282 -

Kansas. Fosselli made one call from it to another disposable, unknown number, Italian area code. Probably didn't have time to get rid of it before I showed up."

Martinelli stared at him. "Do I look like I care?"

"Then we have something in common. I don't care either. I have something better to talk about."

"It's too cold to play games." Roberto narrowed his eyes, wishing Aldo was here to take care of this nuisance so he could get to Sophie. The cells were nothing his attorney couldn't handle, the chain of evidence corrupted, legalese called fruit of the poisonous tree. He'd spoken to Goldberg about the possibility they may show up. If this shit was all he had on him, McDeare's time was up. He yawned. "Get to it already."

"Okay. Your daughter."

"My daughter?"

"Sophie."

There was a roaring in Martinelli's ears. He stopped breathing, his heart drumming in his chest.

*

Before the don could regain his equilibrium, Nick bore down on him. "Sophie Devine. Named after your beloved mother Sophia. Lives in a penthouse in Jersey City with her mother Celine and a stepbrother and stepsister. You visit regularly, often staying overnight. More often now that Celine has a gig with a band playing weddings and bar mitzvahs Saturday nights. Sophie must like her daddy keeping her company when Mommy's gone. No one knows about her. Not your wife. Not your enemies. Not the press. And you'd like to keep it that way. In fact, you're desperate to keep it that way."

His head down, Martinelli rubbed his eyes. Nick waited. When the man looked up, Nick saw a hot light flare in his button eyes. How many people had seen that glint before disappearing?

Pulling a manila envelope from his coat, Nick handed it to Martinelli. The man held it like it would explode in his hand. Finally he slid the photos out, his face blanching.

"Copies of those photos and the cell phones are in the hands of a highly-placed journalist friend of mine. And for the record, it isn't our mutual friend Brianna Fontaine. Anything happens to me, my family or friends, the journalist is instructed to run with it."

*

Numb, Roberto stared at the photos. His sweet Sophie framed with her father in the Jersey City deck window, various shots. His little girl, all innocence and trust, raven curls and big caramel eyes. All about princesses and blue teddy bears.

He was determined to keep it that way. She would never meet the paparazzi, never meet anyone connected with his business, never meet the Roberto who was the head of the last organized crime family in New York City. She would only know the Roberto who was her loving and devoted father.

Roberto had discovered his passion in life late, by accident. The day Celine gave birth to the baby she'd refused to terminate. His passion wasn't being the head of the New York organization, as powerful as any political figure in America.

His passion was being Sophie's adored daddy who could do no wrong.

Everyone had a price. Roberto pulled himself together. He looked McDeare full in the face, those flinty amber eyes staring back at him. "What do you want?"

*

Glued to his favorite bar stool in Hanratty's, Clint was finishing a plate of nachos when images of Barton's funeral flashed across the TV. Fucking bagpipes gave him a headache. How could you play those things and not lose your sanity?

Ordering another scotch, Clint smirked. Everyone had secrets. And he made it his business to know what they were. He knew more about Foxy than his own wife. Adele Foxwell had no idea her crime-fighting husband had just paid for his girlfriend's abortion. You never knew when you'd find yourself in a sticky situation and have to play a trump card. He'd given McDeare that card to play for Martinelli.

Five years ago Clint got wind of Martinelli's hush-hush affair with a luscious lounge singer, Celine Devine. The woman was divorced, living in a tidy Jersey City walkup with her young son and daughter. Clint decided to observe the little tryst. He was handsomely rewarded, adding to his bag of secrets. When Celine gave birth to a daughter nine months later, Clint did a little easy sleuthing, found out the child's name was Sophie. He did more sleuthing, discovered even though the fling had fizzled, Martinelli had moved Celine and her kids to a swanky penthouse on the Jersey waterfront. Celine gave up the nightlife. Roberto took care of all of them, but he doted on his precious little girl.

Curious about the secrecy surrounding Sophie, Clint kept close watch. Affairs among men like Roberto were no big deal, even though Roberto was discrete, flying under the radar. Neither were the kids from those affairs, more often cast aside by their wise-guy daddies than not. But his old friend Roberto was different. He kept Sophie tucked away in Jersey City and went to great lengths to visit her secretly and often. Clint followed pretty Celine through the years, kept track of her activities, her occasional boyfriend, visits by her ex, her staid new job with a band in demand for family celebrations.

Harboring the secret about Celine's daughter for five years, Clint had suspected it would come in handy one day, never imagining just how. He wasn't going soft, he told himself, chugging down his scotch with satisfaction and signaling another. He just wanted to see one little boy in this world get a break at a normal life.

*

"What do I want?" Nick asked quietly. "Leave my family alone. Or your adorable daughter's face hits every print and broadcast news outlet in the country and goes viral. Every detail about your secret love child. The Jersey City address. Your affair with Celine that produced a child. Your enemies will eat it up, salivate over a new target to play with."

"You sick son of a bitch. She's just a little girl."

"And Anthony's just a little boy!" Nick's face grew hot, his anger unleashed. "You've put him—all of us--through hell. You snuffed out my brother's life for a cruise line, a fucking fleet of ships! You killed Lyle Barton's family to silence him, ultimately responsible for his death, too. The bodies are all over the place, Ian

Wexley, Eduardo Santangelo, Steve Bushman, all dead because of you. It ends tonight, for my branch of the bloodbath at least."

The don took a moment, a smile inching across his jowls. "Sun Tzu. A Chinese general and philosopher. Ever read him?"

Sun Tzu? What did he have to do with this?

Martinelli continued. "'Know thyself. Know thy enemy.' You got the enemy part down, McDeare. But the other part needs work. You think you're some hero, the good guy fighting evil. But you and me ... We're alike. We got people we love and people we hate. People get in our way, we step over the bodies to do business. You got blood on your hands, too."

Gianni Fosselli's new face flashed before Nick's eyes. Green eyes. Bald head. Cheekbones sharp enough to cut cheese. That look of shock, lifeless eyes staring up at the moon. He banished it. "You through with the philosophy lesson?"

"I'm through."

"Do we have an understanding?"

Those dark eyes didn't blink. "Yes."

"Then we're finished here. I go home to my son. You go home to your daughter."

*

Speeding down the Henry Hudson Parkway, Martinelli pushed the Honda to the limit. He'd have it checked tomorrow for a tracking device. Nick McDeare had done the impossible, unearthed Fosselli and uncovered Roberto's one vulnerability. Just one, but he'd found it. The link must be Bottoms Up, tracked him from there to Jersey and Celine, followed Celine one day, maybe taking Sophie to preschool. Followed up from there. Nice girl, Celine, good mother, good heart, not very smart. A savvy investigator like McDeare could figure it out. Anyone could figure out anything if they had the balls, the brains, and the motivation.

So McDeare and his people would live under Roberto's protection. His arrogant nemesis would come out of this alive. The rare man to face Roberto Martinelli down and live to tell the tale. Roberto had done what he had to do.

For Sophie. His daughter.

The one person he loved. The one person who loved him back.

*

It had been two hours since Nick had checked in. Jessie paced the bedroom, waiting for her cell to ring. Her stomach upset, heart sinking to her socks, she was going crazy. She should've insisted she go with him, but he'd been so adamant she stay home, safe. She'd given in. Nick had been through too much to argue with him.

Crossing the hall to check on her son, she found Anthony at the window, gazing up at the stars. At his side, Monty gazed out the window, too. Hamlet was perched high on a bookshelf, glaring at the dog. "You should be asleep by now. What's wrong?"

"I keep hoping Daddy Andrew will visit."

"I know you miss him. We all do, but ... remember how tired you were when you got back home from Ohio?"

"Yeah."

- 285 -

"Well Daddy's ten times more tired than that. He's worked hard trying to take care of all of us. He's earned his rest, sweetie."

"You mean he's not coming back?"

"I don't think so, Anthony. He did what he set out to do. He brought Nick into our lives and he … took care of Gianni."

"And he helped Lyle find Barb."

Tears welled in Jessie's eyes as she hugged her son. "Right."

"Jess?" Nick stood in the doorway.

"Thank God you're back!" She flew to him, the words falling from her mouth in front of Anthony before she could stop them. "I've been so worried about you."

"I couldn't call. I was …" He glanced at Anthony, "busy."

Looking from Jessie to Nick, Anthony said, "What's wrong? Where were you, Dad?"

Keeping his tone light, Nick said, "I had some business to take care of."

"And … did you?" Jessie reached for Nick's hand.

Smiling, he brought her palm to his lips and kissed it. "It's over."

EPILOGUE

One month later

It felt good to get the juices flowing again. Nick had been sequestered in his office and on his laptop all day, ever since Jessie left for the theater at noon. She had two performances today, home any minute. He just needed to--

"My God." Jessie's voice startled him. She was staring in horror at his computer screen, THE SILVER LINING at the top of the page. "We talked about this. You know how I feel about that book and why."

"Before you get all worked up, let me explain."

"There's nothing to--"

"Sit." She slouched against the desk, arms crossed, looking so much like Anthony in a snit he had to bite back a smile.

"What, this is funny? You think I don't know when you're trying not to laugh at me?"

"I'm sorry. Calm down and listen to me. I'm revamping the book. It's not about us anymore. It's about a Broadway actor who's murdered ... and an intrepid cop who spends years uncovering the killer."

"Lyle ..."

"Lyle." Nick glanced out the window at Lyle's old apartment. A hole in the ground would be better than seeing those dark lower windows blink back at him, a constant reminder. "I figured if I wrote about him ... I don't know."

"I-I'm sorry for snapping at you, Nick. I've had a terrible day. I love the idea. Love it." Jessie slid onto his lap, brushing the hair back from his brow. "What did your publisher say?"

"He said the book was overdue and he wasn't waiting another six months. I wished him well and hung up."

"Serves him right."

"Then he called back and gave his approval."

"Good." Curling against his chest, Jessie sighed, closing her eyes.

"You're exhausted." He stroked her hair. "How's the new guy doing in the show, what's-his-name?"

"Garrett Wylie, sitcom star. He can't dance. He can't sing. He mugs for the audience and milks every line for a laugh."

"But it's not a comedy."

"Garrett doesn't seem to understand that."

"Just two weeks more."

"Thank God." She let out a deep breath. "And then the role is Valentine's. I just want to be a wife and a mom for a while."

"Any word about Josh?"

Lifting her head, she beamed. "As a matter of fact, today I heard he moved to L.A. But he's not getting many auditions, poor baby. Seems that Josh Elliot's typecast as a song-and-dance man, not a serious actor. I also hear he auditioned for a reality show."

Bursting into laughter, Nick said, "Are you serious?"

"Very. Must be about out-of-work actors." Sitting up, she said, "I've been thinking. How do you feel about the villa in St. John over Anthony's spring break? I need sand and water. We can slather on sunscreen, devour unhealthy food, and toast to the future."

"I feel yes." He rubbed her cheek with his thumb. "I can work down there as easily as here. And maybe you and I can go down a week early. We owe ourselves a honeymoon."

"Sounds good, especially the honeymoon. Now I'm going to bed." Covering his hand with hers, she kissed his fingers. "I'm beat." Jessie pushed herself to her feet. "My feet are killing me from what's-his-name stepping on my toes all night."

*

Stretching, Clint was careful not to hit the horn with his arm. Damn stakeouts were a pain in the butt. He was parked across the street from a Long Island Holiday Inn in Port Washington. Mr. Drinkwater was inside one of those rooms shtupping Mrs. Kaplan. Mrs. Drinkwater wanted all the grubby details before filing for divorce. Clint took a slurp of scotch from the bottle, his camera on the seat next to him. Picking up his cell phone, he finished reading the online news blurb about his old friends, the McDeares. The diva was leaving her hit show to concentrate on being a wife and mother, one little happy family.

If they only knew the full truth about Sophie Devine, the child who'd saved McDeare's ass. Would they be even happier? Or less happy?

Sophie's mama had a secret.

Early in her affair with Roberto, before they were exclusive, back in the day when Celine was a platinum blond lounge singer in Midtown, hair cropped short and sexy ... she had a one-night stand with a drunken patron.

Clint was keeping watch on Celine by then, curious to see where Roberto was going with the enchanting chanteuse. He seemed more than usually enamored. One night she left her nightclub with a good-looking guy, a man obviously feeling no pain. Clint snapped a few photos as they ambled into a hotel, nuzzling each other. Shortly afterwards, Celine, known by her stage name of Fawn Martel in those days, became a steady item with Martinelli. Nine months later she had a baby, let her hair grow long and revert to its natural dark color. The drunken patron would never recognize her from a picture of Celine today.

It had all clicked when Clint began staking out McDeare at the brownstone, that nagging feeling the man seemed familiar ... One look at Clint's photo records told the story.

The drunken patron was one Nick McDeare, former player with any cutie in lipstick and panties.

Sophie's daddy might be Roberto Martinelli. Or he might be Nick McDeare, Roberto's mortal enemy.

Chuckling, Clint upended the bottle for a last gulp. The world was a wicked, wicked place. Celine obviously wasn't talking. He had no idea if she knew her bedmate that night was the infamous Nick McDeare.

Let sleeping secrets lie.

For now.

*

Jessie was asleep as soon as her head hit the pillow. A sleep filled with vivid dreams, one after the other ...

Missing a step, Garrett Wylie fell into the orchestra pit. He wailed for someone to help him up. Jessie couldn't stop laughing ...

Garrett morphed into Andrew, heaving himself up from the pit with one graceful leap and dancing off into the wings with a top hat and cane ...

Nick popped out of a trap door, a seductive smile on his face, beckoning her to follow him ... He led her to a terrace in the tropics ... Bright light ... Hot sunshine ... Nick vanished ... Two men sat at a white wicker table, their backs to her, laughing ...

Beyond them lay the sea, a crystal clear turquoise, the surf sweeping in and skating out with a soft whoosh. Gulls skimmed the surface. A gentle breeze stirred the palms. Tree frogs chirped. So beautiful. Heaven. This is what heaven must look like.

The men turned to look at her. Andrew and Lyle. This is a dream, Jessie told herself in her dream. Amazing. They'd come to talk to her while she was asleep, just like Andrew used to do. Andrew lazily reached out for her, his smile dazzling.

As she stepped towards him the sun disappeared. Smoky clouds raced overhead. The sea began to churn, white caps rocking the horizon. A violent wind whipped Jessie's hair across her face.

Brushing it back, she groped for Andrew's hand ... but it wasn't Andrew.

Eduardo Santangelo!

Grinning. Snapping his gum. In his hand was a gun. His focus shifted to the ground behind her. Jessie looked over her shoulder. Andrew and Lyle were prone on the terrace, their blood staining the tiles.

Enraged, she spun around ... But Eduardo had vaporized...

In his place was a dark faceless shape ... reaching for her!

A silent scream on her lips, Jessie awoke.

*

Nick sat at the kitchen island assembling sushi for dinner. Assorted fish, sticky rice, nori, and wasabi. A Japanese meal in honor of Anthony's first day back at school. Jessie and Monty watched, the dog on alert for scraps falling his way like manna. "Finally shake the dream, Jess?"

"I'm fine." Jessie laughed. "Remind me not to talk about the villa before I go to bed."

Mary placed bowls of cleaned shrimp and sliced vegetables on the counter. "Ready for your tempura."

The front door slammed. Monty sprinted into the hallway, the food forgotten. Anthony burst into the kitchen, dropping his lunch box and books on the counter.

"How was school?" Nick snuck a slice of salmon to the dog, ignoring Mary's dirty look. "Good to finally be back and not have the tutor anymore?"

"Yeah. Everyone was cool, just like Zane said." Anthony bent down to Monty. "Did you miss me, boy? I sure missed you." Monty swiped Anthony's face with his tongue.

"Anthony McDeare." Mary stared into the lunch box. "You didn't eat anything I packed for you."

"Sorry. There's a new lady working in the cafeteria. She made me this great sandwich with ham and salami and a bunch of good junk. And she gave me a strawberry cupcake. She said she read about what happened to me and wanted to do something special."

"Wow, that was nice of her," Jessie said.

"Tomorrow she's bringing me a pie. She has an accent and talks fast. She said I'm cute. I told her guys aren't cute, they're handsome. She thinks I'm funny. She's really pretty." He leapt up and dug through the lunch box. "She gave me a soup bone for Monty." Opening the plastic bag, he presented the bone to his dog. Monty danced away with his prize.

"Do you know the pretty lady's name?" Nick asked, winking at Jessie.

"Yeah." Anthony grabbed his books and started up the steps, Monty at his heels. "I saw her name tag." Running up the stairs, Anthony called down from the top.

"It's Luci!"

About the Authors

Deborah Fezelle trained as an actress at Juilliard in NYC. For 25 years she worked on Broadway, Off-Broadway, and in regional theaters around the country. She began writing at the age of 10, when she penned her first play. THE EVIL THAT MEN DO marked her publishing debut, a story inspired by her sister's untimely death.

Sherry Yanow is the author of COOPER'S LAST STAND, an award-nominated Harlequin romance. She's also been a film and theater critic and an avid soap-opera buff, hosting a soap-opera message board. And then she met Deborah on that same board …

When Deborah decided to check out her favorite soap actor, serendipity took over and she and Sherry began a writing collaboration that has spanned over 10 years, including six staged plays, two web series, and THE EVIL THAT MEN DO, the novel that began it all, published by Shorehouse Books. Since its publication in 2013, EVIL has been selected to be recorded as an audio book for the Florida Talking Books Library Service. EVIL'S sequel is A WALKING SHADOW, published by Shorehouse in 2014. Deborah and Sherry love writing all kinds of popular fiction, from complex tales of love and loss to political thrillers to supernatural karma. In Sherry's "other life," she enjoys her family, her cat, her eclectic classes, and her new home in the beautiful Hudson River Valley. Deborah returned to Ohio, formed a theatrical company, and turned to directing, also serving as acting coach on the feature film UNDERDOGS. She recently moved to North Carolina.

Made in the USA
Middletown, DE
28 July 2020